CHRONICLES OF THE MOON

THE LEGENDS

by Allan Frewin Jones

SCHOLASTIC INC.

New York Toronto London Auckland Sydney
Mexico City New Delhi Hong Kong Buenos Aires

Legend of the Pharaoh's Tomb, ISBN 0-439-80373-X,
Text copyright © 2005 by Working Partners Limited.

Legend of the Lost City, ISBN 0-439-80374-8,
Text copyright © 2005 by Working Partners Limited.

Legend of the Anaconda King, ISBN 0-439-85670-1,
Text copyright © 2006 by Working Partners Limited.

Legend of the Golden Elephant, ISBN 0-439-85671-X,
Text copyright © 2006 by Working Partners Limited.

All books created by Ben M. Baglio
Cover illustration copyright © 2005 by Ed Gazsi
All rights reserved. Published by Scholastic Inc.,
557 Broadway, New York, NY 10012, by arrangement with
Working Partners Limited. SCHOLASTIC and associated logos
are trademarks and/or registered trademarks of Scholastic Inc.

12 11 10 9 8 7 6 5 4 3 2 1   6 7 8 9 10 11/0

Printed in the U.S.A.   23

ISBN 0-439-89741-6

First compilation printing, September 2006

Contents

Legend of the Pharaoh's Tomb   v

Legend of the Lost City   193

Legend of the Anaconda King   383

Legend of the Golden Elephant   571

CHRONICLES OF THE MOON

LEGEND OF THE PHARAOH'S TOMB

"Tremble in dread, thief and interloper: thou art revealed.
The Gods that protect these Halls know thy name,
Intruder in the resting place of Hathtut the Third,
Great King of Upper and Lower Egypt.
Thou hast brought down a curse upon thyself
That shall be visited upon thy family
Even unto the hundredth generation.
Thy first-born son shall die,
And so shall all the first-born sons of thy line,
Until the end of days."

The curse protecting the Funerary Text of
the Scroll of the Dead, found in the tomb of Hathtut III.
Translated by Lieutenant William Christie
of the 21st Light Dragoons, Luxor, August 1883.

PROLOGUE

Egypt, The Valley of the Kings
August 13, 1883

The barren valley was shrouded in the deep shadows of night. The sky was pierced with a thousand points of frozen white fire. And the ancient mountains lay awake, watching and waiting like monstrous, misshapen guardians.

All was silent. There was no wind. The entrance of the old tomb showed black in the cliffside — a deeper patch of darkness in the midnight shadows. It was known by the local people as the Pit of Ghosts.

Suddenly, a flurry of hoofbeats broke the stillness of the night. Three British cavalry officers galloped their horses down the long valley, shouting and laughing as they rode.

Twenty-year-old Lieutenant William Christie drew his horse to a halt outside the ancient tomb. His fellow officers had dared him to spend a night there and he had taken the challenge, throwing the dare back at them: "I'll ride to the Pit of Ghosts at midnight tonight! Who will come with me?"

Two had responded: Lieutenants George Cartwright and Charles Church, both the same age as William, both in high spirits and eager to defy the old legends of ghosts and curses.

The three men dismounted and secured their horses, wrapping the reins around large rocks to stop the animals from straying. Then they paused at the entrance to the tomb, while William struck a match and lit a rag-and-pitch torch. He smiled, amused to see his two companions holding back, waiting for him to make the first move.

A bleak, chill air struck his face as he stepped inside the tomb. The flame of the torch flickered, and for a moment William felt a strange uneasiness, but he shook it off and walked into the center of the chamber. "We'll build the fire here," he said, stamping his boot. His eyes gleamed. "I dare say the ghosts will be glad of the warmth and light." He let out a laugh that echoed within the stone walls. "Let's make ourselves at home."

George and Charles followed him in, carrying bundles of dry tinder. Soon the fire was lit and the three men sat on blankets, passing a flask and talking together in loud voices, their rowdy chatter awakening age-old echoes. The time slipped easily away as they laughed and joked together.

William took out his pocket watch. It was already

half past one. "The ghosts are boring company tonight," he said, getting up to stretch his stiff legs.

"Maybe we scared them away," Charles suggested with a smile.

"Ghosts!" shouted George. "You are neglecting your guests!"

All three men laughed.

William relit the torch and wandered the walls of the cavern. The faint remnants of old paintings were barely visible here and there on the stone. Even as a boy, he had been fascinated by artifacts and lost languages. With his posting to Egypt, William had seized the opportunity to explore the temple ruins and study the hieroglyphic texts of the ancient pharaohs.

He crouched to peer closely at a strange, hybrid creature — part crocodile, part leopard, and part hippopotamus — painted on a stone in the wall. Further investigation revealed that the stone, which was over a square foot in size, was loose, so William took out his pocketknife and dug at the edges. If he could pry it out, he could take it back to the barracks — absolute proof that he had won the dare. "Come over here and help me!" he called to his friends.

His companions joined him and they dug together at the crumbling edges of the stone.

"I can get my fingers around it," George said after a few minutes. "Stand back."

"I don't think so," William replied firmly. "The stone is mine."

"You're welcome to it," Charles told him. "I don't wish to be confronted by such an ugly sight every time I enter my quarters."

"Then you'd best avoid mirrors," William joked. He forced his fingers into the cracks, gripped the stone, and tugged until it came free, and he fell back clutching his prize.

"Look. There's a small chamber," said George, peering closely at the wall. "And something is inside."

William scrambled up. "Let me see."

The others made room for him. He held the torch close to the broken wall and the flickering light revealed an alcove cut into the stone. Within, a small clay jar lay on its side. It was about the size of a man's fist. William reached in and carefully drew it out.

The others gathered around him as he stared at the jar. There was a cartouche on the curved belly — the name of a pharaoh carved in hieroglyphics by some old scribe long ago. The jar had no lid, and the men could see that there was something rolled up inside.

"What is it?" Charles asked. "Is it worth anything?"

"Possibly," William replied. "It must be thousands of years old." He carried the jar over to the fire and leaned down to examine it in the firelight.

"If it's valuable, we will all benefit from it," said George.

Charles rubbed his hands together and held them out to the heat of the flames. "Fair shares for all," he said to William. "Will we be rich?"

"I have no idea," William answered thoughtfully. "Be quiet. I'm trying to read the writings."

George stretched out on his blanket, his arms behind his head. "Let the great scholar work," he said, smiling at Charles. "I will lie here and think of ways to spend my share of the profit."

William frowned, trying to remember the meanings of the ancient hieroglyphs.

"So?" George asked after a few moments. "What does it say?"

"Well . . ." William frowned. "One of the

symbols means *book*." He held the jar closer to the fire. "And there is another I recognize." He paused. "It's the symbol for *the dead*." A strange silence swallowed his words.

William looked up, feeling a sudden chill, as if an icy wind had swept through the chamber. On the other side of the fire, George sat up and he and Charles stared at William through flames that flickered as yellow as poison.

William gazed back at his companions uneasily. He felt horribly cold and moved closer to the fire, noticing that his friends were also drawing in, their faces bleak and their hands reaching forward for warmth. William stretched his fingers almost into the fire. But there was no heat. The flames were cold. He snatched his hand back, startled and alarmed.

He thought he heard voices — whispering voices — coming from the direction of the small alcove. He turned his head to stare at the dark hole, his eyes wide with alarm.

"God preserve us!" Charles murmured. They could all hear the voices now. They could all see the threads of blackness that oozed from the opening and crawled across the sandy floor. The eerie voices grew louder — an incomprehensible babble of anger and menace.

All three men moved at once, scrambling to their feet, backing away from the sinister opening. William glanced at his companions. He saw their faces distorted with fear and felt a cold sweat running down his own face.

The ghastly chorus rose. William thought it sounded like a thousand dead men giving voice to an undying rage. Mesmerized, he watched the crawling blackness reach the fire and snuff it out.

Then, tearing himself away, he snatched up his gear and threw himself toward the cavern entrance. His friends were close at his heels, fighting one another to be free of the tomb.

"The jar is yours!" George shouted to William. "I want nothing to do with it — or with this vile place!"

"Neither do I!" Charles put in, as he reached for his horse. "I beg you to leave it!"

Once outside, they found that the horses were whinnying and straining at the reins, their eyes wide and rolling in fear. Wordlessly, the soldiers mounted up and rode, galloping, away from the Pit of Ghosts.

Vengeful voices shrieked on the wind that howled in the riders' wake.

And then there was no wind. The icy stars stared

down. The mountains watched and waited in the silence of the night.

~~~~~

William sat in his barracks in Luxor. The fear that had sent him and his friends galloping from the tomb had melted away on their return to town. William had ignored his companions' appeals to join them in some crowded backstreet restaurant and waste the rest of the night away. He had work to do. He wanted to learn the secrets of the ancient jar.

An oil lamp cast a pool of light onto his desk. The empty jar stood to one side. It had contained a thick roll of papyrus pages, which William had carefully withdrawn and smoothed out upon the desktop. They were covered with ancient writings.

Slowly he had written out a translation of the first page on a sheet of white paper, consulting textbooks when his memory failed him. Now, at last, the translation was complete.

The Book of Passage Through the Halls of the Dead. William stared down at the extraordinary words that he had scribbled on the notepaper.

Away beyond the sharp-edged hills, the sun was rising, but William was too absorbed in his work to notice. From what William had translated thus far, he knew the papyrus pages contained a sacred text, buried with the dead pharaoh. The pages were meant to guide the pharaoh's immortal soul into the afterlife. So essential was this text that a curse had been placed upon it, so that no one would dare remove it from the tomb.

Thou hast brought down a curse upon thyself that shall be visited upon thy family even unto the hundredth generation. Thy firstborn son shall die, and so shall all the firstborn sons of thy line, until the end of days, William read. Uneasiness crept into his mind. It was a terrible curse.

William wrestled with his fears. His rational mind told him that this was just the superstition of a long-dead people — uncanny, but powerless. But the terror that had consumed him in the tomb came creeping back, and his hand trembled as he held the sheet of white paper to the flame of his oil lamp and watched it burn.

He stood up, walked to the door, and threw it open. The pale blue sky outside was streaked with the amber light of dawn. A trumpet rang out, sounding reveille to rouse the soldiers and, with it, William's fear drained away. "Feebleminded superstition," he whispered to himself. "The curse means nothing!"

Quickly, he returned to his desk, rolled up the papyrus text and pushed it back inside the jar. Then he stashed the jar at the bottom of his footlocker, slammed the lid shut, and turned to face another hot Egyptian day.

Chapter One: The Elephantine Stone

The Valley of the Kings, Egypt
Present Day

The bright sun shone down into the valley, bleaching the hills and beating down upon the bustle and chaos of the great archaeological excavation. Jeeps bounced along dirt tracks, sending up plumes of dust. The slopes of the hills crawled with men in white galabia robes, wielding picks and shovels or carrying baskets of rubble up and down the steep inclines. Donkeys moved surefootedly among the stones, carrying supplies for the broad encampment of tents and trailers. Everywhere, there was noise — of metal striking stone, voices speaking in English and Arabic, and engines struggling in the heat. They were the sounds of the work that uncovered ancient history.

A line of local men were carrying baskets of earth away from a recently opened tomb, cut deep into the hillside. The tomb had been carved into the cliffs at the far end of the western arm of the valley, some distance from the site of most of the royal burials. Inside, the air was still and cool, and a cable snaked along the sloping corridor, powering bright electric lights.

Four people stood in the tomb: twelve-year-old Olivia Christie and her best friend, Josh Welles — just two weeks her junior — along with Olivia's father, Professor Kenneth Christie of Oxford University, and his assistant, Jonathan Welles, Josh's twenty-four-year-old brother. The two men were stooping to peer at some wall carvings.

"Be careful, Josh." Olivia Christie's blue eyes sparkled in the lamplight. "There might be booby traps." She was tall and slim, with long, dark hair and a pale, inquisitive face. Her British accent added a tone of formality even to her jokes.

Josh Welles paused for a moment. From under his blond, shaggy bangs he peered down the long sloping passageway of ancient limestone. He pushed his hair out of his eyes. "Nice try, Olly!" he said. "But I know the tombs around here weren't booby-trapped." He called out to the two men. "It was the pyramids that had all the traps to catch grave robbers, wasn't it? There aren't any here, are there?"

The professor and his assistant were closely scrutinizing a section of the tomb wall that was carved with hieroglyphics. The professor seemed not to hear, but Jonathan turned his head and smiled at his younger brother's question. He had the same warm brown eyes as Josh, and the same shaggy thatch of blond hair.

"Normally, you'd be right," Jonathan said. "But Setiankhra was a pharaoh with a big secret. And a great treasure. He wasn't prepared to rely entirely on the remoteness of the valley and the Necropolis Guards to defend that secret against intruders — so he had the tomb builders add some nasty little devices of his own."

Olly looked at him. "How nasty?" she asked nervously. Her comment to Josh about booby traps had been a joke — or so she had thought. She stared down at the stones beneath her feet. They looked solid enough, but she was beginning to regret her eagerness to come on the guided tour of the recently excavated tomb.

"Come with me and I'll show you some of them," Jonathan offered. He looked at the professor. "Is that OK with you, Professor?"

Kenneth Christie looked up. "What's that?" He had been so caught up in his deciphering that he hadn't heard a word. Olly adored her father, with his untidy graying hair, disheveled clothes, and half-moon glasses on a cord around his neck, but she did find it a little frustrating when he went off into a world of his own and didn't hear a thing that was said to him.

Jonathan repeated the question.

"Yes, that'll be fine," the professor said absent-mindedly, already turning back to the wall. "Some of these writings are very intriguing," he murmured. "Third Kingdom — definitely."

Jonathan led Olly and Josh down to a place where the passageway leveled out. Olly guessed that they must now be at least thirty feet under the towering cliffs of the desolate valley. It was an awesome thought.

The walls and ceilings of the passageway were covered in intricate designs — columns of hiero-glyphic script and drawings of strange and fabulous beast-men with snake-heads and bird-heads and dog-heads. Jonathan shined his flashlight at a par-ticular section of the wall. It was pocked with a series of holes. Josh and Olly stepped closer to look. In the lamplight they could see that each of the holes was blocked by something deep inside — something slender and sharp.

"Those are stone spikes," Jonathan explained. "If a robber triggered the trap, they'd shoot out and impale him. Straight through the gut."

"Wow!" breathed Olly, wide-eyed. "Are they safe?"

"Of course they are," Josh said. "Jonathan and your dad wouldn't let us down here if we were likely to get stone spikes through our heads." He looked at his brother, his voice a little uneasy. "That's right, isn't it?"

Jonathan nodded. "Exactly right," he agreed.

The professor came up behind them. "Impalement was the preferred method of execution for tomb robbers," he said. "To break into a tomb and steal the grave goods was the worst crime imaginable." He frowned, shaking his head. "But someone managed to get in here without falling foul of the booby traps. This tomb was looted a long time ago — probably within a few centuries of its being sealed."

Olly looked at her father. "How would the spikes have been triggered?" she asked curiously.

"I imagine it would have been a mechanism involving wires and pulleys and counterbalances," replied the professor. "It's possible that they wouldn't still work after thousands of years" — he pointed across the floor — "but these stones were placed with great precision," he explained, "balanced to tilt at the pressure of a foot and hurl the unwary intruder into a deep pit."

Olly's eyes widened. She noticed that tapered blocks of wood had been hammered into cracks between the stones.

"Don't worry," her father assured her. "It's quite safe as long as no one removes the wedges."

"But it wasn't just spikes and pits," Jonathan added. "There were enormous stones that would drop from the roof to crush intruders, and poison smeared on door handles, and pitchers of toxic powder carefully positioned to fall and break when a door was opened — not to mention wires stretched across the corridors at neck height, ready to cut a robber's head off."

Josh and Olly exchanged nervous glances.

"They had some pretty unpleasant ways of dealing with burglars back then," Olly remarked.

"They certainly did." Professor Christie had come to the end of the lights powered by the cable from the electric generator. He unclipped a flashlight from his belt and switched it on. The bright beam revealed a second long slope, which he began to descend.

"Professor, I'm going up top for a few minutes," Jonathan said. "I've seen a few things near the entrance that I'd like to check on." He turned and headed up the passage to the small square of daylight that marked the mouth of the tomb.

Josh and Olly looked at each other.

"Do you think they found *all* the traps?" Josh said.

"I hope so," Olly replied. She switched on a flashlight of her own and hurried down the corridor to catch up with her father.

Josh followed. "All the same — you won't *touch* anything, will you?" he said to her. "You know what you're like."

Olly glanced at him, eyebrows raised. "Meaning?"

"Meaning don't go poking around without asking your dad first," he answered firmly. "I don't want to get squashed flat by a great big stone because you've accidentally set off some old booby trap."

"I'm not a complete idiot," Olly said with a laugh. "I won't touch a thing. I promise."

Josh smiled. "Good."

Even though Olly had a talent for being impulsive and often looking before she leaped, she didn't need Josh to tell her to be cautious. The tomb had only been discovered four weeks ago. And it was very big, with at least eighteen chambers. Hardly anything was known yet about the breathtaking, three-and-a-half-thousand-year-old burial site, apart from the fact that it had once housed the mummy of a pharaoh named Setiankhra.

Professor Christie had discovered its location after translating hieroglyphic carvings on a stone he had found on Elephantine — an island in the Nile, known locally as Abu. Immediately after deciphering the stone, the professor had postponed the group's return to England and arranged for them to oversee the excavation of the tomb.

Olly had been on several expeditions with Josh, Jonathan, and her father, but she had rarely seen the professor as excited as when he had found this artifact. They now referred to the priceless object as the Elephantine Stone. Even though it was no bigger than a man's fist, the writings on the stone held great meaning. They had not only given directions to the lost tomb of Pharaoh Setiankhra, they had also referred to something even more astonishing. The writings indicated that within the tomb lay hidden one of the Talismans of the Moon!

This was astonishing because the Talismans of the Moon were the stuff of legend — of film and fantasy. Olly never tired of hearing Jonathan and her father discuss the incredible story attached to them. According to the legend, the Talismans of the Moon had been created in ancient times by priests from different cultures around the world — priests who all served the moon god, or goddess, of their people. Each of these priests crafted a single talisman. And it was said that if all these talismans were brought together, in the right place, then a great secret of knowledge, learning, and time would be revealed.

So went the legend, but the writings on the Elephantine Stone were the first indication that the myth *might* have some basis in reality.

From his research through ancient Egyptian, Assyrian, Greek and Roman texts, Professor Christie had come to believe that the Talismans of the Moon were in fact the key to unlocking the lost Archive of the Old. The Archive was thought to be a structure that contained ancient and secret records of lost civilizations. The Archive of the Old was also the stuff of legend — a legend that the professor had long believed to be true. If the talismans really opened the Archive, then they could indeed be said to reveal a great secret of knowledge, learning, and time — for the Archive of the Old supposedly contained a copy of every magical text of its era.

Since concluding that the Archive really did exist — somewhere — Professor Christie had made it his life's work to find it. And so the possibility that the Talismans of the Moon might *also* exist had filled him with excitement and had brought him — as well as Olly, Josh, and Jonathan — here to Setiankhra's tomb in the Valley of the Kings. Somehow, buried in all this sand, one of the four Talismans of the Moon might truly exist.

Josh and Olly walked gingerly across the wedged, booby-trapped stones and followed the professor down the second corridor. Shadowy chambers opened on either side, and Olly glimpsed stunning paintings and carvings within them.

The professor paused, pointing the flashlight toward an odd, circular painting. "That is a picture of the snake that devours itself," he said. "It's an ancient symbol of eternity. And around it are the seven stars that the Egyptians called the Krittikas — the Judges of Mankind. We know them as the Pleiades."

"Imagine how much work it took to get all this done," Olly murmured in amazement.

"And then they just sealed up the whole thing and forgot about it," Josh put in.

"Yes, indeed," the professor said. "Scores of workers toiled down here, using only wooden clubs and copper chisels. They labored day after day for ten years or more. And their only light came from small, flickering oil lamps." He paused at the entrance to another chamber, shining the flashlight beam from side to side. To the left it revealed a life-sized statue of a jackal-headed man with evil, gleaming green eyes.

"Yikes!" Olly exclaimed, startled by the malevolence in the painted eyes. "Who's he?"

"A shabti warrior," her father told her. "The writings here are spells and incantations intended to bring the pharaoh's magical guardians to life, should anyone attempt to break the great seal and enter his Burial Chamber."

"So this warrior could jump off the wall and come to life? Who'd believe that?" Josh queried lightly.

The professor turned and looked at him. "Never dismiss things simply because you don't understand them, Josh," he said. He moved the flashlight beam over the square entrance way. "Not everything can be scientifically explained."

Olly turned her flashlight to Josh and saw him staring at her father, looking puzzled. Then she shined the light on the shabti warrior and his chamber. The doors stood wide open and the floor was silted and strewn with debris.

"This is the result of flooding," observed Professor Christie. "Every few hundred years this region suffers torrential rainstorms. Millions of tons of floodwater pour into the valley, even seeping into the tombs themselves." He sighed. "It's caused immense damage."

"Is one of those storms due any time soon?" Olly asked. "If I'd known I'd have brought an umbrella." She looked back up the narrow way they had come, imagining a murderous flood of black water roaring down to engulf them.

"I think the meteorologists would have warned us," her father replied, not really acknowledging his daughter's attempt at humor.

"Excuse me," Josh asked, "but if this is the Burial Chamber, where's the sarcophagus?" He knew that the mummified body of the pharaoh, in its gold-encrusted casket, was usually placed within a great hollowed-out stone box — but there was no such box in the chamber. The chamber was empty.

"That's a very good question," Professor Christie replied. "It ought to be in here, but it clearly isn't."

"Maybe the robbers took it?" Olly suggested.

"No, the sarcophagus would have been made of granite or quartzite," her father responded, "and the robbers were searching for gold." He stepped into the room, shining his flashlight on the lavishly decorated walls. "I suspect that there's a hidden doorway." He walked across the uneven floor and stooped to examine some writings. "There must be a clue here somewhere," they heard him mutter.

"When my dad finds the secret door and the treasures, he'll be famous!" Olly told Josh delightedly. "Hey, Dad! I bet there'll be TV shows about you. And books and computer games — maybe even a Hollywood movie!"

Professor Christie stared at her. "I hope not," he replied. "I'd never get any work done with all that kind of nonsense going on."

"No problem," Olly assured him. "I'll do the TV shows for you."

Her father smiled indulgently. "I think you're getting a little ahead of yourself, Olivia," he said. "So far, all I have are riddles and puzzles. It could take years of painstaking research before the secrets of Setiankhra's tomb reveal themselves — if they ever do."

"Of course they will," Olly declared with absolute conviction. "You're a genius, Dad. You'll solve the mystery."

Her father laughed gently and turned to study the cryptic wall paintings again. "Just like her mother," Olly and Josh heard him say fondly.

It was several years since Olly's mother had died in a plane crash during an expedition to Papua New Guinea. Since then, Olly's grandmother had accompanied the father and daughter all over the world, overseeing the domestic arrangements and acting as a stern but affectionate tutor for Olly and Josh.

Josh and Jonathan's mother, Natasha Welles, was a film star. She spent so much time filming in foreign locations, she was often away from home for long periods of time. That was why Josh traveled with his older brother on archaeological expeditions. Besides, Olly's gran also thought it was good for Olly to have someone her own age around.

Olly looked at her friend. "Wouldn't it be great if the two of *us* found the secret doorway?" she said. "I mean, there are only so many walls in here. How difficult can it be?"

Josh looked at her dubiously. "Pretty difficult, I bet," he replied. "Besides, it may not even be in here. It might be in one of those other rooms we saw on the way down. If I were hiding something, I wouldn't hide it in the most obvious room in the whole tomb. I'd be sneakier than that."

Olly looked at him. "You know, that's not a bad idea," she said. Josh was always practical. Sometimes it was frustrating, but she had to admit that it could be helpful, too. She shouted to her father, "Is it OK if we explore some of the other rooms?"

"As long as you're careful," her father called back. "Very careful."

Olly led the way, raking the floor with her flashlight as they headed back up the corridor. They reached a small, square chamber. Paintings and writings covered the walls, some still bright and well-preserved, others smeared and stained and fragmented. Olly pointed her flashlight into the dark corners. Silt was piled against the wall — testament to the ancient floods.

"We should do this scientifically," Josh said. He pointed. "Let's start over there and work our way around. We need to look for regular cracks, and parts of the walls that are sunken or that stick out more than the rest."

They began to pick their way across the debris left by three thousand years of floodwater. The beam of the flashlight lit up a stylized painting of a jackal-headed being.

"He looks like that shabti warrior," Josh said. He glanced at Olly. "What did your father mean about not dismissing stuff just because you don't understand it? Was he talking about the magic spells?" He gave a crooked grin. "He doesn't think they might work, does he?"

Olly's eyes gleamed in the flashlight beam. "You wouldn't think so, but my family is kind of weird," she replied.

Josh laughed. "Tell me about it."

She shook her head. "No, I mean *really* weird."

Josh stared at her expectantly.

"I'm not saying *I* necessarily believe this, all right?" she continued. "But there's a possibility — just a possibility — that there's a curse on my family."

Josh opened his mouth to laugh, but the look in Olly's eyes silenced him. "Are you kidding me?" he breathed. "A curse? Really? That's so cool. What's the story?"

"Well, they say it dates back to the end of the nineteenth century," Olly began solemnly. "It's all the fault of my great-great-grandfather, William Christie."

Josh listened in amazement as Olly told him how William had removed a sacred scroll from an old tomb and then made a translation of the curse.

"So, what happened next?" Josh asked. "Did he die in some weird way?"

"No, *he* didn't die," Olly replied. "That wasn't the curse. His firstborn son, Edmund, was the one who died . . . of tuberculosis in 1907. He was seventeen."

"But that wasn't all that strange back in those days," Josh pointed out. "People died of nasty diseases all the time."

"I haven't finished," Olly said. "William had a second son named Frances. Well, William died in 1939. While Frances and *his* son, Adam — his *firstborn* son — were going through William's things, they found his diaries and this old pot with papyrus pages in it. Frances and Adam read the diaries and learned that the papyrus pages were an ancient text that included a curse on all of the firstborn sons in the family. They also read that William had forgotten all about the curse till his first son died. Then he began to wonder if it was the curse that had killed Edmund."

Josh looked doubtfully at Olly. "And now you're not going to tell me that Adam died, too, are you?"

"You bet I am," responded Olly. She was about to continue, when a strange booming sound interrupted her. It echoed around the tomb, coming from outside the room, further up the passageway. Josh and Olly looked at each other, puzzled by the noise. It was a few moments before they realized that they were hearing the distorted sound of a human voice. Someone was shouting in alarm.

The voice drew closer, and a figure ran past the chamber they were in. Olly was shocked to realize that it was Jonathan. Wondering what possibly could have happened, she and Josh ran after him as he burst into the lower chamber where Professor Christie was working.

"What's all this noise?" the professor exclaimed. "I can't hear myself think!"

"Professor! It's gone!" Jonathan Welles gasped.

The professor and the two friends stared at him.

"What's gone?" Professor Christie asked.

"The stone!" Jonathan cried. "Someone has stolen the Elephantine Stone!"

Chapter Two: Thief!

The city of Luxor lies several miles from the remote, tomb-pocked Valley of the Kings. Two police officers came from there in response to Jonathan Welles's telephone call. Polite and efficient, they examined the trailer from which the Elephantine Stone had been stolen, making notes and asking questions in fluent English.

The small trailer seemed very crowded. Olly and Josh were there, along with the professor, and Olly's grandmother, Audrey Beckmann, who acted as Olly and Josh's tutor while they were on expedition. Audrey sat between the two youngsters, her sharp, intelligent eyes taking everything in. Her gray hair was cut into a short, smart bob. She wore a crisp white blouse, khaki trousers, and stylish but practical suede boots.

There was an air of gloom in the trailer as Professor Christie explained to the police officers the importance of the lost stone. "It is an artifact of immeasurable value," he told them. "Please do everything you can to find the thief and retrieve the stone."

The officer in charge looked at a photograph that had been taken shortly after the Elephantine Stone's discovery. "It is a shame the safe was so easily broken into. Artifacts such as this command very high prices," he said. "It is possible that the stone is already on its way to the illegal markets in Cairo." He saw the look of despair on the professor's face. "But do not fear, Professor Christie, we will ask many questions of many people. *Inshallah* — God willing — we will find the stone and return it to you." The police officers stepped down from the trailer.

"I can't believe it!" Olly wailed. "We were down in the tomb talking about robbers from thousands of years ago, and at the same time someone was up here making off with the Elephantine Stone!"

"At least we've still got photos, and copies of the writings on the stone," Josh pointed out. "It's not like we all have to give up and go home. We can still follow its clues to the talisman."

Jonathan frowned at him. "That's not the point, Josh," he sighed. Olly could understand his frustration. Her father wasn't blaming him, but she knew he must feel responsible for the loss. The safe had been located in his trailer.

Professor Christie lifted his hand. "No, Josh is right," he said. "We must continue our work and allow the police to do theirs."

Audrey Beckmann stood up. "There's obviously nothing more we can do," she said. She looked at Josh and Olly. "You two need to wash that dirt off your hands and come over to my trailer for your lessons."

Olly looked up at her gran in surprise. "I won't be able to concentrate on lessons with all this going on," she said.

Audrey Beckmann frowned. "Oh, I think I'll be able to help you concentrate," she said. "You know the rules, Olly: three hours of class a day during the school year." She headed for the door. "I'll expect to see the two of you in five minutes — with your math books."

The door closed sharply behind her.

Olly looked appealingly at her father. "Maybe we could help look for the stone," she said. "I've been thinking, and . . ."

Professor Christie stared at her in alarm. "No, Olivia," he said firmly. "We'll leave the investigation to the police." He turned to Jonathan. "We shouldn't dwell on this," he said. "There's still plenty of work to be done. I've found some interesting inscriptions in the Burial Chamber. I'd like you to come and look at them with me. And bring the translation of the stone — I think it will be useful."

Olly and Josh left the trailer.

Josh looked at his friend. "So, *what* have you been thinking?" he asked.

"I've got a theory," Olly said, her bright eyes gleaming. "The thief must have kept watch on the trailer, and sneaked in the moment Jonathan's back was turned, right?" She looked at Josh. "Which means it has to be someone who works here — maybe one of the diggers."

Josh nodded. "And *that* means the stone is probably still here," he said excitedly. "Hidden away till the end of the day."

"Exactly," Olly agreed. "So as soon as Gran finishes with us, I propose we search high and low for the stone."

"Sounds like the fastest way to get it back to me." Josh grinned. "Can you imagine the look on Jonathan's face when we hand the stone back to him? It'll be great!"

They stopped to wash their grimy hands and pick up their school books before heading over to Audrey's trailer.

"So, what happened to Adam anyway?" Josh asked curiously. Olly had interrupted the tale of her family curse when Jonathan had announced the theft, and Josh was eager to hear the end — in spite of all that had just happened.

Olly stared at him, her mind still full of plans for finding the Elephantine Stone. "Huh? Oh — how could I forget? Yes, Great-Uncle Adam. He was my grandfather's older brother," Olly explained. "Well, apparently, when he read about the curse, he got really nervous — like you would if you believed in curses and you were the firstborn son who was going to die! His father tried to convince him that the curse couldn't possibly be real, but Adam was totally spooked. He thought he could end the whole curse thing by taking the sacred papyrus text to Egypt and putting it back in the tomb it came from." Olly shook her head. "Big mistake."

"He died?" Josh asked.

"His ship was hit by a really big storm and sank without trace," Olly told him. "Great-Uncle Adam — and the pot and the sacred text and every-thing — went down with the ship." She looked solemnly at Josh. "The curse had claimed its second victim."

Josh frowned. "But Adam only died because he believed in the curse," he said. "Otherwise, he wouldn't have been on that ship in the first place. That's exactly how these curse things work. You tell someone they're cursed, and then the curse comes true. But only because they *believe* in it."

Olly sighed. "Uncle Douglas didn't believe in it. And it got him, too," she said.

Josh stared. "Who's Uncle Douglas?"

They had almost reached the trailer now. The door was opened from inside and Olly's grandmother appeared in the doorway. "Come along, you two," she called. "You won't learn anything by wasting time out there." She withdrew, leaving the door open for them.

"What about Uncle Douglas?" Josh hissed urgently to Olly.

"Later," Olly whispered back. "Don't mention him in front of Gran. She doesn't like talking about it."

~~~~

It was late in the afternoon when Olly and Josh finally escaped the watchful eye of Audrey Beckmann, and Josh was eager to hear the rest of Olly's family history. "So, how did your Uncle Douglas die?" he asked her.

"He was killed in a car crash in 1964," she replied. "He was nineteen. He was my dad's older brother — my grandfather's firstborn son. Dad was born next, then Aunt Anna."

Josh was quiet for a few moments as he took this in. "Why did you tell me not to mention him in front of your grandma?" he asked at length. "She's your *mother's* mother, isn't she? She wasn't directly related to your dead uncle. Why would it bother her?"

Olly shrugged. "Gran just doesn't like anyone talking about the curse. We never mention it in front of her."

"I get it," Josh said. "She thinks the curse is a load of rubbish?"

"That's what Dad says," Olly responded. "But if you ask me, I think it's the other way around. I think she's afraid that the curse is *real*. That's why she won't talk about it."

Josh stared at her. The idea that Olly's level-headed gran might actually believe in the curse was the most alarming thing that he had heard so far. "What does your dad think about all this?" he asked.

Olly frowned. "It's difficult to tell," she said. "He acts like it's all mumbo jumbo, but the reason he got into archaeology in the first place was because of the curse. He did tons of research — following the curse back and checking it out in the archives and so on. And here's the thing: He found some old inscriptions in the British Museum that said that copies of all the old sacred texts, from all the tombs, were kept in the The Archive of the Old." She looked at her friend. "So, you have to ask yourself: Is Dad searching for the Talismans of the Moon because he wants to open the Archive for academic purposes? Or is he doing it so that he can find a copy of the text that William Christie took from Hathtut's tomb, and put it back — like Great-Uncle Adam was trying to do — and end the curse?"

"Wow!" breathed Josh. "You weren't kidding when you said your family is weird."

Olly gave a faint smile. She didn't tell him about what sometimes kept her awake at night. The curse only mentioned the death of firstborn *sons*. But what would happen if no boys were born? Her Aunt Anna had no children, so Olly was the only one in her entire family. Would the lack of boys break the curse? Or would it switch to the firstborn daughter, instead? Olly was a very headstrong girl, and she wondered: If a girl could do anything that boys can do, did that include being plagued by a family curse?

The searing heat of the day had lessened, but the canyon was still as hot as an oven as the two friends walked over to where the diggers were working. Olly looked out across the site. There was no sign of Jonathan or her father. She assumed they were down in the tomb. The laborers were being supervised by Mohammed, a handsome young Egyptian who had been hired for his knowledge of the valley and its history. He was a student of Egyptology from Cairo University, and he spoke fluent English. Olly liked him. He was always polite and courteous, although he was quick to bark orders at anyone who wasn't working hard enough.

"So, where do we start our search for the stone?" Josh asked. "We can't exactly go through everyone's pockets."

Olly looked around thoughtfully. There was a tent nearby where much-needed bottled drinking water was kept. Many of the diggers kept small bundles of possessions there, too, heaped together out of the direct sunlight. "If you keep watch for me," Olly suggested, "I can go into that tent and quickly look through the packs."

Josh's forehead wrinkled. "Are you sure that's a good idea?" he asked.

Olly frowned. "Well, I wouldn't do it under normal circumstances," she admitted. "But we do want to find the Elephantine Stone, don't we?"

"We do."

"And it's not like I'll be prying," Olly continued, "because I'll just feel the packs, and if I come across anything that feels like the stone, then I'll look more closely. That's OK, isn't it?"

"I guess so," Josh said, still feeling uneasy. He shrugged. "Well, this is really important. OK. I'll keep watch — but be quick."

Olly nodded, and with a final nervous glance at the workers, she turned and slipped into the tent.

To her dismay, she found Jonathan standing there, a bottle of water in his hand and a very unhappy look on his face.

"Get in here, Josh," he ordered.

Josh slunk in and stood at Olly's side.

"I can't believe what I just heard," Jonathan said. "You can't just go through people's private possessions! What were you thinking?"

"We want to help find the stone," Olly explained. "We thought it might still be on site."

"You can help by keeping out of the way," Jonathan told her firmly. His eyes moved from Olly to Josh and then back to Olly. "No more bright ideas, OK?"

Olly nodded. "OK," she muttered.

Jonathan herded them out of the tent and went to speak to Mohammed, leaving Olly and Josh rather crestfallen.

"That was terrible," Olly groaned. "Maybe trying to find the stone isn't such a good idea after all." Olly was surprised when Josh shook his head.

"We can't give up yet," he said. "Listen, I have an idea. Why don't we go over to the canteen and have a word with Ahmed? He might know something."

Olly's face brightened. "That's an excellent plan," she said. "We could ask him a few casual questions about the diggers. He knows everything that goes on here. He'll be able to tell us if anyone has been acting suspiciously. Good idea, Josh!"

⌁⌁⌁⌁

The canteen was a large wooden shack at the southern end of the site. It was run by Ahmed Farfour, a beefy, bald-headed man who acted as cook, waiter, and source of all news, gossip, and information for the entire valley. Ahmed had the radio on. It was playing traditional Saidi music, with its reedy swirls of notes and its strong, hypnotic rhythms.

The two friends preferred to go into the canteen through the back entrance. That way they ended up right next to the counter — among Ahmed's tempting snacks. Olly was a particular fan of the thick, syrupy pastries, and the freshly squeezed orange juice, sweetened with sugarcane. Josh liked the freshly baked pita bread and the dipping sauces: hummus, baba ganoush, and spicy tahini.

The back door was ajar when they arrived. Olly stopped so suddenly that Josh almost walked into her. Before he could speak, Olly gestured to him to keep quiet.

Through the narrow crack in the door, Josh heard Ahmed's voice. He was speaking in heavily accented English. At first Josh thought he was talking to someone in the canteen, but after a moment he realized that Ahmed was speaking on a cell phone.

"I cannot get away yet," Ahmed was saying, his voice an urgent, hushed growl. "No, not today. It is impossible. Tell him I will meet him at the market in Luxor at the stall of Khaled the spice merchant. Yes, that's the place. Tell him to be there early — soon after dawn. And tell him that if we can come to an agreement, it will prove profitable for us both. Speak of this to no one else."

The two friends stared at one another. Josh gestured to Olly and they crept away from the building. "What do you think he was talking about?" Olly asked. "It sounded very suspicious to me."

Josh nodded. "Well, if I had to guess, I'd say that Ahmed stole the Elephantine Stone," he whispered. "It sounded like he was arranging to hand it over to someone."

"Amazing!" Olly breathed. "Case solved. We have to tell Dad and Jonathan."

She turned to go, but Josh caught her arm. "I don't think that's such a great idea right now," he hissed. "Ahmed has probably hidden the stone. What if he convinces them that what we heard was totally innocent? They'll go nuts — especially after what Jonathan just said."

"You're right," Olly said thoughtfully. Then suddenly her eyes lit up. "This means we'll have to go to Luxor first thing tomorrow morning, hide near the spice merchant's stall, and catch Ahmed red-handed, selling the stone!"

Josh thought about this. There seemed to him to be a major flaw in Olly's plan. "How are we going to get there?" he asked. "It's four miles away on the other side of the river, and we can't exactly ask Jonathan or your dad to drive us over there at that time of day."

Olly frowned. "Good point," she said. But then she smiled. "Got it! You get along with Abdullah, and *he* looks after the donkeys. Do you think you could persuade him to lend us a couple?"

"He'll want something in exchange," Josh said. "I'll have to think about what we could give him." He glanced at Olly. "You know, we'll need to get up pretty early to be in Luxor by dawn."

Olly groaned. "I'll never wake up in time." They both knew Olly was not a morning person.

"Don't worry, I've got an alarm on my watch," Josh told her, grinning. "I'll make sure you're awake."

Olly frowned at him. "Just wake me gently," she said. "Otherwise I'll be in a terrible mood all morning, and you won't like that at all." And with that she turned and walked off to her trailer.

Josh gazed after her with a quiet smile, wondering what was going to be more dangerous: spying on Ahmed, or waking Olly up in the middle of the night.

Chapter Three:
The Souk at Luxor

The Valley of the Kings was shrouded in darkness as Josh and Olly made their stealthy way toward the donkey pen at the far eastern end of the archaeological dig. Behind a wicker fence, the animals stood quiet and still in the gray gloom. Abdullah, the donkey boy, lay sleeping in his hut, his head pillowed on two comic books that Josh had traded for the loan of two donkeys.

"Which are ours?" Olly whispered, leaning over the fence and patting the nearest donkey. It nuzzled her hand, sniffing for food. "Sorry, donkey — I don't have anything for you," she murmured fondly.

"Abdullah said to take any of them," Josh replied.

A few minutes later, they led two donkeys out of the pen. It took Olly several attempts to mount up — the donkey kept moving every time she tried to climb on board. Josh sat astride his own docile animal, watching and grinning at her efforts.

"This is hard work," Olly puffed, finally getting herself in place on the donkey's back. She pulled the reins and gave the donkey a tap on both sides with her heels. "C'mon, boy," she said. "Let's go!" The donkey didn't move.

Josh made a clicking noise with his tongue and gently twitched the reins. His own donkey responded immediately, trotting obediently forward along the track.

"Hey! Wait for me!" Olly called. "I can't get mine started!" She leaned close to the donkey's long velvet ears. "Listen, boy," she said. "We're on a vital mission here, so could you please get going? I'll bring you an apple when we get back. Is that a deal?"

The donkey lowered its shaggy head and sniffed the ground, as if hoping to find some grass. It didn't move so much as a single hoof.

Olly watched as Josh guided his own donkey back up the path. Without speaking, he caught hold of her reins. He made a small chirruping sound, and the two donkeys began to walk along side by side.

"What are you?" Olly asked with a hushed laugh. "Josh the donkey whisperer or something?"

Josh laughed. "They trust me," he told her. "Animals are smart like that. What can I say?"

Olly smiled, then yawned. "Whose idea was it to get up so early anyway?" she groaned.

"Yours," Josh reminded her. He clicked his tongue and the two donkeys broke into a gentle trot.

A hundred thousand stars filled the sky above, their sharp glitter beginning to fade as the first hint of dawn crept out of the east. The jagged cliffs cast long, forbidding shadows, and as the donkeys trotted down the road, Olly noticed the entrances to the old tombs gaping like black mouths in the hillsides.

Sixty-three tombs had been found in the valley — sixty-three tombs for sixty-three dead pharaohs, Olly thought. She glanced over her shoulder and shivered. In the predawn gloom and silence of the canyon, it was almost possible to believe that wicked, age-old eyes were watching their progress from those dark holes in the cliffs. She was glad a few minutes later when they left the mountains behind and began the descent through the lush green fields that surrounded the town of New Gurna.

It took them about half an hour to reach the Baladi ferry dock. By then, the eastern sky was filling with light. While Josh paid the ferryman, Olly looked back again. The phantoms of the valley had been banished by the dawn, and the cliffs glowed golden in the clear light.

The water rippled under the ferry as it crossed the great river. The trip across the Nile only took a few minutes, and soon the ferry docked on the east bank and the few early passengers disembarked. Olly and

Josh paid a boy to look after their donkeys. From here they would walk.

They skirted the ruins of Luxor Temple with its massive, towering walls and impressive granite statues of Ramses II. From there, they made their way along the Sharia Cleopatra to the Midan al-Mahatta. The souk, a daily market near the center of the city, was already beginning to bustle. It was a maze of canvas-covered stalls selling a huge variety of goods: handwoven rugs, jewelry, brass- and copperware, appliqué wall hangings, leather, perfumes, exotic musical instruments. And seemingly at every step they took, there was a smiling street hawker or a vendor calling out to them to buy something.

"*La! La! Imshi!*" Josh said to a particularly persistent boy who was clawing at his clothes and begging for money. Josh had learned the phrase that meant *No! No! Go away!* from his brother the first time they visited the souk.

"Keep on the lookout for a stall that sells spices," Olly reminded him.

They made their way slowly through the narrow alleys. All around them were men in the loose-fitting galabia robes, old women wearing black with covered heads, and younger women in long gowns of brightly colored cotton.

The clamor of the bartering and talking and shouting was so loud that the two friends could hardly hear themselves think. And that wasn't their only problem. They soon came to a long, winding alley filled with the sights and scents of a hundred different spices, herbs, and dyes. They lay in heaped pyramids — warm yellow saffron, fiery red paprika, and glowing ocher curries. Baskets were stuffed with dates and figs and nuts, oranges and limes and pomegranates. Then there were juicy tomatoes, fragrant bunches of aromatic coriander and mint, piles of green peppers, onions and garlic bulbs, and huge tubs filled with rice.

Josh looked at Olly. He knew if he had really thought this through, he would have found a hundred flaws in their plan. "Which stall belongs to Khaled, do you think?"

Olly blinked at the bewildering scene in front of her. "I don't have a clue," she said helplessly. "Now what should we do?"

"Maybe we should just ask?" Josh suggested.

"No." Olly shook her head. "We need to keep out of sight. Ahmed could turn up at any minute."

"What if we split up?" Josh said. "You can hide at this end of the row, and I'll go and hide at the other. Ahmed will have to come past one of us. Then we can keep tabs on him till he does the deal."

Olly nodded. "Good plan," she agreed. She looked around. An old stallholder in dark blue robes was seated among heaps of oranges and bananas and tomatoes. Behind him, wicker baskets were stacked high. Olly walked down alongside the stall, then slipped behind the stacks of baskets and disappeared from sight. Through the lattice of wickerwork, she watched as Josh made his way quickly along the winding corridor of stalls and vanished.

Olly kept very still, breathing in the bewildering mix of exotic scents and studying the dark faces of the stallholders, wondering which one might be Khaled.

Minutes passed. More people came into the souk. Voices were raised, haggling over prices — the sellers asking too much, the buyers offering too little — in the age-old way of a bartering culture. She found the whole thing fascinating, and was quite surprised when she glanced at her watch and realized she had been waiting for fifteen minutes already.

Hunger pangs reminded her that they had set off on this trip without bringing anything to eat. Bananas were piled temptingly within arm's reach of the baskets. A banana or two would make a pleasant snack, Olly thought, but she couldn't just take them without paying.

She felt in her pockets and drew out some Egyptian money. Then she reached cautiously through the barrier of baskets and helped herself to a couple of bananas, carefully placing the money on top of the remaining pile.

She had eaten the first banana and was in the middle of peeling the second, when she saw Ahmed. Her heart jumped. He walked along the row of stalls and stopped at the one right next to her hiding place.

Olly hardly dared breathe as she watched him. He spoke to the stallholder, calling him Khaled! She grinned. She was in exactly the right place to see and hear everything. She kept as quiet and still as she could and watched Ahmed chatting with Khaled — apparently just passing the time of day.

A couple of minutes had gone by, when a tall thin man in a T-shirt and faded jeans approached the stall. He was much darker than the locals — Olly guessed he might be Ethiopian or Somali.

Ahmed greeted him with a handshake. "Are you Ghedi?" he asked, speaking in English. The man nodded. "Good," Ahmed said. "I have been waiting for you." Olly assumed that this new man either didn't speak Arabic, or spoke in a dialect that Ahmed didn't understand. English was often used as an intermediary language.

Ahmed led the man between the stalls. Olly held her breath and backed stealthily away as they approached her hiding place. She hastily squeezed herself into a narrow space between rough wooden trestles, edging deeper into cover, anxious not to ruin everything by being seen. A tap on the shoulder made her jump and whirl around. It was Josh.

Her heart pounding, Olly put her finger to her lips and gestured toward the two men. Josh nodded and they listened in silence. Ahmed and the other man were conversing in low voices, but the friends could just hear what was being said.

"You have no work permit?" Ahmed asked.

Ghedi shook his head.

"I can help you, I believe," Ahmed told him. "The English will not normally hire anyone without the correct papers, but I can tell them you are a relation of mine and give you a job in the canteen. The pay is not high, and you will need to reimburse me for my efforts on your behalf. You will give me twenty-five percent of your wages. Is that understood?"

Ghedi nodded. Ahmed smiled and took his hand. "Then we have a deal — and I have a new assistant," he said. "Come. If anyone asks, you are my distant cousin from Abu Simbel. You will work hard, but the food is free." The two men shook hands and laughed before Ahmed led Ghedi away.

Olly turned to Josh. "He was only hiring someone without a work permit," she groaned. "I got up early for nothing!"

Josh's face showed his disappointment. "I suppose we'd better get back to camp," he sighed. "If we're gone too long, we'll be in trouble."

As they crawled from their hiding space, the merchant in charge of the stall spotted them.

"*Harami, harami!*" the man shouted in an angry voice. He pointed to the half-peeled banana in Olly's hand. "*Harami!*" he shouted, reaching down to grab them. "*El-Ha'ni! Harami!*"

Olly recognized the words: *Thief! Help! Thief!*

"No! We're not thieves!" Olly yelled, squirming away from his grasping fingers. "I left some money — honestly, I did!" She rubbed her fingers together as a motion for money.

But the stallholder clearly didn't understand English — and he was very angry. He was shouting now, calling out names: "Essam! Bashir!" Olly had

51

no idea how they'd explain themselves without a translator, and no one from the dig site even knew they were there.

The two friends backed away from the old man, only to find that two large, younger men had appeared behind them. Olly had no idea how they'd explain themselves without a translator, and no one from the dig site even knew they were there.

"Run!" Olly yelled. She bobbed under the grasping arms of one of the men and dived to one side. Josh was only a second behind her, slipping past the other man, just out of reach. People were stopping and staring now. Essam and Bashir were shouting as they pursued the escaping friends.

"I paid for the bananas!" Olly yelled. But the continued shouts of her pursuers made it clear her words had not been understood by their accusor.

The two friends ran, ducking and weaving between people, threading their way along the crowded alley, gasping for breath as they ran helter-skelter away from the pursuing men. They jumped over mounds of fruit and vegetables and pounded through stalls draped with colorful robes and embroidered rugs and tapestries. They were trying to find a way out of the souk, but they soon got hopelessly lost in the maze of tangled alleyways. Every street seemed blocked by crowds, and in every direction there were more stalls and more people.

They hurried along a narrow street. There were stalls on one side and sand-colored, single-story shops on the other. Josh pointed toward a small side street.

"Yes!" Olly gasped, desperate to get out of the labyrinth of the souk. They plunged headfirst down the side street. On one side there was a doorway, screened by a striped awning. Josh grabbed Olly by the arm and dived through the entrance.

The friends came to a halt and looked around. They were in a large, dark storeroom of some kind. Carpets and baskets of all shapes and sizes were stacked in profusion, alongside huge pottery urns, carved furniture, and gleaming brass ornaments. Josh dragged Olly down behind a large wooden chest. Panting as quietly as they could, the friends listened carefully for their pursuers. Soon they heard familiar loud, angry voices outside the front of the building.

It was Essam and Bashir — still close on their trail.

"We can't keep running," Josh whispered. "We have to hide." He pointed to some carpet rolls that were heaped nearby. "I know," he said, jumping up and quickly unrolling one of the carpets. "Lie on this!"

Olly stared at him in confusion. "What?"

"Just do it!" Josh panted. "Trust me. Mom did it once in a movie." He pointed to a large papyrus basket with a lid. "I'll hide in there," he said. "Now, hurry up!"

With deep misgivings, Olly lay down on the carpet. Josh grasped the edge of the rug and pulled it up over her. Olly felt Josh heave at the carpet, and then she was being rolled over and over in complete darkness.

She came to a stop face up — fortunately — but totally cocooned by the weight of the carpet. Her arms were pinned to her sides and the heavy material pressed against her face, filling her nose with the smell of newly woven wool. She couldn't move. She could barely breathe! And her nose itched!

She heard Josh's voice coming from one end of the carpet roll. "Are you OK?" he hissed.

"Barely," Olly gasped. "Hide yourself!"

She lay in the suffocating silence for a few moments, hoping that Josh would have time to get under cover. She twisted her head to get her mouth into a position where she could breathe more easily, and saw a patch of light about three feet above her — the end of the roll. Then she heard voices and the sound of footsteps. Their pursuers were just outside the room.

As Olly lay there listening to Essam and Bashir's angry voices, she realized that she was now completely helpless. She was trapped.

Chapter Four: The Plot

Once Josh was sure that Olly was safely out of sight in the rolled-up carpet, he ran for the big papyrus basket, yanked the lid off, and jumped inside. He fitted the lid back in place as well as he could, trying to breathe quietly and hoping that his heart was not beating as loudly as it sounded in his own ears.

Moments after he had secured the lid, he heard Essam and Bashir enter the room, speaking rapidly in Arabic. Soon he could hear other voices, too. Josh guessed that they belonged to the owners of the shop. The conversation rose and fell for a while. Josh didn't know much Arabic so he had no idea what was being said, but he guessed that the main subject was the two young vagabonds who had absconded from the old man's stall.

Eventually the voices moved away. It sounded as if Bashir and Essam were convinced that there were no thieves hiding inside. Josh let out a quiet sigh of relief. He was about to climb out of the basket when he heard new voices approaching. He ducked down again, groaning inwardly and hoping that these newcomers would pass by.

He was out of luck. The voices got louder: Two men, speaking in English, entered the room. Josh could hear that one had an Arabic accent, but the other sounded American.

"We can speak freely here," said the Arab. "The owner is a friend of mine — he will say nothing."

"Will he want a cut of the money?" the American demanded, his voice low and suspicious.

"A small token, that is all," replied the Arab. "A trifle. Once our friend in Cairo pays us what he has promised, there will be enough to satisfy everyone."

"Do you have the stone with you?" the American asked.

"No," responded the Arab. "But it is safe."

The American's voice grew harsh. "What do you mean? Where is it?"

"Have no fear, my friend," the Arab said quickly. "I have hidden it away — in the last place they would think to look: in the tomb of Setiankhra."

Josh held his breath, his mind reeling from what he was hearing. The two men were discussing the Elephantine Stone!

"Are you crazy?" the American snarled. "That place is crawling with people."

"I'll get it for you after nightfall, when the tomb is deserted," said the Arab. "I'll bring it to you then."

"No!" snapped the American. "That's too late. My orders are to hand it over in Cairo this evening. You fool! Why didn't you bring it with you?"

"It was too dangerous."

The American's voice came again, quiet but savage. "I gave my word that he'd have the stone today," he growled. "He doesn't accept excuses. If I let him down, bad things will happen to me." His voice became deadly. "And if bad things happen to *me*, I'll make sure bad things happen to *you*. Understand?"

"Between noon and two in the afternoon, the tomb will be empty." The Arab gasped. He sounded half-choked — as though the American had a stranglehold on him. "The diggers rest at the height of the day then. I'll get the stone for you."

"No. I'll come for it myself," the American growled. "I don't trust you to get this done right."

"But you won't be allowed into the tomb," protested the Arab. "The professor is very cautious — especially since the theft."

"Let me worry about that," replied the American. "I'll be waiting for you in the tomb at midday. Just make sure you're there with the stone. Got that?"

The Arab gasped. Josh assumed he had been released by the brutal American. "I'll be there." He lowered his voice. "Do you have the money?"

"You'll get your share, but not till he gets the stone," said the American. "Now, get lost!"

Muttering a few final words, the Arab left. Josh listened intently, waiting in cramped silence for the American to leave, too. But the man seemed in no hurry. Josh could hear subdued movements — the rustle of cellophane, the faint snap of a cigarette lighter. Then a weight came down on the basket and Josh was squashed into an even smaller space. The American was clearly sitting on Josh's hiding place!

Josh could smell cigarette smoke and hear the man muttering to himself, but he couldn't make out what the man was saying. He bit his lip, his neck aching from the unnatural position he was in. But the agony didn't last long. The American stood up and Josh heard his footsteps moving away.

Josh heaved the lid off his basket and tumbled out. He rubbed his aching legs, crouching on his hands and knees as the numbness in his feet gave way to maddening pins and needles. He tried to stand up, but his deadened feet wouldn't obey, so he crawled over to the pile of rolled carpets. "Olly?" he whispered loudly. "Are you OK?"

"Not really!" came a muffled reply. "Get me out of here!"

Josh got up onto his knees and grasped the edge of the carpet. Then, new voices made him turn in alarm. Someone was approaching and there was not enough time for him to reach the basket. He tried to scramble to his feet, but fell. In desperation, he crawled up the pile of carpets and burrowed down between two of them. He had just gotten himself out of sight when he heard cheerful voices enter the room.

Someone barked orders in Arabic, and Josh felt the heap of rolled carpets shift under him. He lifted his head and peeped out.

Two men were walking out of the room carrying a carpet between them. Josh had to stifle a groan of dismay. The men were carrying off the carpet in which Olly was still hiding!

Quickly, Josh eased himself out of his hiding place and scrambled down the pile of carpets. He ran to the doorway — his feet were working now, although they buzzed and stung as though swarming with wasps — and peered outside. At the end of the narrow side street, he could see a waiting truck. The carpet had been loaded onto the back along with some furniture and ornamental pieces. Josh stared in horror as he heard the truck's engine splutter to life.

Ignoring the tingling in his feet, Josh ran faster than he had ever run in his life. The truck was just pulling away as he made a flying leap for the backboard. His feet dragged for a few seconds as he struggled to pull himself on board, but with a final supreme effort, he managed to haul himself up over the backboard and fall, sprawling, into the back of the truck.

It took him a few minutes to get his breath back. Then he crawled over to Olly's carpet and pulled one end open. "Are you OK?" he called.

"No!" came the muffled reply. "What's going on?"

"We're in the back of a truck."

"I figured that out for myself!" replied Olly's exasperated voice. "Unroll me!"

Josh tried to unwrap the carpet, but it was wedged between two heavy pieces of furniture. He put his mouth to the end again. "I can't. Can you wriggle out?" he asked.

"No! I can't move. I can hardly breathe!"

He reached into the roll and felt Olly's hair under his fingers. He decided that trying to drag her out by her hair wasn't a good idea — but maybe the other end?

The truck was picking up speed now, bouncing and jolting over the uneven roads as it headed south out of the town. Josh clambered down to the other end of the carpet and reached inside. He felt a shoe.

"Olly?" he called into the roll. "I'm going to pull. You try and help me." He got a firm grip on the shoe. "On the count of three," Josh shouted. "One . . . two . . . three!" He pulled with all his strength — and almost fell off the back of the truck as the shoe suddenly came off in his hand!

Defeated, he went back to the head of the carpet. "Olly? You'll have to stay where you are till the truck stops," he called. "Sorry."

"I'll make *you* sorry when I get out of here!" came the muted response.

Josh did his best to make himself comfortable. They had left the town behind now and the truck was moving rapidly along an open road. He had the horrible feeling that this might take a while!

〰️

Josh was right. It was half an hour before they came to a small village. The truck pulled off the main road and began to negotiate small side streets. Eventually, it pulled up outside a large, two-storey house, and the driver and his assistant got out and went to the front door.

Josh slipped quietly over the side of the truck and watched from behind a low wall. The front door swung open, there was a brief conversation, and then the backboard of the van was lowered and Olly's carpet was carried, shoulder-high, into the house.

~~~~~

Olly could guess what was going on. She felt herself tipping at an odd angle, and then the carpet roll jackknifed, folding her up with it. But the change helped. She was finally able to free her arms from their confined position at her sides. She dragged them up across her chest and fought to stretch them out above her head. She had just managed this exhausting feat when the carpet straightened out again, and she was sent crashing to the floor with a jolt that knocked the wind out of her.

Olly listened for a few moments and heard voices receding. She gave a sigh of relief. She was worried they might unroll the carpet right then and there. But it seemed they were happy to leave it rolled up for the time being. She waited a few moments — no voices, so she hoped, no people. She squirmed onto her stomach and began to wriggle slowly along the roll.

Now that her arms were up above her head, it was much easier for Olly to move. It only took her half a minute to get out. She wiped the fluff and sweat off her face, delighted to be free at last.

"Phew!" she breathed, feeling slightly dizzy. "Josh goes in the carpet next time!"

She hobbled awkwardly across the room in her remaining shoe, then decided it would be easier to go barefoot and kicked it off. The other, she assumed, was still on the truck where Josh had removed it.

She was in a bedroom. Olly guessed that it belonged to a wealthy woman, because the bed was draped with colorful silks, the dressing table littered with perfumes and cosmetics. She crept to the open door, keeping herself out of sight and listening intently. It didn't sound like there was anyone nearby. It was time to make her escape from the house. She eased the door open, and almost let out a howl of shock as she came face to face with Josh!

Hurriedly, he pushed her back into the bedroom. "We can't get out that way," he whispered fiercely. "They're coming. I barely slipped past."

"You should have stayed outside," Olly told him.

"I thought you needed rescuing," Josh replied.

Olly grinned. "Thanks, but I managed to rescue myself." She sighed. "And now we *both* need rescuing."

A quick glance round the room soon told her that the window was the only other possible exit. She padded across the floor and flung it open.

"There's a trellis," she said softly. "We can climb down."

Josh tiptoed over. A thick-limbed old fig vine climbed the trellis, making it easy enough for the friends to scramble down. Josh clambered over the windowsill. Olly followed.

"What about your shoe?" Josh asked, looking up and noticing Olly's bare feet above him.

"One shoe's not much use," she replied. "You lost the other one."

"No. I have it in my pocket," Josh said.

Olly rolled her eyes. "*Now* you tell me." She edged back up the vine.

"Olly — no!" gasped Josh, but he knew it wouldn't make any difference.

Olly clambered in through the window, ran across the room and scooped up her shoe. As she was turning to leave, a group of people came in. They looked like a family — a husband, a wife, and two young daughters — and they stared at her in surprise.

Olly waved her shoe at them. "I just came back for this," she explained. "It's a really nice carpet — I hope you enjoy it more than I did," she added, as she raced back to the window.

The man stared at her, then began to speak in rapid Arabic.

Olly didn't stay to listen. She slipped lithely over the windowsill and came down the vine like a monkey.

Four astonished faces stared from the window above as the two friends sprinted along the road and disappeared around a corner.

"Well, that wasn't exactly how I expected things to go this morning," Olly gasped. "But at least we'll be able to catch that American when he turns up to get the stone." She grinned. "I think we did a pretty good job, considering!"

Josh looked at her. "We still have to get back to the dig before midday, or it'll be too late," he pointed out.

Olly nodded. She looked around. "Where exactly are we?" she asked.

Josh frowned. "The middle of nowhere," he replied and pointed. "Luxor is off in that direction. How are we going to get back in time?"

Olly gave him a determined look. "Maybe we can hitch a ride," she said. "Come on — we've got to make tracks if we're going to stop those thieves from getting away with the Elephantine Stone!"

Chapter Five:
Danger from the Past

The sun shone down fiercely from high in the clear blue sky, making the road shimmer in the heat. The Nile lay to the left, silver and sparkling, and a rugged, stony emptiness stretched away to the right for as far as the eye could see. Flies buzzed, and the wheels of the cart rumbled on the road as the donkey trotted steadily along.

Olly sat perched among sacks of beans, chatting away amiably in English to the uncomprehending driver, who gazed out between the donkey's long ears at the endless road ahead.

Josh was nested farther back in the cart, lying back on the sacks and squinting in the dazzling light. "You do realize he can't understand a single word you're saying, don't you?" Josh pointed out.

"I'm sure he recognizes that I'm being friendly," Olly replied. "That's what counts." She looked back. "What time is it?"

Josh glanced at his watch. "It's almost ten thirty."

Olly frowned. They had been on the cart for half

the morning, and there was still no sign of Luxor. The driver, a small, wizened man with only two teeth in his wide smile, had been happy to give them a lift. But Olly had been unable to explain in her broken Arabic that they were in a desperate hurry and had to get back to the Valley of the Kings by midday at the latest.

She decided to try again. "Excuse me."

The driver looked around at her and let out a laughing stream of Arabic. He seemed to find Olly very amusing.

"I'm glad I'm so entertaining," she said patiently. "But is there any way your lovely donkey could be persuaded to go just a little bit faster?"

The driver chuckled and nodded, but nothing happened.

"That's it," Olly said, throwing her arms in the air. "I give up."

"The donkey's probably doing its best," Josh said. "How would *you* like to be hauling us around in this heat?"

"You're right," Olly agreed. "But it drives me crazy when cars and trucks go flying past, leaving us in a cloud of dust. I feel like I've been on this road *forever*." She turned and gazed ruefully at the winding road.

Josh squirmed around on the sacks, trying to get

more comfortable. The donkey trotted on. Time trickled by.

It was a few minutes before noon when they finally got back to the ferry dock. The boy was still there with their donkeys. They had told him they would only be an hour and he was angry at having been stuck there all morning, so they apologized profusely and gave him all the money they still had in their pockets, save their ferry fare. He counted it carefully, then broke into a wide smile and ran off, leaving them with the donkeys.

The ferry was crowded with tourists now. It was approaching the hottest part of the day, and most of the locals were resting in the shade.

Before long, Olly and Josh were across the river and riding back to camp on their donkeys. They were both relieved when they rode up through New Gurna and finally saw the mountain ridges of the Valley of the Kings looming ahead of them.

~~~~~

They dropped the donkeys off with Abdullah and ran toward the trailers. Olly noticed a few diggers sitting in the shade, resting. A trailer door opened as they approached, and Olly's gran stepped down, her head shaded by a wide-brimmed straw hat. Olly could sense trouble ahead.

"I want a word with you two!" her gran said sternly. "We were worried sick until Abdullah told us you'd borrowed two donkeys for a trip to Luxor. What on earth have you been up to?"

"I'm sorry, Gran," Olly gasped. "There's no time to explain. Where's Dad? It's really, really important."

"Your father has driven down to the other end of the valley to do some research in another tomb," her gran replied.

"What about Jonathan?" Josh asked.

"He's working in the office trailer," Mrs. Beckmann said. "But I wouldn't disturb him if I were you — you're not exactly the flavor of the month right now."

"Can't help that, Gran," Olly put in. "We've got vital information." She and Josh ran over to the trailer that had been set up as the site office. Audrey Beckmann followed.

Olly was first through the trailer door, closely followed by Josh. They burst in to find Jonathan frowning over calculations on his laptop. The screen showed a 3-D plan of Setiankhra's tomb as excavated so far.

Jonathan glared at them. "You guys are in so much trouble," he growled as Audrey Beckmann appeared in the doorway behind them.

"But we know where the stone is!" Josh blurted out.

"So *that's* it!" Mrs. Beckmann said. "I should have known."

Jonathan stared at the friends. "What are you talking about?" he demanded, his face grim. "I told you two to stop all this nonsense."

"Yes, but we found out that the stone has been here all along!" Olly explained. "It was stashed in Setiankhra's tomb. And an American man is coming here today — right now — to get it and take it to a buyer in Cairo! If we don't do something quickly, the stone will be gone for good!"

Jonathan stared at her. "An American?" he repeated. "Did you say an American?"

"Yes!" Olly and Josh exclaimed together.

"An American newspaper reporter was here just a few minutes ago," Jonathan said. He looked at Audrey Beckmann. "He told me he wanted to write a big piece on the tomb. He asked if he could take a look around." His eyes widened in shocked realization. "He's in there right now!"

"I'll call the police," Olly's gran said, moving to the desk and picking up the telephone.

Olly shook her head. "They won't get here in time," she pointed out. "We have to stop him *now!*"

"She's right," Jonathan said, jumping up and running for the door. "I'll make sure he doesn't get away!"

Olly glanced at her gran and saw that she was completely immersed in her telephone call. Grabbing Josh by the arm, Olly dived for the door.

"Come on," she said in a fierce whisper. "Jonathan might need help!"

Josh didn't need any encouragement. Together, they jumped down from the trailer and raced toward the tomb entrance.

Jonathan had already disappeared inside by the time Olly and Josh arrived.

Josh caught hold of Olly and brought her to a skidding halt at the entrance. "We won't help by rushing in," he said. "Keep quiet and we'll find out what's going on first."

Olly nodded and they crept silently through the entrance. A few yards down the first passageway, the electric lights began. Olly peered down the rest of the corridor, but it sloped at such a steep angle that she couldn't tell where the hallway leveled out before dropping off again.

Angry voices drifted up to her from the depths of the tomb. Olly swallowed nervously and looked at Josh. His face showed the same uneasiness.

"That is a priceless artifact," they heard Jonathan say. "I can't let you take it."

The American's reply was savage. "That's what you think. Get out of my way!" There was the sound of a scuffle.

Olly and Josh ran down the sloping corridor. An alarming sight met their eyes. Jonathan and the American were locked in a wild struggle, staggering back and forth across the floor of the chamber.

The American was a big man, taller and heavier than Jonathan, and several years older. He was wearing jeans and a brown leather jacket. He had close-cut black hair and wild, dark eyes. Behind him, Olly could see a third figure, small and slight, who she recognized instantly. His name was Habbib, and he was one of the oldest of the hired diggers. His face was tanned and wrinkled by the sun, his hair thin and gray. He clutched a bundle of cloth in his hands, and Olly guessed immediately that it was wrapped around the Elephantine Stone.

Jonathan caught sight of Olly and his brother. "Get out of here!" he gasped.

The American was quick to take advantage of his opponent's distraction. He delivered a crushing blow to the back of Jonathan's neck, which sent the younger man crashing to the floor. A vicious kick then threw Jonathan onto his side and sent him sliding a few feet or so farther down the slope, where he lay gasping and winded. The American took a step toward him.

"You leave him alone!" Olly shouted, too concerned for Jonathan's safety to care about drawing the thug's attention. The American turned toward her, his eyes glinting with menace.

"You're not getting past us!" Josh shouted, his voice shaky but determined.

A cruel grin spread over the American's face. He obviously didn't think Olly and Josh posed much of an obstacle.

Olly acted almost without thinking. The American was standing on the level area between the two sloping corridors. Close to his feet was one of the wedges that had been pushed between the booby-trap stones. Olly sprang forward and aimed a wild kick at the wedge. Her foot struck it hard, sending it skidding across the stones. With a yell of triumph, Olly threw herself backward to safety.

Panting, she stared at the American, expecting the stones to tip at any moment and send him tumbling into darkness. But nothing happened. Olly's desperate gamble had failed. The ancient system of booby traps was no longer working.

"The stone!" the American snarled, shooting a quick look over his shoulder at the terrified digger. "Give it to me!" He reached out, his feet planted firmly, his eyes on Olly and Josh.

The digger stared at him but did not move. Olly could tell from the fear in his eyes that he had not been expecting violence.

"Give me the stone!" the American shouted. Trembling, the digger crept forward and pushed the bundle into the American's hands. He glanced with troubled eyes at Olly and Josh, then backed away again.

The American clutched the bundle of cloth to his chest. His face stretched into a devious grin as he turned toward the two friends. Olly and Josh stood side by side — blocking the corridor. Olly was scared but determined. She wasn't going to let the man get past without a fight — even if the odds were hopeless.

But with his first step toward the exit, the American's foot came down awkwardly. A stone shifted under him, causing him to lose his balance and fall to the floor. At the same moment, Olly heard an eerie, rushing, hissing sound coming from the walls, accompanied by an ominous grinding noise. Her eyes widened as she wondered what was to come. Seconds later, a dozen stone spears shot from the pockmarked wall and flew across the corridor. They struck the far side, cracking and splintering into fragments. Surprised and startled, Olly threw herself to the floor, her arms coming up to shield her face from the flying shrapnel.

The American stared up in shock — if he had not fallen, the spikes would have impaled him! He staggered to his feet, his face distorted with anger as he stared down at Olly. But before he could make a move toward her, the air filled with a wild blast of fine sand. He threw his hands up to protect his face, and staggered backward, blinded and disoriented.

Olly heard the Egyptian let out a frantic stream of Arabic. She peered between her fingers and saw him cowering back from the ancient booby trap. She could see where the sand was coming from — it gushed out of the holes in the walls, cascading into the corridor like water from a burst pipe. But that was not all — blocks of stone began to rain down from the roof, thudding and crashing to the floor with deadly force.

The booby traps had come alive — and they were as lethal as on the day the pharaoh had died!

Chapter Six:
The Tattoo

Olly stared at the mayhem she had created. It had never occurred to her that removing the wooden wedge would cause such chaos. As the booby traps activated around her she scrambled to her feet, deafened by the noise. She and Josh were already ankle-deep in the fine, spreading sand. Some of the falling stones were hitting the floor and crashing straight through to the depths below, their weight dislodging the stones that held the floor together. Sand poured through the gaps. More stones fell away.

Through the storm of fine sand, Olly saw Jonathan stagger to his feet and stumble toward the American, who was poised on the edge of the widening pit.

The floor seemed to be caving in. With a rumble of moving stone, a wide trench appeared in front of Olly. She jumped backward just in time, pulling Josh with her as the ground under his feet gave way.

The stones and sand were tumbling into a deep dark pit. The American was still on his feet, but he was at the heart of the area protected by the booby traps, and the flood of sand blinded him, making it impossible for him to navigate an escape. As Olly watched, the ground disappeared beneath him. As he fell in a sucking avalanche of sand, the wrapped bundle fell from his hands and thudded to the unsteady ground of the tomb.

Jonathan sprang forward and grabbed hold of the American's hand. The weight of the falling man pulled him to the very brink of the gaping pit, but by lying flat on what remained of the floor, Jonathan was able to keep hold of the American and save him from plunging into the chasm.

Olly could see the bottom of the pit far below, faintly lit by the electric light. Row upon row of sharpened stone spikes pointed upward: a deadly trap that had been waiting over three thousand years to claim its first victim.

Jonathan grabbed hold of the American's other hand and slowly hauled him up until he was able to catch hold of the edge of the pit. Relieved of the man's full weight, Jonathan was able to get to his knees, reach down, and drag him back up to ground level.

Olly could see that there was no fight left in the man. He crawled to the side of the corridor and sat with his back to the wall, breathing heavily and nursing the gash in his shoulder.

A strange quiet descended in the tomb. The torrent of sand had lessened until it was no more than a trickle from the holes in the wall. The roof was pocked with gaps left by the fallen stones, and the entire level area between the sloping corridors of the tomb was gone. Instead a gaping hole yawned, threatening to swallow up any unwary intruders.

The terrified digger was crouched against the wall, some way down the lower corridor, staring up toward the booby traps with frightened eyes and muttering anxiously under his breath.

Jonathan stood up and stared across the pit to where Olly was standing in stunned silence. "Olly," he said, wiping an arm across his sweating forehead. "You are something else!"

"I didn't realize all this would happen!" she gasped, her voice apologetic. "I just thought a stone would give way underneath him. Are you OK?"

"I'm fine." He looked around the remains of the corridor. "This place will never be the same again, though." He shook his head. "I can't figure out whether you were incredibly brave or just plain crazy!"

Olly bit her lip. He had a point! But before she could think of a response, they all heard the sound of people approaching from the entrance.

Audrey Beckmann and Mohammed appeared at the head of a group of diggers. "The police are on their way," Mrs. Beckmann said, staring at the debris. "What on earth happened down here?"

Olly blinked at her. "I set the booby traps off, Gran," she said quietly. "And they were a little more spectacular than I'd expected."

Josh looked at his friend. "What am I always telling you about not touching things?" he said. Josh's face was serious, but Olly thought she saw the hint of a grin.

Jonathan picked up the bundle of cloth from the floor and unwrapped it to reveal the Elephantine Stone, still intact. He let out a sigh of relief, holding it up for them all to see. "I think we'll let Olly get away with it this time," he said with a laugh. "What do you think?"

∿∿∿

Half an hour had passed. Habbib and the subdued American were sitting on the ground with their backs to the office trailer, watched over by Mohammed the foreman and a couple of burly diggers. Habbib had his knees to his chest and his head in his hands. He was muttering constantly to himself, obviously traumatized by the events that had taken place in the tomb of Setiankhra. Documents in the American's wallet showed him to be going under the name of Benjamin Carter. He was sullen and withdrawn, offering no further information about himself and refusing offers of food and water.

Professor Christie had been contacted and was on his way back to the site from his research in the tomb of Ramses II. The police were expected at any moment.

Jonathan had led a party of diggers into the tomb to start clearing up the mess. Some kind of bridge would have to be constructed to span the chasm that the booby traps had created.

Olly and Josh were sitting with Audrey Beckmann in her trailer. Olly had the Elephantine Stone in her lap. She stroked it lightly with her fingertips. "I knew we'd find it," she said happily.

"You weren't supposed to be looking for it!" her gran said, glancing sternly from Olly to Josh. "Do you have any idea of the damage you could have done to yourselves?"

Olly looked at her. "Dad won't be mad, will he?" she asked. "After all, we did get the stone back for him."

Her gran's eyes glinted. "It's not your father you need to worry about," she said. "It's me!"

Olly gave her a weak smile. "Oh."

Audrey Beckmann looked gravely at the two friends. "You behaved recklessly and thoughtlessly," she said seriously. She frowned at Josh. "I know Olivia can't always help herself, but you're normally a little more sensible, Josh. And your brother expressly told you to stop interfering."

Olly saw Josh squirm a little under her gran's keen gaze. "We did get the stone back," he said. "You'd think people would be grateful," he added sulkily, under his breath.

"You were lucky," Audrey continued. "You could have been hurt — or even killed. You are never to do anything so foolish again — do you understand me?"

"Yes, Gran," Olly said quietly. Josh nodded.

The awkward interview was cut short by the sound of an approaching Land Rover.

"That's Dad!" Olly exclaimed.

They all came out of the trailer to meet the professor. His face was clouded as he climbed out of the Land Rover. He was clearly worried about Olly and Josh, but Olly quickly managed to convince him that they were both unhurt.

The recovery of the stone delighted the professor and he listened in amazement to Olly's description of the morning's events, and the chaos that had been caused by her activation of the tomb's booby traps.

"The whole roof fell in!" Olly exclaimed, shaking her head. "And just because I moved one little wedge. Those ancient Egyptians *really* had something against burglars!"

"I hope there wasn't too much harm done," her father said.

"Well, the American and Habbib were a little shaken up," Olly replied. "But the rest of us are fine."

Her father blinked at her. "I meant to the tomb," he said.

Olly grinned. Typical Dad!

Only a few minutes after Professor Christie's return, the police arrived to take Habbib and Benjamin Carter into custody.

"Let's hope this is an end to the matter," Professor Christie said to the officers.

Olly noticed her dad staring at the American's wrist as he was put into the back of the police vehicle. Her father was silent and thoughtful as the police car drove away. "What's wrong, Dad?" Olly asked.

He looked distractedly at her. "Very curious. That man had a tattoo on his wrist," he said. "It was the hieroglyphic symbol for Nuit." He took out a small notepad and sketched a strange serpentine symbol.

Josh leaned over Olly's shoulder to see. "What's Nuit?" he asked.

"Nuit was the mother of Isis," Olly said. "I've read about her. She was the sky goddess who swallowed the stars every morning. She also had something to do with the whole resurrection business — they used to paint a picture of her inside the lid of a sarcophagus."

"That's right," said her father, sounding even more professorial than usual. "She married the Earth god Geb, son of Ra, and she gave birth to two sons, Set and Osiris, and two daughters, Nephthys and Isis. She is a sky goddess, and a powerful protector from demons and darkness."

"Why would an American have a tattoo like that?" Josh asked.

"I have no idea," replied the professor vaguely. He gazed toward Setiankhra's tomb. "I must go and see what damage you two managed in removing the stone," he said. "I hope all this trouble isn't going to slow down our work." He slipped the notepad back into his pocket and headed for the tomb.

"I bet I can come up with plenty of explanations for that tattoo," Olly said to Josh. "For a start, that American might be a member of a secret cult, and —"

"I think we can save the guessing games till later," Audrey interrupted, having come up suddenly behind the two friends. "You're overdue for some lessons by now."

Olly stared at her. "We found the Elephantine Stone, got two criminals locked up, and we *still* have to do school work?" she said. "Unbelievable!"

~~~~~

The friends spent much of the rest of the afternoon doing their school work. They surfaced several hours later to find that, under Jonathan's supervision, a team of diggers had already constructed a temporary, plank-built bridge over the chasm in the tomb. More lights had also been installed — the corridors and the Burial Chamber were now fully illuminated.

Josh and Olly walked carefully over the wooden bridge, peering down into the shadowy depths below where the wicked stone spikes waited.

"We almost ended up down there," Josh remarked. "Ouch!"

Olly nodded but said nothing, preferring not

to think about it. Instead, she focused on the remarkable tomb decorations that the extra lights now revealed.

Despite the damage caused by centuries of flooding, the tomb was full of marvelous paintings, their colors bursting into life under the electric lights. The old dyes had held their color to an extraordinary degree. There were rich reds, emerald greens, splashes of pure white, and pools of deep black. Hieroglyphics covered the spaces between the pictures. As Professor Christie had said only a few days ago, the secrets of Setiankhra's tomb looked like they would take months of dedicated work to unravel.

Josh seemed preoccupied as he and Olly wandered back out into the late afternoon sunlight.

"Are you wondering about Carter's tattoo?" Olly asked him. "I am. I'm sure I've seen it somewhere before — only I can't remember where."

Josh shook his head. "No, it's something else," he said thoughtfully. "I didn't want to mention it in front of everyone until I thought it through, but I don't think Habbib was the same person we heard talking to the American in that storeroom in Luxor."

Olly frowned and tried to think back to what she had heard from her hiding place in the carpet. "Now that you mention it, I think you might be right," she said. "The Arab in Luxor sounded like a much younger man, didn't he?"

Josh nodded. "And someone with good English. He said he would meet up with Carter at the dig to hand over the stone, but what if he decided it was too risky to do it himself? What if he sent Habbib along instead?"

Olly's eyes widened. "If that's right, you know what it means, don't you?"

Josh looked grim. "It means the original thief could still be here — waiting for another chance," he said.

"We have to tell my dad about this," Olly declared. "Come on!"

Confronted by Olly and Josh in his trailer a few minutes later, Professor Christie listened in concerned silence. "I don't like the sound of that," he said at last. "I'll call the police and see what they have to say about it. In the meantime, Josh, would you go and find Jonathan for me? I was planning on asking him to drive up to Cairo in the morning and put the stone in a safety deposit box at the museum.

But in light of what you've just told me, I'm going to suggest he drive up there tonight."

Josh discovered Jonathan in his trailer, poring over old documents with the Elephantine Stone safely at his elbow. He agreed with the professor that the safest course of action was to get the stone as far from the camp as possible and, within the hour, he was waving good-bye as he set off in the Land Rover.

By the evening, the adventures of the day were beginning to wear on Josh and Olly. Not long after dinner, they grew tired of watching DVDs and decided to head for bed.

"Sleep well," Olly's gran said. "And remember what I told you: No more stupid risks — do you hear me?"

"Yes, Gran," Olly yawned. "I mean, no, Gran. I mean . . . oh, whatever you say, Gran."

Olly said good night to Josh, who shared the trailer next door with his brother. Then she quickly got ready for bed, switched off the light, and settled down between the sheets. She expected to be asleep in seconds, but her brain wouldn't shut down. It was as if a bright light was shining inside her head and she couldn't turn it off.

She groaned, tossing and turning uncomfortably. In her head she could see the symbol of Nuit that her father had drawn earlier that afternoon. And Nuit was the mother of Isis. She thought that might be important. After all, the talisman they were searching for was known as the Tears of Isis.

It was interesting to Olly that her father had not mentioned the talismans since arriving in the Valley of the Kings. She wondered if it was almost like a superstition, that they didn't discuss the artifacts until they had found some evidence to link them to the site.

Olly wondered what the Tears of Isis might be. She knew the word *talisman* meant some kind of charm that guaranteed good fortune or had magical powers. But the words Tears of Isis sounded enchanted all by themselves. It would be wonderful for her dad if he found this first talisman. They would be a great step closer to locating the archives and reconciling the long-standing Christie curse.

Olly's mind wandered back to the symbol of Nuit. She was sure she had seen a tattoo just like that before — but when, and where?

Olly closed her eyes and desperately tried to remember. She had an image in her mind — simple, but very precise. She could see the ground at eye level and a pair of feet under a long galabia robe. But whose feet? And why was the ground at her eye level? Because she was in a hole, she realized suddenly. And with that, the memory came into focus.

It had been days ago. She had been helping the diggers. She had been in a pit, shoveling earth into a basket, when someone had walked close to the edge, accidentally kicking sand down over her. Olly remembered standing up, ready to give them a piece of her mind — and then she had seen that it was Mohammed, the foreman. He had looked down and apologized profusely before moving away. And it was at that moment that Olly had briefly glimpsed the dark tattoo on the young man's bare ankle.

It was the serpentine symbol of Nuit. The same symbol that her dad had sketched earlier.

And the very same tattoo that Benjamin Carter had on his wrist.

Chapter Seven:
Secrets Concealed
and Secrets Revealed

Josh lay in pitch-darkness, listening to the deep silence of the valley. He was stretched on his back, hands behind his head, thinking over the day's extraordinary events. Jonathan's bed was empty. It was a six-hour drive to Cairo, so the plan was for Jonathan to spend the night in a hotel and hand the stone over to the museum authorities first thing in the morning. He was expected back on site some time in the afternoon.

Josh was glad that the Elephantine Stone was gone. Far better for it to be safe on the road to Cairo than locked up in the small security box that Jonathan kept by his bed. Everyone on the site knew of the box — or could easily hear about it — and Josh was certain that at least one thief was still at large.

He turned onto his side and began to drift off to sleep. But then he was shocked into wakefulness by a small, sharp sound. Josh opened his eyes in the darkness, his senses acutely alert. He was facing away from the door of the trailer, but he felt a breath of air on his cheek, as if the door was open.

Listening intently, his heart pounding, Josh heard the sound of stealthy footfalls moving slowly across the floor. Then he had the creepy sensation that someone was leaning over him. He thought it might be Jonathan, back early, but then dismissed that idea, realizing it wasn't possible — the round trip to Cairo took at least twelve hours.

The next instant Josh guessed what was happening. The thief didn't know that the stone was gone — and he had come to Jonathan's trailer looking for it! Josh realized that this was his chance to discover the thief's identity. Summoning all his courage, he surged up from the bed, grasping the blanket and throwing it over the dark figure. There was a startled squawk as Josh's full weight came down on the intruder, bearing them to the ground. They tumbled together onto the floor, Josh on top, and the thief enveloped in the folds of the blanket.

The thief struggled inside the blanket, and that was when Josh realized that something was wrong. The thief was too small!

Josh sat up, panting. He found the top of the blanket and pulled it off the face of his captive. "Olly!" he exclaimed in surprise.

"Are you crazy?" Olly gasped. "What are you doing?"

Josh rolled off her and switched on his bedside lamp. Olly stared up at him from the floor.

"I thought you were the thief," Josh explained. He saw that she was fully clothed. "What are you up to?" he asked.

Olly got up and sat on the bed. "I remembered where I've seen the Nuit tattoo before," she told Josh. "Mohammed has one exactly like it on his ankle." And she explained how she had come to see the tattoo.

Josh looked thoughtfully at her. He shook his head. "It's a coincidence. That symbol could stand for just about anything," he said. "Mohammed's a really nice person — I can't see him stealing the stone. Besides, your dad trusts him completely, doesn't he?"

Olly nodded. "He does," she agreed. "But right now that tattoo is the only lead we have. I think we should check it out."

"We?" Josh asked dubiously, remembering Mrs. Beckmann's stern words. "Are you sure?"

"Dead sure!" Olly said. "Come on, Josh, we're a great team. Look how well we did today. Are you with me or not?"

Josh sighed. Olly always knew how to get the best of his curiosity. "Count me in," he said, with a reluctant smile. "But what's our plan of action?"

"We need to find out whether Mohammed and Carter were working together, right?" Olly began. "I thought we could wait till everyone's busy at the dig tomorrow, then take a look inside Mohammed's tent."

"What do you think we'll find?"

"I'm not sure," Olly replied. "I doubt there'll be anything obvious — you know, like a diary with an incriminating entry: *Busy day today. Weather hot. Lots of digging. Stole Elephantine Stone.* Nothing like that. But I know Mohammed has a laptop computer and there might be something on that. He must have communicated with Benjamin Carter somehow — and e-mail would be the easiest way."

"You're right," Josh agreed, impressed. "That makes sense."

Olly grinned. "OK, I'm going back to bed," she said. "See you in the morning."

A few moments later, Josh watched from the window as Olly slipped back to her trailer through the quiet stillness of the desert night. It looked like tomorrow was going to be another eventful day, he thought. And if Olly's suspicions were correct, they might even find the evidence they needed to unmask the thief once and for all.

〰〰

It was late the next morning when Olly and Josh sat down for breakfast with Olly's gran. They ate at a table set up by her trailer, shaded by a wide umbrella. Mrs. Beckmann was reading *The Times* — two days old — brought in from England.

Olly poured honey over the yogurt and granola in her bowl and stirred it thoughtfully with a spoon. Josh yawned a lot — still not fully recovered from the activity of the previous day.

Audrey Beckmann lowered her newspaper and peered at the two friends. "So," she said. "Did you both sleep well?"

"Out like a light," Olly said, not meeting her gaze. "Straight to bed and straight to sleep, as per instructions."

"Me, too," Josh said. "Has Jonathan called yet?"

"He spoke on the phone to Olly's father a couple of hours ago when he was about to take the stone into the museum. He said to expect him back some time midafternoon," Olly's gran responded.

"Where's Dad?" Olly asked.

"Your father's been in Setiankhra's tomb for an hour or more already," Mrs. Beckmann said, nodding toward the distant entrance. "And he was up studying old papers till really late last night."

"Is Mohammed with him?" Olly asked innocently.

"I think so," Mrs. Beckmann replied. "Your father took quite a big team over there with him."

Olly looked significantly at Josh. The coast was clear for them to put their plan into operation. She finished her breakfast and pushed the bowl away.

"I think I'll go for a stroll," she said, stretching her arms above her head. "Coming, Josh?"

"OK," he said, bolting the last of his breakfast. "I'll be right behind you."

Mrs. Beckmann looked at them. "What are you two planning?" she asked.

"Nothing," Olly said. "You've got such a suspicious mind, Gran. Why would we be planning anything?"

The older woman's eyebrows lifted. "I meant, what do you intend to do with yourselves this morning?" she said.

"Oh." Olly blinked at her. "Nothing special. This and that."

"Just remember what I told you," her gran warned.

Olly and Josh looked at each other, and Josh nodded to indicate they should make their escape before Mrs. Beckmann started asking more questions.

They had just left the table when one of the diggers, a cheerful young man named Fasal, came running from the tomb entrance. The professor wanted them. "The professor — very excited," Fasal explained as the three of them followed him back to the tomb. "He find writings — on wall. Very good writings — very important, he says."

"I wonder what it is," Olly murmured, but she was thinking that it must have something to do with the Tears of Isis. Only that, or the sarcophagus of Setiankhra would get him that excited.

Professor Christie and Mohammed were in the Burial Chamber. The professor was crouched on the floor with a notepad on his knee, copying hieroglyphics from the wall, lit by a flashlight that Mohammed was holding.

Olly looked at the handsome young Egyptian. He met her eyes and smiled, and Olly felt slightly ashamed for suspecting him of stealing. Maybe her theory was a bit far-fetched.

Professor Christie stood up, his face eager and flushed. "It was sheer luck," he told them excitedly. "I had only been working for a short time when I discovered this." He pointed to the hieroglyphics.

Olly and Josh peered at them. As far as they could tell, the glyphs were no different from all the other writings that covered the walls of the chamber.

The professor pointed to part of the writing. "This is the name of Nuit — not the single symbol we were talking about yesterday, that's just a kind of shorthand — this is the full name. It reads: *Nuit, mother of Isis, lays her blessings upon you, wise wanderer in the winding pathways of the world.*" His voice trembled with excitement. "*I open the chambers of my heart to you.*" He turned to the three, his eyes shining. "And then it says: *You who would gather the tears of my daughter must first unlock the many doors of my house.* Do you see? It must refer to the Tears of Isis. There's no other interpretation. The words in these hieroglyphs are intended to lead straight to that particular Talisman of the Moon!"

"Have you translated the rest?" Olly's gran asked.

"I have," said the professor. He glanced down at his notepad. "It seems to be in the form of a riddle."

Mohammed spoke. "My ancestors often hid their great secrets in riddles and puzzles," he said. "That way, only the wise and the worthy could understand them."

"What does it say?" Josh asked.

The professor read aloud from his notes. As he spoke, his voice seemed to grow stronger and deeper, booming through the empty chambers and echoing in the long corridors of stone. "*In the Chamber of Light, the room that devours itself, the sacred two of the air, and the sacred four of the almond eyes, and the sacred six in black armor shall unite beneath the sacred seven. And the light of the sacred seven will shine upon the head that is whole and the heart that is awake and the eyes that weep.*"

A strange, breathless silence followed.

"Wow!" Olly said softly. "That's amazing."

"Could we have a copy of that?" Josh asked. "I'd like to try and figure it out, if that's okay. Just for fun."

"Certainly," the professor said. "But even if you can solve the riddle, we're still left with another puzzle."

"Let me guess," Olly said. "How do we find 'the room that devours itself'?"

Her father nodded. "Yes. For starters." He turned to Mohammed. "We have more work to do," he said. "Let's hope our luck holds. At least we know one thing for certain: The clues on the Elephantine Stone were genuine — the Tears of Isis talisman is apparently somewhere in this tomb!"

〰〰〰

Olly and Josh walked toward the encampment where the tents belonging to Mohammed, and

99

several of the other diggers, had been pitched. Those diggers who had been recruited locally — from Luxor, New Gurna, and the nearby towns of Armant, Razagat, and Qus — went home at nightfall. But at least a dozen diggers had come from as far away as Aswan or Cairo. They had formed a little camp near to the canteen run by Ahmed. It was hidden from the main excavation site by a thrusting shoulder of the hills.

"What do you think a 'room that devours itself' can be?" Olly asked. "It's just plain *weird*, if you ask me."

"I don't know yet," replied Josh. He frowned. "But I've heard something like it before." Josh might have said he wanted a copy of the riddle just for fun, but he was determined to figure it out. He liked this kind of challenge. Besides, he was good at it.

"I've been thinking," Olly said. "What if the tattoos are a complete coincidence?"

"Then we won't find anything," Josh said simply. He looked at Olly curiously. "Have you changed your mind about searching Mohammed's tent?"

"Well, no," Olly wavered. "I guess not. I just feel a little awkward about it, that's all." She chewed her lip thoughtfully. "The tattoo *is* suspicious, though," she said firmly. "We should check it out. Let's get it over with." She looked around. They were on the outskirts of the small camp. "Which tent belongs to Mohammed?"

Josh pointed at the largest tent. "That one," he said.

"One of us should keep watch," Olly suggested, looking back the way they had come. "Are you OK with that, while I go and investigate?"

Josh nodded. "I'll give you a call if I see anyone heading this way," he said. He clambered up the hump of rock and peered over the top. From this vantage point he could see anyone coming in plenty of time. He turned and gave Olly the thumbs up.

Olly unzipped the flap of Mohammed's tent and crawled inside, pulling the zipper down again behind her. The air was stuffy under the sloping canvas. A simple bed took up one side, and a few personal items sat on a small folding table: one or two books, shaving gear, an oil lamp. On the groundsheet, clothes and other basic items were laid out in neat piles.

Olly looked around quickly for the laptop. She found it on the bed, half-covered by a fold of the blanket. She pulled it out and knelt on the floor to open it and switch it on. The screen lit up.

Olly felt uncomfortable — her conscience was still pricking her. What if Mohammed was totally innocent? What if she'd gotten it all wrong? "He'll never know," she whispered to herself firmly. "Now I'm here, I might just as well get on with it."

There were several folders and icons on the computer screen, most of which seemed to concern Mohammed's university studies, and similar archaeological and historical subjects. Olly rolled the mouse-ball and clicked on the envelope icon to run the e-mail program.

There were lots of e-mails in the inbox and they had all been read. They came from various places — from individuals, from Cairo University, and from several international museums as well. Olly was about to start reading them when a new e-mail arrived.

The sender was *ec@moon-phase.net*. She opened the mail. It was brief, with no greeting and no sign-off at the end. *How does our enterprise fare? Your ten-percent share in the venture is in jeopardy unless things are resolved quickly. I have other contacts willing to take over if you cannot fulfill your part of the deal. Respond immediately.*

Olly raised an eyebrow. Someone out there wasn't very happy with Mohammed right now. He was obviously involved in a business deal that wasn't going smoothly. But did it have anything to do with the Elephantine Stone? The e-mail was too vague for Olly to tell one way or the other.

Olly decided to read a few more e-mails. Now that she looked, there were several from the same address: *ec@moon-phase.net*. They might shed some light on the mystery.

But she didn't get a chance to read any other e-mails because she was interrupted by a frantic voice from outside the tent. It was Josh. "It's Mohammed!" she heard him call. "He's coming! Olly, get out of there, now!"

Chapter Eight:
The Riddle of Nuit

Josh had been daydreaming — gazing up at the cliffs surrounding the Valley of the Kings and turning the phrase "the room that devours itself" over in his mind. He hadn't thought for one moment that anyone would actually come over to the camp at this time of day. He had expected them all to be busy in the tomb. It was lucky that he happened to peer over the hump of rock and see Mohammed walking in his direction. The young Egyptian was already alarmingly close.

Panicking, Josh slid down the bulge of rock and raced for Mohammed's tent. He called a warning to Olly, then turned and sprinted back the way he had come. If he was quick, he would be able to head Mohammed off before he rounded the shoulder of rock. That would give Olly more time to make her getaway — and make up for not keeping a more careful watch.

In fact, Josh almost crashed into Mohammed and made him jump.

"Hello," Josh said breathlessly.

"Hello, Josh," Mohammed replied with a smile. "You are in a hurry, I see."

"Not really," Josh began, thinking fast. "Actually, I'm glad I bumped into you. I've been thinking about that riddle in the tomb. Do you have any idea what it might mean?"

"I've not had time to think about it," Mohammed responded. "But such things were the delight of my ancient ancestors. Far wiser men than I have spent entire lifetimes trying to solve the old riddles." He smiled. "This is an ancient country, Josh. Its sands hide many ancient secrets. Some may never be solved." He nodded politely. "Forgive me, I have to get something from my tent." He sidestepped Josh and continued on.

Josh turned to walk alongside him. "I could get it for you," he offered.

"That's kind of you, but unnecessary," Mohammed said. "It will only take me a moment."

They were just outside the tent now. Mohammed stooped, drew up the zipper and slipped inside. Josh closed his eyes, fearing disaster. But nothing happened. He opened his eyes again and saw something at the edge of his vision: a small, rapidly moving shape.

It was Olly, running at full speed for the cover of the rocks. She had gotten out in time.

~~~~

"Phew!" Olly gasped. "That was close." She looked at Josh, her eyes narrowing. "How did that happen?" she demanded. "You should have been able to see him from way off. I bet you weren't keeping close enough watch!"

"Of course I was," Josh answered defensively. "Anyway, did you find the laptop?"

"I did," Olly said. "Although I only had time for a quick look."

"Was there anything useful?" Josh asked.

Olly frowned. "Not really. There was one e-mail that seemed a bit odd." She explained about the mail from moon-phase.net. "And there were others from the same person, but I didn't get a chance to look at them. When you yelled, I just had time to mark the mail as unread and put the laptop back where I found it."

"So, we're no closer to finding out whether Mohammed and Carter were working together," Josh mused. "Maybe we should take another look in Mohammed's tent?"

Olly shook her head. "I don't think that's such a

great idea," she said. "We barely got away with it the first time. I'm still shaking!"

"So, what do we do now?" Josh asked.

"Let's get a copy of that riddle," Olly suggested. "If we put our heads together, we might be able to crack it." She grinned at Josh. "Wouldn't it be something if we worked out how to find the Tears of Isis before Dad and Jonathan did?"

∿∿∿

Olly and Josh sat at the table by the trailer, eating lunch. Each had a notepad and a pen. The translation of the riddle lay in the middle of the table.

In the Chamber of Light, the room that devours itself, the sacred two of the air, and the sacred four of the almond eyes, and the sacred six in black armor shall unite beneath the sacred seven. And the light of the sacred seven will shine upon the head that is whole and the heart that is awake and the eyes that weep.

Olly had been staring at the riddle for over half an hour, but no matter how hard she concentrated, the words refused to mean anything to her. She pushed her notepad away and sighed as she munched on an apple. "This is giving me a headache," she said. "Let's face it — we're never going to work this out, even if we sit here for a million years!"

Josh looked up at her. He was smiling.

"What's funny?" she asked.

"You are," he said. He tapped his pen on his pad. "Look."

Olly looked. Josh had drawn the rough shape of a snake, curled around into a ring with its tail in its mouth.

"Recognize that?" Josh asked.

"Yes," Olly replied. "It's like that symbol Dad showed us in the tomb."

"And do you remember what he called it?" Josh continued, grinning. "He said it was a picture of the snake that *devours* itself — an ancient symbol of eternity."

Olly leaned forward, interested now. "So, a snake that devours itself is a snake eating its own tail," she said. "But how does a room eat its own tail? It doesn't make sense."

Josh traced his pen around the snake shape. "See? It's a circle," he said. "I'm willing to bet that 'the room that devours itself' is a circular room."

"Josh, sometimes you're almost brilliant!" Olly declared. "That has to be it. You've solved the first part of the riddle. At this rate, we'll have the whole thing worked out by dinnertime! I can't wait to tell Dad."

"You can't wait to tell your dad what?" Mrs. Beckmann asked as she came to join them.

Excitedly, Olly and Josh explained their theory about the circular room. She was obviously impressed. "You're using your brains — I always approve of that — but I'm afraid you'll have to leave the rest for later," she said. "It's time for your lessons now."

Olly frowned. "But listen, Gran," she said firmly. "Seriously now, don't you think that solving this riddle is far more important than boring old lessons?"

"No," her gran replied. "I'll wait for you both in the trailer. Be there in five minutes."

And that was the end of the conversation.

~~~~

Jonathan had arrived back from Cairo by the time Olly and Josh emerged from their lessons. The Elephantine Stone had been successfully deposited in the museum — well out of reach of any other would-be thieves. And Jonathan had some additional news. "We're to expect a special guest," he said. "She's in Italy right now, attending some film festival, but she'll be flying in to see us sometime tomorrow."

"Mom!" Josh shouted in delight.

Jonathan nodded, smiling. "She called me on my

cell phone while I was driving back." He winked at Olly. "Things are going to be pretty lively around here for a while," he said. "You know what these Hollywood stars are like!"

A huge grin spread over Olly's face. If there was one thing that would make this Egyptian adventure perfect, it was a visit from Josh and Jonathan's movie star mother, Natasha. As much as she loved the secrets of the sand and tombs, she would happily take a break for some Hollywood glamor. She couldn't wait.

‿‿‿‿

Josh and Olly were up early the next morning. At breakfast, Olly bombarded Jonathan with questions about Natasha Welles's visit, but he wasn't able to tell her very much more. She would be arriving sometime that day, but she could only stay for a few hours — she was needed back in Rome to start shooting her new movie, a thriller called *Cat's Cradle*.

"She'll probably want a guided tour of the tomb," Josh said. He looked at Professor Christie. "Would that be OK?"

"It would be my pleasure," replied the professor.

"I've got an idea for her next movie," Olly said. "It could be set in ancient Egypt, and she could play the female pharaoh, Nefertiti. She was supposed to be the most beautiful woman in the whole world at the time."

Mohammed arrived and made a low bow. "Excuse me, Professor, but I need your guidance on the clearing of the next chamber."

"Of course, I'll be right there." The professor drained his coffee cup and stood up. "Come on, Jonathan. We've a busy day ahead of us."

They hurried off with Mohammed, and Mrs. Beckmann started to clear the table. "You and Josh can help me with this," she said to Olly. "And it's Saturday today — laundry day — so I want all your dirty clothes in the basket."

Once their chores had been completed, Olly and Josh found themselves a good vantage point from which to watch the road. They were both impatient for the arrival of Josh's mother. Olly knew visits from Josh's mom were more like those from an eccentric aunt. Josh and Jonathan never knew when she'd decide to drop in, but they could always count on her having great stories to share.

"What's that noise?" Olly asked, after half an hour had passed without the sighting of a single car on the road.

Josh listened. It was a strange sound — a kind of

distant throbbing. He stood up, shading his eyes to peer into the distance. He saw a dark pinpoint in the sky and grinned. "It's a helicopter," he announced, with a laugh. "Mom's arriving in a helicopter!"

The arrival of the helicopter at the archaeological dig caused a major stir. Word had already gotten around the camp that a Hollywood movie star was coming, and the diggers threw down their tools and crowded around as soon as the rotors stopped spinning, all of them eager to catch a glimpse of the celebrity.

Natasha Welles stepped down from the helicopter, smiling and waving — every inch the movie star. Olly gazed at her in awe. Somehow Josh's mother always managed to look as if she was on a movie set — even now, when she was only dressed in jeans and a simple white blouse, with her long auburn hair tumbling loose down her back.

Josh and Olly pushed forward through the crowds as a second figure appeared at the door of the helicopter. "She brought Ethan with her," Josh remarked.

"Oh, is that bad?" Olly asked, recognizing that Ethan was the name of Natasha's latest boyfriend.

"No, Ethan's great," Josh replied happily. He

reached the front of the crowd and his mother opened her arms to greet him.

Olly knew about Ethan — anyone who read magazines, or watched TV, knew about Ethan Cain. He was a handsome, self-made millionaire who had earned a fortune in computer software. He now traveled the world as a modern-day adventurer. His name had been linked with Natasha Welles for several months now. There was even talk of a wedding, although both celebrities denied making long-term plans. Ethan was also dressed casually in a shirt and jeans. When no one else emerged from the helicopter, Olly realized that Ethan must have been the pilot. If any guy was cool enough for Josh's mom, Olly thought Ethan Cain just might be the one.

Natasha shook hands and gave autographs and made her way gradually through the crowd, her arm around Josh's shoulders. Jonathan was waiting for her by the trailers. They hugged and Jonathan shook Ethan's hand.

"Trust you to make a spectacular entrance," Jonathan said to his mother.

"You know me," Natasha replied with a laugh. She hugged Olly and Mrs. Beckmann. "It's lovely to see you all again," she said. She looked around. "And what an amazing place this is. I'm so glad Ethan persuaded me to take time off to come down here."

"There's lots to see," Olly said. "Do you want to visit the tomb? You'll never believe what's been going on — it all started when my dad found this old stone with —"

"For goodness sake, let Natasha catch her breath," said Mrs. Beckmann. "Come on into the trailer, I expect you could do with a rest and some lunch after your flight."

Natasha put an arm around Olly's shoulders. "Just let me get settled in, Olly," she said. "Then I want you to tell me everything that's happened." She gave Josh and Jonathan a knowing look. "My own children never tell me anything, so I'm relying on you to give me the full story."

~~~~~

Olly and Josh had a great time over lunch. The professor missed it altogether, he was so wrapped up in his work, but Ethan was friendly and funny, talking of whitewater rafting in India and bungee jumping in New Zealand and scuba diving in Malaysia; his life seemed to be an endless series of exciting escapades. And Natasha clearly enjoyed being away from the pressures and expectations of her working life. She seemed happy and relaxed, and delighted Olly especially, by showing an interest in her adventures with Josh and chatting away like an old friend.

Both Natasha and Ethan were particularly fascinated by Josh and Olly's tale of the Elephantine Stone — its theft and spectacular recovery. Natasha laughed uproariously at Olly's description of her time inside the rolled-up carpet, and Ethan was riveted by the chaos caused when the ancient booby traps were triggered.

"And right now," Olly told them, "we're working on a riddle that my dad found in the tomb." She showed Ethan and Natasha the translation of the riddle, and Ethan seemed particularly intrigued by it.

"I think the first part means a circular room," Josh said, and explained his reasoning.

"Yes, I can follow that," Ethan agreed. "But what are the sacred two, four and six?"

"We're still working on that," Olly told him.

"It reminds me of the riddle of the Sphinx," Ethan said thoughtfully.

"Oh, yeah," Josh put in, looking at the others who sat at the table. "The one that initiates into the priesthood had to answer: What animal goes on four legs in the morning, two legs during the day, and three legs in the evening? The answer is 'human beings.' They crawl when they're babies — that's the morning of life. They walk upright as they grow up — that's the daytime of life. And they use a stick, like a third leg, when they're old — in the evening of life." He looked at the riddle. "So, do you think this could be similar?" he asked Ethan. "Two — four — six. Do you think they're supposed to be legs?"

"Yes, that's it!" Olly said. "A bird has two legs. Four legs would belong to some kind of land animal." She frowned. "And six legs could mean an insect."

"The Egyptians held the scarab beetle sacred," Jonathan pointed out. "That could be the answer. Two — four — six. Bird — animal — beetle."

"And seven?" Natasha asked.

Olly grinned. "An old beetle," she joked. "With a walking stick!"

Ethan laughed. "I don't think so."

Olly jumped up. "Me neither. But we've got most of it," she said to Josh. "We should go and tell Dad. He's going to be amazed!"

"And he might be able to help us make sense of the part about the sacred seven," Josh added. "We should ask him to take another look at the riddle on the wall of the Burial Chamber — I've got a feeling it might hold some more clues."

Chapter Nine: Moon-phase

Ethan Cain and Natasha Welles gazed up in awe at the beautiful paintings that covered the walls of Setiankhra's tomb.

"They're breathtaking," Natasha said, her voice hushed, her eyes wide. "I never realized they would be so colorful — or so detailed."

Olly smiled. "They *are* pretty impressive," she agreed. She was on her best behavior, in part because she was in the presence of a movie star, but also because she and Josh had been reminded that the tombs were not only sacred, but potentially dangerous. Ever since Olly set off the booby traps, the two friends had not been allowed in the tombs without an adult. She turned back to Jonathan and her father, who were examining the hieroglyphs of the riddle. "Have you found anything?" she asked.

They seemed to have been scrutinizing the glyphs and muttering quietly to each other for ages.

The professor stood up. "I can't see anything to suggest what the sacred seven might be," he said.

"There may be clues elsewhere, but it could take weeks to find them."

"That's too bad," Josh said. "I suppose we'll just have to keep working on it."

"But do you think we've got the rest right?" Olly asked her father. "Is 'the room that devours itself' a *circular* room?"

"It's a good theory," Professor Christie agreed. "Except for the fact that a circular room would be very unusual. The Egyptians seldom used curves in their architecture. A circular room would be quite unique."

Ethan stepped closer to the wall and looked at a hieroglyph to the left of the riddle.

"This bird image," he said, "it's a *benu*, isn't it?"

"Yes, a phoenix on a solar disc," Jonathan replied, coming up alongside him. "It's a frequent New Kingdom image."

"There are similar images in the tomb of Ramses the Fourth," Ethan murmured. "Have you worked out what it means in this context? Isn't that obelisk icon alongside it thought to be an embodiment of Osiris, the ruler of the Underworld?"

"Yes, it is," the professor confirmed. "I had no idea you were interested in Egyptology, Mr. Cain."

"Please, call me Ethan," he said. "I'm no expert,

Professor; I'm just an enthusiastic amateur. But I have a few interesting items that I've collected over the years, and I enjoy the research." He looked more closely. "Have the writings in this cartouche been translated yet?" He examined the ancient brushstrokes. "These symbols — they indicate *road*, don't they?"

Jonathan nodded. "Yes, the literal translation of this seems to be: *under me the backward road* — but we have no idea what it means."

"No." Ethan's voice was soft. "They certainly were a cryptic people."

Natasha laughed. "I know that tone, Ethan," she said. She looked at Olly, standing at her side. "His voice always gets that hazy sound just before he vanishes into one of his projects. It's a waste of time talking to him then — he's off in a world of his own."

Olly nodded. "Tell me about it," she sympathized. "Dad's just the same."

Natasha put an arm around Olly's shoulders. "Ethan, I'm going up top now," she said. "This place is incredible, but it's a little claustrophobic for my liking."

Ethan, Jonathan and the professor were over at the far wall, heads together, deep in conversation.

Natasha laughed. "See what I mean?" she said to Olly. "He's gone, already." She smiled at Josh. "Now then, do you two guys want to stay down here, or do you want to come with me and hear about my new movie?" For once, it was no contest. The three of them headed up the corridor to the surface.

"I want to hear all the latest Hollywood gossip," Olly said to Natasha.

"Well, I don't think there'll be time for *all* of it," she replied, laughing. "But I'll fill you in on all the juiciest parts." She looked over her shoulder. "Josh, are you coming?"

The three of them had been walking along together, but Josh had suddenly stopped to stare at the wall.

"What is it?" Olly asked, walking back. He was gazing at the depiction of the snake eating its own tail — the painting that had given him the idea of the circular room. He pointed to the stars that surrounded the snake. "Remember the professor mentioning these?" Josh asked.

"Yes," Olly replied. "They're the Pleiades. Except that the ancient Egyptians called them something else."

"The Krittikas," Josh told her. "Count them."

"One, two, three, four, five, six — oh!" Olly gasped. "*Seven!*"

"Seven sacred stars," Josh agreed. "*Seven* — just like the riddle says."

"We have to tell Dad," Olly said excitedly.

"We can tell him when he comes up," Josh said. "After all, the riddle only tells us what to look for once we're in the room that devours itself. Jonathan and your dad still have to figure out how to find that room."

Natasha was looking over their shoulders. "I'm sure they'll work it out," she said. "And Ethan might even be able to help. He was being rather modest down there — he's really quite an expert on this stuff. He has several hundred items on display back home, and a whole library full of reference books."

~~~~

Time flew past for Olly and Josh as they sat with Olly's grandmother, drinking iced lemonade and listening to Natasha talk about her upcoming movie. It was midafternoon before Jonathan and Ethan emerged from the tomb and joined them under the umbrella.

"Professor Christie is still down there," Ethan said. "He's busy translating more of the writing."

"What have you people been doing?" Jonathan asked, pouring himself a glass of lemonade.

"Just chatting," Olly said casually. "Oh — and solving the last part of the riddle, as well."

Jonathan stared at her. "Excuse me?"

"We've figured out what the sacred seven are," Josh told him gleefully. "They're stars."

"The Krittikas!" Ethan said, leaning forward eagerly. "Of course! A sacred bird, a sacred animal, a sacred scarab and seven sacred stars." He laughed. "You two are amazing!"

"Aren't we, though?" Olly said with a grin. It wasn't every day that they received a compliment from the likes of Ethan Cain. She looked at Jonathan. "Now all you and Dad have to do is find that room."

"Easier said than done," Jonathan replied. "It could take six months to translate all the writings down there."

"But the clues must be there," Ethan said.

"I'm sure they are," Jonathan agreed. "Every aspect of the burial of a pharaoh had to be covered by protective spells — and every spell had to be written out in full. If the Tears of Isis were put in the tomb for safekeeping, then spells would have been placed around them to protect them from desecration."

"You mean from tomb robbers?" Josh asked.

Jonathan nodded. "But the spells weren't simply there to keep unwanted humans out," he said. "They were also there to stave off supernatural danger. The mythical world of the Egyptians was a dodgy place — if you didn't protect everything with very carefully worded and detailed spells, all kinds of bad things could happen. The pharaoh could lose his way on his journey to the next world, or his food could be poisoned by demons, or his heart could literally be stolen from him! Getting from this world to the next wasn't easy."

"I know you and Dad will find the Tears, eventually," Olly said. "And then they'll be put safely in a museum until we need them to open the Archives." She noticed a frown cross Ethan's face as she spoke, but it soon cleared.

"Which museum will you donate the Tears to, if they're found?" he asked Jonathan.

"The Egyptian Museum in Cairo," Jonathan replied. "Professor Bey, the Museum Director, has been kind enough to give us full access for research purposes."

"Natasha told me that you were on your way back from the museum when she called you," Ethan went on. "She said you put the Elephantine Stone there

124

for safekeeping. I wish I could have seen it before it was locked away — it sounds fascinating."

"It's a shame I didn't call Jonathan before he handed it over," Natasha remarked. "I'm sure he'd have been happy to let you look at it." She turned to Jonathan. "Ethan was in Cairo, you know. That's where I met up with him to come down here. He's been there for several weeks."

"I've been looking into a real estate deal," Ethan said. "I'm thinking of opening a branch of my company there." He smiled. "But that's boring stuff. Has Natasha told you about some of the stunts she'll have to do in the new movie? They're pretty wild."

Josh looked impressed. "You didn't say you were going to do your own stunts, Mom! What kinds of stuff will you do?"

Natasha laughed. "Whatever they ask me to, I expect," she said. "Within reason, of course." And soon they were all enthralled by more tales of moviemaking.

The afternoon passed quickly, and all too soon for Josh and Olly, Natasha began to talk about the journey back to Rome.

"Can't you stay for just one night?" Josh asked. "It feels like you've only been here five minutes."

"We still have another hour or so," Ethan said.

He looked at Olly and Josh. "I've brought my camcorder with me, and I'd love to take some footage of the valley from the helicopter. I can't pilot the chopper and make a movie at the same time — would you two be interested in coming up with me to shoot some film?"

"Oh, yeah!" Josh said. "I can handle the camera."

"And I could do the commentary," Olly put in quickly.

Ethan smiled. "That's fine with me," he said.

Jonathan stayed with Natasha and Olly's gran, while Ethan led the two friends to the helicopter.

Once Josh and Olly were safely strapped in the back, Ethan climbed into the pilot's seat up front. Josh took command of the camcorder as Ethan gunned the engine. The noise rose to a steady, throbbing roar as the rotors began to turn — slowly and heavily at first, then faster and faster until they were just a dark blur.

Josh lifted the camera to his eye and pointed it out of the window to take some footage as the helicopter rose into the air.

"Whee-oo!" Josh whistled, as the land dropped quickly away below them. "This is great! I'm going to have to ask Mom to buy me one of these for my birthday."

"Which?" Olly asked. "The camcorder or the helicopter?"

"Both!" Josh replied laughing.

"Are you guys OK back there?" Ethan called.

"We're fine," Olly shouted back.

The helicopter circled and the landscape stretched out beneath them like a 3-D map. The mountains flung long shadows across the rugged terrain in the early evening sunshine and the Nile sparkled like a thread of silver. The little riverboats with their triangular sails lay on the water like resting butterflies. Olly spied New Gurna, nestling among green fields, and across the river, small and remote, she made out the broken temples and narrow streets of Luxor.

Ethan banked the helicopter and turned to the south, following the line of the valley. Olly leaned close over Josh's shoulder to call out the names of the tombs as they flew over them.

"That one to the right — point the camera over there, Josh — that's Ramses the Fourth's tomb, and right ahead of us and to the left is the tomb of the sons of Ramses the Second. It's called KV5, and it's where Kent Weeks found a whole bunch of secret chambers," Olly said.

"Just like what we'll probably find in Setiankhra's tomb," Josh added.

"And to the right is the tomb of Ramses the Second," Olly continued. "And directly ahead of us is the tomb of Tutankhamen."

The helicopter swept the length of the rugged valley, turning this way and that so that Josh could get clear shots of all the tomb entrances that dotted the craggy hills. The last tomb, deep in the shadow of overhanging cliffs, belonged to Tutmoses III.

Finally, Ethan swung the helicopter around and they headed north, back toward the excavation site.

"So, what turned you on to Egyptology, Ethan?" Josh asked.

"I suppose it was the remoteness and the grandeur of it," he replied. "And the epic scale of it all — the complexity of their civilization." A longing tone came into his voice. "They were a great people. Imagine if you could go back there to watch the pyramids being built — to learn all their lost secrets firsthand."

"Someone should invent a time-travel machine," Josh said.

"Yes," Ethan agreed. "Someone should."

The helicopter started to descend. "And so," Olly said, leaning over Josh's shoulder again, "we return to the newly discovered tomb of Setiankhra.

Inside, even as I speak, the famous British archae-ologist, Professor Kenneth Christie, and his assistant, Jonathan Welles, are working to decipher the cryp-tic clues left by the ancient people of this land, and to find their way to the circular chamber that houses the Tears of Isis. Pictures supplied courtesy of Josh Welles. Your captain for this flight was Mr. Ethan Cain. And this is Olivia Christie, signing off. Thank you for your attention."

Olly noticed Josh roll his eyes at her, obviously thinking that her voice-over was a little much. She couldn't help but think that Josh lacked his mom's flair for the dramatic. Josh lowered the camcorder as Ethan brought the helicopter in to land, amid billow-ing clouds of dust.

"That was great," Ethan declared. "I loved the voice-over, Olly. Let's hope Josh got some good footage to complement it."

"I'm sure I did," said Josh. "It'd be pretty hard not to around here.

They clambered out of the aircraft and began to make their way back toward the trailers, where Olly's grandmother and Natasha were still chatting.

"I just want to check that everything's OK for the flight back to Cairo," Ethan called to the two friends. "You go ahead, I'll only be a few minutes."

Olly turned and nodded, but as she looked back at the helicopter, something caught her eye. Behind the door to the fuselage, a logo was painted on the side of the aircraft. It was a silver oval containing a silver crescent moon in one side and a silver full moon in the other. Beneath the logo, Olly read the word "Moon-phase."

"What's up?" Josh asked. He had stopped to wait for his friend.

Olly pointed at the logo. "Moon-phase," she said.

"That's right," Josh agreed. "I think it's a part of Ethan's computer firm. So what?" His eyes widened suddenly. "Oh! You're not thinking of that e-mail on Mohammed's laptop, are you?"

Olly nodded — momentarily speechless with surprise. The e-mail had said *ec@moon-phase.net. Could the "ec" have stood for Ethan Cain?* Olly wondered.

Ethan Cain at Moon-phase?

Chapter Ten:
The Hidden Door

Olly and Josh stared at each other. Olly felt as if the world had suddenly turned upside down and inside out. She couldn't be absolutely certain that the e-mails from moon-phase.net had been sent by Ethan, but if they weren't, it was an extraordinary coincidence. *But why would Ethan Cain be sending e-mails to Mohammed?* Olly wondered. How would they even know each other? And, more to the point, exactly what kind of business venture would they be involved in together?

She looked again at the silver logo on the helicopter, and then back at Josh. "We shouldn't say anything," she murmured to him as they drew near the trailers. "Not till we've had time to think about this."

Josh nodded.

"I'll think of an excuse so we can get a few minutes on our own," Olly whispered. Then she waved at Natasha, Jonathan, and her gran, who were still sitting around the table outside. "That was a great trip!" she called as she and Josh walked over.

"Ethan's just checking out the helicopter," Josh said.

Natasha sighed. "Then we'll probably be on our way soon. What a pity. I'm having such a lovely time."

"That voice-over was thirsty work," Olly said. "I'm going to get myself a drink. Would anyone else like one?"

"Just bring a jug of water out, please," said Audrey Beckmann. "And some fresh glasses."

"I'll give you a hand," Josh offered, and the two friends hurried inside together.

As soon as the door closed behind them, Olly turned to Josh. "What on earth is going on around here?" she asked. "Is everyone in the world trying to get their hands on the Elephantine Stone? Even Ethan?"

Josh opened the fridge and took out a large bottle of mineral water. "It could all be perfectly innocent," he said.

"Hmm," Olly murmured dubiously. "A coincidence that Mohammed and that American thug have the same tattoo? A coincidence that part of Ethan's company is called Moon-phase, and that Mohammed is getting e-mails from someone at moon-phase dot net? A *coincidence* that all three of them happen to be in the same place at the same time?" She frowned. "I don't think so!"

"But even if you're right about the e-mail, Ethan might be doing some perfectly ordinary business with Mohammed," Josh suggested. "After all, Mohammed's an archaeology student, and Ethan's interested in archaeology."

Olly shook her head. "In which case, why hasn't Ethan mentioned that he knows Mohammed?" she asked. "Do you want to know what I think? I think Ethan's got something to do with the Elephantine Stone being stolen."

Josh shook his head. "He wouldn't do something like that," he protested. "He's a millionaire. If he wants something, he can just buy it. He doesn't have to steal stuff."

"He can't buy stuff that isn't for sale," Olly pointed out. "The Elephantine Stone *definitely* isn't for sale. And I just remembered something; Carter said he had a buyer lined up for the stone in Cairo. And Ethan has been in Cairo for the past few weeks, hasn't he?"

Josh stared at her. "You think Ethan was the *buyer*?" he gasped.

Olly nodded as a pattern began to form in her mind. "Maybe Mohammed and Carter were both working for Ethan," she breathed. "Mohammed's job was to steal the stone and hand it over to Carter. Then Carter was supposed to take it to Cairo and give it to Ethan. But the plan fell apart when *we* overheard Carter's plans and got the stone back!"

"That might have been why Ethan suggested to Mom that they come and visit us down here," Josh added. "Maybe he had an ulterior motive." Then he shook his head. "But Ethan seems like a really great guy. Besides, there are lots of artifacts around. Why would he want to steal this one?"

"I don't know. Maybe he wants things he can't have," Olly said grimly. "Or, maybe he wants the stone for the same reason we do."

"To help find the Tears of Isis?" Josh questioned. "But he had never heard of the Tears before we told him." Olly remembered Ethan's reaction to their explanation of the talismans. "He could just be a good actor," Olly suggested. "He's dating one."

Josh gazed at her, temporarily at a loss for words. "Even if you're right," he said at last, "we can't just go and tell everyone. They'll think we're out of our minds. Mom really likes Ethan. She's never going to believe he was involved in stealing the stone."

"True," Olly agreed thoughtfully. "And if we do say anything, Ethan and Mohammed will just deny it and we'll end up looking like idiots." Her forehead creased in concentration. "Maybe we're just jumping to conclusions," she said. "After all, Ethan knew the stone was safely locked away in Cairo before he came here. Your mom told him, remember? Besides, they're getting ready to leave now," she added. "If he was hoping to find the Tears, he'd need to stay here longer than one single day."

"Yes, but —" Whatever Josh had been intending to say was interrupted by the sound of the trailer door being opened from the outside.

Ethan appeared in the doorway. "I'll have some water, please, guys," he said. "Although I could use something a little stronger!"

Olly hastily poured the mineral water into a jug, while Josh got out the glasses. "Is there a problem?" she asked.

Ethan nodded. "There's a fault with the chopper's engine," he said. "We were lucky it didn't show till we were back on the ground. I'm going to have to send for a replacement part." He smiled ruefully. "It looks like we're going to be imposing on your hospitality a little longer than expected. Natasha is going to make some calls and reorganize her schedule. Jonathan will drive her back to Cairo in the morning, but I'll be staying here till the engine part arrives. But hey, every cloud has a silver lining; it'll give me more time to explore the tomb." He gave them a friendly wink. "You never know, I might even be able to help the professor find the room that devours itself."

He took the jug of water from Olly's hands and left the trailer.

Olly looked at Josh. "I bet there's nothing wrong with the helicopter," she hissed. "It's just an excuse for him to stay longer." Her eyes narrowed determinedly. "We're going to have to watch him every minute, day and night."

Josh nodded. "You're right. Poor Mom," he said. "She really likes him."

"Well, he's a rat," Olly said firmly. "And we're going to do everything we can to *prove* that he's a rat!"

〜〜〜

It was early evening, and long shadows were reaching out across the valley. The sun had dipped behind the western cliffs, but the sky was still bright. There were another two hours till dusk.

Olly and Josh were sitting at the table with Olly's grandmother, Josh's mother, and Ethan Cain. Natasha had just finished a call to her agent in Hollywood. She flipped her cell phone shut. "Judy is going to see that everything is reorganized for me," she told them. "If Jonathan and I head off early in the morning, I should still be able to catch the midafternoon plane from Cairo to Rome." She smiled at Olly. "Meanwhile, you can tell me more about that movie idea you have for me. Who would I be playing?"

"Nefertiti," Olly told her. "She was a really beautiful female pharaoh."

"If you're going to talk movies, I think I'll go and stretch my legs," Ethan said. He got up. "I'd like to see how Jonathan and the professor are getting along in the tomb."

The diggers were only employed for a half day on Saturday, but Olly's father and his assistant had decided to do some more exploring on their own. There was plenty of work to be done in Setiankhra's tomb that didn't require hired laborers.

Olly and Josh watched Ethan as he strolled past the trailers and turned out of sight at the end of the row. Josh wanted to stay and talk more with his mom, but his suspicion got the best of him.

"I think I'll go for a walk, too," Josh said, standing up.

"Me, too," Olly added.

Natasha gazed at them with a crooked smile.

"Everyone's abandoning me," she wailed. "Was it something I said?"

"Don't mind them," Audrey Beckmann commented. "They can't keep still for five minutes." She looked at the two friends. "Don't lose track of the time," she said. "I'll be starting dinner in an hour or so. I want you back here, washed, and ready to eat by eight."

"OK," Olly agreed. She smiled at Natasha. "We can talk about the movie over dinner. I've had some great ideas."

"I'll look forward to that," Natasha replied.

Josh and Olly wandered off after Ethan. "We can't just follow him," Josh whispered to Olly. "He'll see us."

"I know," Olly whispered back. "This way." Josh followed, and in moments they were peering from between the trailers.

"There he is," Olly whispered.

Ethan was heading toward the tomb entrance.

"Maybe he really *is* just going to see how Jonathan and your dad are getting along," Josh suggested.

Olly wasn't so sure. "Wait!" she hissed. Halfway to the tomb, Ethan gave a quick glance over his shoulder and then turned and strode briskly in the opposite direction — away from the tomb and toward the campsite.

"Got him!" Olly whispered sharply. "I'll give you two guesses who he's going to see."

The friends followed Ethan carefully, keeping low and sticking to the shadows as much as possible. As a result he got way ahead of them, but at least he didn't realize he was being tracked.

He rounded the shoulder of rock and disappeared from sight. Josh and Olly raced after him, scrambling up the side of the rocky outcrop.

"Keep your head down," Josh warned as they neared the crest of the ridge. They both peered cautiously over the top, and Olly let out a soft hiss of satisfaction.

Ethan Cain was only a few yards away from them, and Mohammed was with him. The two men were speaking together in low voices. The urgent murmurings drifted up to the friends, but neither of them could pick out any actual words that were being said. However, one thing was very clear from the tone of the men's voices and the way they were behaving: The two men knew each other and had far more pressing issues to discuss than the weather.

Their conversation lasted only a minute or so.

Mohammed gestured back the way Ethan had come, Ethan nodded sharply, and the two men turned and headed back together.

Olly and Josh flattened themselves against the rocks. They were well above the men, and unless either of them happened to glance upward, there was a good chance that the two friends wouldn't be spotted.

Olly watched as Ethan and Mohammed passed them and made their way toward the tomb. Mohammed was carrying a large flashlight.

"What do you think they're up to?" Josh whispered.

"No good, that's for sure," Olly replied. "Let's go."

They kept their distance as they trailed their quarry. The men were walking quickly, both of them looking around every now and then, as if to check that they weren't being observed. Olly and Josh's pursuit consisted of wild dashes from one point of cover to the next. It wasn't long before the men were a long way ahead of them, but they didn't dare draw any closer for fear of being seen.

Olly watched from the shadows of a long, low rock as Mohammed and Ethan entered the tomb of Setiankhra. "I wish we could have heard what they were talking about," she said. "What if they're just going down there to see how Dad and Jonathan are doing? That won't prove anything!"

"There's only one way to find out," Josh said. "Come on." He ran the last twenty yards to the tomb with Olly close behind. The entrance showed up clearly, a flare of electric light in the gathering dusk. "Slowly now," Josh murmured.

Olly nodded, knowing they were going against orders by entering the excavation on their own.

They stepped into the tomb, moving as quietly as possible, both of them listening intently for any telltale sounds of the two men. Silently, they crept across the wooden bridge and down the second corridor. As they neared the bottom, they heard voices.

Olly paused, her heart pounding.

Josh looked at her and put his finger to his lips. They pressed against the wall and edged a little closer to the entrance of the Burial Chamber.

"They've found it!" It was Ethan's voice, quiet but excited.

"They must have gone through," Mohammed said.

Olly came to the entranceway and peered around the corner of the chamber. There was no sign of Jonathan, or her father, but she could plainly see Ethan and Mohammed. The two men were standing together at the far end of the shadowy room. But it was something else that completely took her breath away.

Where the wall of the chamber previously had been smooth and flat, there was now a square opening, about three feet wide and slightly more than three feet tall. It was just below the place where the professor had pointed out the hieroglyphics that mentioned the sacred protector Nuit.

Olly's heart pounded. Her father and Jonathan had somehow found the hidden doorway! As Mohammed had said, they must have gone through to explore because there was no sign of them on this side of the doorway. How could they resist?

"I had no idea they were so close to finding the hidden entrance," Ethan remarked. "We must follow them."

Mohammed gripped Ethan's arm as the older man ducked to go through the door. His voice was suddenly low and urgent. "Look!" he said, pointing to the writings over the door. "Do you see the hieroglyphs?"

"I don't have time to translate," Ethan snapped. "What do they say?"

Mohammed moved closer to the wall. Something in his voice sent shivers up Olly's spine as he translated. *"This shall be the gift of Nuit to thee, traveler on the backward road. Thou shalt not die. Thou shalt move through all the ages. Thou shalt have one foot in the future and one foot in the past. Deathless traveler, thou shalt live for a hundred million years."*

Ethan let out a slow, triumphant breath. "Ahhhh!" He gripped Mohammed's shoulder. "Just as I'd hoped!"

But Mohammed backed away from the wall, his eyes uneasy. "I will not go through there," he said. "The danger is too great. Night is coming, and a powerful moon is rising. This is not the time to desecrate a tomb protected by Nuit." He shivered, staring around warily. "I feel her presence all around me in this place," he muttered. Then he turned and looked intently at Ethan. "There's still time to give this up — to go away from here and forget."

Ethan moved purposefully toward him. "Forget?" he murmured. "Forget something I've been searching for all my life? I don't think so. I have as much right to it as anyone."

"Then you must travel the road alone," Mohammed told him. "I will have nothing more to do with it." He turned and walked out of the chamber. He rushed right past Olly and Josh, and headed up the corridor to the surface.

Olly flinched away, treading on Josh's feet as she tried to keep out of Mohammed's sight. Josh caught her hand and pulled her quickly into one of the side chambers.

"I'm going in," they heard Ethan snarl at Mohammed. "And I need you to come with me."

Mohammed paused just beyond the entrance to the side chamber. "No, not tonight," he said, defiant. "It isn't safe." The writings on the wall had clearly unnerved him.

Olly saw Ethan stride after Mohammed. She sidled to the entrance of the chamber and peered out.

Ethan had caught up with Mohammed just a little farther up the passage. "Think about what we might find!" he was saying, his voice urgent and persuasive. "Are you really willing to give up the chance to claim the Tears of Isis?"

The Egyptian's footsteps faltered. Ethan's words had obviously had an effect on him. He turned back uncertainly. And then his eyes locked on Olly!

Ethan whirled around, searching the tomb. When he caught sight of Olly, he lunged.

"Josh! Time to get out of here!" Olly yelled, running away from Ethan and down into the Burial

Chamber. Josh raced after her, with both Ethan and Mohammed close on his tail.

The friends tumbled into the stone chamber as an angry shout from Ethan echoed off the walls behind them. They were trapped — there was no way out. No way but one!

Olly caught hold of Josh's sleeve and dragged him through the darkened doorway in the chamber's wall. "Help me!" she gasped. And, together, she and Josh heaved the heavy stone doorway closed, just as Ethan hurled himself toward it.

In spite of Ethan's momentum, the door thudded shut, plunging Olly and Josh into deep, impenetrable darkness.

Chapter Eleven:
Secrets of the Tomb

A thin beam of bright light cut suddenly through the darkness. Josh had pulled a small flashlight from his pocket. The light illuminated a gray stone wall and a floor strewn with rubble. They were in a narrow corridor that stretched away to the left and right, parallel to the Burial Chamber.

"We need to find Dad," Olly said.

Josh raked the beam of light along the featureless corridor in both directions. "Which way?" he asked.

They heard the grinding sound of stone grating on stone. Josh aimed the flashlight at the doorway. It was being pushed open from the outside.

Olly didn't wait to think. "This way!" she said, running to the left.

Josh followed, taking a quick look over his shoulder as he ran. He saw a crack of light in the wall — Ethan and Mohammed would soon have the door open again.

Olly was in the lead. "Give me the flashlight!" she gasped. Josh handed it over. Olly grazed one hand along the wall as the thin white beam stretched out ahead of them, lighting up the rough floor and the narrow gray walls.

A black slit appeared in the wall to their right. They ran past it. There was another, and another — dark passageways leading off at right angles to the main corridor.

A flare of light behind them threw their shadows forward. They were caught in the bright beam of a powerful flashlight. Ethan and Mohammed were chasing them along the corridor.

Olly caught hold of Josh's arm and pulled him into one of the side passages. This new corridor was exactly the same as the other: a straight, gray tunnel, a little more than shoulder-width, and around six feet high.

But then they came to something different: a small chamber. Olly shined the flashlight around. The walls were covered in intricate paintings. Animal-headed figures sat in profile on chairs, watching as a jackal-headed figure — which Olly recognized as Anubis — weighed a human heart against a feather on a set of simple scales. The crocodile-headed god, Thoth, waited nearby. Olly knew his task: to gobble down any hearts that failed the test and were heavy with misdeeds. Rows of hieroglyphs filled the spaces between the paintings.

"Wow!" Olly breathed.

"No time for 'wow'," Josh panted. "Which way out?" Five identical tunnels led off in every direction, like spokes from the hub of a wheel.

"Beats me," Olly gasped. She tried to go over their route in her head. Left from the doorway, then a right had brought them here. If they wanted to work their way back around to the doorway in the Burial Chamber, she figured they should go right and right again. With some luck, that would take them full circle.

Olly flashed the light into the tunnel that led off to the right. "This one!" she said.

They ran along the stone passage deeper and deeper into the heart of the mountains. Olly kept looking for a corridor that went to the right, but there was none, so they kept running. Soon, she noticed that the walls here were inlaid with green jasper. And painted cobras, with gleaming jeweled eyes, reared up the sides of the corridor.

The friends came to a sharp bend. The wall ahead was covered in a huge painting of Osiris, god of the Underworld, holding a crook and flail. His wife, Isis, stood behind him, and ahead of them were the four sons of Horus.

In spite of the fear of pursuit, Olly had to be

dragged away from the wall painting. She had spent all her life learning about ancient Egypt from her father — and now she was seeing ancient master-pieces that had lain hidden for thousands of years. It felt to Olly as if they were running through a kalei-doscope of Egyptian mythology, going ever deeper into a dead world that their presence was bringing back to life.

"We're going down," Josh commented.

"I know," Olly replied. The tunnel had been sloping for some way now. Olly didn't like to think of how far under the surface they must be. "Not again!" she gasped.

They had come to another chamber with six exits leading out of it. Here the paintings depicted green boats sailing across an azure sky. Seated in the larg-est boat was a man with a scarab for a head. A lion lay — sphinxlike — shaded by papyrus plants that were entwined with cobras.

Again, Olly chose the tunnel to the right. If her mental picture of the place was accurate, she thought, they should now be heading back to the main part of the tomb. There was only one problem: How deep under the ground were they now? The passage ran level for some time, but then it dipped alarmingly, shooting down like a ramp into a well of darkness.

Olly pointed the flashlight down, but the tunnel fell away beyond the beam. "This can't be right," she panted. "We're too deep. We should go back and find a passageway that heads upward."

Josh stared back up the tunnel. "Can I have the flashlight?" he asked.

Olly handed it to him. He sent the beam skidding back the way they had come. A thousand almond-shaped eyes glittered at them from the walls. "Listen!" Josh said.

Olly held her breath and strained her ears.

"Hear it?" he asked.

She nodded. It was distant, but unmistakable: the sound of feet pounding on stone, echoing down through the corridors and chambers. Ethan and Mohammed were still in pursuit.

"We can't go back," Josh said. "We might run straight into them."

"Where are Jonathan and Dad?" Olly wailed.

"They must have gone another way," Josh said. "There were lots of side tunnels. They could be anywhere!"

"Great!" Olly took a deep breath, exasperated. "We'd better keep going then," she decided.

They hurried on, side by side, down the slope. The corridor tilted as steeply as a child's slide, making it difficult for Josh and Olly to keep on their feet. Then Olly brought her heel down on a piece of loose stone that skidded away beneath her. She slipped and fell into Josh, and soon they were both sliding down the shaft, the flashlight skimming the walls and ceiling as they plunged downward.

Their fall was halted by a bank of loose, dry sand and rubble. They tumbled into it, breathless and bruised. It was a few moments before Olly could catch her breath enough to speak. "Are you OK?" she asked.

"I think so." Josh groaned, sitting up. Sand cascaded off his clothes. He shined the flashlight beam around them. "Look at that." He pointed the beam at the top of the bank of sand and stones where it reached the ceiling of the passage. The roof had fallen in and the heaped sand and rubble was the result of the collapse. "It's completely blocked!" Josh said. "We'll never get through. And listen . . ."

Again, they could hear the telltale sounds of pursuit. And now, mixed in with the echoing footfalls, they could also hear voices, weirdly distorted, drifting down the long slope toward them.

"Well, we can't go back," Olly said. "Shine the light here." Josh turned the flashlight back onto the sand and rubble. Olly crawled up to where the debris met the roof and began to dig, scooping out the sand and throwing the lumps of stone down behind her.

"What are you doing?" Josh asked.

"What does it look like?"

"But the tunnel could be blocked for another twenty yards!" Josh pointed out.

Olly ignored him. She was working hard, shoveling the sand away with both hands.

Josh shook his head. "This is crazy," he sighed. But he scrambled up the slope and joined Olly, holding the flashlight under his chin and using his hands to dig away the sand and rock.

The pair worked in dogged silence for some minutes. Sweat was pouring off them onto the sand and they were both gasping for breath. They had moved forward about three feet, and then, quite suddenly, Olly wrenched a lump of stone away and found a hole. They had reached the place where the roof had caved in.

They renewed their efforts, revealing a broken-edged gap that expanded to the full width of the roof. Olly took the flashlight and squirmed up through the hole. "It goes up about six feet," she called down to Josh. "I can see exits to either side — and a roof. I think it's another passage running right above this one!"

They cleared away more debris and soon stood side by side in the hole.

"Cup your hands," Olly said. "Help me climb up."

Half a minute later, the two friends were standing in the higher tunnel. Josh had the flashlight now. He pointed the beam to the right. "Uh-oh!" he said. This corridor ended in a flat stone wall, about twelve yards away. He turned the beam the other way and sighed with relief. The tunnel continued ahead for twenty yards or so, then there was a black square — an entrance or an exit.

The friends hurried on together, and stepped through the entrance. They found themselves standing on a platform of white stone slabs, flanked by life-sized shabti warriors made of shining quartz crystal. Josh moved the flashlight beam around the chamber they had entered. It was huge, the roof soaring up and away in a high arch of faintly glowing white rock. Olly saw that the walls were carved with bas-relief depictions of the soul's journey to the afterlife.

Two immense stone columns, decorated with carved palm fronds, held the roof up. At the base of each pillar sat a huge black statue — at least ten feet tall — of Osiris, the god who watched over the netherworld. Next to him sat a statue of his son,

Horus, with a falcon's head and eyes of gold and silver — to represent the sun and the full moon.

Behind these two majestic gods a vast chasm opened up, splitting the chamber in two.

"Can you believe this?" Olly murmured as she slowly crossed the chamber.

Josh didn't reply. He was gazing around in awe.

They walked together to the edge of the chasm. Josh pointed the flashlight at the far side. It was easily five yards away. The light also revealed a slender stone bridge spanning the gulf, just wide enough for a person to cross. There was no handrail or support. Beyond the bridge was another platform of white stones, and a dark, square gateway in the far wall of the chamber, also guarded by shabti warriors. Their green jeweled eyes glinted menacingly in the flashlight beam.

Josh stepped forward and shined the flashlight down into the chasm. Many feet below he saw a forest of sharpened stone spikes and, with a shudder, he noticed that human skeletons lay among them. He looked at Olly. "That's not a comforting sight," he said quietly.

Olly pursed her lips and stared at the thin, white stone bridge. "We can do it," she said. She glanced at Josh. "Do heights bother you?"

"Do they bother *you*?" he returned.

Olly shook her head.

"That's good, then," Josh said firmly. "I'll go first." Olly nodded and Josh stepped carefully out onto the bridge. He shined the light down at his feet. Olly swallowed hard, trying not to think about the spikes and skeletons below as she edged onto the bridge behind him. The stonework was narrow and smooth, but it looked safe.

Slowly they approached the middle of the bridge. "How are you doing?" Olly asked, surprised to find that her voice was shaking.

"It's easier than I expected," Josh replied. "And by the way, I *don't* like heights."

Olly smiled. "You're doing fine," she told him.

"Thanks," Josh said, glancing over his shoulder. But it was a bad move. Momentarily distracted, Josh stumbled. Olly reached forward to catch him as he tripped, but she missed. He fell hard. His fingers managed to catch the bridge, but the flashlight fell from his hand.

Olly watched in horror as it plummeted into the chasm.

Chapter Twelve:
The Golden Doors

Josh heard a crack as the flashlight hit stone somewhere far below, and then the chamber was lost in utter blackness. He lay sprawled on the cold stone bridge, facedown, his heart hammering. His fingers gripped the edges of the bridge while his mind whirled. He had dropped the flashlight! They were lost and blind and one wrong move could send them plunging down to the deadly spikes below.

He felt Olly's hands on his legs and heard her voice. "Josh — are you OK?" she asked.

"Yes. You?" he answered.

"I'm fine," Olly replied. "But we need to get off this bridge." Josh knew she must be terrified, but her voice sounded calm. "I'm going to back up. We'll just have to hope Ethan and Mohammed find us. At least they've got a flashlight. We'll never get out of here without a light."

"No." Josh felt himself growing calmer. His brain was beginning to work again. "Stay where you are." He rose cautiously to his hands and knees and then sat back on his heels. He fumbled in his pockets until his fingers found the piece of candle and box of matches he carried with him.

His hands trembled as he opened the box and struck a match. The light flared and grew steady. Josh touched the match to the candlewick, which caught and burned brightly. He was pleased by how strong the flame was. Now he could see the ground at his feet — though the shadows hemmed him in on all sides.

He turned. Olly was staring at him, her eyes bright in the candlelight. "You carry a candle?" she asked incredulously.

Josh nodded. "Jonathan gave it to me. He always carries matches and a piece of candle in the tombs. Just in case."

"Smart," Olly said. "Remind me to thank him. Could we get off this bridge now?"

Very carefully, the pair made their way to the far side of the chasm. Josh felt an overwhelming sense of relief when he finally stepped off the narrow bridge. He lifted the candle to see the exit from the chamber and headed toward it. Olly followed, and the dark raced in behind her as though it was giving chase.

Beyond the exit the tunnel was no more than ten feet long. It opened into another chamber so huge that Josh and Olly couldn't see the far walls or the roof. On either side of the entrance stood massive obsidian statues, each with the head of a hawk.

"That's Horus," Olly remarked nervously as she gazed up into the god's fierce face. "The patron of the living pharaohs." The statue's black eyes stared out over Olly's head, its haughty gaze fixed eternally on the engulfing darkness. She touched the cold, shining stone of the statue. "When was the last time anyone saw this?" she murmured. "It must have been thousands of years ago."

Josh raised the candle. The walls that stretched away on either side of the entrance were covered with immense bas-relief sculptures, depicting mythical scenes of gods and men and animals. Their colors shone in the flickering candlelight — red and gold and green, blue and yellow and white — eventually disappearing into the darkness.

Awed by the vastness of the place, Josh and Olly moved farther into the room. And then they both gasped in wonder and disbelief, because piled around the towering pillars that supported the roof lay golden treasures! Plates and jeweled goblets, statuettes and swords, shields and bowls, all glittered and gleamed and threw back the candlelight.

Josh's head spun with the wonder of it all. He

felt small and insignificant among such wealth and beauty and grandeur. The light of the candle seemed a tiny flicker in that great lost hall of treasures.

"It's as if they're watching us," Olly said, her voice low with awe.

Josh turned and saw that she was referring to two great statues that had emerged from the gloom ahead of them. They *did* seem almost alive, he thought. As if at any moment a head would turn and a hand lift, creaking with the weight of years. It was scary, but it was wonderful at the same time.

They walked between them and found themselves in a colonnade of warrior statues, all facing inward. A wall appeared at the end of the guarded aisle. It was covered in richly colored paintings. This time, all the people and animals were facing to the right.

"It's like a kind of procession," Olly said, approaching the painting. "I wonder where they're all going."

The wall arced, and Olly followed the painted procession around the curve. "Josh?" Olly's voice was breathless with excitement. "This is a curved wall!"

"Yes, I noticed," Josh replied. He knew what Olly was thinking — the same thought had occurred to him. Did the wall form a circle? And if so, what lay inside?

The procession ended. Two women in white robes knelt at the feet of a tall figure with the head of a jackal — the god Anubis, who escorted souls on their journey to the Underworld. At his back was a mass of hieroglyphic writings. And beyond that was a pair of huge, closed doors, made of gleaming, beaten gold. Josh could see a tawny, rippled reflection of his own face in the shiny metal.

For some time, the friends just stood there, staring up at the golden doors, speechless with amazement, all thought of their pursuers forgotten. Olly was the first to break the silence. "I think this is it," she whispered reverently. "I think we've found the room from Nuit's riddle!"

Chapter Thirteen: The Chamber of Light

"How do we get in?" Olly whispered, staring up at the doors.

Josh held the candle closer, searching for a handle or a lever. There was nothing. He winced as the candle guttered and a rivulet of hot wax burned his fingers. He looked down anxiously. The candle was already half eaten away by the flame. It wouldn't be much longer before it became too short to hold. And then what? He had matches, but they were only good for a few seconds each. And once the matches were gone, the darkness would swallow them whole, and that would probably be the end of them. He decided not to share his thoughts with Olly.

She was moving back and forth, running her hands over the doors, as if hoping to find something invisible to the eye. She pushed against the doors. They didn't move. "There has to be a way to get them open," she said.

"Open sesame!" Josh intoned solemnly. Nothing happened.

"That's Arabian legend, not Egyptian," Olly said, dropping to her knees. "Give me some light."

Josh crouched beside her. She was at the join between the doors. Here, the stone floor had been hollowed out to make a small hole. Olly pushed her fingers in under the doors. "I can feel something," she said. "It's hard and sharp and—" There was a loud metallic click and Olly saw the doors shiver slightly. She stood up and pressed her hand against them. They swung smoothly inward.

Together, the two friends moved forward into the room, all thought of danger temporarily forgotten in astonishment and delight. The room was like the inside of a huge golden bell. The enclosing walls and the vaulting ceiling were made of panels of highly polished gold, which glowed dark yellow in the candle flame. The panels were etched all over with fine drawings and writings. Even the floor was gold.

Olly looked at Josh, her eyes shining. "How did the riddle go?"

Josh handed Olly the candle stub as he rummaged in his pocket, then unfolded the sheet of paper. "'In the Chamber of Light, the room that devours itself, the sacred two of the air, the sacred four of the almond eyes, and the sacred six in black armor shall unite beneath the sacred seven,'" Josh recited. "'And the light of the sacred seven will shine upon the head that is whole and the heart that is awake and the eyes that weep.'"

"OK, we think the two and the four and the six represent legs, and the seven are the Pleiades," Olly said. "But what does the rest mean?"

"I don't know, yet. But look!" Josh pointed across the room. On three slender gold bases stood three small gold sculptures. Olly and Josh walked toward them. One was an ibis — a tall, long-beaked, spindle-legged bird. Its wings were spread wide and its sinuous neck arched down and forward, support-ing a flat golden plate which rested on its wing tips and head.

The next was a sitting cat, slender and elegant with a haughty, Abyssinian face. Between its ears was a strange kind of headpiece, almost like a crown, with a smooth, flattened top.

The last of the golden sculptures was a beetle with a golden dish on its back.

"Two legs, four legs, six legs," Olly said happily. "It's them. What about the seven?"

Josh shook his head. He began to circle the room, peering at the etched pictures as they flashed in the guttering light of his failing candle. The wax had burned down almost to his fingers now. It would only be a matter of minutes before he couldn't hold it anymore.

Something sparkled in the light. He held the candle closer. There was a pattern of white jewels set into the gold of the wall — seven white diamonds arranged in the same formation as the Pleiades! And about three feet below them was a small golden shelf. "Bring the statues over here," Josh called.

Olly lifted the heavy, golden cat off its base.

"No!" Josh directed. "The bird first."

Olly nodded and quickly exchanged the cat for the ibis.

Josh pointed and she rested it on the shelf.

"Now the cat."

Olly brought the cat over and placed it on the gold plate on the bird's head. Its base nestled perfectly on top of the plate. She ran back for the beetle. The sacred insect sat right on the cat's headpiece, the dish on its back in line with the lower stars in the arrangement of diamonds. "Now what?" she demanded.

"I don't know," Josh replied. "It looks as if something should fit into the dish on the beetle's back." He looked around the room. "Is there anything else?"

"I don't think so," Olly responded, also gazing around.

"What else do we have to do?" Josh asked. "Why hasn't anything happened?" He racked his brains. What had they missed? The three sacred animals had been united under the seven jewels. They had fit together perfectly. So why weren't the Tears of Isis revealed?

Olly gave a sharp hiss and whipped around to face the doors, which still stood open.

"What is it?" Josh asked.

Olly ran to the doors and peered out. "I can see a flashlight beam coming this way," she said. "It must be Ethan and Mohammed."

"Close the doors," Josh instructed.

Olly heaved against the doors and they swung closed with a clang.

Josh winced at the noise. "If they didn't know we were here before, they do now," he remarked.

"I couldn't help it," Olly snapped, leaning against the doors to hold them shut. "Get working on the riddle. I'll try and keep them out."

Josh stared at the seven jewels. "The light of the sacred seven," he muttered under his breath. "What light? What does it mean?"

Something hit the outside of the doors. The blow vibrated through Olly's back. She flexed her legs, digging her heels in. "Josh!"

Ethan and Mohammed obviously weren't bothering to look for the release mechanism — they had resorted to brute force.

"Try to find something to wedge the doors shut," Josh suggested, thinking furiously. He had only one goal: to solve the riddle before the two men burst in. For once, he wasn't thinking about what might happen afterward.

Boom! Another blow struck the doors.

Olly ran toward the slender base that had held the cat statue.

Boom! The doors shuddered.

"What light do they mean?" Josh yelled in frustration.

"Try the candle!" Olly shouted. "It's the only light we've got."

Josh looked at Olly and smiled. It was worth a try. He placed the small candle-end in the dish on the scarab's back and stepped away. The flame flickered. For a moment Josh thought it was going to go out. But then it grew stronger, flaring up with a heart as bright as sunlight.

The seven jewels caught the light from the swelling candle flame. They burned with a blinding intensity, their white light building and building as it reflected and rebounded from the polished surfaces of the golden room, until the whole chamber blazed like the sun.

This must be why it's called the Chamber of Light, Josh thought, shielding his eyes with his hand, as a beam of light leaped across the room from the seven jewels to strike a panel in the far wall. A rumbling noise filled the room. He watched in amazement as the golden wall panel slid back to reveal a recess. There was a statue in the secret alcove — the figure of Isis, made entirely of gold. Her hands were together, palms upward. And as the light touched them, it scattered into myriad different colors that bounced and rebounded off the walls, roof, and floor, in a dazzling rainbow of light.

At that instant, the doors flew open and Ethan Cain and Mohammed burst into the room. Ethan's eyes were bright and feverish as they focused on the statue. "Ah! The Tears of Isis!" he cried. "At last!"

The two men moved toward the statue of Isis, stumbling directly into the brilliant beam of light. Immediately, they fell back — blinded — trying to protect their eyes.

As Josh stood frozen in shock, staring at the two men, he saw a movement out of the corner of his eye. Olly held one of the golden bases in her hands. She swung it and, with both arms, threw it across the room. The heavy golden column spun through the air and struck Ethan on the shin. He let out a bellow of pain and crumpled to the floor, dragging Mohammed down with him. The Egyptian dropped the flashlight as he fell and it skidded across the floor toward Josh.

"Come on!" Olly yelled to Josh as she ran to the statue. In her open hands, Isis held a small, golden casket. The lid was open, and inside glittered two enormous, pear-shaped, blue sapphires. Olly snatched the casket up, and as she did so, the lid fell shut, instantly extinguishing the lights. A split second later, Josh's candle flickered and died. The only light now came from Mohammed's flashlight.

Josh ran forward and picked up the flashlight, then he and Olly skirted the two men and raced for the door.

"The Tears of Isis. At last?" Olly muttered to Ethan as she and Josh pushed the doors shut. "I don't think so!"

As the doors came together, Josh caught a last glimpse of Ethan through the crack. He was clambering to his feet, his face twisted with pain and anger. He shouted something, but the words were lost behind the clanging doors.

The friends ran, Josh in the lead with the powerful flashlight, Olly right behind him.

"We need to go back the same way we came!" Josh shouted.

"We'll never find it!" Olly yelled.

Josh realized she was right. The golden room was encircled with avenues of guardian statues. It would take them forever to find the original row and retrace their steps to the surface — even if they were able to remember the way.

They hurried on through the hall of treasures, until the beam of the flashlight hit a far wall and revealed a doorway. As they neared the exit tunnel, Olly paused for a moment and looked back over her shoulder.

"What's wrong?" Josh asked.

"Just making sure it's real," Olly said with a smile.

They emerged into a corridor that sloped gently upward. Josh and Olly could hear no sounds of pursuit, so they slowed to a brisk walk.

"This must lead somewhere important," Olly said hopefully after a while. "And we're going upward all the time — that's good news."

"How far do you think we've come?" Josh asked.

"I don't know," Olly replied, then stopped for a

moment, listening. She shook her head. "I can't hear anything back there," she said. She looked at Josh. "Once we're out, we're going to have to get someone to help us rescue those two. We can't leave them down there without any light."

Josh nodded. "But we have to get ourselves out first," he said. "Show me the Tears again."

Olly opened the casket and the sapphires sparkled in the flashlight beam.

"Aren't they fabulous?" Olly breathed.

"Amazing," Josh agreed. He grinned. "I can't wait to show them to Jonathan and your dad."

"Then we'd better get moving," Olly said. She shut the casket and the glorious blue light went out.

They walked on. Several minutes later, Josh saw something ahead of them. A small square of blacker darkness, some way in the distance. He began to walk more quickly. Olly kept up with him and soon they were both running. The square of darkness grew.

They burst out into a large square chamber. The floor was silted and scattered with debris, and the walls were covered in paintings and hieroglyphs. A flight of ten large stone steps led to the roof. The foot of the stairway was guarded by grim shabti warriors of black granite.

Josh shined the flashlight around the chamber. There didn't seem to be a way out.

"Those steps must be there for a reason," Olly said, staring up to where the steps met the ceiling of stone blocks. She moved toward the stairway.

"Watch where you walk," Josh warned her. "There might be traps."

Olly slowed down. "I'll be extra careful," she said. At the foot of the stairs she stopped and looked up. "It seems safe enough," she murmured and brought one foot down tentatively on the bottom step. She looked over her shoulder at Josh. "It's fine," she told him. But as she put her weight on the step, it slid downward a few inches with a grating sound. "Oh, please — no. Not another booby trap!" Olly breathed.

A low rumble sounded from above her head. Josh shined the flashlight upward. Sand was filtering down from between cracks in the stone roof. Loud grating and grinding sounds now filled the chamber. "Move!" Josh shouted.

Sand began to cascade down, with small stones that bounced on the steps and struck Olly on her head and shoulders. She threw herself backward as a large block came crashing down, striking the stairs and breaking them as it tumbled to the floor. In its wake, sand and rubble cascaded out of the rift in the ceiling.

Breathing in a mouthful of dust, Olly thought, *This is it. This is the Christie family curse, taking its turn on me, the firstborn girl.*

"Olly!" Josh shouted in panic. He heard her scream, but then she vanished from sight — suddenly hidden by the flood of debris that poured from the broken ceiling and rushed in a torrent down the steps.

Chapter Fourteen: The Tears of Isis

Dust billowed in thick gray clouds, clogging Olly's lungs and sending her reeling backward as the roof of the chamber fell in.

"Olly!" she heard Josh shout, but her mouth was thick with grit and she couldn't reply. She scrambled into a corner of the chamber and rolled herself into a protective ball as dirt and stones showered down over her. She expected to be crushed at any moment by a falling stone block.

But it didn't happen. The noise lessened and the surge of debris dwindled to a trickle of sand and pebbles. She took her arms away from her head and stared upward. At first she couldn't understand what she was seeing. It looked like dark blue velvet scattered with diamonds. *It must be another ceiling*, she thought, *above the chamber roof — painted to look like the night sky.*

A breath of air touched her cheek. Her vision cleared and the roof of stars suddenly leaped away into the far, far distance. She realized that she was gazing up at the sky — the *real* night sky!

"We did it!" she breathed. "We escaped!"

She looked across the chamber for Josh. The clouds of dust were thinning and she saw him pressed against the far wall, staring at her in shocked relief.

"I thought you were killed!" he said.

Olly grinned. "Not me," she replied. But she was only too aware of how lucky she had been. The booby trap had clearly been set to catch anyone climbing the stairs. The fact that she had thrown herself backward, away from the steps, had saved her life.

Josh came over to help Olly to her feet. Together, they climbed over the wreckage and scrambled up the stairs.

"Fresh air!" Olly said. "Can you smell it?"

"Yes," Josh replied with a happy sigh.

Earth and sand sloped up to ground level a few feet above their heads. It was late evening and a rare whisper of breeze came over the western mountains.

"I wonder where we are," Olly said.

The crater hole was several yards across. They began to climb out.

"Olivia! Josh! What on earth is going on? How did you get down there?" came a familiar voice from above.

"Gran?" Olly said in surprise. Her head came up

174

above ground level and she instantly saw where she and Josh had surfaced. They were in front of the trailers, not far from the table and chairs. Natasha Welles and Audrey Beckmann were gazing down into the chasm that had opened up almost under their feet.

"Josh!" Natasha gasped.

"I'm OK, Mom," Josh called.

Mrs. Beckmann stared into the hole. "What have you been up to?" she demanded as she helped Olly out. "You're not supposed to be in there by yourselves. You could have been killed! And if you've caused any damage down there your father will never forgive you."

Natasha offered a helping hand to Josh, looking at the two disheveled friends in astonished disbelief.

Olly grasped her gran's hands, her face glowing. "It's huge down there, Gran — bigger than you'd ever believe," Olly explained. "We found the room that devours itself. But Ethan and Mohammed were chasing us. They're still down there, and —"

"What are you talking about?" her grandmother interrupted. She frowned at Josh. "What is all this nonsense?"

"She's telling the truth," Josh said. "Ethan wants the Tears for himself." He looked at his mother.

"I'm sorry, Mom, but it's true. We need to find Jonathan and the professor."

Natasha looked completely bewildered. "Surely they're still down in the tomb," she said. She frowned at Josh. "I don't understand — what was that about Ethan?"

Olly impulsively gave her grandmother a hug. "We've got so much to tell you," she said. "But right now I have to find Dad." She drew back and pulled the golden casket out of her pocket. "You see, we've found the Tears of Isis!" And with that, she broke away from her gran and raced toward the main entrance of the tomb. Josh chased after her.

The two stunned women looked at one another for a moment, and then they, too, began to run toward the tomb of Setiankhra.

〜〜〜

Olly and Josh tumbled into the Burial Chamber, just as Jonathan and Professor Christie were climbing out through the secret doorway.

"You're safe!" Olly exclaimed happily. "I was afraid they might have done something to you."

"Olly, marvelous news!" exclaimed the professor. "We've found the sarcophagus of Setiankhra!" He gestured toward the doorway. "It's in a chamber through there. It's the most wonderful thing!"

Jonathan looked at the two friends. "What happened to you?" he asked, staring at their grimy faces and dirty clothes. "*Who* might have done something to us?"

"Ethan and Mohammed," Josh told him.

Olly ran forward. "And Dad, we've found the Tears!"

Both men stared at her incredulously. Olly held the golden casket out on the palm of her hand and raised the lid. The beautiful sapphires glittered and shined. Jonathan and the professor drew closer, gazing at the jewels.

"What is this, Olivia?" the Professor breathed. "Where did you find these?"

"In the room that devours itself!" Olly replied, grinning.

"Which way did you turn when you went through the secret door?" Josh asked.

"To the right," Jonathan told him.

Olly shrugged. "We went left — and you're not going to believe what we found!"

"But first we have to warn you about Ethan and Mohammed," Josh said.

"*What* about them?" Jonathan asked.

At that moment, Natasha and Audrey Beckmann came running breathlessly into the chamber.

"They're after the Tears of Isis!" Josh said. He glanced at his mother. "Both of them! Ethan was behind the theft of the Elephantine Stone. Mohammed was helping him." He pointed toward the secret door. "They chased us in there. It's a long story, but we managed to get their flashlight and find our way out."

Natasha stared at him in disbelief. "This is insane," she said. "Ethan isn't a *criminal*."

Jonathan looked hard at Josh. "Are they still down there without any light?" he asked sharply.

"Yes," Olly nodded. "We left them in the Chamber of Light."

Josh opened his mouth to speak, but Jonathan silenced him with a gesture of his hand. He looked at Professor Christie. "We need to get in there and find them," he said.

"Ethan!" Natasha suddenly exclaimed.

Everyone followed the direction of her gaze. She was looking at the secret door and Ethan Cain was there, doubled over, one hand against the wall. His clothes were dirty and torn and there was a raw, bloody graze on his cheek. Blood trailed from the corner of his mouth and his lips were swollen and bruised. "Help me," he panted, almost falling into the room. Jonathan and Natasha ran forward to catch him. He seemed dizzy and breathless. "Mohammed," he murmured. "You have to stop Mohammed before he gets away. He stole the Elephantine Stone!"

"Don't trust him!" Olly shouted. "Mohammed was working for him."

Ethan stared at her in surprise. "That's not true," he protested. "I tried to stop him." He gestured to his face. "He did this to me."

"No," Josh said, glaring at Ethan. "You were working together to steal the Tears of Isis."

Ethan shook his head. He pulled himself upright with a visible effort. "I let Mohammed think I'd help him steal the stone." He looked at Professor Christie. "I thought I could get him to reveal himself if I played along with him," he said. "I was stupid. When I confronted him, he went crazy. I thought he was going to kill me."

"That's not true, Dad," Olly said. "He's lying to you!"

Ethan coughed weakly. "No, Olly, really I'm not," he insisted.

"Then why were you chasing us?" Josh demanded.

"Mohammed was determined to go after you," Ethan said. "I couldn't risk letting him hurt you. So, I went with him."

"That's not how it happened!" Olly exclaimed in exasperation.

Ethan smiled kindly at her. "I don't blame you for being confused, Olly, but I'm telling the truth. There was a long chase through the dark." He glanced up at the professor. "It's immense down there — dozens of rooms and probably miles of corridors. It's a stupendous find!"

"So I've heard," said the professor. "But what about Mohammed?"

Ethan frowned. "Well, we found Olly and Josh in a golden room," he said. "There was a bright light which completely dazzled me. I couldn't see a thing. Then something struck my legs and I stumbled into Mohammed. We both fell. Before either of us could get up, Olly and Josh had taken our flashlight and left. Mohammed was crazy with anger. I could tell he was prepared to hurt Olly and Josh to get the Tears from them. I tried to reason with him, but he attacked me. He had another, smaller flashlight, so he left me there on the floor and went after Olly and Josh. It was a few minutes before I could walk." He shook his head. "I tried to follow him, but I couldn't see which way he had gone. In the end I used my cigar lighter to find my way out." Ethan pulled free from Natasha and Jonathan. "But we must find

Mohammed now," he said anxiously. "There's no time to lose!"

"You're far too badly hurt," Natasha argued. "We need to get you to a doctor."

"You don't actually believe his story, do you?" Olly exclaimed.

Natasha frowned at her. "Stop it, Olly!" she snapped. "Ethan's right — you're just confused." She looked at Josh and her voice softened. "Who wouldn't be after what you've been through? But Ethan got hurt trying to protect you, can't you see that?"

Josh stared speechlessly at his mother.

Olly was lost for words, too. She looked from face to face and realized that no one believed their story. Ethan had won everyone over.

"It doesn't matter," Ethan said, smiling weakly at the two friends. "It was all a misunderstanding." He took a step toward them. "But I have to know one thing: Did you find the Tears of Isis?"

Olly stared at him. He was so persuasive that for a moment she almost believed him. She almost believed that she had conjured up all of the evidence against Ethan in her head. Then she remembered the ferocious look of greed she had seen on his face in the Chamber of Light. However, she knew it was pointless to keep accusing him when everyone else was convinced that she and Josh were just mistaken. Looking coldly into his face, she showed him the golden casket.

Ethan's eyes gleamed as he gazed at the fabulous jewels. "Beautiful," he said. He looked around at the professor. "Congratulations, Professor. There are chambers of treasure back there," he said. "This is the greatest find since Tutankhamen — possibly the greatest untouched hoard ever discovered in Egypt! You're going to be famous."

"That can wait," said Mrs. Beckmann, taking charge of the situation. "First, we need to call the police and tell them about Mohammed. Jonathan — deal with that, please. Natasha and I will take Ethan to my trailer. He can rest there and we'll clean him up and see how much damage has been done." She turned to the youngsters. "Olivia, you can help us. Josh — I'd like you to run over to the diggers' camp. Wake a few of them up and tell them the professor needs them immediately." She looked at the professor. "They can mount an overnight guard on the place, just in case Mohammed is still in the vicinity."

While Olly was still reeling from the turn of events, her father stepped up to her and lifted the

casket out of her hands. "These need to be put somewhere safe," he said, closing the lid. "Go with your
gran now, Olivia. Tomorrow, we'll study the Tears
of Isis to see what secrets they hold."

Olly stared at Josh, stunned by the way the adults
had taken over and by how easily Ethan had fooled
them all.

Josh gave her a blank, helpless look that showed
he was feeling the same way. Then he turned and
ran off on the errand that Olly's gran had given him.

〰〰

It was a busy night. The police arrived with some
bad news of their own. Benjamin Carter was
gone — he had bribed a guard and escaped from his
cell. A hunt was on, but so far there had been no sign
of him.

Police officers examined Mohammed's tent, but
found it stripped of his possessions. He had beaten
them to it. The laptop — the final shred of evidence
that Olly and Josh had hoped might link Ethan Cain
to the theft of the Elephantine Stone — was gone.

And the dig supervisor himself seemed to have
melted into the desert night. The police promised
to do all they could to track him down, but they
didn't seem hopeful. One officer stayed at the site to
keep watch over the tomb.

Professor Christie didn't enter the tomb again that night. He spent the evening in his trailer, making calls to Cairo University and the Egyptian authorities, informing them of the find, and inviting them to join him in exploring the extraordinary lost catacombs of Setiankhra's tomb.

It was midnight before the camp began to settle down. Beds were found for Natasha and Ethan. The golden casket that contained the Tears of Isis was locked away in the security box, and Jonathan slept with it by his side.

Neither Josh nor Olly found it easy to sleep. Olly lay wide-eyed far into the night, torn between the almost unbearable excitement of their discovery and her deep dismay that Ethan Cain had fooled everyone. *At least his schemes failed and we beat him to the Tears of Isis*, she told herself. *We have the first Talisman of the Moon.* And comforted by that thought, she eventually drifted into a shallow, restless sleep.

~~~~~

It seemed only a few minutes later that Olly was woken by somebody shaking her shoulder. She snuggled deeper under the covers. "Go away, Josh," she mumbled. "You're such a pain!"

"Olivia!" It was her gran's voice. "Wake up, now, dear."

Olly forced her eyes open. Audrey Beckmann was leaning over her.

"What time is it?" Olly asked.

"It's still early, but Natasha and Ethan are leaving shortly. I thought you'd want to say good-bye. I've already woken Josh."

Olly was suddenly wide awake. "I thought Ethan was staying till the helicopter was fixed," she said as she hopped out of bed.

"Change of plans," said Gran, picking up her clothes from the floor and handing them to her. "They're both catching a flight from Luxor airport this morning. Apparently there's some kind of problem at Ethan's head office and he has to deal with it personally." She frowned. "How many times have I told you not to throw your things all over the floor when you get undressed?"

Olly was climbing into her clothes. "Sorry, Gran," she said.

Her gran sat down at the end of her bed. "Now, Olly," she began. "I don't want any more nonsense about Ethan." She raised a warning finger. "Make sure you're on your best behavior. And be quick, now." She got up, patted Olly on the back, and left the room.

Olly frowned. Best behavior! If only her gran knew what had *really* happened down in Setiankhra's tomb. But she didn't, and that was that. Olly sighed. At least she and Josh had found the Tears and wrecked Ethan's plans. She'd remember that when she had to wave him good-bye.

Natasha and Ethan were ready to leave by the time Olly appeared. One of the diggers was going to drive them to the airport in the Land Rover. Jonathan, Josh, Audrey Beckmann, and the professor were saying their farewells to the glamorous couple as Olly came up.

"Well, it's been quite a visit, hasn't it?" Natasha said, giving Olly a hug.

Olly smiled. "I'll say." She exchanged a knowing look with Josh.

Ethan turned toward the two friends. "No hard feelings about our little misunderstanding," he said, smiling cheerfully at them. "You should both be very proud," he continued. "You've discovered something that other people have spent entire lifetimes searching for. I only wish I could spare the time to explore the tomb with you."

Olly looked steadily into his eyes and smiled sweetly. "Why do you have to go?" she asked. "Couldn't you stay a little while longer?" She knew the real reason he had changed his plans: Now that the Tears were safely under lock and key, he had no hope of getting his hands on them.

Ethan met her gaze. "Business has to come first," he sighed. He leaned toward her, smiling. "But I'll be following your father's quest for the other Talismans of the Moon with great interest," he told her. "And you never know — I may even find time to visit you now and then and see how you're all doing."

Olly stared at him — for a moment she caught a glint in his eyes that wasn't at all friendly. Then he turned and climbed into the Land Rover with a final wave.

The little group watched and waved as the Land Rover headed down toward the river.

"Did you see that look he gave me?" Olly whispered to Josh.

"Yes," Josh whispered back. "And I didn't like that comment about watching your father's search for the other Talismans with 'great interest'!"

"Me neither," Olly agreed. "I'm sure we haven't

seen the last of him. But we beat him this time, and if he comes back for more, we'll just have to beat him again."

"What are you two whispering about?" Mrs. Beckmann asked.

"Nothing, Gran," Olly replied lightly. "When's breakfast?"

〰〰

It was shortly after breakfast that the first of the visitors arrived on site. Professor Khalil Fehr, Head of Egyptology at Cairo University, was a tall, courteous man with gray hair and a face as dark and wrinkled as a walnut. He brought with him a team of archaeologists and scientists who had flown in to examine the great discoveries. Professor Christie was in his element among so many experts on ancient Egypt. Soon he was lost in conversation and debate with his eminent colleagues.

Olly was desperate to go down into the tomb again. She couldn't understand why it was taking so long for her father to get around to it.

"A lot of important people need to be involved," her gran explained. "We're visitors in this country, Olivia, remember that. Your father wants to do this right."

Over the next hour, various Egyptian dignitaries

and government officials began to arrive from Luxor, Aswan, and Cairo. They greeted Professor Christie enthusiastically, congratulating him on his find, all of them eager to see the ancient treasures that had been discovered.

"It's not me you have to thank," the professor told them all modestly. "My daughter, Olivia, and her friend Josh made the most astonishing finds."

At last, everyone gathered around the hole through which Olly and Josh had escaped the tomb the previous night. Jonathan had been up since shortly after dawn, supervising a team of diggers who had worked to make the hole safe. The roof was now shored up with timbers, and more steps had been added to make the descent into the chamber easier.

"This is not the method by which we first entered the tomb," the professor explained. "But the other route is much more difficult and dangerous."

"I'll say," muttered Olly, thinking of the shattered skeletons beneath the bridge.

"Shh!" hissed Josh. "He's talking about us!"

"My daughter, Olivia, and my assistant's brother, Josh, are the ones who actually found the Chamber of Light and the Tears of Isis," the professor was saying.

All eyes turned to the two friends. Olly grinned and seemed to glow with pride, while Josh, embarrassed by so much attention, endeavored to hide behind his shaggy blond hair.

"We will now enter the tomb of Setiankhra," Professor Christie continued. "And I would like Olly and Josh to be our guides."

Olly and Josh stared at each other in astonishment. Neither of them had expected this.

"You're the only ones who know the way," Jonathan pointed out to them quietly, smiling at their shocked expressions.

The friends soon recovered from their surprise, and side by side they led the way down into the catacombs of Setiankhra's tomb.

As they made their way through the spectacular hall of treasures, they heard gasps of amazement from the group behind them. Josh looked at Olly and grinned.

"I can see that being heroic explorers is going to take up an awful lot of our time," Olly said to him thoughtfully.

Josh nodded. "You're right. I mean we still have all the other Talismans of the Moon to find for a start. Then we'll have to figure out how they reveal the Archives. I don't know when we'll be able to fit in schoolwork."

A determined look crossed Olly's face. "I don't think eminent explorers should have to do school-work anyway," she said firmly.

Josh laughed. "I can't wait to hear it when you attempt to convince your gran," he told her.

They had reached the golden doors at the heart of the hall of treasures. Here they stopped and turned to the party of archaeologists. "Ladies and gentlemen," Olly announced. "Welcome to the Chamber of Light!"

And as she and Josh opened the doors, the crowd of scholars waited in silent anticipation to share the friends' brilliant discovery.

CHRONICLES OF THE MOON

LEGEND OF THE LOST CITY

PROLOGUE

The Legend of the Moon Goddess

In ancient days in China, it was said that ten suns lived in the giant Lau Shang tree that grew in the Heavenly Lands beyond the Eastern Horizon. These ten suns were the offspring of the Sky God, Di Jun, and the Goddess, Xi He. Their mother decreed that only one sun should burn in the sky at a time, and she decided the order in which her sons would cross the heavens, each taking their turn in Di Jun's chariot. But the unruly suns became discontented with their mother's discipline, and they came up with a plan to break free of their tedious duties.

One morning, all ten suns appeared together, blazing defiantly in the sky. They ignored their mother when she called for them to return to the tree. They did not even heed the mighty voice of Di Jun, their heavenly father. They were free at last, and they were determined to remain so.

At first, the people of Earth greeted the ten suns with delight, but soon their crops began to wither under the fierce heat, their rivers dried up, and their lands became parched. The Emperor of China implored Di Jun to help the people and to restore the old order of one sun a day.

Di Jun sent messengers to Earth: a mighty archer named Hou-Yi, and his beautiful wife, Chang-O. Di Jun gave Hou-Yi a red bow and a quiver full of white arrows. He hoped that the arrows would help Hou-Yi frighten the ten rebellious suns back to their duties. But when Hou-Yi saw the scorched and thirsty earth, he grew angry and, one by one, he shot down nine of the suns from the sky.

The people were delighted and proclaimed Hou-Yi a hero, but Di Jun was angry at the deaths of his sons, and he condemned Hou-Yi and Chang-O to remain on Earth and become mortal.

But Hou-Yi refused to be mortal. He went into the Uttermost West and sought the help of the Queen Goddess. She gave him a pill of everlasting life and told him to prepare himself with twelve months of prayer and fasting before taking the pill.

After returning to his home, Hou-Yi hid the pill and began his long preparations. One night, his wife Chang-O was awoken by the delightful fragrance of flowers. She rose and noticed a single white moon-beam, and she followed it to find that it was shining from the pill. Chang-O picked up the pill and swallowed it — and found that she could fly.

She flew through the house and out into the lotus-scented garden, singing joyfully as she soared beneath the full moon. Her husband awoke and, when he realized what Chang-O had done, he became terribly angry. Chang-O fled her husband's wrath, but he pursued her over mountains and plains, through bamboo forests, and across great rivers, until, in her fear, she flew up to the moon seeking refuge.

Her only companion on the moon was a magical hare that pounded medicinal herbs with a mortar and pestle. Regretting her actions and seeking to appease her husband, Chang-O coughed up half the pill. She then commanded the hare to pound up the half-pill and make a new pill that she could take back to Hou-Yi.

Each year in China, at the Festival of the Moon, the people eat mooncakes to symbolize the pill made by the hare and to honor the moon goddess, Chang-O.

Chapter One: The Journey

Olivia Christie stopped reading the legend and looked up from the book, her blue eyes shining. "Well," she said, "what do you think of that?"

Josh Welles smiled. "Nice story, Olly," he replied, glancing up from his laptop computer. "So what happened? Did Chang-O find Hou-Yi? Did he ever become immortal again?"

"I don't know," Olly said. "I haven't read that far. But I will."

Twelve-year-old Olly and her best friend, Josh, were seated side by side in a large passenger airplane. Olly had been reading aloud the story of Chang-O, the Chinese moon goddess, as preparation for their trip. Josh's eyes were trained on his laptop, which showed a map of Asia. A red line indicated their flight path. Their party had boarded a plane at London Heathrow before dawn that morning. A quick transfer in Paris, just as the sun was rising, had brought them aboard their present aircraft for the ten-hour flight to Beijing, China.

While they were halfway to the Chinese capital,

that was not their final destination. Their trip would include two more plane rides, the first stop being in the Sichuan Province at the ancient city of Chengdu. From there, the party would begin the final leg of their extensive journey to the ancient ruins that had recently been revealed along the banks of the mighty Minjiang River.

Olly's father was the renowned archaeologist Professor Kenneth Christie. The Chinese authorities had requested his presence at this historic dig, and Olly was traveling with him. Her mother had died two years ago, and, since then, Olly had frequently accompanied her father on his international expeditions, where she was looked after and tutored by her grandmother, Audrey Beckmann. Olly — short for Olivia — loved traveling with her dad. The exploration and archaeological digs were a good match for her adventurous nature, much better than staying home in England. She especially liked trips like this one, where they would be seeing part of an ancient world that had been lost for centuries. The old secrets and stories — like the myth of Chang-O — fascinated her. Besides, she had a very personal reason for being interested in things like curses and myths.

Professor Christie's assistant, a talented

archaeological student named Jonathan Welles, was Josh's twenty-four-year-old brother. Their mother was the famous movie actress Natasha Welles. Because her career did not provide Josh with a very stable home life, it had been arranged that he would accompany his brother and the Christies on their continent-hopping adventures. This arrangement worked out well, because he and Olly had soon become the best of friends.

Audrey Beckmann was more than happy to tutor Josh as well. In fact, Audrey often stated that she was relieved to have Josh around since he was far more reliable and practical than her headstrong granddaughter.

Olly peered out of the small porthole. The airplane hung in a clear blue sky above an endless panorama of barren, snowcapped mountains. As she stared down at the breathtaking but forbidding wildlands of the Alatau Mountains, Olly felt the wonderful knot of excitement in her stomach that always accompanied the start of a new quest.

It was only a few weeks ago that they had been in the Valley of the Kings in Egypt, excavating the ancient tomb of Pharaoh Setiankhra. Olly almost couldn't believe that she and Josh had actually been the ones to find the golden room deep under the cliffs — the room known as the Chamber of Light. In spite of ancient booby traps and deadly rock-slides, the two friends had escaped the tomb with the two sapphires that were known as the Tears of Isis. And, according to legend, the Tears of Isis was one of the priceless Talismans of the Moon.

If the legends were true, then the Talismans of the Moon were created thousands of years ago by the moon-priests of ancient civilizations in different parts of the world. Each culture made its own talisman, and it was said that if they were all brought together at the right time and place, then great wonders would be revealed. Together, the talismans could answer age-old secrets.

In the course of his recent archaeological investigations, Professor Christie had found evidence that the talismans might be more than mere legend. Ever since then, he had been determined to track them all down and unlock their secrets.

Olly breathed a sigh of pure joy and settled back in her seat, thrilled to be on a new adventure. She turned the page of her book on Chinese mythology and read on. "According to some versions of the myth," she related to Josh, "Chang-O never got the pill of everlasting life to give to Hou-Yi. Some say the hare is still pounding away on the pill. But other versions say that the hare completed the new pill, and that it hardened into a disc of pure moonstone." She frowned. "What's moonstone?"

Josh opened a search engine on his laptop and tapped at the keyboard. "Let's find out," he said a moment later. "*Moonstone is a semiprecious gem with a white or blue sheen. It reflects light in a distinctive shimmering way. It is found in Brazil, India, the USA, Madagascar, and Mexico.*" He grinned. "And on the moon," he joked.

Olly laughed. "In this other version of the myth, Chang-O got the pill and took it down to Earth. She searched for Hou-Yi, but she never found him. It's said that she still has the moonstone with her in her final resting place — which, according to legend, is the lost city of Yueliang-Chengshi." She looked at Josh. They both knew from overhearing the professor and Jonathan that the lost city was supposed to be close to where the new ruins had been found. "And Dad is pretty convinced that if we find some kind of moonstone there, then it's got to be the Mooncake of Chang-O, one of the Talismans of the Moon." Olly and Josh exchanged another knowing glance.

Then Jonathan Welles's face appeared over the

back of his seat, his long, light brown bangs falling into his warm brown eyes as always. "How's it going?" he asked. "Having fun?"

"I was just reading Josh the Myth of Chang-O," Olly told him. She looked up at Jonathan curiously. "What makes Dad think we're going to find the talisman at this particular dig?" she asked.

Jonathan looked over at Audrey Beckmann, who appeared to be engrossed in a novel. Olly's sixty-three-year-old grandmother was a tall, elegant woman with gray hair cut into a neat bob. She supervised the day-to-day running of the small party — ensuring that the group ate properly and had clean clothes to put on, as well as keeping a stern but affectionate eye on Olly and Josh.

Olly guessed what Jonathan was up to. Olly's grandmother had given strict orders that Olly and Josh were not to trail off on their own investigation this trip. Any searching of the ruins was to be supervised. Jonathan didn't want Audrey to think he was giving them too much information for their own good.

Jonathan looked back at Olly and his younger brother. "It all goes back to a map that was discovered a few years ago," he explained. "The map was carved on an earthenware pot, and it showed the lost city of Yueliang-Chengshi. Many people thought the city was just another ancient myth."

"Yeah," Josh continued for his brother, "but the map pictured the old city at a bend in the Minjiang River, which appears to be close to where we'll be."

Olly frowned at him. "How do you know that?" Josh laughed. "Your dad told me," he replied.

"Well, you could have said something!" Olly sighed.

"What's all the noise?" asked a new voice to the conversation. Professor Christie's head appeared around the side of his seat, his graying hair an untidy thatch, his bright eyes glinting over half-moon glasses. "I'm glad for your interest, but I don't think everyone on the plane wants to know about our plans. You need to keep it down."

"They were just discussing the finding of the map, Kenneth," Audrey Beckmann explained.

Olly looked at her grandma, surprised that she had been following the conversation.

"Why don't you tell them the most recent news, and then we'll all be quiet," Olly's grandmother suggested.

"Well, yes." The professor nodded enthusiastically, marking the place in his book.

Olly loved hearing the excitement in her father's voice when he talked about his work.

"Just yesterday there was a big discovery." Professor Christie explained. "An inscription found among the ruins indicates that these might be the remains of the lost city of Yueliang-Chengshi. If so, then it's more or less exactly where the terra-cotta map indicated it would be. It's evidence that the city might not just be legend. It could be real."

"The translation of the inscription reads: *Here Hou-Yi finally lost Chang-O — she who fled to the moon*," added Jonathan.

"And the myth even says that Chang-O's final resting place was in Yueliang-Chengshi!" Olly exclaimed in delight. "So that's where we'd find the moonstone talisman."

"Let's hope so," said the professor, turning back to his work. "And let's hope we can find more evidence before the river rises again."

The Minjiang River flowed down from the mountains of the Tibetan Plateau until it spilled into the huge Yangtze River. But the rains had not come that spring, and the river had dwindled to half its normal size, revealing broad banks that had not been dry land for a thousand years. And from the mud and silt of those exposed riverbanks, the eroded ruins of ancient buildings jutted like broken brown teeth. If not for the drought, they would not have been discovered.

The Chinese authorities had invited a few internationally renowned archaeologists to come and excavate the site — but it was a race against time. When the rain finally did come, the mountains would empty millions of tons of floodwater down into the valley of the Minjiang River and the ruins would be lost again.

Olly took another look out the window. The vast mountain range still stretched away beneath them. "This is taking forever," she said. "I want to get there and start searching for the talisman!"

"I think not," her gran said firmly. "On this trip, I'm determined to make sure you two behave yourselves and keep out of trouble."

"Spoilsport," Olly said with a grin. She exchanged a secret glance with Josh, knowing that once they were on site, he would be as eager as she was to join in the hunt for the fabled Mooncake of Chang-O.

Chapter Two:
The Sacred Mountain

It was late in the afternoon of the following day and they were airborne again.

They had landed at Beijing Capital International Airport at three in the morning, local time, disoriented by the shift in time zones and exhausted by over eleven hours of traveling. Then, far too early the next morning for Olly's liking, they had been roused from their beds to take the domestic flight to Sichuan Province.

Then another, much smaller aircraft was waiting for their party when they touched down at Chengdu Shuangliu Airport several hours later. It was an elderly twin-prop plane, which Olly thought looked like an antique. It was just large enough to take the small party and their baggage.

The old plane made flying a dramatic event. It flew low, hugging the land, the fuselage vibrating to the roar of the engines. There were no luxuries on this flight and the seats were hard and narrow — but Olly loved it. It made her feel as if the adventure had really begun.

She and Josh leaned together to look out the window as the scenery passed swiftly below them, the landscape changing from rice paddies to bamboo forests and then to orchards and fields of corn and wheat. They pointed down excitedly to towns and villages of traditional wooden houses with roofs of tile or bamboo thatch. And all the while, the foothills of the vast Tibetan Plateau drew closer, and the land began to rise and fall in deeply forested hills and lush valleys. Occasionally, on a wooded hillside, they would glimpse the elegant, curved roof of an isolated Buddhist temple emerging from the trees. And in the distance, they could see the mountains looming on the horizon.

Jonathan leaned over to speak to the two friends. "We should see the river soon," he told them. "I've just been talking to the pilot. We'll be approaching the site from the north, following the course of the Minjiang."

It was only a couple of minutes later that Olly and Josh caught sight of the river. Here, the effects of the drought were alarmingly obvious: The once ample waterway had dwindled to less than half its usual width, shrinking to a murky brown thread no more than thirty feet across that ran between deep sloping banks of cracked earth.

An ancient irrigation system kept the cultivated land green and growing but, in some places, entire stretches of the countryside were no more than parched brown earth.

The sight unsettled Olly's conscience. She looked at Jonathan. "All I've been thinking about is how great it's going to be for us to see the old ruins," she said sadly. "I didn't really think about what it must be like for the people who live here."

Jonathan nodded. "It's been rough for them," he replied. "If the drought goes on much longer things will get pretty bad."

Josh frowned. "It gives you mixed feelings, doesn't it?" he said. "I mean, we'd like the rain to hold off till we can find out everything there is to know about the ruins, but at the same time, you can't help hoping the rain comes as soon as possible."

Olly smiled ruefully. "Let's hope there are plenty of diggers on site," she declared. "That way we can get the work done really quickly — and then it can rain as much as it likes." She looked at Jonathan. "Do we know who's in charge down there?"

"Professor Andryanova," Jonathan told her. "He's a Russian — very well thought of by a lot of people." He leaned closer and dropped his voice.

"But just between the three of us, I get the feeling the professor doesn't think much of him."

Josh looked surprised. "So he's not very good?" he asked.

"He's good," Jonathan said. "He would never have been appointed team leader otherwise. But he has a reputation for cutting corners to get quick results. And he's a great self-publicist who tends to turn a dig into something of a media circus. Fortunately, the man who's cofunding the dig with the Chinese authorities has insisted on minimum publicity."

"Who exactly *is* putting up the money?" Olly inquired. "These things are expensive. Gran told me it was an American billionaire." She looked sharply at Jonathan. "You don't think it's Ethan Cain, do you?"

Jonathan gave a soft laugh. "No, I don't," he replied. "And even if it was, I thought we cleared up that misunderstanding you had with him in Egypt." He put his hand on Olly's shoulder. "Trust me," he said, "Ethan Cain is not out to steal the Talismans of the Moon from under your father's nose — and he never was!"

Olly and Josh said nothing. They knew better than to say anything more about their strong suspicions about the superficially charming Ethan Cain. They were convinced that the Californian computer billionaire had been behind various criminal activities that had plagued their search for the Tears of Isis in Egypt. But no one believed them, and what made things even more awkward was that the wealthy computer genius was actually dating Josh and Jonathan's mother. Olly and Josh had liked Ethan until they realized he had hidden motives and that he'd willingly steal the artifacts if that's what it took. Jonathan, like the rest of the adults, still believed that Ethan Cain had just been in the wrong place at the wrong time.

"So, who *is* paying for all this?" Josh asked.

"A man named Augustus Bell," Jonathan said. "From what I've heard, he's a Texan oil baron with plenty of cash to spare. He's not known in the usual archaeological circles, so I suspect he's funding the dig in order to buy himself into history."

"Oh, I get it," Olly put in. "Everything we find will end up in the Augustus Bell wing of a Chinese museum somewhere."

Jonathan laughed. "Something like that," he agreed. He nodded toward the window. "Keep your eyes peeled. You should see something pretty spectacular shortly," he said, and then moved back to his own seat.

"So, Ethan is definitely not involved in any way?" Olly whispered to Josh.

He shook his head. "When Mom called us from location in Acapulco the other day, I asked her whether Ethan had shown any interest in the ruins. She told me he was up to his eyes in work in California and hadn't even mentioned them to her."

"Good!" Olly said emphatically. "The farther Ethan Cain is from here, the better."

"Shhh!" hissed Josh, glancing over his shoulder. "If your grandma hears you saying stuff like that, we'll get another lecture about not accusing innocent people of being criminals."

Olly nodded and turned to stare out the window. "Wow!" she exclaimed, all thoughts of Ethan Cain driven from her head.

Josh leaned over her shoulder. "Wow!" he agreed breathlessly.

Here, the river was lined by tall cliffs of rust-colored stone. Carved in the solid rock-face was a huge statue of a man, seated, with his massive feet planted firmly apart and his hands resting on his knees. His hair was sculpted into a bun, and he appeared to be gazing serenely over the river.

Thickets of tall trees grew around his enormous shoulders. He was the full height of the cliffs.

"Look at the people down there," Olly said, staring down at the small shapes clustered around the feet of the statue. "They're tiny!"

"They just *look* tiny," Josh responded, "because the statue is over two-hundred feet tall. It's the Grand Buddha," he continued. "It was carved during the Tang Dynasty in the eighth century."

Olly looked at him. "You're beginning to sound like a tour guide," she laughed. "I hope you're not expecting to get paid for all this info."

"No, it's all free," Josh replied. "I've been looking up stuff on the Internet," he explained. "Jonathan told me about a site. The next big thing we see will be the sacred mountain."

"It's called Si-houzai-shan," Olly told him with a grin. "See? I know some stuff, too. I read about the mountain because it's right next to the place where we're going to be digging. Right by the bend in the river."

"But do you know what the mountain's name means?" Josh asked.

Olly frowned, trying to remember so Josh didn't one-up her. "Dad told me," she said thoughtfully. "It has something to do with fire."

"Dead fire mountain," Josh declared, happy to have won at this round of trivia. "Si-houzai-shan is an extinct volcano."

"'Extinct' means totally dead, doesn't it?" Olly queried anxiously. "I don't like the idea of hanging out near a volcano that might go off."

"That's something I asked Ang-lun about that the last time I e-mailed him," Josh told her. "He said it hasn't erupted for hundreds of thousands of years — so I think we're pretty safe."

Ang-lun was the twelve-year-old son of a Chinese archaeologist, Dr. Feng Zhe-hui. Dr. Feng was a close colleague of Olly's father and the man who had organized Professor Christie's trip. Dr. Feng and his son would be meeting them at the landing strip and taking them to the dig site.

Olly and Josh had started e-mailing with Ang-lun over the past couple of weeks. They were looking forward to meeting him at last and exchanging gifts. Ang-lun was learning English, and from his e-mails he seemed to be very fluent already. Josh and Olly were bringing him a copy of *Treasure Island*, which he had told them was his favorite book, but he had only read it in Chinese so far.

The small plane continued its journey south along the shrunken course of the Minjiang, and it wasn't long before Olly and Josh could clearly see the tall slopes of the sacred mountain looming on the horizon.

"We'll be landing soon," Jonathan called. "Seat belts on, everyone."

The plane lifted suddenly, soaring high up into the clear blue sky, leaving Olly's stomach somewhere far below. She and Josh had their noses pressed against the window as the mountain grew to fill the entire skyline, its upper reaches shrouded in mist and clouds. The pilot was climbing to fly over the mouth of the volcano.

The mountain was a broad rugged cone of gray-brown rock, treeless and raw in the slanting afternoon sunlight. The summit was a ring of broken peaks, several miles across. The wide crater that lay within the broken crown of the mountain was filled with a dense blanket of white mist that veiled whatever lay beneath.

"The mountain is considered a sacred place by a lot of the local people," Josh said.

"I can see why," Olly replied, enchanted by the sight of the ancient volcano and its cover of dense mist.

The plane skirted the mountain peak and began to circle downward. Olly strained against her seat belt, watching as the ground rose swiftly up to meet them. They had come to a place of brown, baked earth, wrinkled and folded and dry.

A flat stretch of land lay directly ahead. The world was rushing past now, and the small aircraft was rattling and vibrating as the pilot throttled back and came in to land. There was a bump and a lurch as the wheels hit the ground. The plane rose again for a heart-stopping second, then came down with a thump. Olly and Josh were jolted in their seats as the plane came to a shuddering halt.

Olly grinned at Josh. "Phew! That was exciting," she said.

The next few minutes were spent getting everyone safely off the plane and piling the luggage by the side of the makeshift runway.

Olly looked around. There were a couple of dilapidated old buildings nearby and a simple dirt road that snaked off among the hills — but there was no sign of life anywhere. "I thought Dr. Feng was going to meet us," she remarked. "Where is he?"

"I'll find out," Jonathan said. He dialed a number on his cell phone.

"We could do some exploring while we're waiting," Olly suggested.

"No, stay put," said her grandmother. "I don't want you getting lost in the first five minutes."

The professor shielded his eyes against the fierce sunlight as he scanned the horizon. "That's strange," he said. "We landed right on time, and Dr. Feng definitely said he'd be here to meet us. Perhaps he's running a little late."

"I hope he comes soon," Josh murmured. "We can't lug our gear to the site on foot." He looked at Jonathan. "It's over a mile away, isn't it?"

Jonathan nodded, but he was frowning. Obviously there was no answer to his call yet.

"I don't think it will come to that," Audrey Beckmann said. "Now then, would anyone like something to drink while we're waiting? I've got some bottles of water around here somewhere." She rummaged through one of her bags.

Olly wandered to a high point a little ways away, where she could see farther along the gray dirt road. "Someone's coming!" she called. A battered and dust-coated old Jeep was making its way toward the landing strip.

Olly ran back to join the rest of the party as the vehicle came to a halt. A Chinese man stepped out. He looked like he was in his forties. His clothes were dirt-encrusted and his hands and face were grimy. Olly guessed that he had come straight from the dig without having had time to clean up.

The professor greeted him with a smile. "Dr. Feng," he said. "It's a pleasure to see you again."

But Olly saw that the doctor's face was troubled. "I am sorry I am late," he apologized. "But there has been a terrible accident at the site. People have been injured. Professor Andryanova has been taken to the hospital." He looked around the stunned group. "The local diggers are saying that the ruins are cursed, and many have abandoned the site," he added. "They say that if we continue to violate the sacred mountain, we will all die. It is a disaster."

Olly and Josh stared at each other, stunned by Dr. Feng's troubling news. It seemed as if more than just a drought was afflicting the land that lay in the shadow of Si-houzai-shan, the dead fire mountain.

Chapter Three: The Curse

Olly's high spirits had plummeted upon hearing Dr. Feng's news of the accident at the dig. The Christie party was subdued as the Jeep took the last bend in the rough earth road, and they saw ahead of them the wide, sunbaked banks of the Minjiang River.

As Josh had shown Olly on a map, the river made a wide loop around the sacred mountain, running through a wilderness of hills and valleys that grew more steep and rugged as they neared the foot of Si-houzai-shan.

The volcano dominated the landscape. The late afternoon sun had dropped away behind it, throwing much of its mass into deep shade, but its outer contours were highlighted with shining gold. The wisps and tatters of cloud that hung around its barren upper slopes glowed with an eerie, translucent light. Seeing the moody landscape reminded Olly of the recent tragedy among the ancient ruins.

The Jeep pulled into the camp at the archaeological dig site and came to a dusty halt. Olly climbed out and stood staring up at the mountain's majestic bulk, feeling suddenly very small and insignificant beneath its long shadow. She could understand how people might believe the mountain was sacred. There was something about it that inspired awe — and a little fear.

"Don't just stand there gawking, Olivia," snapped her grandmother. "Help us unload."

Olly tore her eyes away from the mountain as her grandma pushed a heavy bag into her hands. She looked around, taking in the rest of her surroundings. The Jeep was parked on the long gentle slope of the dry riverbank. The brown river flowed sluggishly through rocks and boulders thirty or more feet away. Off to one side, Olly saw what they had come all this way to investigate. The broken walls and towers of an ancient town rose out of untold centuries of river silt and mud. In the other direction, a cluster of temporary wooden huts and cabins had been constructed for the archaeologists to live in while they worked. A few dusty cars and trucks were parked behind the buildings, alongside three industrial digging machines.

Olly had imagined that the place would be bustling with activity, but the small number of people who remained were standing or sitting in small, subdued groups. Some were obviously locals, dressed in simple shirts and pants of brown and tan and orange. Olly noticed that they were all quite young. She assumed that they were the only ones who had not deserted the site because of the curse that Dr. Feng had mentioned.

There was also a group of downcast field archaeologists who sat silently together, obviously badly affected by the accident. Some were Chinese, but Olly knew that the rest came from a variety of other places, including Russia, America, and Europe.

A section of the ruins had been sectioned off with red-and-white tape. That was obviously where the accident had occurred.

While they were still unloading their luggage, a man approached them from the huts. He looked Chinese, but he was not dressed for work on the site. He was wearing a gray tunic and trousers that Olly thought had a somewhat military look. His eyes were hidden by dark glasses. Two men in similar dress appeared and stood behind him — one of them Chinese, the other European or American, from the look of him.

"This is Charles Lau," Dr. Feng told Professor Christie.

Mr. Lau shook the professor's hand unsmilingly. "We've been expecting you, Professor," he said in perfect, American-accented English. "I hope you had a pleasant journey. I am Mr. Bell's personal representative at this excavation. My job is to ensure that the work moves forward and to prevent any potential problems between the people working on the dig and the people who live nearby."

Olly looked at the dour-faced man, thinking that he seemed curiously out of place here. She didn't like the fact that his eyes were concealed behind dark glasses — it made him look as if he had something to hide.

"Why should there be any problems between us and the local inhabitants?" Jonathan asked.

Mr. Lau gave him a humorless smile. "There shouldn't be," he said. "But a few local people are angry that foreigners have been brought in to plunder their land. They believe that they should benefit from whatever is found here. They do not understand that the work you are doing is for scientific purposes rather than profit. They are disorganized and ignorant farmers, that is all. They present no difficulty to my people — all of whom are highly trained professionals. However, I recommend that you keep to this immediate area. I cannot guarantee the safety of anyone who wanders off alone."

Olly didn't like the tone of disdain in Lau's voice

as he spoke about the local people. And she could tell from the look on his face that Josh had also taken a strong dislike to Augustus Bell's "personal representative."

Audrey Beckmann stepped up to the man. "Are you suggesting we might be in physical danger?" she asked.

"I lead an elite team," said Lau. "I can assure you that we will not allow you to be inconvenienced by a few troublemakers." He nodded briefly to Dr. Feng and to Professor Christie, then turned sharply on his heel and marched off toward the huts. His two men followed.

Jonathan frowned after them. "What do you think?" he said. "They look like security guards to me. Why would Bell feel the need to hire men like that?"

"Unfortunately, there is some local unrest," Dr. Feng admitted. "But don't be alarmed by Lau. The people who farm around here are poor and are suffering badly from the drought, but they are kind and not aggressive in the least. I can assure you that they will do nothing to interfere with our work."

"I hope you're right, Doctor," Professor Christie said with a frown. He looked toward the ruins. "Before we do anything else, perhaps we should see how the accident happened," he suggested.

Dr. Feng led Jonathan and the professor over to the ruins. Olly and Josh followed them while Audrey bustled off to start unpacking.

The red-and-white tape surrounded the shell of a building. There were signs that some major digging had already taken place. Within the broken walls, a pit had been excavated, some thirteen feet deep. To one side, a whole section of the ancient wall had clearly fallen in. Rubble and debris covered the ground.

"The walls have not been properly propped up," Olly heard her father murmur to himself as he examined the excavation. "That's not the work of a curse. It's poor planning." He shook his head. "And this isn't the first time I've seen Andryanova cut corners." He frowned and fell silent as he noticed an interesting carving and bent to examine it more closely.

"Was anyone seriously hurt?" Olly asked, peering down into the deep trench.

"Professor Andryanova broke his leg," Dr. Feng replied. "Thankfully, the others only suffered cuts and bruises. The real problem is that most of the people we hired locally have deserted us. As you can see, only a few of the younger ones stayed behind, and if anything else goes wrong, I think we'll lose them, too. It will take several days to bring in new workers from towns farther away — if they will come at all once news of the accident spreads."

"Do you mean because of the curse?" Olly asked. "Why do they think the place is cursed?" She had heard her father denounce the idea, but she was still curious.

Jonathan shook his head. "That's not important right now," he said. "Our real problem is how to keep the dig running with so few workers. We don't have much time."

Professor Christie had wandered to the far end of the roped-off area, stooping to scrutinize a section of the wall. Dr. Feng approached him. "While Professor Andryanova is in the hospital, would you be prepared to take over as the team leader?" he asked.

Josh and Olly listened with mild interest as Dr. Feng convinced a reluctant Professor Christie to take over as temporary leader, and Jonathan promised to get the remaining workers to make the site safe.

As they all headed back toward the cabins, Olly walked alongside Josh. "Great," she said gloomily. "We've come all this way, and now we can't do anything." She frowned at her father and the others, deep in conversation. "I know Jonathan said it wasn't important, but I'd really like to know why some of the local people think this place is cursed," she added.

As they approached the cluster of buildings, a Chinese boy burst out from one of the cabins and ran toward them. He was wearing jeans and a T-shirt, and his face was bright with a full smile.

"That's Ang-lun!" Olly exclaimed, recognizing him from an e-mailed exchange of photographs. She looked at Josh. "Where's the present we brought for him?"

Josh took the hardcover copy of *Treasure Island* from his bag.

"Hello Olly, hello Josh," Ang-lun said, grinning. "I have very looked forward to meeting you. I have been helping to prepare food for everyone. I will show you where you will be sleeping. Then we can eat."

"This is for you," Josh said, handing Ang-lun the book. Olly noticed that Josh was careful to hold the book in both hands as he passed it to Ang-lun, since her father had told them that Chinese people saw this as an especially respectful gesture.

Ang-lun was clearly delighted by the gift and he cradled it in his arms as they walked toward the buildings.

The Chinese boy explained that he and his father were staying nearby at his grandmother's house in Banping, a small village a mile or so to the north. He showed Olly and Josh to a two-room cabin. Josh and Jonathan were to sleep in the larger of the rooms, and Olly in the other. The professor and Audrey Beckmann were sharing an adjacent building. The rest of the archaeological team was staying in the various other huts, which were gathered around a much larger cabin used for cooking and eating. There was another hut for washing and several more for storing equipment.

Mr. Bell's representative, Mr. Lau, and his men had their own quarters a little farther away. According to Ang-lun they kept very much to themselves and even prepared and ate their food separately.

Having shown them around the campsite, Ang-lun presented Josh and Olly with a rolled scroll. Olly unrolled it to see a colored illustration, drawn on paper made from bamboo pulp. A man in bright red traditional Chinese costume was standing on a hillside, his arms raised, his face astonished. Hovering in the air above him, her feet in the clouds, was a woman. She was wearing traditional dress and a jeweled tiara, her long silken ribbons fluttering in the wind as she smiled serenely down at the man in red. The sky was dark blue, and behind the woman's head was the full moon.

"They are Chang-O and Hou-Yi," Ang-lun

explained. "Chang-O is about to fly off to the moon. My grandmother painted it for you when I told her that you were interested in the story."

"It's wonderful," Olly said, enchanted by the delicate picture. "I've read the myth many times, so it is amazing to see this. Please thank your grandmother for us."

"You will be able to thank her yourselves at the festival," Ang-lun told them.

"There's going to be a festival?" Josh asked.

Ang-lun looked surprised. "Didn't you know?" he replied. "The Festival of the Autumn Moon will be taking place in Chung-hsien in two days' time. It's a celebration of the moon goddess, Chang-O. There will be lion dances and dragon dances, and music in the streets." He grinned. "And lots of mooncakes to eat. Then, at the end, there will be many fireworks. Chung-hsien isn't far away. You must all come — it's great fun."

"We wouldn't miss it," Olly said, her eyes shining at the thought of a traditional Chinese celebration.

Josh looked thoughtfully at Ang-lun. "Mr. Lau said we should stay away from the local people," he said. "He told us some of them don't like us being here. Is that true?"

Ang-lun's face clouded. "A few are unhappy that

the old city has been found," he explained. "They believe that it is cursed. They think the ruins should be left alone, and that if we continue digging, the sky god will show his anger by refusing to let it rain ever again."

"Why do they think the city is cursed?" asked Olly.

"They believe that the sky god made the river rise on purpose to cover the city," Ang-lun continued. "The Shan-ren said that it was to punish the people for letting Chang-O stay here after she had stolen the pill of everlasting life." He shook his head. "Some of the older people are very superstitious."

"What's the Shan-ren?" Olly asked, trying to piece the puzzle together.

Ang-lun looked at her. "The Shan-ren were the guardians of the sacred mountain," he said. "But they died out a long time ago."

"You mean they were a kind of secret society?" Josh exclaimed.

Ang-lun nodded. "Some of the older people still believe in the Shan-ren's teachings, but the younger people aren't very interested." Ang-lun smiled. "And I don't believe in curses."

"Don't be too sure about that," Josh warned. "Olly's family has a curse on it. At least, that's what I'd call it."

Olly glared at him. "Thanks for bringing that up," she said. She turned to Ang-lun, who was gazing at her in surprise. "It's nothing, really," she told him, trying to downplay the situation. "An ancestor of mine took a scroll from an old tomb in Egypt. The scroll had a curse on it, that's all." She shrugged and fell silent, hoping it would be enough of an explanation. She didn't like to talk about it. She had only told Josh, her best friend, within the last month.

"Tell him the rest," Josh urged. He looked at Ang-lun. "The curse said that the firstborn son in each generation of the family would die young. So far, they all have — including Olly's uncle Douglas, that's her father's older brother. In fact, that's one of the reasons why the professor is here. If he can find all the Talismans of the Moon, he thinks they'll lead him to the Archive of the Old. Then he can get a copy of the Egyptian scroll, put it back in the tomb, and break the curse before anyone else dies," he finished triumphantly.

Ang-lun looked confused. "I don't understand," he said. "What is the Archive of Old?"

"It's an ancient library," Olly explained. "No one knows where it is, but it's supposed to have copies of every sacred writing that was ever made back in ancient times." She sighed, wishing Josh had never brought this up. "Back in the last century, my great-uncle Adam believed that if the scroll was taken back to the tomb, then the curse would be lifted. Unfortunately, Adam *and* the original scroll were both lost at sea when the ship he was on went down in a storm." She narrowed her eyes thoughtfully. "I don't think my dad really believes in the curse — but it was finding out about it that got him interested in archaeology in the first place."

She paused and looked at Ang-lun. "It's like this. There are four Talismans of the Moon. The Mooncake of Chang-O is supposed to be one of them," she explained. "If someone possesses all four of the talismans, that person is supposed to be able to open the Archive of the Old."

Ang-lun looked at Olly. "But you told me you have no brothers," he said to her. "So, even if the curse was real, it can't do you any harm."

Olly didn't reply. She didn't want to mention the dark thoughts that sometimes kept her awake at night. For three generations, the firstborn of the Christie family had met a sudden and tragically early death. They had all been sons — but what if there were no sons for the curse to destroy?

What if there was only a daughter?

What if there was only Olly?

Chapter Four: ◉ The Ruined City

Josh slept soundly that night, worn out by the long journey and the change in time zones. A good sleep helped to adjust his body clock a little, and the enticing smell of cooking that came in through the open window of his bedroom the following morning soon had him up and dressed.

Jonathan's bed was empty. Josh assumed he had risen early to get working on the site.

Yawning, Josh thumped on Olly's bedroom door. "You up?" he called. Josh heard grumbling from within. Olly was not at her best first thing in the morning — especially when eight o'clock in the morning in Sichuan Province was one o'clock in the morning back home. "Get up!" Josh called. "You'll miss breakfast."

He stepped out of the cabin. The morning was fresh and clear. Above him, the sky was a lovely pale blue and cloudless. He could see activity over at the ruins; people were busy with long timbers and sheets of boarding. He could see Jonathan perched on a section of walling, wielding a hammer. The sound of the hammer blows drifted on the faint breeze.

A couple of Mr. Lau's men were standing nearby on a crest of high ground, watching the workers.

Josh hurried over to the dining cabin. Professor Christie and Dr. Feng were huddled together at a corner table, poring over documents and talking eagerly together in low voices. A young Chinese woman was at the griddle, tossing a thick, sweet-smelling pancake while Audrey Beckmann watched.

"Hello, Josh," Olly's grandmother said. "Did you sleep well? Are you hungry?"

"Yes and yes," Josh replied. "I called Olly, but she just moaned at me."

"I did not moan," came Olly's voice from the doorway. "I just don't like being yelled at, especially not in the morning." She was dressed and attempting to look bright-eyed. "What's for breakfast?"

"Wei-li is making us *jian bing*," Audrey Beckmann said. "It's a kind of crepe. Go and sit down. I'll bring the food over to you."

Their first Chinese breakfast began with a bowl of *mian cha* — thick, sweet porridge made from millet. It was topped with sesame paste and sprinkled with sesame seeds. Josh and Olly ate it hungrily with broad china spoons, and drank fresh milk from delicate porcelain cups.

Audrey Beckmann brought them the *jian bing*, plump and browned from the frying pan. "When you've finished eating, you can come over to my room for your lessons," she said firmly.

Olly frowned at her. "Gran, do we have to?" she asked. "I was hoping we could help Dad and Jonathan. It is our first day, after all."

"You've already missed two days of lessons. Besides, I don't think Jonathan will want you anywhere near the site until he's finished making sure everything is safe." Audrey gave them a stern look. "I want you both in my room with your schoolbooks in a half an hour, OK?"

Olly and Josh nodded. There was no point arguing with her. Once Mrs. Beckmann had made a decision, not even Olly's powers of persuasion could change her mind. Besides, as Olly pointed out to Josh while they finished their breakfast, once lessons were over for the day, they would have the whole afternoon to explore.

~~~~~

By midday, when the two friends emerged from their makeshift schoolroom, the sun was burning bright and hot, filling the air with fine red dust and causing objects in the distance to shimmer in a heat haze.

The dining area was much busier than it had been at breakfast time. Jonathan was there eating lunch along with a team of field archaeologists and eight or nine locals — young people who had returned to the site to work, either because they didn't believe in the curse or — as Jonathan pointed out to Olly and Josh — because they needed the money.

The two friends had a quick lunch of noodle soup before checking with Jonathan that it was safe for them to go and explore the ruins.

"That's fine," he told them. "Just be sensible. Stay within sight and don't go near any of the areas I've taped off. You can check out the finds hut, too — you can see everything that's been uncovered so far."

This sounded like a good idea, so before they went exploring, they took a detour to the cabin where everything found on the dig was gathered for cleaning and cataloging.

It was an extraordinary collection. There were countless shards of earthenware, but much more interesting were the golden cups and plates and bowls. Most of them were damaged—eroded and distorted from centuries under the ground—but some looked as bright and perfect as when they had first been made. There were exquisite statuettes of green jade, and figurines of bronze and ivory. A young archaeologist named Nadia was working in the hut. She spoke English with a thick Russian accent, and was excited to tell them that the artifacts dated back nearly three and a half thousand years.

Even more eager to explore, Josh and Olly next headed for the ruins. From what Josh could tell as they approached, Jonathan had secured about a quarter of the area so far. The rest was still taped off.

They stepped down into the first of the long trenches and, with a real sense of wonder, they entered the dead city. In some places, the only trace of the building that had once stood there was a single row of stonework or a section of flooring. But, elsewhere, entire stone walls towered over Josh and Olly's heads, cracked, broken, and discolored from centuries under the rushing waters of the Minjiang River, but solid and impressive nevertheless. Here and there, they were able to enter rooms or corridors, and walk on newly excavated floors where no one had set foot since the river had risen in ancient times.

Olly stood in the middle of a large room with high stone walls. "I can see why some people might think this place is cursed," she remarked to Josh. "It's a bit creepy — and it's so cold."

Josh also noticed the strange chill that lingered in the ruined buildings — a coldness that seemed to seep from the stones and flow through the rooms and corridors despite the intense heat of the sun.

He scrambled up a chunk of timeworn masonry, and stared out toward the mountain, shading his eyes from the sun. "If this really was a city, where's the rest of it?" he called down to Olly. "All the buildings they've found so far wouldn't really make a decent-sized town." He spotted a solitary stone building a few hundred yards away among the hills. "I wonder what that is?" he said, pointing. It was on higher ground than the ruins, and although it was obviously old and damaged, it didn't have the battered and worn look of the old city.

There was no reply from Olly. Josh looked down and saw that she had wandered off. "Keep away from the taped-off areas," he called.

"I will," came Olly's reply.

Josh continued to explore on his own, making his way gradually toward the stone building in the hills. He climbed down into a long trench with freshly dug stonework in the sides and floor. He moved slowly, hoping to spy some telltale color or shape that would turn out to be a previously missed but priceless artifact. He smiled to himself, thinking how envious Olly would be if he found something amazing.

Suddenly, he realized that he was now close to the strange, solitary building he had seen from the entrance of the ruins, *and* that he was near the place where the accident had happened. He climbed out of the trench and stared down into the pit where Andryanova and his team had been working when the wall collapsed. A scaffolding of timber framed the walls now.

Josh noticed that a similar pit had been excavated next to this one. It was surrounded by a waist-high wall, broken and decaying and about one and a half feet thick. The excavation was still taped off. Josh bent down and found himself peering into a sunken chamber. He guessed the drop was about twenty feet onto a floor of silt and crumbling earth.

He was about to draw back and go in search of Olly, when a glint of something caught his eye. It was in the wall of the room — only two and a half feet below where he was standing. He leaned farther over, trying to make sense of what he was seeing.

It was about the size of his hand and it was set back in the wall. It had only been revealed because a great chunk seemed to have recently fallen away. There was no tag to show that the artifact had been spotted by anyone else, and it struck Josh that perhaps the collapse of the other wall had caused vibrations that had made the mud fall away. If that was the case, then he was the first person to see this thing for thousands of years!

He hesitated for a moment. Perhaps he should go and tell Jonathan about it. That would probably be the sensible thing to do, he thought. On the other hand, if he leaned just a little bit farther over, it would be within arm's reach.

Josh couldn't resist trying. He leaned farther over, lying across the wall and reaching down as far as he could. His fingertips were only inches away from the shining object. As he touched it, another chunk of mud fell off, and now he could see even more of the object. It looked like a circle of gold — and he was sure there were some kind of markings on it.

He strained to reach down those last few inches. His fingers clawed at the object, and more earth broke away. He lifted his feet off the ground so he could creep forward on the broad top of the wall. Now his fingertips could actually touch the cold metal. He grinned — almost there!

And then, as he stretched downward to get a grip on the object, he slipped forward. For a horrible moment he hung there, knowing he was going to fall but unable to pull himself back. Then the balance tipped and, with a loud yell, Josh toppled headfirst into the chamber below.

Chapter Five: Missing!

Josh twisted as he fell, landing heavily on one shoulder and rolling on the soft earth. He lay gasping for breath and grimacing in pain for a few moments. Then, realizing he wasn't badly hurt, he opened his eyes and stared around at the walls of the chamber. They were smooth and featureless and there were no window holes. There was a doorway, but the door itself had long since decayed away, and the exit was blocked by a solid wall of packed earth.

"Nice going, Josh," he groaned to himself. "That's the last time you act like Olly!" He looked down at his clothes. "*And* it's the last time you wear a white shirt on a dig!" he added. And then he realized that there was something under his right hand — something cold and smooth. He sat up, ignoring the aches and pains, and picked the thing up. It was a golden disc, about eight inches across. Somehow he had managed to grab it out of the wall as he had plunged past.

He grinned, forgetting his problems for a moment as he studied the beautiful artifact. He had been right about the markings; a series of little dimpled depressions had been punched into the surface of the golden disc and, from what Josh could tell, they formed a street plan of a large city.

"What are you doing down there?"

Josh looked up, startled by the voice from above. Olly's head and shoulders were dark against the sky as she looked out over the top of the wall into the pit.

"I slipped," Josh responded. He got to his feet and lifted the golden disc up toward her. "But look what I found."

"What is it?"

"I don't know," Josh said. "But I'm pretty sure it's made of gold."

"Wow!" Olly breathed. "Come on up so I can see it."

Josh blinked up at her. "How?" he asked.

She frowned and looked around the walls. "Can't you climb out?" she asked after a moment.

Josh shaded his eyes against the bright sky. "Could *you?*" he demanded pointedly.

"I wouldn't have fallen down there in the first place," Olly retorted. "What were you thinking, Josh? I'm going to have to go and get help. And then Jonathan and Dad will skin us alive. You did know this place is still taped off, didn't you?"

"I know," Josh said ruefully. "I didn't fall down here on purpose. Can't you just get a rope or something without telling anyone?" Josh didn't need her to point out that finding a golden disc would not be a good enough excuse for putting himself in danger. He didn't like to think about what Mrs. Beckmann would have to say. She'd likely say that it was more like something Olly would have done, Josh considered.

"I'll see what I can do," Olly replied. She disappeared for a moment, then her head popped back over the wall. "Don't go away," she added with a grin.

"Oh, ha-ha," Josh called up. "Just hurry up, please, before someone comes."

Olly vanished again and Josh sat down cross-legged on the ground. He held the golden disc in his hands and leaned over it, studying the intricate markings, waiting to be rescued.

~~~~~

Olly ran back through the ruins toward the camp. She needed to rescue Josh quickly before the others finished their lunch and headed back to the site. She smiled to herself — it was unusual for Josh to get himself into trouble like this. It had been fun teasing him. Nine times out of ten, she would have been down the hole, and Josh would have had to rescue *her*. And he certainly wouldn't have spared her the embarrassment.

She felt a little envious that he had found the golden disc — but she was more intrigued than anything else. She couldn't wait to get Josh out and take a good look at it.

She headed for the equipment huts. There was bound to be rope in there somewhere. She glanced over at the dining cabin, fearing she'd see the team coming back out to work. But, the door was closed and there was no sign of anyone.

She found a coil of thick rope, slung it over her shoulder, and ran back to the ruins. "I'm back," she called. "I'm just going to tie one end onto something, then I'll let the rope down." Her mouth curled in a wry smile. "I suppose you know how to climb a rope?" she added.

There was no reply.

She frowned. "I was only kidding," she called, assuming Josh hadn't been impressed by her joke.

Still nothing.

She peered over the wall. "Oh!" She stared down into the sunken room, hardly able to believe her eyes. Josh was gone.

She assumed he must have managed to climb

out on his own, so she stood upright, and looked around. "Josh?" she called.

But he was nowhere to be seen.

She shouted, "Josh!"

Nothing.

Olly's eyes narrowed. It was dawning on her that maybe Josh had only *pretended* he couldn't climb out. He was getting back at her for making fun of him. "I bet I know what he did," she muttered to herself. "He took that golden thing to show to Dad without me." She snorted. "And there's no way he'll mention how he found it!"

Forgetting the rope, she trudged irritably back to the camp. As she arrived, she saw Jonathan's team leaving the dining cabin. "Where is he?" she asked Jonathan. "Is he in there with Dad?"

Jonathan gave her a puzzled look. "Do you mean Josh?"

"Of course I mean Josh," she said. "I suppose he's been showing off with that thing."

"What thing?" Jonathan asked. "What are you talking about, Olly? I haven't seen Josh since the two of you went off together half an hour ago."

"Oh." Olly stared at him in surprise. "I thought . . ." She frowned. "Is Dad still in there?"

"Yes, he's talking with Dr. Feng and Mr. Lau," Jonathan replied.

"And you haven't seen Josh at all?" Olly queried.

Jonathan looked suspiciously at her. "What have you two been up to?" he demanded. "Has he wandered off somewhere?"

"No," Olly answered quickly. "We were just exploring the ruins, and I kind of lost track of him."

"What's this *thing* you were talking about?" Jonathan asked.

"He found something," Olly replied. "I thought he'd come here to show it to you and Dad."

"No, he didn't," Jonathan said, still regarding Olly dubiously.

Olly decided it was time to go before Jonathan asked any more awkward questions. "Maybe he went back to the cabin," she said. "I'll just go and check." She ran over to their cabin, a small knot of anxiety forming in her stomach. Where on Earth had Josh gone?

She pushed open the door to Josh and Jonathan's room. Josh wasn't there. "OK," Olly said to herself. "This is getting silly. He has to be somewhere."

She ran over to the hut with the washrooms. Still no sign of him. Really worried now, she ran from hut to hut, but Josh was nowhere to be found. It was as if he had just vanished.

"What's going on?" Audrey Beckmann's voice brought Olly to a halt. "Jonathan tells me that Josh has disappeared."

Olly was now too concerned about Josh to bother hiding the truth. "He fell into a big hole," she said, waving an arm toward the ruins. "I went to get some rope to haul him out, but when I got back, he was gone!"

"Come and show me where you mean," Mrs. Beckmann said.

By this time, Jonathan had explained the situation to Professor Christie. So Olly led the professor, Dr. Feng, her gran, and Jonathan over to the ruins. Mr. Lau followed silently behind them.

"He was down there," Olly said, pointing into the sunken room.

Jonathan stared down into the pit. "He shouldn't have been anywhere near here," he said. "What did I tell you about being careful and staying in sight?"

"I know," Olly said miserably. "But he saw something sticking out of the wall, and when he leaned over to try and get it . . ." She didn't need to finish the sentence.

Mr. Lau stepped forward and stared into the room below. "What did the boy find?" he asked Olly.

She looked at him. "It was some kind of golden disc," she said, holding her hands apart, "about this big."

Mr. Lau took out a radio and spoke rapidly into it in Mandarin. Then he turned to the professor. "I don't think the boy could have climbed out on his own," he said. "The walls are too smooth. Someone else must have been here. I'll have my men begin a search." He turned to Olly. "How long ago did this happen?"

"Only a few minutes," Olly replied.

"Good, then they won't have gotten far — unless they have some kind of transport. Let's hope that's not the case."

"Mr. Lau," Audrey Beckmann broke in. "I'd be very grateful if you'd explain what you mean."

The man turned to face her, his eyes, as ever, hidden behind his dark glasses. "I think the boy has been kidnapped," he said flatly. "Possibly they only wanted the golden disc, but they may intend to hold him for ransom. This is the first time any outsider has dared to come on the excavation site. It certainly won't happen again." He stalked off, talking rapidly into his radio.

"We should search, too," Jonathan said. "I'll organize everyone into groups. With any luck, Lau's wrong and we'll find Josh somewhere nearby."

"I'll help," Olly said.

"No, you won't," her gran contradicted. "You'll go straight back to your cabin and stay there."

"But . . ."

"Do as you're told, Olivia," said her father.

Frustrated, annoyed, and very worried for Josh, Olly miserably made her way back to the huts. Could Lau really be right? Had Josh been kidnapped? It didn't seem possible. But what other explanation could there be for his strange and sudden disappearance?

~~~~~

Half the afternoon had passed, and Olly was practically climbing the walls in frustration. She ran from window to window in the cabin, hoping to see someone coming back with Josh. She could see people in the distance — search parties scouring the hills. She chewed a fingernail, wishing she could be out there with them. The uncertainty and inactivity was driving her crazy.

She saw Jonathan approaching and leaned out the window. "Any sign of Josh?" she asked, already guessing the answer from his face. He looked tired and anxious.

"Nothing so far," Jonathan replied.

Olly looked at him, trying not to sound as frightened for Josh as she felt. "Maybe Dr. Feng was right — and this place really is cursed."

"Don't be silly, Olly," Jonathan said, frowning at her. "It's more likely that Lau is right and Josh has been kidnapped." He set his jaw. "Your grandmother has called the police in Chung-hsien. They should arrive soon. In the meantime, all we can do is keep looking." He looked up at her. "You've got your cell phone, don't you? So you can call me if he turns up."

Olly nodded.

Jonathan turned and set off up the long, dry riverbank at a steady jog.

Olly sank down on one of the beds. Sitting around and waiting for news went against every instinct in her body. She wanted to be out there. She wanted to find Josh.

For a long minute, she gazed out the window, her eyes scanning the hills, her fingers rattling impatiently on the windowsill while she thought through the options: Wait here, or go and help.

Eventually, she got to her feet, her mind made up. Waiting was impossible. She ran across the room and slipped out the door. She would be very careful — and if she saw anything suspicious, she had her cell phone to call for help. She decided to search for some clues back at the sunken room where she had last seen Josh. The search parties were ranging farther out into the countryside now, and the ruins were deserted.

Fortunately, the coil of rope was still lying where Olly had dropped it. She quickly looped the rope around a jutting chunk of masonry and knotted it. She let it out into the room and climbed down.

The first thing that struck her was how chilly it was down among the ruins. The day was so hot and humid now that the cold took her by surprise. She shivered as she looked around at the walls. The ancient stonework was smooth and precise — the joints between the big blocks of stone would not even allow for a finger to be inserted. There was no way Josh could have climbed out — not unless someone else had helped him.

She crouched to examine the floor. The ground was soft in places. She could see the print of Josh's shoes quite clearly here and there. But, in other places the earth was sunbaked and hard. The sun was sinking now in the western sky, throwing long, cold shadows across the room.

Something glinted by the wall on the other side of the room, catching her eye. She walked over to it and picked it up, turning it over in her fingers. It was a white shirt button — quite clean and new. She frowned. Josh had been wearing a white shirt. She looked up at the wall next to the button. The stonework was as sheer as it was on all the other walls. She was sure Josh couldn't have climbed up here.

But then she noticed a crevice in the rock at shoulder height. She stepped forward and peered into the hole. All she saw was blackness. She took her small pencil-flashlight out of her pocket and, switching it on, directed the powerful narrow white beam into the hole. Still, she could see nothing. The beam illuminated the sides of the hole, but did not reveal how deep it was.

She pushed her forefinger into the hole and felt something very cold and smooth against her fingertip. It wasn't stone, she was sure. It felt more like metal.

She pressed her fingers against the metal thing and heard a soft, sharp click. The wall moved slightly and she snatched her hand away in surprise. A section of the wall, about seven feet high and three feet wide, had moved smoothly inward.

Cautiously, she pushed this section of the stone wall with one hand. It gave, swinging open silently to reveal a deep, dark space from which cold, clammy air flowed. A hidden passage! She pointed her flashlight into the darkness. It illuminated some kind of small, dusty room.

"Josh?" Olly called tentatively. "Josh, are you in there?" She stepped forward nervously, her mouth dry, her stomach knotting. "Josh?" she called again, lingering in the stone doorway.

She hesitated. Maybe she should go back and get help. Then, out of the corner of her eye she saw a movement.

A figure was lurking in the shadows to one side of the door. Before she had time to react, the figure lunged forward, knocked the flashlight out of her hand, and pulled her into the room. Olly stumbled and fell to the ground. And the stone doorway swung silently closed behind her, shutting out the light.

Chapter Six: 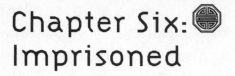 Imprisoned

A voice spoke sharply in Olly's ear. She could not tell if they were words of warning or command, but she was sure they were in Mandarin. She scrambled toward her flashlight, which was lying on the floor, its beam lighting up a section of the far wall.

Before she could reach it, a bright light flashed in her face. She lifted an arm to shield her eyes. "Stop that!" she snapped.

The flashlight angled away from her face and more Mandarin was spoken. Olly got to her feet and backed against the wall, staring at the man in front of her. He was tall and wiry, and the lower half of his face was hidden behind a red silk scarf. Deep-shadowed eyes stared unblinkingly at her from beneath a leathery, lined forehead. Olly guessed that the man was in his forties at least. He was wearing a simple shirt and trousers.

He watched her with deep, intent eyes. She licked her dry lips, wondering how she could escape. She stooped and picked up her flashlight. Then, she sidestepped toward the entrance, keeping her back to the wall. The man tracked her with the beam of his own flashlight.

Once she was close, Olly bolted for the doorway and struggled to get some kind of grip on the stonework, but it was smooth and featureless. She turned and looked back at the man, noticing as she did so that there was a black pictogram on the scarf that masked his face.

"I am Olivia Christie," she said firmly, trying to sound as if she had everything under control. "I want you to let me out of here right now." She wracked her brains for something to say in Mandarin, but the beginning lessons her gran had given her did not prepare her for this. "*Qing!*" she said at last. *Please!*

The man spoke again.

"*Wo bu dong,*" Olly said, remembering more of the words from the list of frequently used phrases. "*Ni hui jiang yingyu ma?*" *I don't understand. Do you speak English?*

The man shook his head. He had understood her. That was something.

"OK," Olly said slowly. "I know how to say hello, good-bye, please, and thank you, but I'm not sure any of that is going to help much." She pointed to the door, making a gesture that she hoped he would understand meant she wanted out.

Again he shook his head, this time aiming his flashlight toward an open doorway in the far side of the room. He nodded toward her and pointed at the doorway again.

Olly was beginning to recover from her initial fright. The man didn't seem to mean her any immediate harm. His voice was quiet and calm, and his behavior was not especially threatening. "You want me to go that way?" she asked, also pointing.

He nodded.

She looked at him. "I don't suppose I have much choice, do I?" she sighed. Then she frowned. "Who are you? What are you doing down here?"

The man spoke sharply, gesturing for her to move. She pocketed her flashlight and walked toward the far doorway, glancing over her shoulder to see him following close behind.

The doorway led to a narrow corridor. Occasionally, another doorway led off to one side or the other, but the man put a hand on Olly's shoulder, keeping her to the main passage.

Olly remembered the cell phone that she had in her pocket. That made her feel better. As soon as she got the chance, she would try and call in a rescue party.

She turned to look at the man. "You've got Josh,

too, don't you?" she said. What was the Mandarin word for boy? *"Nanhair?"* she said. "Boy? Are you taking me to Josh?" She frowned. "Well, I hope you are. And when we get out of here, you're going to be in trouble, mister — that's a promise."

The man didn't speak but pressed his hand down on Olly's shoulder, bringing her to a halt. She looked around. There wasn't an obvious doorway nearby, but then he reached into a square cavity and a section of the wall slid away to reveal a block of darkness.

Assuming this was their way forward, Olly moved toward the opening. But the man stopped her with one hand, and patted her pockets with the other. He found the bulge of her cell phone and took it out.

"Here, wait a minute," Olly said. "You can't do that."

But the man simply stepped aside and gave Olly a firm shove in the small of her back. She stumbled forward into the darkness. The doorway swung closed at her back and the flashlight beam was cut off.

Olly turned and hammered on the cold stone. "Hey! Let me out!" she shouted.

"Don't bother," came a weary voice out of the darkness. "I tried that. He won't come back."

Olly spun around. "Josh?" she gasped. She fished

in her pocket for her flashlight. At least the strange masked man had left her with that.

She switched it on. Josh was sitting in a corner of the small stone room. He lifted both hands to cover his eyes. "Ow!" he said. "Too bright!"

"Sorry." She moved the light away, shining the beam around the room. It was windowless and doorless — a sealed stone box no more than thirteen feet square.

Josh stood up and squinted at her.

"Are you OK?" she asked.

"Oh, fine," Josh said dully. "I'm having a great time. How long have I been here?"

"Several hours," Olly told him. "What happened?"

"I was grabbed from behind by two men and dragged through a doorway in the wall. They brought me here and then left." He gestured to a chunk of bread and a bottle of water. "They left me something to eat and drink," he said. "But they took the gold disc. I think that was what they really wanted."

"Did they have scarves over their faces?" Olly asked.

Josh nodded.

"My guy, too." Olly crouched and used her finger to draw the pictogram she had seen on the man's scarf in the dust that covered the stone floor. It was a simple symbol — like a capital *E* lying on its back, with the central stroke elongated, and an inverted *Y* over the top.

Josh squatted at her side. "Yeah, I saw that," he said. They looked at each other. "Do you know what it means?" he asked.

Olly shook her head. "Mr. Lau thinks you were kidnapped by criminals," she remarked. "I suppose it could be some kind of gang marking." She stood up and walked over to the featureless section of stonework that hid the secret doorway. "Whoever they are, we have to get out of here," she said firmly. She ran the flashlight beam over the wall, hoping to spot some crack or hole or fissure that might contain another opening mechanism.

Josh joined her, and together they scoured the walls with their eyes and hands.

"What do you think they're going to do with us?" Josh asked as they finished examining the final wall.

"I don't plan on hanging around to find out," Olly muttered. She aimed the flashlight upward. The low ceiling was also made of stone blocks.

"We might be able to smash our way out if we can find something heavy to hit the wall with," Josh suggested. He pointed to the corner of the room where a large stone slab lay on the floor. "That might make a good battering ram."

Olly rested the flashlight on the floor and they both stooped to try and lift the stone. It was impossible for them to get their fingers under it, so they tried shifting it out of the corner, heaving and dragging with all their strength.

The stone moved a few inches. Josh got behind it and pushed with all his might. It moved again with the harsh grating noise of stone on stone. Josh suddenly found himself staring down at a black hole in the floor big enough to swallow him whole. He let out a startled yelp and jumped back.

An odd sound echoed up from the depths: a rushing, chattering, roaring sound — familiar but misplaced.

Olly knelt down and pointed her flashlight into the hole. It was a stone shaft, possibly ten feet deep and, at the bottom, rippling and glinting in the flashlight beam, was a stream of flowing black water. "It's some kind of well," Olly announced. "I guess this water runs into the river."

"It does!" Josh agreed with sudden excitement. "I saw it on the plan."

Olly stared at him. "What plan?"

"I forgot to tell you; there was a design etched on

the gold disc. It looked like the street plan of a city. I think it was *this* city — the lost Yueliang-Chengshi. It showed a waterway running through the center and down to the river." He pointed at the rushing water below. "This might be it."

Olly looked thoughtfully at him. "Which means that water down there is heading straight for the river, right?"

Josh nodded. "We could throw something in — a message to tell people where we are. It would end up in the river and someone would see it." His eyes lit up. "We'd be rescued."

Olly looked at him. "Except that we don't have anything to write on or anything to write with, or anything to put a message in so it wouldn't get wet." She raised a single eyebrow. "Apart from that, great plan."

Josh sighed. "You're right," he said. "It doesn't help us at all."

"Unless we jump in, of course," Olly suggested.

Josh gave a bleak laugh. "Yes," he said. "We could always do that."

"No. I mean it," Olly insisted.

Josh looked at her. "You want us to jump down the well?" he asked incredulously. "Then what?"

"We swim," Olly replied calmly, as if she was just suggesting a stroll over the hills.

"And what if there's no air?" Josh asked.

"We hold our breath," Olly responded. She shined her flashlight down into the hole again. "Look how fast the stream's going," she said. "We know the river isn't far away, so it can't run underground for long. We'll probably only have to hold our breath for a few seconds." She looked at Josh. "Unless you can think of another way to get us out of here — bearing in mind that this stone slab is too heavy for us to pick up, let alone use as a battering ram."

Josh shook his head dubiously. "How long can you hold your breath?" he asked.

"Long enough," said Olly.

"You're not the greatest swimmer in the world, Olly," he pointed out.

Olly frowned at him. It was true; as versatile as she liked to consider herself, swimming had never been her thing. "And you are, I suppose?" she countered.

"I'm not saying that. I just think it's crazy to jump into the water without any idea of what's down there. We could both end up drowning."

"Or, we could sit here doing nothing till we're just a bunch of old bones," Olly argued. "Except that I'm not going to wait for that to happen. I don't care what you think. I'm going to give it a try."

Josh looked thoughtfully at her for a few moments. "Maybe we could do it," he said. "But we need to think it through. First, you need to learn how to properly hold your breath underwater."

Olly sighed. "I know how to hold my breath," she said.

"Look, I can swim the full length of a swimming pool underwater," Josh pointed out. "What about you?"

"I don't know."

"Exactly. The thing is, we only breathe with the top two-thirds of our lungs. So, you have to pant really fast before you take a big breath. That way, all the carbon dioxide that's lying around in the bottom of your lungs gets stirred up and comes out, which leaves more room for oxygen."

Olly stared at him. "You know the weirdest things, Josh," she said. "Will the flashlight survive underwater?"

"It's supposed to be waterproof," Josh replied. "Now, do the panting thing," he instructed. "Then, take a big breath and I'll time you to see how long you can hold it."

Olly breathed in and out rapidly for a few seconds, then took a big gulp of air. Josh looked at his watch. Olly began to feel a tightness in her chest. It grew until she couldn't stand it anymore. She forced herself to hold on for a few seconds longer, and then she let out breath and gasped in some fresh air.

"That was only forty seconds," Josh told her. He looked anxious. "That's not very long. Maybe you should practice panting some more."

Olly rolled her eyes and breathed in and out quickly for a few seconds before taking a second big gulp of air. Then, ignoring the look of surprise and dismay on Josh's face, she slid her legs over the edge of the well and pushed off with both hands.

Olly shut her eyes as she hit the water. It closed over her head, wrapping her in an icy darkness and filling her ears with the clamor of its rushing. Her feet touched bottom with a shock that jarred through her. The flashlight fell out of her fingers and she felt herself being buffeted by the fast-flowing water. After the initial shock, it wasn't as cold as she had feared, but it was far stronger than she had anticipated. She floundered blindly and felt the bottom under her feet again.

She pushed up, thrusting her arms forward, then forcing them back in a swimming motion. She felt herself moving along with the flow of water and felt a sense of relief. It was going to be OK. Despite losing the flashlight, she knew she could do this.

The tightness was beginning to grow in her chest, but not so fast that it worried her.

Her confidence was short-lived. She hit the wall of the tunnel hard with one shoulder. Bubbles of air escaped her lips and, grimacing with pain, she tried to writhe clear of the wall. But the current caught hold of her and twisted her around and around.

It was several moments before Olly managed to regain control of her body. Then she touched the bottom with her hands and feet again and felt some kind of debris gathered in the base of the channel. She realized she had to get clear; she couldn't risk getting snagged underwater, so she flexed her legs and pushed up hard — too hard. Her head struck the roof of the channel. She felt a rush of blood in her ears and, completely disoriented by the blow, she was tossed and turned in the torrent.

The pain grew in her lungs. Olly realized she had no idea which way was up. She began to panic. Then she felt something catch her foot. She struggled to free herself, but there was something tangled around her shoe and she couldn't pull herself away. Red lights exploded behind in her eyes. The pain in her chest grew more intense. And Olly realized, in a horrible moment of clarity, that she wouldn't get to the surface in time. She was going to drown.

Chapter Seven: Deep Water

"Olly!" Josh snatched at her clothes as she dropped down the well, but it was too late. The last thing he saw before he was enveloped in darkness was Olly's figure entering the water with a loud splash. A moment later, the flashlight went out.

"Olly!" A spray of cold water flew up the well, spattering Josh's face. He had to follow her — there was no choice. But he forced himself to count slowly to five before he moved. He didn't want to risk crashing down on top of her. It was dangerous enough without that happening. Why did she have to be so reckless?

"I'm coming!" he called. He sat on the edge of the well, filled his lungs with air, and dropped.

The water was a shock, but Josh kept his head. His feet struck bottom, and he guessed the depth of the channel wasn't much more than his own height. He pushed off carefully, allowing himself to be carried by the powerful current, but also wary of hitting his head as he rose. He reached up blindly and felt smooth masonry against his groping fingers. Then, in spite of his caution, his back hit the roof so that the breath was almost knocked out of his lungs.

Josh struck out, swimming strongly, feeling the curved roof of the channel scraping against his back and heels. He was surprised that, even with the drought, the tunnel was filled to the top with water, leaving no breathing room whatsoever. He expected at any moment to feel Olly's feet or legs ahead of him. He forged ahead, carried by the current, staring blindly into the swirling black water and hoping desperately to reach air before his lungs gave out.

And then, suddenly, the water was full of brightness. Josh pushed upward and emerged into daylight. He gasped, treading water and flicking his head to get the hair out of his eyes as he looked around for Olly.

He had surfaced in a deep channel about twenty feet wide with high banks. Olly wasn't there.

His heart hammering, Josh took a huge breath and plunged back down, turning underwater and swimming back the way he had come. He guessed that Olly must still be down in the channel and he forced himself not to panic. There was still a chance. He estimated that he had not been under the water for much more than half a minute.

But now Josh had to fight against the powerful current. He forced his way deeper into the black tunnel, his eyes straining against the darkness, his hands feeling desperately for Olly.

His groping fingers brushed against something. It was Olly's arm. Josh turned, bracing his feet against the bottom of the channel and leaning back into the current. He tugged at the arm and, for a dreadful moment, he thought he would not be able to pull Olly free. But then, with a rush they were tumbling through the water. He kept a tight hold of his friend as he headed for light and air, determined that he wasn't going to lose track of her again.

They burst out of the water. Olly coughed and choked as Josh helped her to the bank. Together, they crawled up the slope and lay panting side by side on the mud.

It was several seconds before Olly was able to speak. "Piece of cake," she gasped at last. She turned her head and smiled at Josh. "What did I tell you?"

"What happened?" Josh asked.

"My foot got caught in something down there," Olly replied. She frowned. "It was getting pretty nasty."

Josh sat up and pushed wet hair off his face. "I suppose I saved your life, then," he commented.

Olly grinned and punched his arm. "My hero," she said. She stood up, her legs shaking, and looked around. "Where are we?"

Josh followed her gaze. The channel came out from underneath a big, half-ruinous, stone building. He recognized it as the solitary old building he had seen from the ruins earlier that afternoon. It seemed like a lifetime ago that he had noticed the building and set out for it. He stood up. "We'd better get back to camp," he said. "It's this way."

Olly nodded, and they helped each other up the long slope to ground level.

Climbing to a high point, they saw that they were at the southern end of the ruins. The waterway they had used to escape seemed to run in a straight line under the old building and on into the river. They couldn't see where the water was coming from, but they assumed it was flowing from the mountain.

Josh shivered as they walked back to the cabins. The sun was going down behind the mountain, and his wet clothes were cold and heavy on his body.

As they neared the huts, they saw a door open. Olly's gran stood on the threshold. She stared for a moment, then shouted and began to run toward them. She took out a cell phone and yelled into it as she ran. Josh guessed that she was telling either Jonathan or Professor Christie the good news.

Audrey Beckmann came to a halt in front of them, her face filled with relief.

"Hello, Gran," Olly said with a tired grin. "Look who I found! Someone had locked him up in a cellar back there." She gestured toward the building. "We had to swim through an underground tunnel to get out."

Audrey Beckmann looked from one to the other, momentarily speechless. Her expression of relief changed to one of concern as she studied Olly's friend. "Are you all right, Josh?" she asked him.

"I'm fine," he said. "They didn't do anything to me." He frowned. "Except swipe the gold disc I found."

"That's the least of our worries right now," Audrey Beckmann replied in classic grandmother tone. "Come with me and we'll get you cleaned up and into some dry clothes. The police will be here soon, so you can tell the full story then. And under the circumstances, Olly, I'll ignore the fact that you were told very clearly to stay in the camp."

As they walked to the huts, Audrey Beckmann put her arms around their shoulders. "I was so worried about you two," she said, hugging one and then the other. "I'm glad you're both safe."

Olly and Josh looked at each other. She wasn't the only one.

~~~~

It was early evening. Olly and Josh were in the dining cabin, working their way through large bowls of spicy Kung Pao chicken. The professor was with them at the table, along with Jonathan, Audrey, and Dr. Feng. The police officers from the nearest town had recently departed, having taken statements from the two friends with Dr. Feng acting as translator.

Olly and Josh had taken them to the sunken room from which Josh had been abducted. Jonathan and the police officers had gone down into the hole, but in spite of Olly's instructions on how to open the hidden door, they had been unable to get the mechanism to work. Finally, they had allowed Olly down to demonstrate, but to her surprise and frustration, she found that the small metal tag within the hole was missing. She supposed that one of the mysterious masked men had come back and removed it.

The police had insisted that the wall be broken down, so Professor Christie had given instructions for Jonathan and two members of the archaeological team to carefully take the wall apart. The professor had looked on, wincing as the stones were lifted out one by one. Olly knew that, under normal circumstances, the area would have been painstakingly excavated over several days, or even left entirely intact.

Finally, the room beyond the wall had been revealed. A brief exploration of the tunnels and rooms had turned up no clue to Josh's captors. The rooms were either empty, or more often, had collapsed in on themselves. The tunnel that led to the old building where Olly and Josh had been imprisoned petered out in ever-larger rockfalls.

In their prison room itself, there was nothing to prove that anyone had been down there for centuries, except for the remains of the bread and water left for Josh.

Olly had drawn the pictograph she had seen on the men's scarves to show the police officers. She had the impression that one of the men had recognized the symbol, but he had shaken his head and said nothing. Then, suppertime arrived and the police officers had gone.

Those who remained went to the dining cabin and sat together. As she ate her food, Olly looked at

Dr. Feng. She had the curious feeling that he had also recognized the symbol. "Is there any way of finding out what that means?" she asked him, nodding toward the sheet of paper with the pictograph on it.

"There are over fifty-six thousand characters in Chinese writing," Dr. Feng said. "Many of them are no longer used. I suspect this pictograph is some ancient character that has been adopted by a criminal gang. It is clear that they saw what Josh had found and stole it to sell."

"I'm sure you're right," said Olly's father. "There's a lucrative international market in stolen antiquities; it's a pity."

"Well, let's hope they're caught quickly," said Olly's grandmother. "I will sleep a lot easier once I know they're all under lock and key."

At that moment, the door to the cabin opened and Mr. Lau stepped inside. He walked up to the table where they were sitting. "I have informed Professor Andryanova of the incident with the two young people this afternoon," he said. "He has instructed me to tell you that you are all to consider yourselves under my protection from now on."

Jonathan frowned at him. "Meaning what?" he asked.

Lau smiled coldly. "Meaning that no one should leave the immediate site without informing me first," he said. "I will need to know the dig schedule, as well as if anyone is investigating new areas. My men will be on guard twenty-four hours a day." He looked at Olly and Josh. "And from now on, I suggest that if the two young people want to go out for any reason, they should be accompanied by one of my men."

Olly glared at him in annoyance. The idea that she and Josh wouldn't be able to set foot outside their cabin without one of Lau's men on their tail did not appeal to her one bit.

"We will do as you ask, of course, Mr. Lau," Professor Christie agreed. "And I'm grateful for your concern over the welfare of Josh and my daughter." He frowned. "I intend to begin working tomorrow morning in the areas that my assistant has secured." He looked at Lau. "I trust your men won't get in the way?"

Mr. Lau nodded briefly. "Your work will not be interrupted, I can assure you," he said. He gave another curt nod and left.

Olly looked at her father. "Do we *really* have to ask his permission every time we want to go out?" she asked.

"It's probably best for the time being," replied the professor. "Dr. Feng has been in contact with the authorities at Chengdu, and we're hoping some officials will be here tomorrow or the day after. They will be better able to advise us of how we should behave."

"Meanwhile, perhaps it would be best if Josh and Olly leave?" Mrs. Beckmann suggested. "I could take them to stay in Chengdu while you finish the dig."

"No!" Olly and Josh chorused in dismay. While Chengdu would be interesting — the great mountainside Buddha that they saw from the plane was located there — it still couldn't compare with being on the site of an active dig.

Olly looked imploringly at her gran. "We won't be in any danger with Mr. Lau's men on guard," she said, and turned to her father. "Please don't send us away. It's just not fair. We'll miss everything!"

Professor Christie looked thoughtfully at Olly and Josh. "No," he said at length. "I won't send you to Chengdu — not for the time being anyway."

Olly and Josh looked at each other in huge relief.

"It's a pity that Josh didn't come and tell us about that golden disc when he first saw it," Jonathan commented, eyeing his younger brother with a frown.

Josh's forehead wrinkled. "I'm sorry," he said. "I should have done that but I was so excited that I didn't really think."

"We won't worry about that now," Professor Christie put in. "What's done is done, as long as you are sure to think in the future." He looked at Josh. "Can you remember any of the markings? You said they looked like they showed the plan of a city?"

"I only had a minute or two before I was grabbed," Josh began, "but it looked like the city was much bigger than the ruins we've found so far, and the main part of it seemed to be farther away from the river. I couldn't quite make it out, but it seemed to have a wall around it."

"What kind of wall?" Olly asked.

Josh shrugged. "It was just a couple of lines running right around the main part of the city. Maybe it wasn't really a wall. It could have been a big road or a moat or a ditch or something like that. But the water channel was definitely shown — the one under the building. And it appeared to go through the wall."

"Well, that building is certainly no more than five or six hundred years old," Jonathan said. "It couldn't have been part of the original city. It was probably a mill of some kind."

"The building wasn't on the plan," Josh confirmed. "But the waterway was. What do you think it is? Where does it come from?"

"I should think it's a natural tributary of the river," the professor replied. "Probably sourced from a spring in the mountain."

"But it isn't natural," Olly pointed out. "It's made of stone. You just can't see much of that now because of all the mud and stuff."

"Ah, well, you see, the people who built the city would have constructed an artificial channel to control the flow of the water," Professor Christie explained. "We will investigate it further, when we have time," he continued. "But, our priority must be to get all the information we can from the ruins in the riverbed while we have the chance."

~~~~~

Olly said good night to Josh and went into her room. She opened her traveling bag and withdrew a cherished new piece of electronic equipment that her gran had bought her only a few weeks ago. It was a digital recorder. All she had to do was press a button and speak into the microphone slot each evening, and she would have a digitally recorded diary of the entire dig.

She yawned, worn out by the events of the

extraordinary day. She had made her first entry last night, describing their long flight and arrival on site. She had intended to add an update every evening, but now she just wanted to throw on her pajamas and climb between the sheets. She put down the recorder, deciding that she would record her update in the morning.

She was just about to get undressed when something at the head of the bed caught her eye. A small, black, oblong shape was lying on her pillow. Puzzled, she walked over for a closer look.

To Olly's surprise, the small black object was the cell phone that the masked man had taken from her in the secret tunnel.

And tied around it was a slender ribbon of red silk.

Chapter Eight: ⊛
A Secret Revealed

Olly threw Josh's door open and waved the cell phone at him. "They brought it back!" she yelled. "I'm going to tell Dad." Without waiting for him, she pelted across to the dining cabin. Professor Christie, Jonathan, and Audrey Beckmann were still there, talking at the table.

Olly ran in and thumped the phone down in front of her father. "I found it on my pillow," she said. "What kind of thieves give things back?" She stared around at the startled faces. Moments later, Josh arrived barefoot, wearing jeans and his pajama top.

The return of Olly's cell phone caused surprise and puzzlement in everyone. No one could make sense of it.

"We'll have to let Mr. Lau know," Jonathan said. "Whoever put it in Olly's room must have walked right past his guards." He snorted. "So much for his protection!"

But the question still remained: If the masked men were a band of thieves, then why return something that they could have sold? Even if they were thieves intent only on stealing the golden disc, why not just throw the cell phone away? Why take the risk of coming right into the camp to give it back? And why were they in the underground chamber in the first place?

"We're obviously not going to get to the bottom of this tonight," said Audrey Beckmann. "Jonathan, could you go and tell Mr. Lau what has happened? Suggest to him that his men need to be far more vigilant from now on." She looked at her grand-daughter and Josh. "You two should go back to bed," she said. "I'm sure there won't be any more unwelcome visitors, but I want you to keep the doors and windows shut and locked." She stood up. "Off you go now, and get some sleep."

As the two friends headed back to their cabin, Olly looked thoughtful. "If you ask me, they brought my phone back to show us that they aren't just a bunch of thieves."

Josh stared at her in disbelief. "They kidnapped us and locked us up, remember?" he demanded.

"But they didn't hurt us, did they?" Olly pointed out. "And they left food and water for us. For all we know, they might have come back and let us out once they'd hidden the golden disc." She looked at

Josh's dubious face. "I think that was all they wanted — the golden disc."

Josh frowned but didn't reply; Olly had given him a lot to think about.

~~~~

It was a long time before Olly was able to sleep. She lay in her darkened room, staring wide-eyed at the ceiling, trying to make sense of it all. She toyed absently with the red ribbon, while her mind raced. She knew that foreigners often considered Chinese people to be somewhat cryptic, but this was ridiculous!

She eventually drifted off, still no closer to understanding the motives of the extraordinary kidnappers, who had risked capture in order to return her stolen phone.

It was very strange.

~~~~

Josh's sleep was also disturbed, but he was puzzling over something else — something that he had not remembered until now.

The plan on the golden disc had seemed to show that the lost city was divided into two sections. There was a small outpost on the banks of the river, and then a much larger area behind, presumably built up in the foothills of the mountain. But, the important point was that the two parts of the city were linked by the water channel. Josh lay in the dark and thought that, if the waterway was tracked back toward the mountain, surely it would lead to a lot more of the lost city, lying undiscovered maybe only a few inches below the earth.

He finally fell asleep, imagining himself finding the first piece of masonry that would lead to the spectacular discovery of the whole of Yueliang-Chengshi. And, with luck, the talisman known as the Mooncake of Chang-O.

<center>~~~~~~</center>

By the time Josh woke up the next morning, Jonathan was already up and out. Josh got dressed and went to Olly's room. He found her sitting fully clothed on her bed and talking into her digital recorder. She pressed the stop button and listened as he told her what he had remembered about the plan on the golden disc.

Her eyes lit up as he spoke. "We should follow the channel all the way back and see exactly where it goes," she said excitedly.

Josh nodded. "That's exactly what I think," he agreed. "I'm going to tell Jonathan and the professor about it right now."

Olly shook her head. "No, I mean *we* should follow it — you and I," she said. "I'm sure Dad will want to investigate the watercourse later, but right now everyone's concentrating on the buildings by the river, in case the rain comes soon. So," she said with a dramatic pause, "why don't we do some exploring on our own?"

"Because last time we went off on our own, we both got kidnapped," Josh pointed out. "They'll never let us out alone."

Olly smiled. "But we won't be alone," she said. "We'll be together."

Josh's face broke into a broad grin as he looked at her. "The waterway leads toward the mountains. In order to follow it, we'll have to get off the site without anyone noticing," he said. "And that means getting past Mr. Lau's men."

"We can outwit them," Olly said confidently. "No problem."

Josh nodded. "Of course we can," he said. Then he frowned. "But if we see anything suspicious out there, we run for it, OK?"

"OK," Olly agreed.

There was the sound of footsteps in the adjoining room. A moment later, Audrey Beckmann put her head round the door. "Lessons in thirty minutes," she said. "You just have time for breakfast. Don't be late."

Olly looked at her. "You do remember that today is the Festival of the Moon, don't you?" she said. "It's a public holiday in China. People take the day off, you know. So, I was wondering . . ."

"Nice try, Olly," Mrs. Beckmann broke in. "But you'll still have to do schoolwork this morning."

~~~~~

As it turned out, Olly's gran had come up with a special lesson plan that day. A large part of the morning was devoted to learning more about Chinese history and the yearly Moon Festival.

Olly and Josh learned that, according to the Chinese lunar calendar, the festival always took place on the fifteenth day of the eighth month. Though it was held to celebrate the moon goddess, it was also a celebration of the harvest.

"We are all going to the festival, aren't we?" Olly asked.

Mrs. Beckmann nodded. "We can go together to Chung-hsien this evening," she said. "The festivities don't really get going until after nightfall. Not that the farmers around here have a great deal to celebrate this year. Still, I expect they'll make the best of it. Apparently the dragon dance and the lion

284

dance are especially interesting. The dragon dance is supposed to protect the people from sickness and disease, but the lion dance is meant to bring rain." She looked at them. "And I'm sure they will be hoping the lion does his job particularly well this year."

After lunch, Josh and Olly went to their cabin. Mrs. Beckmann had driven to the nearby city of Chung-hsien for supplies — and she wasn't expected back for several hours. Practically everyone else was busy in the ruins. Jonathan and a small team were putting the last safety measures in place, but almost everyone else was involved with the new excavation by the river — everyone except Lau's men, who were standing guard.

Josh borrowed his brother's binoculars, then went to join Olly in her room.

"How are we going to get past them?" Josh asked, watching one of Lau's men from the window. "They probably won't pay any attention to us while we're on-site, but as soon as they see us following the watercourse off into the hills, they'll stop us for sure."

"Then we have to make sure they don't see us," Olly said. She pointed. "Do you see that line of boulders behind the dining cabin?" Josh looked where she was indicating. Several large rocks jutted from the dry gray mud. "If we can get down behind them, we can use them as cover all the way up the bank," Olly went on. "Then all we have to do is get to the other side of that hill and we'll be out of sight."

Josh looked uncertainly at the long bare hillside. "If any of Lau's men happen to look in that direction while we're on the slope, they'll definitely spot us," he said.

"There's no other way," Olly replied. "Unless you think we should go and ask their permission."

Josh shook his head. "Let's do it," he said, fueled by his own curiosity. "I just hope we find something to make this worthwhile."

"We will," Olly said. "I've just got a feeling we will."

They slipped out of the cabin and made their way carefully through the camp without being seen. Olly pressed against the wall of one of the storage huts and peered quickly around the corner. "OK," she said softly. "I can see one of Lau's men, but he's facing the other way. I'll make a dash for the rocks, then you follow once I'm safe."

Before Josh could speak, she had gone. He watched from cover as she ran at a crouch toward the line of boulders. She threw herself onto the ground behind them. The guard had seen nothing.

Taking a deep breath, Josh raced after her, expecting to hear a shout from behind him at any moment. He reached the boulders and ducked down out of sight.

Olly was grinning. "Piece of mooncake!" she said. "Now, follow me, and keep your head down." She crawled up the dry riverbank with Josh close at her heels.

A minute or so later, they had come to the end of the natural cover. They were above the line of the river and ahead of them was a bare slope about sixty-five feet long. As Olly had said, once they were on the other side, they would be able to use the natural contours of the land to make their way unseen to the watercourse, but as Josh stared up the slope, it looked like a long way to run.

Olly lifted her head cautiously over the rock. "It's OK," she whispered. "He's still looking the other way. Let's go!" She took off like a gazelle, racing wildly up the slope. Josh was right behind her. He risked a quick glance over his shoulder. The guard was still facing the other way. It looked like they were going to make it.

Olly leaped over the crest of the hill and made a slithering landing on the far side, skidding down in a cloud of dust. Josh dropped down just behind the ridge, breathing hard from his run. He lifted his head over the crest, wanting to be absolutely certain that they had not been seen.

His heart jumped into his mouth. The guard had turned. He was staring toward the hill. Had he seen them? The man had his radio in his hand and was obviously speaking to someone.

Josh ducked down again and slithered to join Olly at the foot of the hill. "He saw us!" he gasped.

She stared at him. "Is he coming?"

"I don't know," Josh replied. "He was talking on the radio."

An anxious look clouded Olly's face. "Maybe we should go back?" she suggested.

"Not after you've dragged me this far," Josh told her. "Come on, let's get out of here before they turn up."

She blinked at her friend and then grinned. "Great idea."

They ran side by side along the narrow valley between two ridges of land. Keeping low to the ground, they quickly made their way up from the river and closer to the sacred mountain.

They lay on one of the higher slopes and finally risked lifting their heads to peep over the top. They had come several hundred feet from the river. The folds of the land prevented them from being able to see most of the ruins of the city, but far off to their right they could see what remained of the old mill. Their plan was to pick up the waterway behind the mill, and then follow it back into the hills to its source. There was no sign of pursuit.

"I told you we'd lose them," Olly laughed, scrambling back down the slope.

"We still have to get back without getting caught," Josh reminded her.

She looked at him, her eyes gleaming. "We won't have to worry about that if we find something spectacular," she said.

Still keeping low, they made their way toward the back of the old mill.

At last they were standing on the high bank, looking at the rushing water as it flowed down from the hills and into the mill.

Josh climbed to higher ground. He put the binoculars to his eyes, trying to make out where the canal came from, but the folds of the land were in the way. "We'll have to follow it," he called down to Olly. "I can't see where it starts."

Just then, Josh heard a sharp voice from below. He turned quickly, staring over his shoulder. Mr. Lau was standing on a high bank of land, about two hundred feet away, with his back to him. He was holding a cell phone or a radio to his ear. He made wide gestures as he spoke, and his words sounded like commands. Josh got the strong impression that he was giving orders to his men — organizing a hunt for Josh and Olly.

Josh dropped to the ground, his head low, watching intently. Lau gave more orders and beckoned sharply. Moments later, a second man joined him on the hilltop.

Josh slithered helter-skelter down the hillside.

"What's wrong?" Olly asked.

"They're getting close," Josh gasped.

Olly's eyes widened. "We better get out of sight," she said. She pointed to the bank below them. "We can hide there." The bank was undercut, leaving an overhang of earth matted with dry grass. They dropped down onto the steep slope of the canal and scrambled under the dry turf.

Josh's heart was hammering in his chest as he lay there on the ground. He held his breath, listening intently. It wasn't long before he heard the voices of two men speaking rapidly together in Mandarin. They were close — too close.

Mr. Lau's voice sounded directly overhead. Josh

realized the security chief must be standing right above his hiding place. Dirt rained down over Josh's face, but he didn't dare wipe it away for fear of attracting attention.

Mr. Lau shouted something and received a faint reply from some distance away. It was impossible to tell what the men were saying, but Josh assumed that they were trying to figure out where the two friends had gone.

Then the tone of Lau's voice changed — as if he was speaking to someone much closer by — and Josh realized with surprise that he was now speaking in English.

"Yes, sir, we think the two of them may well have found something of significance. We're close behind them. They cannot have gone far. We'll find them," he said.

Josh thought at first that he must be speaking on a cell phone to Professor Christie or to Jonathan — although Lau had never called either of them "sir." But then Lau's words took a strange turn.

"No, sir, we don't have any more news about the disc; we have people searching for it. Yes, it's only a matter of time." He paused, and then said something that made Josh catch his breath. "We will do everything we can to locate the disc, Mr. Cain. Leave it to us."

Josh's brain reeled with shock. He wondered whether he had misheard. Could Mr. Lau really be talking to Ethan Cain?

Chapter Nine: Pursuit

Olly lay perfectly still in the confines of her narrow hiding place — but her brain was whirling. She had heard Lau speaking on the cell phone, and leaped to the same conclusion as Josh: The security chief was talking to Ethan Cain!

She listened as the second man joined Lau and they spoke in Mandarin for a few moments. Then they moved away. As far as Olly could tell they headed down the waterway toward the old mill.

"Olly!" It was a frantic whisper from Josh. "Did you hear what I heard?"

Olly squirmed out of her hiding place and climbed up onto level ground. Josh emerged — covered in dust — and joined her, his eyes wide.

"Ethan Cain," Olly confirmed grimly.

Josh's eyes narrowed. "So much for that reclusive Texan oil millionaire funding this dig," he said. "There's probably no such person as Augustus Bell. I bet it's been Ethan Cain all along. I expect he hired Professor Andryanova to run the excavation for him." Then he frowned. "But my mother said he wasn't even interested in this dig," he said. "She told me he was working flat out on some big project in California. She wouldn't lie to me."

"No, she wouldn't," Olly agreed. "But Ethan wouldn't worry about lying to her! And he knows about the golden disc. Lau must have been passing him information about everything that's been happening."

Josh let out a low whistle. "It sounds like he must think the disc is pretty important."

"Maybe he knows something we don't," Olly suggested.

Josh shook his head. "How can he? I only found it yesterday."

"Was Mr. Lau around when you were describing it to everyone?" Olly asked.

Josh thought hard. "Yes," he replied. "I think he was."

"Lau probably got on the phone to Ethan and told him all about it," Olly said. "And if Ethan thinks that the plan on the disc might show where the Mooncake of Chang-O is hidden, then he'll want to get his hands on that disc at all costs."

Josh frowned. "But why are they following us? We don't have it."

"No, but maybe he guessed that we'd learned

something from it. Maybe that's why it was so easy for us to get out of the camp; they let us out on purpose. And they weren't following us to drag us back — they wanted to find out where we were going!"

Josh grabbed Olly's arm. "We have to get back and tell Jonathan and the professor."

Olly shook her head. "They won't believe us," she said.

"Why would we lie about it?" Josh asked.

Olly smiled. "They won't think we're lying, Josh," she said. "They'll just think we've got it all wrong again, like in the Valley of the Kings. Remember how Jonathan reacted a couple of days ago on the airplane when I mentioned Ethan Cain? He said we should forget all about the 'misunderstanding'! I'm sure Ethan has given Mr. Lau orders to keep his involvement totally secret. If we go charging in there telling them all that Augustus Bell is really Ethan Cain, they'll just think we've gone mental."

Josh looked thoughtfully at her. "And we can't prove it, can we?"

She shook her head. "No, we can't."

Josh kicked frustratedly at a stone. It tumbled down the steeply curved bank and splashed into the water. "Well, what *can* we do, then?" he asked.

"We can find out where this water comes from," Olly said firmly. "That's what we came out here to do, so let's do it." She looked at him. "And let's hope we find something to lead us to the Mooncake of Chang-O before Ethan's men get there. Because that's what he's after, Josh; he wants the talisman, and we've got to make sure he doesn't get it."

They followed the slow winding of the water-course up through the rising hills. Here and there they saw places where there had been landslips into the canal, leaving rocks and boulders and earth-banks around which the rapid water swirled and foamed.

"How far do you think we've come?" Olly asked, eventually.

"I don't know," Josh replied. He looked at his watch. It was mid-afternoon. They had been away from the camp for nearly two hours. "Do you think we should head back?"

"Not just yet." Olly found a high point and lay on the top, scanning the land ahead of them with the binoculars. Josh kept watch behind them. So far they had been lucky and remained undetected, but he was convinced that the guards were still out there somewhere, scouring the hills for them.

Olly tracked the course of the canal and caught sight of something strange in the distance. She couldn't quite make it out. Then she realized what she was seeing. At first glance, it seemed as if the waterway ran straight out of the mountainside, but as she focused more carefully, she saw that the water was pouring out of a black archway. And she could even see that there was a ridge that ran alongside the rushing water — like a pathway. It led under the arch and into the mountain. "Josh," she called down, her voice breathless with suppressed excitement. "The channel goes into a tunnel."

"What kind of tunnel?" Josh asked, climbing up to where she lay.

"See for yourself." She handed him the binoculars. He put them to his eyes.

"That can't be natural, can it?" Olly said. "Someone must have made it."

Josh nodded. "Let's find out where it goes," he suggested eagerly.

A shout broke the still air. Startled, they both turned. One of Lau's men was standing on a ridge of rock above them. He gestured to them — a signal that plainly meant they should stay where they were. Then he began to clamber down the hillside toward them. A few moments later, a second man appeared against the skyline.

Olly looked at Josh. "Do you want to stay here and get marched back to camp by Ethan Cain's goons?" she challenged. "Or do you want to lose them and find out where that tunnel goes?"

Josh took a final glance at the two approaching men, then grinned at Olly. "Let's lose them," he replied.

The two friends ran along the canal side, searching for a place where they could cross without having to swim. There were more shouts from behind them. They came to a place where a whole chunk of the hillside had crumbled away, strewing rocks and boulders into the canal. Olly went first, jumping from boulder to boulder, arms spread for balance. She glanced over her shoulder and saw that Josh was right behind her.

The two men shouted again. Olly ignored them. "We have to lead them away from the tunnel," she called to Josh breathlessly. "They can't find out about it. They'll tell Ethan."

She jumped to a rock that was just under the surface of the rushing water. But the stone was slippery. Her foot slid from under her and she fell into the water. Josh dropped to his knees and snatched at her, catching hold of her arm. But he didn't have time to get a sure footing, and her weight sent him, too, slithering off the rock and into the fast-flowing water.

Shaking water from their eyes, they swam to the far bank and scrambled out.

"Are you OK?" Josh asked.

"No, I'm not!" Olly snapped, obviously annoyed with herself. "Look at me, I'm soaked! Now what do we do?"

"I have an idea." Josh replied. "Come with me." He scrambled up the hillside and down the far slope. Olly followed.

"Where are we going?" Olly gasped as they ran.

"Banping!" Josh told her. "The village where Ang-lun told us his grandmother lives. It's just on the other side of the volcano. It can't be far away."

"Ang-lun will help us lose those creeps," Olly said, her voice brightening. "Good thinking, Josh."

Josh looked back as he reached a hilltop. The two men were still following. They must have made the jump from rock to rock across the canal. And from a different direction, he now saw Mr. Lau running toward them, too.

"There it is!" called Olly. Josh turned back. Below

them, nestling in the foothills under the shadow of the mountain, was a small village of huddled, gray-walled buildings with roofs of split bamboo.

Olly and Josh hurtled down the hillside and ran into the village. An elderly woman dressed in loose blue overalls and carrying a battered kettle smiled and stared at them with interest, her dark eyes bright under a blue turban. A man in faded denims also stopped to stare, and a woman in a long red dress, carrying a baby, paused at the door of a house and called something back to those inside.

"Ang-lun!" Olly shouted. "*Qing! Qing!*" Please! Please!

An old man stepped toward them, speaking rapidly and pointing to a house at one side.

"Ang-lun?" Josh asked.

"Ang-lun," the man responded, nodding. "*Song-ai-mi!*"

"I'm sorry, I don't understand," Josh said.

The man pointed to the house, repeating the same words. "*Song-ai-mi.*"

And then, to Josh and Olly's relief and delight, Ang-lun himself appeared at the door of the house. He ran out to meet them, his face surprised and puzzled. "You're wet," Ang-lun said. "What are you doing here?"

"We'll explain later," Olly promised. "Can you hide us?"

"What's wrong?" Ang-lun asked.

"Lau and some of his men are following us," Josh explained. "We don't want them to find us."

Ang-lun nodded. "Come with me," he ran back into the house with Josh and Olly at his heels. They came into a small room with a brick floor and simple bamboo furniture. The white walls were decorated with hanging scrolls — some covered with Chinese script, and others with beautiful, intricate illustrations.

"Stay here, out of sight," Ang-lun said, and then he stepped out into the open again and walked into the dusty street. He turned and looked in the direction from which Olly and Josh had come. Lau and his two men were in sight now, running at a trot down the hillside toward the village.

Olly and Josh watched from the window as Lau and his men approached their Chinese friend. Lau spoke in English, his voice harsh. "Where are they?"

Ang-lun shook his head and replied in his own language.

"Speak English," said Lau. "I don't understand your dialect."

"You are not welcome here," Ang-lun said in English. "Go away." He made a dismissive gesture, as if ordering the men to leave the village.

Lau gave a hard bark of laughter. The men walked toward Ang-lun. Olly held her breath, wondering what would happen next, wondering to what lengths Lau would go in his hunt for her and Josh.

Ang-lun stood his ground as the three men approached him.

"I have to take the girl and the boy back to camp," Lau said. "It's for their own safety. Tell me where they are, or I'll search this entire village."

Ang-lun stared defiantly into Lau's face. He spat out a single word. It wasn't English.

Lau's eyes blazed. Olly got the impression he understood that word just fine — and didn't like it at all! He snatched at Ang-lun's clothes, grabbing him by the collar. "We aren't leaving this place until we've found them. Now tell me where they are, or do you want me to beat the truth out of you?"

Ang-lun glared up fearlessly at Lau's angry face.

"We can't let them hurt him," Olly cried. "We've got to stop this." She and Josh rushed to the doorway and stepped outside.

"We're here," Olly called. "Let him go!"

Chapter Ten: ◈
The Shan-ren

Lau and his men turned at the sound of Olly's voice. A look of cold satisfaction crossed Lau's face. He gave a curt nod. "You'll come with us," he said.

There was nothing else to be done, Olly thought. They had been caught, and now they would be taken back to camp to face the music. She realized that she and Josh had nothing to show for their illicit expedition into the hills. They didn't even dare tell anyone what they *had* found, because once Mr. Lau knew about the mysterious tunnel into the mountainside, he would waste no time in telling Ethan Cain. However Olly looked at it, things were not going to go well for them when they returned to the dig site.

The two friends were about to walk over to the security guard, when Ang-lun tore free of Lau's grip and stepped back with a loud cry.

Suddenly the small street was full of movement. Men and women appeared in doorways and from between buildings. Some of them were carrying sticks and farm tools. All of them were staring at Lau and his companions.

Olly and Josh looked around in surprise.

"I told you that you were not welcome here," Ang-lun said simply. "Olly and Josh are our guests. They do not want to go with you. Turn around and leave while you can."

Mr. Lau grimaced and made a lunge at Ang-lun, who jumped back out of reach. There was a rising murmur from the crowd of villagers. One man stepped forward with a pitchfork. He held it in front of him, his arms taut as if he was ready to strike.

Mr. Lau stared around, clearly assessing the situation. The villagers were slowly closing in on the three security men, and many of them held potential weapons in their hands. The security guard must have decided he didn't want a full-on confrontation, for he turned toward Olly and Josh, his mouth set in a tight, grim line of resignation.

"We're fine here for the time being, Mr. Lau," Olly said to him cheerfully. "You don't need to worry about us."

He didn't reply. The circle of villagers had now almost completely surrounded him and his men, leaving them only one clear exit from the village — back the way they had come. Mr. Lau turned and walked away without another word. His men followed. As he walked back up into the hills, Olly saw that the man was already speaking on his cell phone.

"I wonder who he's talking to," she murmured to Josh. "Someone back at camp? Or Ethan Cain?"

Ang-lun said something to the villagers, and they laughed, looking kindly at Olly and Josh before returning to their fields and homes.

"What did you call Lau that made him so mad?" Josh asked Ang-lun.

"*Zei*," Ang-lun said with a grin. "It means 'bandit.'"

"Thanks for getting rid of him for us," Olly said.

"Come inside again and meet my grandmother," Ang-lun suggested. "And then you can explain why you didn't want to go with him — and why you're both so wet."

Ang-lun led them through into a second room. A small, elderly woman knelt at a low desk. She looked at Josh and Olly with the same amiable curiosity they had seen in the faces of the other villagers. Her skin was tanned and wrinkled, and her dark eyes were bright. She was dressed in a simple orange tunic and trousers, and her gray hair was cropped close to her head. In front of her was a sheet of red paper and a pot of black ink. She was using a brush to paint beautiful Chinese pictograms onto the paper. As in the first room, Olly saw that the walls through here were hung with writings and illustrations.

The old lady stood up, smiling and nodding at Olly and Josh as Ang-lun spoke to her. She said something to them, holding out a small yet surprisingly strong hand for them to shake.

"My grandmother asks if you would like to take tea," Ang-lun explained. "She says we should sit on the terrace where the sun will dry your clothes."

"That would be lovely," Olly replied. "And can you please thank her for the gift she made us? You can tell her it's on my bedroom wall."

The little old lady smiled and nodded again as Ang-lun led Olly and Josh into a little sunny courtyard behind the house. There was a small, low table and some stools.

While they waited for Ang-lun's grandmother to bring the tea, Olly and Josh told Ang-lun about their adventure and the archway in the mountainside from which the canal water flowed.

"I didn't even know it existed," Ang-lun told them, obviously fascinated. "It must be very old."

"That's what we think," Josh said. "When the channel is at its normal level, the arch would be completely covered in water. It probably hasn't been visible for hundreds of years."

"That's why we didn't want Lau and his henchmen to know about it," Olly added. "He'll tell Ethan Cain and then there'll be a whole world of trouble."

Ang-lun looked puzzled.

"We'd better explain about Ethan," Josh put in. He told Ang-lun of their previous encounter with the Californian billionaire, and of his attempt to get the Tears of Isis. "He's trying to do the same thing here, we're sure of it," he finished.

"But the real problem is that no one believes us," Olly continued. "They all think Ethan is a nice guy." She looked at Josh. "We can't tell anyone back at camp about the tunnel," she said. "If we tell them, then Mr. Lau will find out, too. And once he knows, he'll be right on the phone to Ethan! We can't risk it."

"So what's our plan?" Josh asked.

"We have to investigate the tunnel ourselves," Olly said. "If there's anything important to be found in there, then we need to find it first."

Josh looked at his watch. "Your gran will be back

from Chung-hsien soon, if she's not already," he remarked. "She'll notice we're missing, and they'll all go crazy if they think we've both disappeared again."

"Yes, we should go back to camp soon," Olly agreed. "But we should plan to investigate that tunnel the first chance we get."

Ang-lun's grandmother came out of the house with a bamboo tray in her hands. On it stood a delicate china teapot and four small white china bowls patterned with brightly colored, curling dragons. A few moments later, Olly and Josh were sipping the fragrant green tea.

"Did your father tell you about the golden disc?" Josh asked Ang-lun.

Ang-lun nodded. "He believes it was stolen by bandits."

"If we draw the symbol the thieves had on their scarves, do you think your grandmother might know what it means?" Josh inquired.

"She might," Ang-lun replied. "I'll go and get something for you to draw with."

After a moment, he returned with brush, ink, and paper. Josh took the brush and dipped it in the ink. Carefully, he drew the curious lying-down *E* and upside-down *Y* symbol.

The old lady looked at it and then gave Olly and Josh a strange, inquisitive glance. "*Shan-ren*," she said. Then she turned to Ang-lun and continued.

Ang-lun's eyes widened as he listened. "My grandmother says this is the symbol of the Shan-ren — the guardians of the mountain," he told Josh and Olly.

Josh stared at him. "I thought you told us they died out centuries ago."

Ang-lun spoke again to his grandmother. Her reply seemed to surprise him.

"What is she saying?" Olly asked eagerly.

Ang-lun smiled at her. "She said — I'm not quite sure how to translate it — she said that old trees have deep roots."

Olly blinked at him. "Excuse me?"

"I think I know what she means!" Josh exclaimed. "The Shan-ren didn't die out — they just went underground." He looked at Ang-lun. "You said that the Shan-ren were the guardians of the mountain. But why does the mountain need to be guarded?"

Ang-lun translated Josh's question for his grandmother.

She shook her head. "*Laocheng*," she said. "*Mimi! Mimi!*" She smiled at Olly and laughed softly.

"My grandmother says it is a secret. I'm afraid she won't tell you," Ang-lun explained.

Josh looked thoughtfully at the old lady. "If the disc was taken by the Shan-ren, then maybe they thought there was something on it that gave the secret away," he mused.

"What secret?" Olly asked. And then she reached out and gripped Josh's arm as an astonishing thought struck her. "What if the secret is the location of the Mooncake of Chang-O?" she said. "What if that disc wasn't just a street plan — what if it was a *treasure map?*" She fixed Josh with a fierce gaze. "You have to remember everything you can about that plan — every little detail."

Josh bit his lip as he struggled to remember. "It showed part of the town near the river. And then the rest of the city a little ways away, surrounded by some kind of thick wall or something. That's about it."

A car horn suddenly blared from the street outside, interrupting the conversation.

"What's that?" Olly asked Ang-lun.

"I'll go and see," Ang-lun replied in a protective tone. "You wait here." He disappeared into the house.

His grandmother was watching Olly with her bright dark eyes.

"*Xiexie*," Olly said carefully, pointing to the tea. *Thank you.*

The old lady smiled and gave a slight bow of her head. Then they heard footsteps in the house coming toward the back door, and they all looked around.

Audrey Beckmann stood in the doorway, her face grim. Olly opened her mouth to speak, but her gran raised her hand. "Thank Ang-lun's grandmother for her hospitality," she said, her voice very calm and controlled. "Then come with me to the car." She turned and walked back through the house.

Olly and Josh looked at each other, and Olly swallowed. She had never seen her grandmother look quite so angry before. She was starting to think it would have been safer to go back with Mr. Lau and his men. "We are in big trouble!" she said.

Chapter Eleven: Into the Tunnel

All the way back to camp, Olly and Josh waited for the ax to fall, but Olly's grandmother was worryingly silent. It was not until they arrived that they learned what their punishment was to be.

"Not only did you leave the camp when you were expressly told to stay put," Mrs. Beckmann told them in a cold fury. "But you enlisted the help of Ang-lun to make a fool of Mr. Lau. You have probably stirred up who knows what resentments between the villagers and Mr. Lau's men, and you've made a difficult situation a great deal worse." Her eyes blazed. "You will not be coming to the festival with us this evening. I'm sorry I have to be so hard on you both, but you must learn to obey the rules."

Neither of them argued.

Jonathan was sympathetic when he heard. "You two don't think things through sometimes," he said later when they were alone with him in their cabin. "What made you wander off like that when you know there are dangerous people out there?"

"But they aren't dangerous," Olly argued. "The men who took the golden disc are Shan-ren. They weren't going to hurt us. They just wanted to keep their secret."

Jonathan frowned. "First of all, I think you're missing my point. Secondly, the Shan-ren died out centuries ago," he said. "Where did you get all this nonsense?"

"Ang-lun's grandmother recognized the pictogram on their scarves," Josh explained. "She seemed very sure that it was the symbol of the Shan-ren."

"And just because some people decide to wear the same symbol, you assume they're members of an ancient secret society that doesn't even exist anymore?" Jonathan demanded incredulously. He shook his head. "You never should have gone out to the mountain."

Olly and Josh exchanged a quick glance. "We were just exploring," Olly said lamely.

"We wanted to find out where the watercourse went," Josh added.

"And did you?" Jonathan asked.

"Not really," Olly replied quickly, before Josh could respond to his brother's question. "We didn't have time. Lau and his men found us."

"And that's another thing I don't understand," Jonathan declared. "Why run away from Lau? What did you think it would achieve?"

"We don't like being followed around," Josh said. "And we don't like Lau."

"He's not here to be likable," Jonathan retorted. "He's here to protect us." He shook his head. "You're acting like little kids."

Olly felt a rush of blood to her face. She hated that Jonathan thought badly of them. "Lau isn't what he seems," she murmured.

"What on Earth does that mean?" Jonathan demanded.

Olly looked at him. She desperately wanted to tell him the whole story — how Lau was working for Ethan Cain, and how she and Josh were absolutely convinced that Ethan was manipulating them all, hoping they would find the Mooncake of Chang-O for him. But she couldn't. She knew Jonathan would not believe her. It was a horrible, hopeless situation.

Then the time came for everyone to leave for Chung-hsien. Olly watched gloomily from the cabin window as the archaeologists and workers piled into their vehicles. "I hope they have a nice time," she muttered bitterly.

Josh sat on the edge of her bed, resting his chin on his hand. He couldn't even bear to watch.

The only ones left at the camp were Lau's men — and Olly and Josh. Olly sighed as the vehicles drove out of sight. She could see one of the security men on the riverbank nearby, and another standing over by the ruins. She knew that there were others dotted about the site, including one standing right outside the cabin door.

Olly stalked the room like a caged tiger, frustrated that they had been so close to making a major discovery when Lau had caught up with them. She had seen the tunnel from which the water flowed, and there had been a footpath running alongside the rushing water — a footpath that might lead to who knows what wonderful secrets. And now, instead of exploring the tunnel, they were stuck in the cabin, with one of Lau's men guarding the entrance. It was frustrating.

Josh watched her as she marched to and fro past the bed. "I've been thinking," he began. "It's only going to be a matter of time before someone else spots that tunnel. And as soon as it's found, Lau is bound to tell Ethan all about it."

Olly nodded gloomily. "And Ethan will be as eager as we are to know where it goes," she said. "So then there'll be a race to see who gets there first: Ethan Cain's people, or us."

"Exactly!" Josh agreed. "And we have to make sure it's us. So we need to go back there right now! This is the perfect time — while everyone is away. There are still a few hours before the sun goes down. That's plenty of time to get there and take a look around. And the festival doesn't finish till late, so we'll be back here before anyone even realizes we're gone."

"That's a great plan, Josh," Olly cried. But then her face fell and she pointed to the door. "But how are we going to get past him?"

Josh frowned. "That's a good question," he said. "Have you got any ideas?"

Olly sat down, looking thoughtful. Then she leaped to her feet again in delight. "I've got it," she declared. "We can play my diary recordings to make the guard think we're still here, then we can slip out of the window and off into the hills!"

"Excellent," Josh said, getting up. "Now, help me make the bed so it looks like someone's asleep in it. Then we can do the same in my room." He grinned. "That way, if the guard gets nosy and decides to check up on us after your recordings have run out, he'll just think we've gone to bed."

"Josh, if I wasn't worried about you getting a swollen head, I'd say that was almost brilliant," Olly declared, getting to work on the bedspreads.

A few minutes later, all the preparations were in place. Clothes and bags had been bundled up under the bedcovers in both rooms, to give the impression that the beds were occupied, and Josh had found a flashlight. The only problem was that both their watches were suffering from water damage, so they'd have to guess the time.

Olly set the digital diary on a chair close to the door and pressed the playback button. Her voice sounded. "Testing, testing. OK, this is Olly Christie's private and personal diary. So, if you're listening to this, you shouldn't be. It's August the fifth and I've just finished packing my stuff for our trip to China. The whole gang is going again, and I'm really looking forward to it. I'd never tell Josh this, but I really like it when he comes along with us, because . . ."

"OK," Olly said, bundling Josh toward the window. "We'd better get going."

"Wait a minute, I want to hear this," Josh protested.

"It's private and personal," Olly said firmly. "Now get out of that window before I have to push you out."

Josh climbed through the window and dropped to the ground. A few moments later, Olly let herself down beside him. She reached up and pulled the window closed. She left the catch undone — so they would be able to get back in that way — but to anyone who didn't look too closely, the window would appear to be shut.

"OK," Olly whispered. "Let's go!"

〰〰

The early evening sun threw the great mountain into dark shadow as Olly and Josh made their way along the course of the waterway. The old volcano loomed above them, dominating the pale sky, its peak, as ever, shrouded in white mist.

They were soon tired from scrambling over the rocks, but the fear of being seen and followed had lessened as they moved farther away from the camp. At last they found the same piece of high ground from which Olly had first seen the tunnel. She put the binoculars to her eyes.

The dark tunnel mouth leaped into her circle of vision. In the late afternoon light under the mountain, the stream of water seemed as black as oil. White crests of foam showed where the flood broke against rocks and earth-banks.

Olly smiled. "We're almost there," she said.

They had to slither down a steep incline to reach the place where the water flowed out from the mountain. Here, the land formed a natural bay. From the staining on the rocks, it was clear that the water level was normally ten feet higher, and that the tunnel entrance would certainly have been hidden from view.

The stonework had suffered from centuries under running water. Sharp edges had been worn into smooth curves, and here and there a stone had fallen, leaving a black gap. A coldness crept out of the tunnel, making the friends shiver as they stared into the echoing darkness.

Josh switched his flashlight on. The seething black water glittered eerily in the light. Olly noticed that the walls of the tunnel had a greenish tinge, and roots and stems hung from the curved roof where plants had forced their way between the stones. A stone-flagged path followed the canal on both sides, stretching away into darkness, beyond the beam of the flashlight.

"Look!" Olly said, pointing to the keystone in the high arch, seven feet above their heads. Carved deep into the time-worn stone, but still clearly visible, was the symbol of the Shan-ren.

Josh and Olly looked at each other. Then Josh

took a deep breath and plunged into the tunnel. With a final glance back at the rosy evening sky, Olly followed.

⁓⁓⁓⁓

They soon lost all track of time and distance in the endless night of the tunnel. The half-moon of light from the entrance had gradually dwindled away behind them, and now it was gone. All around them as they walked steadily forward in the light of Josh's flashlight, the roar of the water echoed and re-echoed.

"How long have we been in here?" Olly asked.

"I don't know," Josh replied. "Half an hour?"

"More like an hour, I'd say," Olly responded. "How far do you think this tunnel goes?"

Josh turned to look at her. "Do you want to go back?"

"No. Not yet," Olly said.

They walked on in silence.

"What's that?" Olly asked after a few moments. The flashlight beam had picked out a dark slot in the side of the tunnel. It was the first time that they had seen any break in the endless monotony of the stonework.

Josh shined the flashlight into the gap. "They're stairs," he said, aiming the light up a flight of steep, narrow stone steps that rose between walls of solid rock. The treads were uneven and broken in places.

They gazed up the stairway. "What do we do?" Josh asked. "Should we keep to the waterway, or see where these stairs go?"

Olly felt torn with indecision. Obviously the stairs had been carved through the solid rock for some purpose, but she was reluctant to abandon the original plan of finding out where the water came from. "Let's follow the stream for, say, one thousand more steps," she suggested. "If we don't find anything by then, we can come back and try the stairs."

As it turned out, the decision was forced on them sooner than they had expected. Olly was counting the steps in her head, and she had gotten to four hundred when Josh stopped in his tracks. She peered ahead and saw that the flashlight beam had revealed a serious cave-in. The water foamed and bubbled over large chunks of stone and forced its way between them, hissing and splashing. The stone walkways on either side of the stream were completely blocked.

Josh looked at Olly. "The stairs?" he asked.

She nodded. "The stairs."

They returned to the staircase and started up the

steps. It was a tricky climb. Olly found it easier to use her hands and feet on the ancient stones and, more than once, she stepped on an edge that crumbled away beneath her foot, almost making her fall. She could hear the loosened stones, tumbling down into the well of darkness behind her.

Olly gave up counting steps at three hundred. But then, just as she was wondering if the stairway would ever end, she came to the final step and found herself staring down a long tunnel filled with a strange, silver light.

She sat on the top step, rubbing her aching legs and getting her breath back. Josh joined her, and they gazed along the tunnel together. The curious light was coming from the far end. It didn't seem like daylight — and besides, it must surely be dark outside by now — but Olly couldn't think of what else it might be.

Without speaking, they both got up and walked along the passage. After a little while, Josh turned his flashlight off. The light was strong but hazy. It reminded Olly of car headlights shining through thick fog. And the closer they came to the end of the tunnel, the brighter the light became, until it was almost dazzling.

"Careful!" Josh said suddenly, catching hold of Olly's arm as they came to the tunnel mouth.

Olly looked down at her feet and saw that the stones had come to an abrupt stop. The tunnel appeared to end in a vast, misty cliff-face. She couldn't see how far the drop was because wisps of cloud swirled about her feet, obscuring whatever lay below. She glanced up and gave a gasp of wonder. Beyond more shreds of mist, the sky was black above her and filled with bright stars. And overhead, larger than she could ever remember seeing it before, shined the full harvest moon.

But then Olly noticed a dark outer edge to the sky. It curved all around her, sending up black fangs into the net of starlight. "Josh," she breathed, her voice trembling. "We're inside the mountain!"

Josh didn't reply — he was gazing around in awe — but his fingers tightened on her arm.

Now Olly understood the strange silver light. It was the moonlight, shining down upon the layer of cloud that filled the crater of the extinct volcano. They had seen it before — when they had flown over it in broad daylight — but under the full moon, it glowed with a pearly sheen that was like something from another world.

And even as Olly gazed down into the cloud, it drifted as if disturbed by a silent wind. The silvery veil swirled and parted and, that very moment, Olly found herself staring down onto a sight that took her breath away.

Chapter Twelve: Yueliang-Chengshi

Far below, glimpsed fleetingly as the mist lifted, Olly saw buildings. Not broken ruins, but perfect buildings with pearly walls and spiked silver towers and elegant, curved, gray roofs.

Then the clouds moved again and the vision was lost.

"Yueliang-Chengshi," Josh murmured.

Olly stared at him. "The lost city?"

He nodded. "It was inside the volcano the whole time," he said. "Remember the lines I saw around the city plan on the golden disc? I thought it was a wall — but it was actually the mountain!"

Olly stared down into the swirling silver mist. "This is the secret that the Shan-ren have been protecting," she said softly. "That's why they took the golden disc — they knew it gave away the exact location of this city." She looked at Josh. "The Mooncake of Chang-O must be down there somewhere."

"Yes," Josh agreed. "And that's why we have to explore as much of the city as we can before we go back. There's no way this place can be kept secret now, and as soon as we tell Jonathan and the professor about it, Lau will pass the news on to Ethan Cain."

"You're right," Olly said. "And I'm *not* going to let him find the Mooncake first!" She looked around for some way down from the ledge. A narrow, winding stairway of stone carved into the sheer mountainside descended into the cloud to one side.

Olly moved to the stairway and took a first cautious step down. The stone held firm under her foot. She began to descend, one hand pressed against the rock-face for support. She looked around.

Josh was right behind her. "Watch where you're going," he said anxiously. "I don't want to have to explain to your gran if you fall and sprain your ankle."

Olly made a face. If she were to fall down these steps, she'd do a lot worse than sprain an ankle! She willed her eyes to adjust to the hazy light and concentrated on her descent. She could make out the mountain wall at her side and a few steps above and below her — but the rest of the world was already disappearing in a dense blanket of bright white cloud. The air was cool and damp against her skin as thick tendrils of vapor curled around her body.

The constant shifting of the mist was disorienting,

and it was very disturbing to have to lower herself, step by step, into nothingness. But as she descended, Olly gradually noticed that she could see farther. She was coming out under the cloud layer.

And then, quite suddenly it seemed, the mists cleared and she saw the fabulous lost city of Yueliang-Chengshi.

Somehow the light of the full moon penetrated the clouds, giving the whole city a lustrous, radiant glow — as though all the buildings were made from trapped and molded moonlight. There were towers and spires of silver stone, gleaming in the beautiful, luminous light. There were walls that glowed as though they had an inner fire. There were graceful minarets and cupolas and soaring pagodas amid streets of silver. And shining courtyards stretched away, filled with statues of men and women and dragons and lions.

But now that Olly was closer to the city, she could see that it was deserted and abandoned. From the high ledge, it had looked perfect under the light of the moon, but from here she could see that much of it was in ruins.

Josh was right behind her. "The cloud is getting thinner," he said. "That must be why it's so bright down here."

Olly looked up. Veiled in wisps of cloud, she could see the white disc of the huge full moon. Then she paused as a faint scent reached her. "Can you smell flowers?" she asked.

Josh sniffed. "No, I can't smell anything," he replied.

Olly frowned and sniffed. "Neither can I now," she remarked. "I must have imagined it."

She walked down the last couple of dozen steps and passed through an ornate archway that led to a wide courtyard of gray stone. It was ringed with statues — life-sized terra-cotta soldiers wearing full traditional Chinese armor of linked stone discs. Some of the figures were cracked or broken — and many had lost a limb — but of those that were still intact, Olly noticed that every face was different, as if the ancient craftsmen had given each of the men a unique personality.

At the end of the courtyard, a covered gateway was formed by the lithe body of a rearing dragon. The creature was carved from white stone, with ivory claws and teeth, and jeweled eyes that glittered like fire. Olly stopped in her tracks, gazing at the beautiful sculpture. But then she caught another whiff of flowers — jasmine, she thought, or possibly lotus blossom. But she could see no flowers of any kind, and then the scent was gone again.

"Did you smell it that time?" she asked Josh.

"No. What?" Josh replied, looking puzzled.

Olly shook her head. "Nothing," she murmured. "It doesn't matter." She walked on across the court-yard, between the ranks of silent soldiers, with Josh at her side.

"No wonder no one knows this place is here," he commented, looking up at the thin white veil of cloud. "We flew right over the mountain and we didn't see a thing."

Olly looked around. "It's a very strange place," she said thoughtfully. "From above, it looked abso-lutely perfect — as if people could come walking out of the buildings at any moment. But it's all fall-ing to pieces once you get closer."

"It's still amazingly well-preserved, though," Josh said. "Especially when you think of how old it must be."

Olly's eyes lit up. "And we're probably the first people to see it for thousands of years," she breathed.

Through the dragon gate, they found a building with a forecourt of ornate sculptures. Long-necked birds seemed to be dancing to the music of stone musicians playing exotic instruments.

"Those birds are cranes," Josh told Olly. "I've read about them. The ancient Chinese people thought cranes were immortal."

"Why are musicians playing to them?" Olly asked.

"To keep them happy," Josh replied. "So they won't fly away. They believed that if the cranes stayed, then the people would live forever as well."

Olly looked at the dancing birds. "They seem happy enough," she remarked. She gazed around at the deserted city. "But it doesn't seem to have worked for the people, does it?"

Pearly water trickled from fountains and ran in narrow rivulets, filling the still air with a soft rippling sound. Olly was just about to move on, when once again she smelled the heady fragrance of flowers. "This is getting ridiculous," she muttered, looking around for flowers. There were none to be seen. "Where is that smell coming from?"

"Flowers again?" Josh asked. He sniffed deeply.

"Can you smell it now?" Olly inquired hopefully.

Josh frowned. "I'm not sure. There might be something — but it's very faint." He shook his head. "No. It's gone."

"I've had enough of this," Olly said. She marched off determinedly. "I'm going to find those flowers."

They turned a corner and found themselves on a broad avenue of fabulous palaces. Olly followed the fleeting scent along the silvery roadway that stretched ahead of her. The avenue rose gradually in a long, gentle slope and, at the far end of the street, standing high on a hill of white marble steps, was a solitary building that seemed to be made of shining moonlight.

"I've seen pictures of buildings that look like that," Josh said. "I think it's a temple."

"Let's go and find out," Olly suggested, her natural curiosity taking over.

Together they walked quickly up the long road and climbed the gleaming marble stairs. The white stone walls of the temple reflected the moonlight, giving the building its dazzling radiance. Carved on the walls, the friends could see moon-symbols inlaid with jade, ebony, turquoise, and agate.

"There are some flowers here," Josh said. He pointed to the pillars and doorposts of the temple, up which stone flowers climbed, inlaid with gems that sparkled in the light.

Olly frowned and leaned close to one of the

carved blossoms. She sniffed experimentally, but there was no scent. "Stone flowers don't smell," she said to herself. "That's just silly." But as she passed through the high doorway, she caught the faintest hint of jasmine.

Inside, the ceiling was of black lacquer, inlaid with opalescent stars and a mother-of-pearl moon. The walls were also a lustrous, shining black.

"How has all this survived for so long?" Olly wondered.

"I suppose the volcano has kept the city hidden from humans and protected it from the worst of the weather," Josh replied.

Olly nodded and moved on through to an inner chamber. Here, on platforms and tables all around the room, were bowls of bronze, carved wooden chests bound in gold, and bright bells and gongs of silver.

Olly paused to gaze at the carvings on a large door at the end of the room. Inset in silver on the white stone of the door itself was a curious picture. It seemed to be a stylized depiction of the city: The high walls of the volcano were clearly shown, and from the city, a woman with shreds of cloud at her feet was flying up toward the full moon.

"It's Chang-O," Olly murmured, her voice soft

and reverent. "This must be a temple to the moon goddess."

Josh nodded and gently pushed the door, which swung open easily. The friends walked on into a small oval inner chamber, its pearly walls quite plain and unadorned. Over to the left, there was an altar or stone table set on four broad stone steps. A statue lay on the table, reminding her of the images of the dead that Olly had seen, lying on top of their own tombs, in English churches.

But the stonework of this statue was painted in bright colors. It was a woman dressed in red robes, her face white and her glossy black hair hanging down over the end of the altar — so long that it reached the floor. A single moonbeam shined down onto the woman's face, from a circular hole in the ceiling above her.

Olly and Josh walked silently toward the statue. As they got closer, Olly began to realize that the red silk gown and the radiant fall of black hair were not carved and painted stone at all. "Is she *real*?" Olly whispered in awe.

"I don't know," Josh murmured, the confusion obvious in his voice.

They climbed the steps and looked into the

beautiful face. It was white, but perfect, as though the woman had only just closed her eyes and drifted into a peaceful sleep. There was a delicate tiara of silver across her forehead and, set into the center, was a moonstone disc that shimmered with an inner light.

"She must be Chang-O," Olly said softly. She pointed to the moonstone on the woman's forehead. "And that must be the Mooncake," she added. "Josh — we've found it!"

Gently, Olly reached out and touched the moonstone. It felt slightly warm under her fingers, and it easily came free from its silver setting. Olly lifted it in the beam of bright moonlight and gazed at the surface. It was ringed with flying cranes holding trailing garlands of flowers in their beaks. In the center was etched a crescent moon and a flaming sun.

Olly could feel Josh leaning over her shoulder. "Should I do this?" she whispered, caught by a sudden doubt.

"I don't know," Josh replied. "But we can't leave it here for Ethan Cain to find."

Olly moved the stone out of the light. Immediately the moonbeam faded and the whole room darkened. "What's happening?" Olly asked.

Far above them, they heard a distant peal of thunder. A moment later, great heavy raindrops began to fall through the hole in the roof of the temple.

"We should go," Josh said. He caught Olly's arm, and pulled her down the steps toward the exit.

As they neared the doorway, Olly heard what seemed to be a gentle sigh. She turned. Chang-O's body was surrounded by a soft glow, through which Olly could see the raindrops falling like sparkling diamonds.

And then, as Olly watched, the glow faded and Chang-O's body seemed to turn to stone.

Chapter Thirteen: The Storm

The thunder roared, echoing and reverberating in the crater of the ancient volcano, until Josh and Olly had to put their hands over their ears as they ran through the Moon Temple. It was darker now — not pitch black, but dark enough to make them stretch out their hands as they ran, in case they should stumble into unseen things in their path.

They came out onto the broad stone steps. The rain was falling in torrents, lashing the white stones and bouncing on the steps. The city was a dull gray now. The strange light that had made it so beautiful and unearthly had vanished, as if washed away by the rain.

A jagged fork of lightning blazed across the sky, thunder bellowed, and the rain hammered down on the stones with a sound like hissing snakes.

"This is amazing!" Olly yelled above the noise. She ran out into the pelting rain, splashing through the puddles and stretching her arms up to the deluge.

She tilted her head to let the pellets of water patter down on her face.

Josh watched from the shelter of the temple's doorway with a grin on his face. "You're crazy!" he called.

"Think of the farmers!" Olly shouted back. "They'll be so pleased. They're all going to be OK now that the rain has come. This is the best thing that could possibly have happened."

"What about the dig?" Josh reminded her. "It'll be washed away."

Olly danced toward him. Her clothes were sticking to her, her hair hung in her eyes and her face was running with water, but she didn't care. "I know," she said, laughing and spinning in the rain, the talisman clutched tightly in one hand, "but we've got the Mooncake now! That's the really important thing."

Olly skipped back up the temple steps to Josh. She wiped the water out of her eyes and gazed out at the city. It was awash. Already, puddles of rainwater were spreading across the stone streets. The temple was on a small hill, but all around it the ground dipped before rising again toward the crater walls. Puddles were beginning to combine into large gray pools.

A long groan of thunder shook the air.

"I think we better head back and show Jonathan and the professor what we've found," Josh suggested.

Olly nodded and pushed the precious moonstone into her pocket. "OK," she said. "Let's go!"

They ran down the temple steps. Olly had never known a storm like it; the whole world seemed full of falling water. It was cascading from roofs, streaming through the streets, gushing and spilling over statues and sculptures until it seemed as if the city was melting around them.

Lightning sizzled across the clouds with thunder at its heels. "Isn't this the most amazing storm you've ever seen?" Olly shouted. "I've always loved really big thunderstorms!"

Josh wiped water out of his eyes with a soaking sleeve. "I prefer watching them from indoors," he confessed.

Olly laughed. A tidal wave of rainwater couldn't have dampened her spirits. They had found a city, lost for thousands of years, and she had the Mooncake in her pocket. Very soon she would be able place it in her father's hands and see the look of surprise and delight on his face. Everything was wonderful!

They turned the corner and ran back past the statues of cranes and musicians. The seated musicians were waist-deep in water now, and the birds seemed to be wading as Josh and Olly rushed on toward the stairs.

When they reached the dragon arch, they found it shrouded in fine spray, and the courtyard of soldiers beyond was a foot deep in swirling floodwater. Josh and Olly joined hands and waded across the expanse of drowned flagstones. It was heavy going, but at last they were through the first arch and the long stone stairway rose ahead of them, water leaping and bouncing down the steps.

"Be careful," Josh shouted as Olly began to climb.

"It'll be fine," she called back as more thunder crashed above them.

They scrambled up into the gray clouds. There was no moonlight now to make the mist shine, and Olly could see nothing. She felt wet, slippery rock under her feet and heard the constant splash and patter of the rain as she climbed ever upward.

Eventually, Olly emerged above the clouds. It was a little lighter here, and above her, Olly could see the storm clouds racing across the sky. The rain was still falling, but the thunder and lightning had stopped — for a while at least. She clambered up the last stone stairs until she came to the shelf of rock that led into the mountain.

"Oh my gosh!" Josh said, staggering out of the rain and pushing his wet hair out of his eyes. "It's crazy out there!"

Even Olly had to admit that it was a relief to be out of the battering rain. But there was a curious, roaring noise in the tunnel. She turned to Josh. "What's that?" she asked.

"I don't know," Josh replied. "But I don't like the sound of it."

~~~~~

The echoing rumble sounded ominous to Josh. He led the way along the tunnel, but as they neared the stairs, the din got louder and louder. Josh took out his flashlight and played the beam along the passage. He walked to the top of the stairway and listened to the noise that echoed up from the depths. He looked at Olly. "I've got a bad feeling about this," he muttered grimly.

She listened. "It's nothing," she said hopefully. "Just the rain."

"I hope you're right," Josh replied, and together they began the long climb down to the waterway.

They had been on the stairs for only a few minutes, when the flashlight beam suddenly shined on dark floodwater only a couple of steps below. Waves surged up the stairwell, white water heaving and churning over the steps, one by one.

Josh and Olly drew to a halt, staring down into the flood.

"Well, I don't think we can dive down and get out this time!" Olly exclaimed.

Josh nodded. "You're right about that," he said. "If the water has risen this far, then the entire canal will be flooded, too."

Olly blinked at him. "So, what do we do?"

Josh turned and shined the flashlight back up the stairs. "We'll have to look for another way out," he declared.

"*Is* there one?" Olly queried.

"I don't know," Josh replied.

They climbed the stairs in silence. For a moment, Josh almost wished he had stayed back at camp in the warmth and comfort of his cabin. But then he thought of beautiful Yueliang-Chengshi, and the moonstone safe in Olly's pocket, and he knew it would all be worth it — if they could find a safe escape from the volcano!

The roar of the rising flood lessened as they climbed. "I'm getting really sick of these stairs," Olly puffed.

"Tell me about it," Josh agreed. But at last they reached the top of the stairway. Josh looked toward the far end of the tunnel and saw a cascade of falling water. He and Olly made their way along the passage and gingerly edged out through the water onto the rain-washed ledge.

Olly turned to look up at the cliff-face above them. "We'll never climb out that way," she called to Josh. "You'd need to be able to fly, like Chang-O, to get over the mountain."

"That's it!" Josh exclaimed. At Olly's words, an image had flashed into his mind. "Remember that picture on the door in the temple?" he reminded her. "The one of Chang-O flying to the moon? I think it showed a route up the inside of the crater." He looked at her. "Another way out!"

"Are you sure?" Olly asked.

Josh nodded. "I think so. Besides, what choice do we have? Let's go and look at it again before the water gets too high."

Olly frowned at him. "If we end up getting drowned down there, I'll never talk to you again!" she warned.

He smiled grimly. "Fair enough."

This time it was Josh who took the lead down the stairs and through the cloud bank. The silver city was afloat in a rolling ocean of water now, and the flood came almost to their waists as the friends struggled to wade across the courtyard. The soldiers simply stared ahead impassively as the water rose around them.

Josh and Olly fought their way through, half wading, half swimming, until they could see the temple on its hill. The sight of the beautiful white building — still standing proud above flood, on its stone steps — gave them renewed determination, and they began to make their way up the long avenue toward it.

They were almost there when suddenly Josh felt Olly being dragged away by the flood. She had lost her footing in the racing water, which now threatened to sweep her away entirely.

Olly's head vanished beneath the water. Josh clung on tightly to her hand, but felt his own feet losing their grip in the rising tide. Olly surfaced, coughing and gasping for air as Josh felt his feet being lifted off the ground. He lunged forward, dragging Olly with him, in a last desperate attempt to reach the steps.

It was with huge relief that he felt stone beneath his feet again and dragged himself out of the deluge. He helped Olly to her feet, but the flood was rising swiftly now, and they had to climb another step to get away from the lapping water. Josh gazed out over the city and felt a rush of panic. The temple hill was an island in a rising sea. They had just about reached the building — but were they ever going to be able to leave it again?

Chapter Fourteen: The Man in the Demon Mask

"Well?" said Olly. "Now what?" They stood under the shelter of the temple gateway, watching the rain falling on the drowning city.

Josh didn't reply. He stared up at the clouds for a moment, then turned and walked into the temple.

Olly stayed there beneath the arch of the doorway, imagining that Chang-O herself might once have stood in the very same spot, old and tired from her long hunt for her husband, holding the Mooncake in her hand. Maybe she, too, had gazed out over the city, but had seen it alive and bustling with people and animals now long gone.

Olly fingered the talisman in her pocket. It still felt curiously warm against her skin. Her brain told her that taking the talisman from Chang-O's crown could not have brought the rain, but she did wonder if maybe she had been *meant* to find the Mooncake. And some strange instinct told her that she and Josh would be kept safe by it. Chang-O would watch over them, Olly thought, and then smiled to herself, imagining how Josh would react to such a fantastical idea.

"Olly!" Josh called from inside the temple.

"Yes?" Olly replied, tearing herself away from her view of the city and heading inside.

"I think I've figured it out," Josh told her as she joined him at the door of the innermost chamber. He pointed to the picture. "See?" he continued. "I know where this building with the two spires is. You can see those spires in the distance from the steps outside. They're in the opposite direction from the way we came." He traced the pathway that the long-dead artist had threaded through the city. "If we take this direct line from here to the building with the two spires, it should lead us to the path up the mountain." His finger came to the base of a zigzag line that led up to the mountain peaks, from which Chang-O was depicted flying to the full moon. "There's only one problem," Josh finished. "How do we get across the city?"

"We swim for it if we have to," Olly replied.

Josh looked at her. "That didn't work too well last time we tried it, if you remember," he pointed out.

Olly smiled. "We didn't have the talisman then," she said.

346

Josh gave her a puzzled look.

"Everything will work out fine," Olly told him. "I have a feeling."

They ventured out into the endless rain again and made their way around to the far side of the temple. Olly saw the building with the two spires far off in the distance. It stood on a ridge of high ground above the flood. But between that building and the temple, the waters ran wild and deep, rushing and roaring through the streets.

Olly stepped down to the water's edge and stared into the swirling waters, gathering her courage for the plunge. Her fingers tightened on the talisman. She took a long, slow breath and stepped down again, the water teeming at her ankles. Another step, and it was up to her shins. And then, with the third step, something astonishing happened.

Olly's foot jarred against something. It was higher than she had been expecting. She stepped out again cautiously, and still the ground remained level beneath her. She turned and looked at Josh. "There's some kind of pathway just under the water," she told him. "It's like a wall or something." She stooped, trying to see the path through the troubled floodwater. She could dimly see a faint white line under the surface, and she laughed with delight, because the path seemed to be leading them straight to the building with the two spires. "Come on in," she called to Josh. "The water's fine!"

Josh grinned as he came down the steps to join Olly and, side by side, they waded out toward the spires.

~~~~~

"I think the rain is beginning to ease off," Josh said, staring up at the clouds. He looked back at the city. Water was still pouring off the roofs and cascading through the streets, but the fierceness of the downpour did seem to have lessened.

They were standing on a flat terrace of white stone that jutted out from the mountainside. Above them, a narrow path made its jagged, zigzag way up the inside of the crater. The friends had another hard climb ahead of them.

"What time do you think it is?" Olly asked.

"Midnight?" Josh suggested. "Maybe even later."

Olly gazed out over the city. "I hope the water doesn't do too much damage," she murmured. "It's such a beautiful place."

"It'll be a while before any excavations can be carried out," Josh commented. "It'll probably be weeks before all that water drains away."

Olly turned her head sharply and stared at him.

"What?" he queried, surprised by the look on her face.

Olly shook her head. "Nothing," she said. "I'd just like to get back to camp and put some dry clothes on, that's all."

"If the camp is still there," Josh remarked. "With this amount of rain, the whole place could be underwater by now."

He set off up the zigzag path. Water was flowing down the track, making it slippery, but it was an easier route than the stone stairway had been. Every now and then the climb was relieved by a wide paved area. The friends rested on those high galleries, catching their breath and giving their legs time to recover.

Eventually, they came to the cloud bank. The city faded away into a gray haze beneath them and was lost from sight. "I've got the weirdest feeling we'll never see it again," Olly said.

Josh looked at her. "Of course we will," he replied. "Once we tell Jonathan and the professor about it, they'll want us to show them the way in. The dig will probably be extended for months. There must be an incredible amount of stuff down there — enough to fill an entire museum."

Olly just nodded thoughtfully.

They soon emerged from the cloud bank and again saw the fangs of the mountain all around them. The thunderclouds seemed less threatening now, and the rain was much lighter, as if the storm's fury had worn itself out.

They came to a final platform. Bronze dragons guarded an ornate archway made of glowing jade. Josh took his flashlight out again and shined the beam through the arch and into the tunnel beyond.

"Look at this!" he exclaimed. He had expected to see a simple passageway hacked through the rock, like the one by which they had entered the city, but the flashlight beam was reflected by a thousand jewels, set in panels of onyx and jade and ivory that lined the entire length of the passage.

There were stone shelves set in the paneled walls, holding sculptures made of stone and bronze, silver and pottery. Josh gazed in fascination at dancing figures and long-necked birds. Horses and lions and dragons.

Josh and Olly were cold and tired and completely wet, but they forgot their fatigue and discomfort as they marveled at the ancient treasures of Yueliang-Chengshi. Josh noticed that many of the sculptures and carvings showed a man with a bow and arrows, while others seemed to depict Chang-O either afloat in clouds or gazing up to a full moon. All along the tunnel, the walls were inlaid with representations of the moon — from crescent to full, wrought in silver and bronze and gold.

It was almost a disappointment for the friends when the flashlight beam showed the tunnel narrowing to a dark exit onto the mountainside. The mouth of the passage was a narrow and curved slit like a huge cat's eye.

Josh squeezed through first. He emerged about a third of the way up the mountain, and found himself staring out through fine rain over a landscape that he didn't recognize. Olly appeared at his shoulder. Below them, clustered among the foothills, was a mass of bright lights: a town.

"Is that Banping?" Olly asked.

"I don't think so," Josh replied. "It's too big. It must be Chung-hsien." As if to confirm his words, a rocket, trailing fire, suddenly soared up from the town and burst in a shower of gold and silver sparks. A second and a third blaze of light followed, one exploding in red fire, the other opening up like a golden flower. A few moments later, the sizzle and crackle of the fireworks reached their ears.

"It's the Moon Festival!" Olly exclaimed happily.

Josh turned to look back at the fissure through

which they had emerged. He frowned. The rock-
face seemed smooth and featureless with no sign of
an opening. He took a step back to investigate, shining his flashlight beam over the rocks.

~~~~

Olly watched the fireworks for a few moments,
then she turned to speak to Josh. He was gone.
"Josh?" she called. Even without the light of his
flashlight, she could see very well. And there was
absolutely no sign of him.

"Josh!" She couldn't understand where he'd gone.
A few seconds ago he had been standing right beside
her. Her heart leaped into her mouth. Maybe something had happened to him. Had the Shan-ren
taken him again? She looked around anxiously and
then realized, with a jolt, that the cleft through
which they had exited the tunnel had also vanished.

"Josh!" there was an edge of panic in her
voice now.

"What's the matter?" Josh asked, sounding quite
normal — and very close by. "What are you yelling
about?"

"Where are you?" Olly asked, staring at the
rocks.

"I'm here." Suddenly, right in front of her eyes,

Josh shimmered into sight. Olly let out a yelp of surprise.

Josh was grinning from ear to ear. "I think it must be some kind of optical illusion," he explained. "You can't see the entrance to the tunnel from the outside." He stepped back, dissolving into thin air. A moment later, he stepped forward and reappeared. "See?" he said.

"Please stop doing that," Olly begged. "It's weird!"

"Don't you get it?" Josh asked. "That's why this place has never been found. You'd have to know exactly where the entrance is to be able to go through it." He frowned. "We should leave some kind of marker here, or we won't be able to find it again."

"Leave your flashlight," Olly suggested. "We won't need it now."

"Good idea." Josh switched his flashlight off and laid it on the ground in front of the secret entrance, so that it pointed to the hidden fissure. "There," he said. "Now we'll be able to get back to the city, even if the canal is underwater again after all this rain."

"Come on," Olly said. "I want to go and show Dad what we've found. And he's probably down there in Chung-hsien."

Josh nodded, and they set off down the mountain toward the welcoming lights of Chung-hsien, all thoughts of exhaustion and cold forgotten.

It wasn't long before they could hear the sounds of the festival — music and laughter, and the constant hiss and roar as more fireworks were launched into the sky.

"They've really got something to celebrate now that the rain has come," Olly said elatedly. She looked slyly at Josh. "Do you think we had anything to do with making it rain?"

He frowned at her. "Hardly."

Olly grinned. "I'm not so sure," she said. She put her hand in her pocket and touched the Mooncake. "I think Yueliang-Chengshi is a very strange place," she continued thoughtfully. "And I think we were meant to find the talisman."

Josh eyed her dubiously. "Let's hope Jonathan and your father think the same," he said.

Olly laughed. "Oh, they'll forgive us for leaving camp when they see the talisman," she said. "I can't wait to see my dad's face! This will be the second Talisman of the Moon that we've found." She grinned at Josh. "We'll have to write a book about —"

An alarmed look on Josh's face silenced her. She turned to see what had startled him.

Two of Lau's men stood in front of them, as if they had appeared out of nowhere.

"Oh, *rats!*" Olly muttered. She and Josh both turned to run, but two more men in gray stood barring their way back. One of them was Lau himself.

"You are difficult people to find," he remarked, his voice smooth and cold.

"We're going to see my father," Olly told him defiantly. "You can't stop us."

"I think you'll find I can," Lau retorted. He spoke briefly in Mandarin, and a moment later both Olly and Josh were held securely by Lau's guards.

Olly glared at Lau. "If you don't take us to my father, you're going to be in a lot of trouble," she said. "I know who you really work for — and he doesn't scare me."

"Please come with me," Lau said calmly. He turned, beckoning to his men.

Olly and Josh were bundled along in Lau's wake. Olly struggled in vain. She thought of shouting for help, but the noise of the festival was too loud. She would never be heard. For the time being, she decided, they had no choice but to do what Lau wanted.

They came to a large wooden house on the outskirts of the town. Lau led them into a room lit with

355

a rainbow of brightly colored lanterns. A figure in a traditional robe of blue and white silk stood with its back to them at a window, apparently watching the festivities.

Lau motioned to his men to bring Olly and Josh forward.

"Let us go!" Olly demanded, struggling again.

The figure at the window turned slowly to face her. Covering his head was a Chinese demon mask, the eyes blazing red under fiercely frowning brows, the mouth distorted into a fearsome grin that displayed pointed white fangs.

Olly and Josh stared at the apparition in shocked silence. Olly swallowed hard. "Who are you?" she asked.

The figure raised his hands to the mask and carefully lifted it off. "Hello, Josh. Hello, Olly," he said pleasantly. "This is a nice surprise."

Olly's head spun.

It was Ethan Cain.

Chapter Fifteen:
The Dragon Dance

Olly stared at Ethan in unconcealed dislike. "What are you doing here?" she demanded, though she had already guessed he was looking for the Mooncake of Chang-O.

Ethan nodded toward the window. "I came to watch the Festival of the Moon," he replied. He gestured toward the mask. "And to join in the festivities a little in my own way." He smiled at them, but Olly saw a ruthless gleam in his eyes. "The lion dance is intended to bring on the rain," he commented. "Did you know that?"

"Yes," Josh snapped.

The American half-turned to the window again, and traced a raindrop down the glass with one finger. "It seems to have worked," he remarked. "Very nice for the local farmers, but something of a blow for your father, Olly, I should think. I don't imagine he's even close to finding the talisman yet." He smiled. "I wonder if you've had more luck." His gaze flicked to Josh. "Luck was obviously with you when you found that golden disc."

"We're not afraid of you," Josh stated defiantly.

Ethan raised an eyebrow in an expression of puzzlement and surprise. "What an extraordinary thing to say, Josh," he said mildly.

"*You* stole the disc!" Olly spat. "It was you all along."

He gave a dismissive wave of his hand. "I didn't steal it. It was someone else altogether. Someone with a very different motive, I'm sure." He looked from Olly to Josh. "Tell me, what do you know about the Shan-ren? I was under the impression that they had died out, but I keep hearing that name." His eyes narrowed. "Do they still exist?"

"As if we'd tell you!" Olly declared scornfully, realizing she wanted to defend the guardians of the mountain, even if she wasn't sure if they did exist. "We know you put up the money for this dig — and you deliberately used a fake name so nobody would know it was you."

The American grimaced, as though hurt. "Why do you persist in misunderstanding me?" he asked. "I have a fascination with archaeology. I kept my name out of the proceedings to prevent media interest. The Chinese authorities didn't want swarms of reporters descending on the site, so they asked that I remain anonymous." He smiled at Josh. "Being the son of a celebrity, I'm sure you know how inconvenient it can be to be famous."

Josh didn't reply.

"We know exactly why you're here," Olly muttered darkly. Then she let out a harsh laugh. "And you're too late, so you might just as well turn around and go straight back home again!"

"Just a second here." Ethan glided across the floor to Olly's side. "What do you mean, I'm too late?" he demanded icily.

"She meant the rain will close down the dig," Josh put in. "That's what she meant."

Ethan Cain fixed Olly with a piercing gaze. She lifted her chin and looked him boldly in the eyes, her mouth set in a determined line.

"Did she mean that?" Ethan mused in a low whisper as he stared at Olly. "Or did she mean something else entirely?"

A shiver of unease ran through Olly. She had the horrible feeling that he had guessed the real meaning of her words. She could feel the talisman heavy in her pocket. All he had to do was search her and he'd have it.

She held his gaze for a long time, and it was Ethan who looked away first. He turned and walked back to the window. Olly glanced quickly over her shoulder. Lau and his men stood behind her, blocking the way to the door.

"What were you doing on the mountain?" Ethan asked quietly, still with his back to the friends.

"We went for a little walk," Josh replied.

"No," Cain said flatly. "You made up your beds to give the impression that you were still at the camp, and then you left without being seen." He looked at Olly. "Your grandmother had told you to stay there," he murmured thoughtfully. "Mrs. Beckmann is a formidable woman. I trust you wouldn't have disobeyed her without good reason. I believe that Josh saw something on the golden disc that sent you out on the mountain — twice — without permission. I think it has something to do with the old watercourse, because that's where Lau lost track of you the first time. And I suspect you were looking for something. My guess is that you thought you had a clue that would lead to the Mooncake of Chang-O." He wheeled around suddenly. "You're both resourceful people. I remember that from our little adventure in Egypt. So were you lucky, I wonder?" he continued. "Did you find it? Or something that would lead you to it?"

Olly exchanged glances with Josh. They both

knew better than to say anything. A few tense moments passed.

"I'd like to go and find my father now, if that's OK with you," Olly said calmly, breaking the silence.

A flash of anger crossed the American's face. "Search them!" he ordered.

Olly turned to see Lau and his men moving forward. But, suddenly, the window shattered and the air was full of broken glass. Ethan threw his arms up to protect his face just in time, as fragments of glass flew around him. And there was something else — something that shot across the room, trailing smoke. It came crashing to the floor at Mr. Lau's feet.

He stared down at it for a moment. And then an explosion of white light and noise sent him staggering backward. The thing had split into burning, sparking fragments that began to career wildly around the room, giving off earsplitting shrieks and bangs.

Olly realized what it was: Someone had thrown a bundle of large firecrackers in through the window. She grabbed hold of Josh's hand and together they ran for the door. Josh snatched it open and slammed it shut behind them. They raced along the corridor toward the main entrance of the building. They could hear pounding feet behind them; Lau's men were already in the corridor. And above the continued explosions from the firecrackers, they could also hear Ethan Cain shouting commands.

Reaching the front door, they leaped from the building and plunged down an alleyway. "Who threw the firecrackers?" Josh gasped.

"I didn't see," Olly said. "I don't know."

They rounded a corner, their feet slipping on wet earth. A long passageway between two buildings led to a brightly lit street. They ran toward it.

But a figure melted out of the shadows in front of them, barring their path. They slithered to a halt. The man was dressed in red and across the lower half of his face he wore a red scarf. On the scarf was the now-familiar Shan-ren pictogram.

The man pointed to one side, and spoke urgently in Mandarin. Olly saw that there was a narrow open door in the wooden wall. She didn't have time to think it through, but she had a hunch that the man was trying to help them, so she dived through the doorway with Josh only an instant behind.

The man followed and shut the door. The room was in darkness, lit only by the light that filtered in between the wooden slats of the wall. Their rescuer stood silent and alert with his back to the door, listening.

They heard running feet in the alley getting closer and then running on past.

The man let out a sigh of relief and then spoke again in Mandarin.

"*Wo bu dong*," Olly replied. *I don't understand.*

A sudden light illuminated the room. The man held a flashlight in his hand. He untied the scarf from around his face and smiled at Olly and Josh as he let out another stream of Mandarin. Olly liked the man's face; he looked honest and kind. He smiled again and pressed his hands together, bowing slightly.

"I think he's on our side," Josh whispered.

The man held his hands up, making a circle with his fingers. "Chang-O," he said. He looked from Olly to Josh. "Chang-O."

"Yes," Olly agreed, moved by a sudden sense of understanding. "Yes, Chang-O!" She put her hand in her pocket and drew out the Mooncake. "We found it in the old city in the mountain," she explained. "The Shan-ren have been keeping the city a secret for thousands of years, haven't they?" The man gazed at the moonstone then looked inquiringly at Olly, as if trying to understand what she was saying. "And now we've found it," she added thoughtfully. "And soon the whole place will be full of strangers." She frowned. "It's all wrong," she said decisively, turning to Josh. "We shouldn't do this."

Josh frowned. "What do you mean?"

"The old city has been kept secret for so long, Josh," she replied. "We can't tell. It would be wrong."

"You mean we shouldn't tell *anyone?*" Josh queried. "Not even Jonathan and your dad?"

Olly gave him a crooked smile. "Is that crazy?" she asked. She wasn't sure where her thoughts were coming from. She just had an image in her mind of the beautiful old city being ransacked by greedy men like Ethan Cain. She turned back to her Chinese rescuer. "Did you throw those firecrackers into the room?"

The man stared at her blankly. Olly did a pantomime of the firecrackers banging and leaping around. "*Ni?*" she asked. *You?* The man smiled and nodded.

Hardly understanding why she did it, Olly suddenly held the Mooncake of Chang-O out to the man from the Shan-ren. "Take it," she said. "Put it back where it came from."

The man shook his head. He reached out and closed Olly's hand around the moonstone, pushing it away from him. He carefully replaced the scarf over his mouth and nose, and opened the door onto the alley. Then he gestured for them to leave.

As they stepped out into the fine rain, he put a hand on Josh's shoulder. Olly saw something being pressed into Josh's hand, then the door closed on the man and they stood alone in the alley.

Josh held the object up. It was a flashlight.

"Why did he give you that?" Olly asked.

Josh was looking at it with an extraordinary expression on his face. He looked up at her. "Because it's mine," he said simply.

Olly looked confused and Josh gave a breath of laughter. "It's my flashlight, Olly," he explained. "The one we left on the mountain — to mark the passage."

"Oh!"

"I don't think he wants us to find our way back to the city," Josh mused.

"But he let us keep the Mooncake," Olly said bemusedly. "What does it mean?"

"I *think* it means that the Shan-ren are OK with us finding the talisman, but that they don't want the city disturbed," Josh said. "I agree with you; we can't tell anyone about it. We can say we found the talisman in the canal."

Olly lifted the moonstone. "Let's go and find Dad," she said. "The quicker this is somewhere safe, the happier I'll be."

They made their way to the end of the alley and came out into the brightly lit street. It was filled with revelers and noise, and hung with lanterns and streamers. Food and drink were being sold from colorful wooden stalls, musicians were playing traditional tunes, and people were dancing in the muddy streets, delighted that the rain had come.

Fireworks were still going off all over town. Rockets shot into the sky and exploded in colored fire. Firecrackers jumped and whirled with flashes and bangs. And showers of silver, green, and gold sparks streamed down from upper windows.

Olly caught a glimpse of one of Lau's men in the throng. He was speaking on a cell phone. He didn't seem to have noticed them. Quickly, she caught hold of Josh's arm and pulled him in the opposite direction.

The two friends darted through the revelers, constantly on the lookout for pursuit. Olly saw another of Lau's men on the far side of the street. Before she could duck out of sight, he spotted her and reached for his phone. She slipped behind a stall. "They've seen us," she said to Josh.

He nodded. "I know — and there's one over there, too." He pointed to a corner where another security man was standing, scanning the crowd for the two friends.

Olly and Josh slipped away down a side road. They emerged in a central square that was so crowded they could only just push their way through the throng. The bamboo houses surrounding the square were strung with glowing lanterns, and the music here was loud and very rhythmic.

Josh wiggled his way to the front of the crowd, with Olly hanging onto his shirt so they wouldn't get separated. A dragon dance was taking place. The great creature swayed and writhed across the square, chasing a masked man in a vivid red costume, who bounded athletically ahead of the monster, performing cartwheels and somersaults. The dragon's head was beautifully made with golden horns, snapping red jaws, and a long golden beard. Its eyes rolled and swiveled as it chased the man in red, while drums thundered and cymbals crashed.

Under the flowing silken body and tail, Olly could make out at least ten pairs of legs, expertly following the intricate choreography of the dance as the great beast swept around the square, its head rising and falling to the rhythm of the drums.

Mesmerized, Olly watched the man in red veer away as the dragon almost caught him. The fearsome creature wheeled and sped after him, its body undulating as if it were alive, trailing long silk streamers from its horns and ears and tail.

Olly was so absorbed by the rhythm of the dragon's movements that she didn't notice Lau approaching until he put his hand on her neck. She started violently, then squirmed free and tumbled out into the square, pulling Josh with her.

The masked man saw them and ran forward, gesticulating wildly, shouting and leaping. Olly scrambled to her feet and looked around frantically. She saw Lau making his way toward her through the crowd, and more of his men closing in from other directions. There was no way out.

The masked man grabbed Olly's wrist and dragged her toward the middle of the square. She struggled, and Josh ran to rescue her, but the man caught his arm, too. He spoke from behind the mask. "Go to the dragon," he said in English with a heavy Chinese accent. "He will protect you. Go!"

There were shouts and calls and cheers from the crowd as the masked man led Olly and Josh toward the dragon. It was coiled in the middle of the square now, writhing and rolling its eyes.

Dazed and bewildered, Olly allowed herself to be pushed toward the dragon's snapping jaws. At the same time the body and tail came snaking around her and Josh, effectively blocking Lau and his men from reaching them. A section of the silk that formed the dragon's body lifted high and the friends found themselves drawn in under the bamboo framework.

A gong sounded. The dragon roared and began to move. Olly saw that Josh had caught hold of the dancer directly ahead of him and was trying to mimic the man's movements. She did the same, doing her best to follow the path of the dragon dance. She couldn't see what was going on; her whole world consisted of the black-clad dancers and the bamboo frame with its covering of colored silk. But somehow she managed to keep in step as they took a zigzag course across the square.

She heard shouts and laughter and saw the feet of spectators as they ran from the dragon. She realized they were at the far side of the square now. The dancer directly behind Olly spoke briefly and pushed her. She and Josh came stumbling out from under the dragon's skirts and were quickly absorbed into the crowd.

"Were they Shan-ren?" Josh gasped, breathless from the wild dance.

"I don't know," Olly panted. "But they got us away from Mr. Lau, whoever they were."

"Let's find the professor," Josh said. "Before Lau catches up with us again."

They made their way through the festive streets, desperate to catch sight of Jonathan or the professor. Smiling vendors offered them mooncakes and hedgehog buns and fresh noodles, but they had no time to enjoy the sights and sounds of the festival. Olly just wanted the talisman to be safe. And Lau's men seemed to be everywhere, while there was no sign of anyone from the camp.

"Maybe we should find somewhere to hide?" Josh suggested. "Just till things calm down. If they can't find us, maybe Lau's men will think we've gone back to the dig site."

Olly nodded. "Good idea," she said. "It's got to be better than running around until we get caught again." She stopped and looked around her. They were in a narrow alley, cluttered with bicycles and bins and even several baskets of chickens. "How about this place?" she suggested.

"Why not?" Josh agreed. "We could duck down

behind the baskets and just lie low till the festival is over."

"I think we'll be safe here," Olly said, heading over to the baskets Josh had indicated. She took the Mooncake of Chang-O out of her pocket, feeling again its curious warmth in her hand. "Ethan won't get his hands on the talisman now."

"I'm not so sure," Josh replied in a low voice.

Olly turned back toward him and saw five of Lau's men approaching from the end of the alley. "Run!" Olly yelled. She swung round, prepared to make a dash for it, but a figure blocked her way — a figure with outstretched arms, dressed in long blue and white robes. Olly stared up into the fiendish grin of a demon mask.

Ethan Cain had them trapped.

Chapter Sixteen:
The Keepers of the
Great Secret

Ethan stepped forward and stretched out his hand. "I'll take that, thank you, Olivia," he said.

Olly and Josh shrank together in the narrow street. Only a short distance away, they could see the bright lights and hear the joyful music of the continuing festival, but with Ethan in front of them and Lau's men behind, there was no escape.

Olly realized that she still had the talisman in her hand, the white moonstone glowing between her fingers. "No!" she shouted breathlessly. "You can't have it!"

The American grabbed Olly's arm. She twisted in his grip, struggling to break free. And then her feet slipped on the wet ground, she lost her balance, and the talisman flew from her fingers.

It arced through the fine rain, shining like a miniature moon. Olly watched in silent dismay as a figure stepped around the corner of the narrow street and instinctively caught the object that came hurtling toward him. The moonstone landed squarely in his palm and he closed his fingers around it. Olly looked up at the newcomer's face, and her eyes widened in surprise. It was her father!

Professor Christie stared in complete astonishment at the moonstone disc that had fallen into his hand. And Olly tore herself loose from Ethan Cain and ran to him. "It's the talisman," she shouted joyously. "It's the Mooncake of Chang-O! We found it. Josh and I found it!"

More men appeared from around the corner. One was Dr. Feng, but there were other Chinese men with them that Olly and Josh had never seen before.

"Good heavens, Olivia, what do you mean?" the professor asked in bewilderment.

"Look at it, Dad!" Olly told him.

The Professor peered at the moonstone and his face lit up with surprise and delight. "I think it is," he gasped. "Olivia, where on earth did you find this?"

"We were searching the canal," Josh put in hurriedly.

The professor stared at him. "The canal? You mean the old waterway?" He gazed at the talisman, then at Olly and Josh. "Oh my," he said again, clearly at a loss for words.

Dr. Feng and the other men crowded around to look at the talisman. And Ethan Cain took off his mask and stepped forward, his face stretched into a side smile. "Professor Christie," he said. "So nice to see you again — and at such a moment!"

Olly caught a fleeting glimpse of suppressed anger and greed in Ethan's eyes — but a second later it was gone, hidden behind the phony grin.

Looking a little dazed, Professor Christie shook the American's outstretched hand. "Ethan!" he exclaimed. "What brings you here?"

"I have a confession to make, Professor," Cain said. "I'm the man co-funding the excavation of the ruins. As soon as I heard about the accident, I dropped everything to come and visit Professor Andryanova in the hospital, and to see how things were going." He smiled. "I never hoped to arrive on the very day that the Mooncake of Chang-O was discovered!"

Josh and Olly exchanged glances. They knew better than to try and reveal Ethan's real motives for turning up. He would talk his way out of any accusations, and everyone would think they were being foolish, suspicious, and immature. That's what had happened on their last expedition, and, until Ethan Cain was caught red-handed, it would probably happen again and again.

"Where's Jonathan, Professor?" Josh asked.

Professor Christie had pulled a magnifying glass from his pocket and was minutely examining the moonstone. He was so absorbed by the talisman that Josh asked twice without getting a response.

"Your brother went back to camp to check that everything was all right," Dr. Feng eventually told him. "The rain was so heavy we thought the camp might be in danger of flooding. Mrs. Beckmann went with him." His eyebrows rose as he smiled at Josh and Olly. "I believe she intended to reduce your punishment and allow you to come for the end of the Moon Festival. She will be worried that you are not at your cabin. Maybe I should call her and let her know that you are safe and sound."

"Oh." Olly's face reddened. "Yes, would you, please? And don't forget to tell her about the talisman."

Dr. Feng stepped to one side and took out his cell phone.

Olly looked at Josh. "Gran will forgive us when she hears that we found the Mooncake of Chang-O," she whispered. "Won't she?"

Josh nodded, smiling. "You mean she'll probably only ground us for a year."

"Something like that."

Ethan had moved across to speak with the Chinese men who accompanied Olly's father. One of the men was interpreting, and from what Olly could make out, they were officials from Chengdu who had come to confer with her father and to check on the dig in the wake of the accident.

Olly listened in disgust as the American smooth-talked the Chinese officials. "That guy is such a creep," she muttered to Josh. "If only they knew the truth about him!"

"I don't want to talk about it," Josh growled. Olly looked at him sympathetically. She knew that he had more reason than she did to loathe the charming California billionaire. Josh glowered at Ethan. "It's not just that he's underhanded and greedy. I mean, it's obvious that he doesn't think twice about lying to my mom," he murmured under his breath.

Their subdued conversation was interrupted by the sudden arrival of Jonathan. He was out of breath and anxious. "It's not good back at the camp, Professor," he said. "The river is already rising." Then he caught sight of the moonstone talisman in

Professor Christie's hands. "Is that what I think it is . . . ?" he gasped.

Josh ran up to him. "It's the Mooncake of Chang-O!" he said proudly. "Olly and I found it."

Jonathan looked hard at the two friends. "You should call your grandma, Olly. Right now. She's frantic with worry."

"Dr. Feng is calling," Olly muttered sheepishly. "I'll make it up to her."

Jonathan turned back to gaze at the Mooncake. "Where did you find it? *How* did you find it?"

"We followed the course of the canal," Josh explained. "And there it was! It was just luck, really."

Olly noticed that Josh was carefully avoiding telling any direct lies. "The place where we found it is probably underwater by now," she added. She glanced at Josh. "It was dark and we couldn't really see where we were. I don't think we'd be able to find the same place again."

Josh nodded his agreement.

Dr. Feng joined them. "I have spoken with Mrs. Beckmann," he reported. "She says she is glad that you are both safe and sound, but she has a few words to say to you about your midnight wanderings!"

"Did she sound angry?" Olly asked.

Dr. Feng shook his head. "She was more concerned with supervising the evacuation of the camp. But she said you are not to leave Professor Christie's side under any circumstances."

"That's fine by us," Josh said with a grin.

The professor held the talisman up between his fingers. "It's a wonderful piece of craftsmanship," he said. "I believe there are pictograms among the engraved pictures. We must get them translated as soon as possible." Then his face clouded and he looked at Dr. Feng. "Did you say the camp was being evacuated?"

"That's right," Jonathan confirmed. "The river is already rising. The water was only a few feet or so from the lower huts when I left. Audrey stayed behind with some of the team to start moving things to higher ground. I think we'll have time to rescue everything, but the ruins are already suffering. The lower pits are full of water, and if the river keeps rising at its current rate, I'm afraid the whole site will be underwater by morning."

"The farmers must be happy, though," Olly pointed out, seeing the disappointment on her father's face. "And we *have* found another Talisman of the Moon."

The professor nodded. "Yes, you're quite right,

Olivia. We can't be selfish; the rain is a real blessing. And we can thank our lucky stars that we have the talisman — and a great many other priceless artifacts."

Olly could feel Ethan's eyes on her. She turned and smiled at him. "It's great, isn't it, Mr. Cain?" she said innocently. "I bet you're delighted that my father has the talisman."

He smiled suavely back at her. "You know exactly how delighted I am, Olly."

Olly looked him squarely in the eyes. "Yes," she said. "I do."

~~~~~

Usually the Festival of the Moon in Chung-hsien began to wind down at midnight, but not tonight. The people from the town, the local villages, and the farms were far too excited to let the celebrations stop. After months of drought and uncertainty, the rain had come. The mighty Minjiang would soon flow at full strength again and all would be well.

Olly's dad had given the friends permission to wander the streets with Ang-lun, watching the dancers and musicians, and buying sweet moon-cakes to munch as they walked happily among the noisy crowd.

It was well past midnight when Ang-lun took them to see his grandmother again. The elderly lady was sitting on a low stool near a trio of musicians who played a lilting theme on traditional Chinese instruments. Ang-lun told the friends the names of the strange instruments: the *ruan*, a moon-shaped four-string lute; the *zhong-hu*, a long-necked, two-stringed violin; and the *di-tsu*, a bamboo flute.

The rippling music formed a gentle backdrop to their conversation with Ang-lun's grandmother. The old lady seemed delighted to see Olly and Josh, taking their hands and smiling and nodding at them as she drew them down to sit with her. She poured them some green tea, still chatting away in Mandarin.

Ang-lun listened and translated. At first, his grandma only seemed to be speaking about the miracle of the rain, but then Ang-lun looked at Olly and Josh curiously, and Olly thought she caught the word "Shan-ren" in the tumble of incomprehensible Mandarin.

"What did she say?" Josh asked.

"I don't really understand what she means," Ang-lun replied slowly. "She wants me to thank you for keeping the secret." He shook his head. "I don't know what she means — and she won't explain — but she says that you are now the Keepers of the Great Secret. She says you have done a good thing."

Olly looked into the woman's wise face and saw a brightness and a knowingness in her eyes. "*Xiexie*," Olly said in her faltering Mandarin. "*Xiexie*." *Thank you. Thank you.*

The old lady smiled and took Olly's hand, speaking softly as she leaned over the upturned palm.

"My grandmother wishes to tell your fortune," Ang-lun explained.

"Am I going to be rich and famous?" Olly asked curiously.

The old lady spoke rapidly.

"My grandmother says you will have an exciting life," Ang-lun told Olly. "But she says that you must beware of a dangerous enemy. She also says you will have many adventures and that a good friend will always be with you."

Olly looked at Josh. "That'll be you," she said with a grin. She turned again to Ang-lun. "Could you ask her whether we'll find any more Talismans of the Moon?"

A few moments later, Ang-lun translated his grandmother's reply. "She says that very soon you will travel over wide oceans and tall mountains to an ancient city in a faraway land."

"Wow!" Olly said. "That sounds great! And will we find the next talisman there?"

The old lady laughed as Ang-lun translated Olly's question.

Ang-lun smiled. "She says that only the gods can answer that question."

Their conversation was brought to a sudden halt by the screech and roar of fireworks. A hundred rockets had been sent soaring into the night sky, where they exploded into shining flowers of sparkling silver light. Everyone watched, mesmerized, as glittering white fire rained down over the rooftops in a spectacular finale to the Festival of the Autumn Moon.

The fireworks marked the perfect end to their mission, Olly thought. The Mooncake of Chang-O had been found, the rain had come at last, and — if Ang-lun's grandmother was right — it sounded like it wouldn't be long before they were off on a quest for the next Talisman of the Moon.

Olly sighed happily as she gazed up into the glittering sky. She couldn't wait!

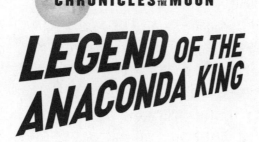

CHRONICLES OF THE MOON

LEGEND OF THE ANACONDA KING

PROLOGUE
The Amulet of Quilla

In 1538, the Spanish Conquistador Don Hernando Pizarro led an expeditionary force into the Inca heartlands to the south of Lake Titicaca. There he found vast wealth in silver and in gold, which he gathered and sent back across the Atlantic Ocean in great galley ships to the King of Spain. He learned from the native people that riches beyond the dreams of man were held in the sacred temples on the Island of the Sun and the Island of the Moon that lay in Lake Titicaca. Don Pizarro visited the islands, and his people claimed much treasure from them, but the greatest prize of all eluded him: the Amulet of Quilla, who was the Incan goddess of the moon.

Fearing that the amulet would be lost forever to the invading Spaniards, Coyata, the loyal handmaiden of Quilla, had secretly fled the island by night. She took the precious amulet to a hidden location in the rain forests of the Incan lands. For long, weary years the Spaniards searched for the amulet, but it was never found. . . .

Chapter One: Incan Adventure

Olivia Christie looked up from the notebook she had been reading. Her father, an eminent professor of archaeology, had copied the history of the highly prized Amulet of Quilla from sixteenth-century documents he had discovered in the Spanish National Archaeological Museum in Madrid. In a few short days, he and his team would be in South America, taking up the ancient search for the sacred amulet of the Incan moon goddess.

And she would be with him. She could hardly wait.

~~~~~

Olly swam slowly downward through the transparent waters of the vast lake, gazing out through her scuba mask in fascination and delight. Air was coming steadily to her through the oxygen regulator, but still her heart was pounding. She was taking her first open-water scuba dive after weeks of training back home in England, and it was very exciting.

At last she was putting all her practice and hard work into action.

She lifted her head. Above her she could see the waiting boat — a dark leaf shape on the surface of the lake, its outlines wavering in the endless, glittering, sunlit motion of the water. She looked down again into the depths — below her the water grew darker where the sunlight could not penetrate, and the lake floor was green and mysterious.

She was diving at a gentle slant, her body sheathed in an orange wet suit, broad fins strapped to her feet to help propel her through the water. Up above, the air was hot and dry, but underwater Olly felt pleasantly cool. She was hardly aware now of the weight of the oxygen tank strapped to her back. Her equipment had been thoroughly checked before the dive, and she felt perfectly safe — especially since she had two experienced divers along with her. She turned her head and saw her friend Josh Welles in his yellow wet suit, streams of bright bubbles rising up from his head, his legs working smoothly as he descended.

"Olly?" The voice was an electronic crackle in her ear. "How are you doing?"

She turned her head the other way, to look at Josh's twenty-two-year-old brother, Jonathan. He was the team leader; he had been scuba diving all over the world. Twelve-year-old Josh had been diving for a couple of years, but Olly — two months older than Josh — had only learned to dive earlier that summer.

Olly gave the universal OK signal with her hand — finger and thumb together to form an *O*.

Shafts of shining blue light pierced the water, making her slow, careful dive down to the bottom of the lake seem like a magical journey through some mysterious other world.

She heard Josh's voice. "This is better than a swimming pool in Oxford, isn't it?" he said.

"It's fabulous," Olly agreed.

A couple of months ago, when the trip to the high Andes Mountains and a dive into Lake Titicaca had first been mentioned, Olly had not been very excited. She wasn't a great swimmer, and she had some uncomfortable memories of being underwater. When her father, Professor Kenneth Christie, had led an archaeological expedition to China earlier that summer, Olly had gone with him. But she had struggled trying to swim in an underground channel. There were no air pockets, and the distance had proven too long for Olly. If it hadn't been for Josh coming to her rescue, she might have drowned.

But Josh had encouraged her to learn to dive. "You can do it," he had told her. "In fact, you've *got* to do it, Olly. There might be ruined buildings under Lake Titicaca — ruins that are thousands and thousands of years old." Josh had looked at her solemnly. "You don't want to miss something as amazing as that, do you?"

Olly didn't, and so she had decided that she *would* learn to scuba dive. She was determined to see for herself whether there really were ancient ruins deep beneath the surface of the lake.

And now, just a few weeks and several intense scuba lessons later, she was diving confidently into unknown waters in Bolivia, and beginning another adventure in the ongoing quest to find all the fabled Talismans of the Moon.

Long, long ago, so the legend went, in different civilizations spread throughout the world, the priests and priestesses of the moon gods had called for the beautiful Talismans of the Moon to be made. Fashioned by expert craftsmen out of precious metals and priceless jewels, these talismans were said to hold an ancient and marvelous secret — a secret that would only be revealed when they were all brought together in the correct place.

Olly's father had discovered references to the legendary talismans in his studies of archaic writings. Gradually, he had begun to believe that the talismans were not simply the stuff of legends, but real artifacts that actually existed.

Since then, with his brilliant assistant Jonathan, Professor Christie had focused on discovering the talismans and unlocking their secret. Already, two had been found: one in the Valley of the Kings in Egypt, the other in the remote heartlands of China. Professor Christie now believed that clues which would lead him to a third Talisman of the Moon — the Amulet of Quilla — would be found amidst the ruins of Tiahuanaco. Jonathan had told Olly and Josh how to pronounce the city's name by breaking it down into syllables: "Tee-a-wah-na-co." This ancient city had originally been built on the shores of Lake Titicaca, but it was now stranded ten miles inland due to the gradual shrinking of the lake.

But there was an intriguing additional element to this expedition that Olly was excited to investigate and that had prompted her to learn to dive. Some archaeologists believed that there was a ruined city beneath the waters of Lake Titicaca — evidence of a society so old that, if real, its existence would completely change everything scientists believed about the origins of human civilization on Earth.

Olly knew that her father was skeptical about these extraordinary claims. As a scientist, he would require proof before he accepted that vast cities had existed in the world twenty thousand years earlier than anyone had previously thought. But Jonathan was fascinated by the theory.

"Olly! Josh! Can you see that dark ridge over to your left?" Jonathan's voice crackled in Olly's ear again, interrupting her thoughts. She turned her head. Jonathan was pointing toward the lake bottom. She swam toward him and peered down where he was indicating.

At first, all she could see was a formless mass of dark green in the water. Small, silver fish, striped with black, moved in swift shoals below her, skittering out of the way as she, Josh, and Jonathan slowly approached.

As Olly drew closer, she saw that beneath the thick vegetation and algae that covered the bottom of the lake, there appeared to be some solid shapes. Her eyes widened with astonishment as she realized she was looking at a great wall-like structure that stretched out across the lake bed.

"Wow!" she heard Josh exclaim in her ear. "Look at that!"

"I'm looking," Olly replied. But she could hardly believe her eyes. Being told by Jonathan that there might be a ruined city under the lake was one thing. Actually seeing signs of it in front of her eyes was something else.

As they swam together, only a few feet above the lake floor, more and more huge shapes began to emerge from the green gloom, half-covered in deep silt and dense vegetation.

Olly saw Jonathan unclip his camera from his belt and begin to take pictures.

"It is a city, isn't it?" Olly asked.

"It looks like one to me," Josh replied.

Olly heard Jonathan's voice. "Or it could be natural rock formations that look like ruined buildings," he said. "I really can't tell one way or the other at the moment."

"What do you mean?" Olly demanded. She pointed to where a sunken cleft stretched off into deeper waters like a long, straight road. "That has to be man-made!"

"But if this is a city," came the crackle of Josh's voice in her ear, "then it must have been built before there was ever a lake here. And the lake has been here since before the last ice age. That's thousands of years."

"And from what we know of human evolution," Jonathan's voice came in, "at that time our ancestors were wearing animal skins and living in caves, not building cities."

Pondering this information, Olly struck out strongly with her legs, gliding down between two green walls to follow the gulley. The bottom was flat between high sides.

"This has to be a road," she murmured. "What else could it possibly be?"

"I don't know," Jonathan's voice replied sharply in her ear. "But don't go too far. This is your first dive — I don't want you getting into trouble."

"I'll be fine," Olly replied. "I just want to see where this goes."

"By the look of it, it goes into much deeper water, Olly," Jonathan said. "Too deep for us."

"What we need is a bathyscaphe," Josh remarked. "One of those small submarine things that can go into really deep water. Then we could go right down to the very bottom. Olly — did you know that the lake is nearly nine hundred feet deep in some places?"

"No, I didn't," Olly said abstractedly, "I leave all that kind of stuff to you." She laughed. Her friend had a natural ability for collecting useless facts. She peered down the algae-covered valley along which she was swimming. The water was filled with bits of vegetation that drifted around her, making the water slightly murky.

"What do you mean by 'that kind of stuff'?" Josh questioned indignantly. "It's good to know something about the places we explore."

Olly looked up and around. She couldn't see Jonathan or Josh now. The high sides of the gulley enclosed her like a tunnel. If it wasn't for Josh's friendly voice in her ear, she would have found the experience rather eerie and disquieting. She could almost imagine that ancient eyes were peering out at her from among the rippling weeds.

She was certain the trench had been man-made. It seemed obvious to her that it was an ancient road. She pictured the people of a lost, drowned civilization, moving up and down this road thousands upon thousands of years ago, under a clear blue sky. She wondered how they had been able to build a city at a time when other humans were still learning how to make the simplest of stone tools.

"Did you know, for instance," came Josh's

voice again, "that the name *Titicaca* means 'rock of the puma'?"

"No, I didn't," Olly said, suddenly interested. "I like pumas. I like all big cats — but I think I like pumas best. Do they live around here?"

"What? In the lake?" Josh asked, sounding amused.

"No, in the Altiplano," Olly said, using the name given to this isolated region high in the Andes. "Oh!" she gasped suddenly. "What's that?" She had glimpsed a dark outline in the algae below her.

"What's what?" Josh asked.

"Just a second, I'm not sure," Olly replied. She swam downward until she was skimming the tall green fronds.

"Where are you, Olly?" came Jonathan's urgent voice. "You know you're supposed to stay within sight of me."

"I'm fine," Olly said. "I'm just following the road."

"Well, come out of there so I can see you," Jonathan ordered. "Don't start getting adventurous; you could wind up in trouble."

"OK," Olly promised. "Just a minute."

The tall waterweeds swayed around her as she cut through them. She had almost reached the dark object now.

She gave a gasp of shock, and bit back a scream as the weeds parted to reveal eyes! Something was watching her through the quivering weeds. She hesitated, and an undercurrent drew the curtain of green farther aside so that, for a fleeting moment, Olly clearly saw the face that stared at her.

It was the exquisitely carved face of a cat.

Chapter Two: ∿
The Island of the Moon

Olly broke the surface and swam toward the waiting boat, the curious artifact with the cat's face on it tucked into her belt. A hand reached down and helped her climb the short ladder into the vessel. The boat belonged to a local man named Carlos. He smiled down at her as she clambered awkwardly out of the lake. He had the dark skin, broad cheekbones, and jet black hair of the native Aymara Indians.

Olly unstrapped the heavy oxygen tank and Carlos slipped it off her back. Then Olly collapsed in the stern of the boat, catching her breath. "Look what I found!" she said after a moment, holding the artifact out to Carlos.

It was about the size of her hand, thin, curved, and carved into the shape of a cat's face with wide, staring eyes. It was green-tinged and felt a little slimy from being so long under the waters of the lake.

"It is a puma," Carlos said.

Olly's eyes widened. "Really?" she breathed,

surprised that she and Josh had been talking about pumas only seconds before she found the thing.

A splashing sound drew Carlos to the edge of the boat, and a few moments later Josh climbed aboard, followed closely by Jonathan.

"What have you got there?" Jonathan asked.

"It's a puma," Olly told him proudly.

Jonathan sat down beside her. "So it is," he said, gently lifting it out of her hands. He turned it over. "Very nice."

Olly frowned. "Is that all you can say?" she responded. "I bring up a priceless archaeological find from the bottom of the lake and all you can say is '*very nice*'?"

Jonathan laughed. "I'm sorry, Olly," he said. "But lots of these things have been found. It's made of pottery and was probably part of a chalice of worship or an incense burner."

"How old is it?" Josh asked, peering over his brother's shoulder.

"It looks like it predates the Incas," Jonathan said. "It could be anything from eight hundred to fifteen hundred years old — maybe even older. It's a lovely find, Olly — but it's not all that unusual."

"Does that mean that I can keep it?" Olly asked eagerly.

"Sorry," Jonathan said. "It'll have to go to a museum. But I don't see why we can't ask them to include a little display card with 'Found by Olivia Christie' on it."

Olly liked the sound of that.

Jonathan looked from Olly to Josh. "So, are you two worn out yet, or would you like to see the ruins now?"

"I'm not worn out at all," Olly said. "Let's go!"

Jonathan warned them that with the thin air at this high altitude, they would tire more quickly. Olly had felt a little breathless at times, but she was determined not to let it stop her — especially when there was something interesting to explore.

Lake Titicaca lay in a lofty valley of the Altiplano — the Bolivian high plane — which rose almost twelve thousand feet above sea level. All around the plateau, snowcapped mountains soared to over seventeen thousand feet. Up here the air was clear and thin, and all activity was an effort.

Jonathan asked Carlos to take them to the Island of the Moon. As the motorboat sped along, Olly and Josh struggled out of their wet suits. By the time the boat reached the island, they were all toweled down and changed into T-shirts and shorts.

The group waved to Carlos, then jumped into

the shallow, crystal clear water and waded up onto dry land. The island reared sharply out of the lake and required a steep climb to get up off the beach. The sun-bleached rocks were broken up by patches of pale, wiry grass and scrubby bushes.

Olly would never have admitted it, but she found the climb difficult — the thin air was catching up with her, and the midday sun beat down on them relentlessly. But at last, they stood on the highest point of the island. Olly ran an arm across her sweating forehead, and paused to get her breath back. It was some comfort to her to see that Jonathan and Josh were also panting.

Behind them, she could see the mainland stretching away into the distance, some twenty miles from the island. In the other direction, she could see the long, dark ridge of the much larger Island of the Sun, and beyond that — gray-blue in the haze — the farther shores of Lake Titicaca.

Once they had recovered, Jonathan led the way along the high back of the island and down a rough slope. He pointed. "Welcome to Inak Uyu," he said. On a broad, terraced plateau, halfway down the slope, Olly saw the remains of thick stone walls jutting from the surrounding undergrowth.

"These are the remains of an Incan Moon

Temple," Jonathan explained, as they made their way down to the plateau. "It dates back about eight hundred years — but it was built on an already-existing site. Recent findings have proved that people have lived on this island for at least four thousand years."

"I read that, too," Josh added. "The pre-Inca people are known as the *Tiwanaku*. And before them were the Pucara people, and before that —"

"Did you know that the Moon Temple was staffed entirely by women?" Olly interrupted, eyeing Josh with amusement. Sometimes he acted like he was the only one who knew anything! "They were called the *Mamacona* — the Chosen Women. Men weren't allowed here at all, except to make sacrifices to the moon goddess, Quilla."

Josh grinned. "You've been doing some research," he said.

"I have," she responded. "You're not the only one who can read."

Jonathan laughed at their lighthearted rivalry. "Come on," he said, "let's explore."

Olly hadn't realized just how massive the ancient stone walls were until she was in among them. The perfectly shaped blocks of masonry reared high above her head.

The main part of the temple consisted of three long, broken walls around what had once been a large courtyard. The walls were punctuated by several curious doorways that seemed to lead nowhere.

"What are these for?" Olly asked, standing under one of the great square entrances. It was as if, for some reason, the ancient architects had set four doorways inside one another, each one a little smaller than the one before it. The final, smallest doorway was blocked by a flat wall of stones.

"They're called niches," Jonathan explained. "We haven't really worked out their role in Incan rituals, but we've seen them in several different locations. We think they may have been special places where the high priestess sat during important ceremonies."

They walked through the ruins while Jonathan explained how, for millennia, pilgrims would have come from all over the region to worship at the Temple of the Moon and the Temple of the Sun, and make sacrifices to their gods.

"Sometimes it was something as simple as a handful of corn offered up to please the sun god," Josh told them. "Or woven clothes might be burned in a sacrificial fire. But sometimes animals were killed. It was very important to keep the gods happy."

They spent an hour or so in the ruins before heading back to Carlos and the boat. They set off under a clear, blue sky. Olly leaned over the side, letting the sun-dappled water run through her fingers as they headed for the mainland.

"Carlos?" she called. "Can't you go a bit faster?"

Carlos grinned at her. "Sí, señorita, I go very fast for you."

He was true to his word. The boat took a leap forward, cleaving the water as it scudded across the lake, leaving a broad white wake of foam behind them.

Olly let out a yell of delight, her long dark hair floating in the wind, the air whipping past her face and ripping at her clothes. "That's more like it!"

Josh was grinning, too, as the wind caught his shaggy blond hair and dragged it across his face. "Go for it, Carlos!" he called. "As fast as you can!"

"No, no," Jonathan groaned. "No faster, please."

Olly looked at him. He was clinging grimly to the back of the boat, and looking rather green.

"But this is fun!" she shouted above the high-pitched roar of the motor. The boat clipped a wave, rising and falling as the spray splashed Olly's face. "Whooo!" she gasped, hanging on tight. "See what I mean?"

Jonathan seemed to go a slightly deeper shade of green.

"Some people just don't know how to enjoy themselves!" Olly yelled heartlessly as the small motorboat sped across the brilliant blue waters under the blazing afternoon sun.

∿∿∿

Olly had been accompanying her father on his continent-hopping archaeological adventures ever since her mother had died in an airplane crash in New Guinea two years ago. On these trips, Olly's grandmother, Audrey Beckmann, kept an eye on Olly and her father, making sure they ate properly and had clean clothes to wear. She was an intelligent and determined woman — and a qualified teacher — who acted as tutor for both Olly and Josh.

Jonathan and Josh's mother, Natasha Welles, was an internationally famous movie star. She was always having to travel to different locations for filming, so Mrs. Beckmann had suggested that Josh accompany his brother and the Christies on their expeditions. Josh and Olly were best friends, so the arrangement worked very well.

Olly loved this exciting, freewheeling life, although, in her opinion, her grandma was a little too insistent on keeping up the schoolwork, while she and Josh would much rather spend time exploring. Even the fact that the two friends had been directly involved in finding the first two Talismans of the Moon didn't hold any sway with Audrey Beckmann, and all Olly's persuasiveness was wasted once her grandmother had made up her mind. Olly and Josh loaded their scuba gear into their Land Rover, and then Jonathan drove them the fifteen miles to the small town where they were staying. As they sped along the arid dirt road, the starkly beautiful landscape of the Andes spread out around them, — the sunburned rock and rough pastureland were dotted with grazing llamas and alpacas. Far away, they could see snowcapped mountain peaks. Even in the high-noon sun the view of the icy High Sierras gave Olly a chill.

They were staying in a beautiful house owned by a friend of Josh's mother, a retired actress named Jazmine Romero. It had white, adobe walls and a roof of curved terra-cotta tiles. Josh and Olly had adjoining second-floor rooms, with a shared balcony from which they could look out over the picturesque buildings of the town and watch the comings and goings of the local Aymara Indians.

The group arrived at the house to find Olly's father already there. While they had been scuba diving in Lake Titicaca, Professor Christie had set off to explore the ruins of the ancient ceremonial site of Tiahuanaco.

Usually, the professor's expeditions included field archaeologists, experts, and local diggers, but this trip was on a much smaller scale. He had to be back in England in two weeks to attend an important international seminar. There simply wasn't time for a full excavation — but his recent research in Madrid had convinced him that even a brief trip to Bolivia might yield some useful clues as to the whereabouts of the long-lost Amulet of Quilla.

The professor and Olly's grandmother were sitting at a table under the wide veranda of the house, drinking fresh juice from tall, chilled glasses. Mrs. Beckmann was reading a newspaper, elegantly dressed as always in a cream silk blouse and khaki linen trousers. Olly's father sat opposite her, his gray hair a wild thatch, his clothes rumpled and dusty. He was totally absorbed in the papers he was reading.

Typical Dad! Olly thought fondly. Completely lost in his own academic world, the professor was unaware of his unkempt appearance.

Mrs. Beckmann looked up. "Did you enjoy your swim?" she asked.

"We had a great time," Olly replied. "I found this." She placed the pottery puma face delicately into her grandma's hands. "It's going to be displayed in a museum. There'll be a note next to it with my name on it."

"Well, that's lovely," her grandmother said with a smile. "It's a cat!"

"It's a puma, actually," Olly said, throwing herself down in a chair and reaching for the jug of juice that stood on the table with a couple of empty glasses. "How about you, Dad? Find anything amazing?"

There was no response from her father.

"Earth to Dad!" Olly called in a much louder voice. "Come in, Dad!"

Professor Christie peered absentmindedly at her through his half-moon spectacles. "Oh, hello there," he said vaguely.

Now that she had his attention, Olly asked her question again.

Her father frowned. "It's been good and bad," he told her.

Jonathan and Josh joined them at the table. The

ice clinked as Olly poured them each a tall glass of juice.

The professor glanced at Jonathan. "I was able to see the Puma Punku Stone — the engraved slab that Pizarro mentioned in his letters to the King of Spain."

"That's great news!" Jonathan exclaimed, leaning forward excitedly. "And did the markings match what Pizarro had claimed?"

"Yes," the professor confirmed. "The designs engraved on the stone do seem to be a coded depiction of the handmaiden Coyata's journey from the Temple of the Moon as she escaped with the Amulet of Quilla. But as Pizarro said in his letters — the stone is incomplete." He frowned. "I spoke with the curator of the site, and he told me that over the years a great many people have searched the area for the missing part of the Puma Punku Stone."

Olly looked at him. "So, what do we know so far about the Amulet of Quilla?" she asked, sitting back and stretching out her legs.

"We know that Coyata took it from the temple on the Island of the Moon to keep it out of the hands of the Spanish Conquistadors," her father began. "She first took it to Tiahuanaco, but Coyata knew it wouldn't be safe there for very long. So she waited in hiding for a moonless night, and then she journeyed to a forested area by a great river." The frustration showed in his voice. "But we have no idea in which direction she traveled to reach this forested area, or how far she journeyed."

Olly frowned. "A river that runs through a forest, huh?" she said. "Well, it's a start."

Jonathan shook his head. "Bolivia is a big country, Olly, and it's full of rivers," he told her. "Most of them pass through rain forests at some stage. You could search for a lifetime and not even come close to finding the place where the amulet was taken."

"Then the answer's pretty obvious," Olly said firmly. "We have to find the missing piece of the stone so we can read the rest of Coyata's story." She nodded thoughtfully, and fixed her father with a stern gaze. "You'll need some sharp-eyed people on this mission," she said. "Here's an idea: Josh and I will go with you to Tiahuanaco in the morning, and we won't give up looking till we find it!" She lifted her eyebrows. "What do you say?"

"It's a tempting offer, Olly," her father said with a smile. "But I don't think it's going to be lying around anywhere obvious. Pizarro's men realized the significance of the Puma Punku Stone — and they searched very thoroughly for the missing piece. My worry is that the stone didn't originate in the city of Tiahuanaco at all, but was brought there at some later date. The missing section could have been left behind or lost on the journey."

"You could be wrong," Olly pointed out hopefully.

"Yes, I could," her father admitted. "Which is why I've invited a local expert to come and examine the site with me." He turned to Jonathan. "Doctor Vargas is coming up from La Paz tomorrow morning. I'm hoping he will be able to shed some light on the problem."

"Then you two will definitely be staying with me," Mrs. Beckmann put in, eyeing Olly and Josh. "The last thing your father will need is the two of you racing around getting in everyone's way. Besides, you have lessons in the morning — you know that."

"But we could help," Olly urged. "Studying can wait, just this once, can't they?"

Mrs. Beckmann arched an eyebrow. "If I had a dollar for every time you've said that, Olivia, I'd be a rich woman," she said. Olly opened her mouth to speak again, but her grandma lifted a silencing hand. "Besides," she went on. "I have something rather interesting planned for the two of you tomorrow."

"Oh, OK," Olly replied. That didn't sound so bad.

"What is it?" Josh asked.

"We're going to the market," Mrs. Beckmann told him, "where you're going to get a chance to watch the local weavers at work. I'm told it's quite fascinating."

Olly and Josh looked at each other in disbelief. Olly had very serious doubts about how fascinating weaving could be.

Chapter Three:
Legends and Looms

"Do you know what's really exciting about weaving?" Olly asked Josh the following morning as the two friends sat on the veranda steps, waiting for her grandma.

Josh looked at her in surprise. "No, what?"

"Absolutely nothing!" Olly declared.

Josh laughed. "It won't be that bad," he said. He was happy that today's lessons involved a trip outside. It could have been worse: It was a gloriously sunny morning and they might otherwise have been stuck indoors struggling with math or geography.

Josh and Olly were both wearing hats to shield them from the fierce sun. The air quickly heated up once the sun climbed above the mountain peaks, but at night, under a clear sky shining with frosty stars, temperatures plummeted dramatically. The Altiplano was a place of extremes, where you could sunbathe at noon and freeze to death overnight.

Jazmine's house stood on high ground overlooking the town. Directly below, simple, rustic buildings jostled for space, while farther down the hill the buildings were larger and more ornate. Josh could see that the broad marketplace in the middle of the town was already filling with people.

"Is everyone ready?" Audrey Beckmann asked, arriving on the veranda.

Josh and Olly got up and followed her down into the town. The place was full of activity, and they were quickly caught up in the hustle and bustle of the crowd.

The local Aymara women wore bulky, brightly colored skirts and woolen shawls. The men were dressed in colorful ponchos and wore close-fitting, pointed, woolen caps. Olly and Josh noticed that some of the women carried babies in woven slings across their backs.

The broad marketplace was packed with produce. There were a few large stalls, but many of the merchants simply occupied a space on the ground, their wares spread out in heaps on thick straw mats. Josh saw a huge variety of things for sale, from corn on the cob, haba beans, watermelons, and tomatoes to balls of colored yarn, metal pots and pans, and woven fabrics. Children ran in and out of people's legs, laughing and calling to one another. Meanwhile, the delicious smells of soups and stews drifted through the air from outdoor kitchens, making Josh feel hungry even though it hadn't been long since he'd had breakfast.

As he gazed around, Josh noticed a man who seemed, for a moment, to be standing watching them. He wasn't an Indian — he was dressed in a white linen suit that showed off his golden tan, and he had white hair that was swept back from a high forehead. But an instant later, he was lost in the crowd, and Josh was distracted by the calls of the market sellers.

They made their way slowly across the busy market, following Olly's grandma, who threaded a path through the crowds. Josh felt quite relieved when they finally emerged from the riotous marketplace and entered a less hectic area of small workshops and enclosed stalls.

"This way," Mrs. Beckmann said, leading them into an adobe building. The large, open room was piled high with fabrics woven in a seemingly endless variety of colorful patterns. The walls were hung with more lengths of material, a little like flags — although Josh had never seen flags with such amazingly intricate designs on them.

A woman wearing a traditional pollera skirt and a white blouse came to greet them. Josh guessed that she was in her forties, and took an instant liking to her round, smiling face and bright eyes.

"You must be Olly and Josh," the woman said, smiling at the two friends. "I have heard all about you. My name is Fabiola." She looked at Olly's grandma. "Audrey says you wish to learn how to weave?"

Olly opened her mouth to speak, but Josh stopped her just in time with a discreet poke in the ribs. It would be just like Olly to say something embarrassing about what she really thought of weaving.

Fabiola shepherded them across the room. "Come, come, I will show you."

"I'll leave them with you for the time being, Fabiola, if that's all right," said Olly's grandmother. "I have a few things to buy in the market." She turned to Olly and Josh. "I won't be long," she said. "You can tell me all about it when I get back."

"Are you enjoying your visit to our country, Olly?" Fabiola asked.

"It's absolutely wonderful," Olly replied enthusiastically, as she followed Fabiola toward a doorway into a wide courtyard, where rows of women sat on mats on the ground, working at small, horizontal, handheld looms.

"Here we weave mantras," Fabiola explained. "A

416

mantra is one of the most prized possessions of an Aymara family. It is useful as well as decorative. It can be slung across the shoulders and used to carry things."

"I saw that in the market," Josh said. "There were women carrying babies in them."

Fabiola nodded. "Babies or firewood or vegetables — a mantra can be used for everything. They are also spread on the ground and used as mats, and as you can see, they make wonderful wall hangings." She pointed to one of the flag-shaped mantras that hung above the doorway. "Each town has its own designs," she explained. "The patterns are passed down through generations — many go back hundreds and hundreds of years."

Josh gazed up at the mantra over the door. It had a complex inner design of red, black, and yellow symbols, and a border of green and blue squares, many of which contained squat, stylized figures with their arms held in various positions.

"That mantra was woven by my great-grandmother," Fabiola told him. "It is a very ancient design." She looked at the friends, her eyes twinkling. "Would you like to try some weaving yourselves?"

"We'll probably make a mess of it," Olly said.

But Fabiola simply laughed and led them over to a couple of spare looms in one corner of the courtyard. "These are backstrap looms," she told them. "Aymara women have been using them for a thousand years or more."

Josh looked at the simple looms in fascination. Around the courtyard, each woman sat with her legs stretched out in front of her. The far end of the loom's framework was attached, by a cord, to a peg set in the ground about a half yard beyond her bare feet. The other end was held firm by a belt fastened around the woman's waist. There was a steady click and thud as the weavers worked.

Fabiola called an elderly woman over to help, and Olly and Josh were soon strapped into their own looms. Fabiola sat at Josh's side. The other woman, Beatriz, helped Olly.

Both looms already held a half-finished length of cloth. "Mantras are made in two halves," Fabiola explained to Josh. "Each half is woven separately, and then the mantra is stitched together. On the loom, the long threads are called the warp, the crosswise threads are the weft." She leaned across him, her long, brown fingers moving nimbly as she showed him how to weave the threads.

Josh watched carefully, bewildered at first by the speed at which Fabiola was working. But gradually, as the minutes passed, he began to grasp the rhythm and pattern of it. "Could I do a bit of the design you showed us on that mantra above the door?" he asked. "The one with those funny men on it." He liked the little stumpy figures with their arms going in different directions — it kind of reminded him of a football referee, almost as if the different positions might mean something.

Fabiola nodded and watched carefully as Josh made his first clumsy attempt at weaving. It was demanding work, but Fabiola was encouraging and patient, and slowly Josh began to get the hang of it.

He heard Olly laugh. "I'm hopeless at this!" she sighed. "My fingers are all thumbs. How are you doing, Josh?"

Josh didn't look up or reply. He was too busy concentrating on his work.

"He is doing very well," Fabiola said. "He has a real feel for it."

"Really?" Olly said. "Good for him. Weave me a mantra, Josh."

"Sshh!" he hissed at her. "I'm going to lose my place if you keep chattering."

"I'm sorry, Beatriz," Olly said. "I'm obviously not cut out to be a weaver. Is it OK if I just sit and watch Josh?" She shuffled over and sat cross-legged beside her friend.

"Keep quiet, OK?" Josh told her.

"Of course," Olly muttered, sounding slightly miffed.

But it wasn't in Olly's nature to sit in silence for any length of time. "I found a piece of pottery on the bottom of Lake Titicaca when we went scuba diving yesterday," Olly told the two women. "It had a puma's face on it."

"The puma was always a divine animal to the Aymara people," Beatriz remarked wisely, in her cracked old voice. "Many people still believe that eclipses are caused by a sacred puma biting pieces out of the sun and the moon. There are not so many pumas in these parts nowadays because there are so many people. But the pumas live on in legends."

"I'd like to know more about the history of Bolivia," Olly said. "About the Incas and the con-quistadors. The Incas had a really powerful empire at one time, didn't they? But then the conquistadors invaded."

"That was because of the wickedness of Atahualpa," Beatriz said. "He stole the kingship from his brother, Wascar, and imprisoned him. In doing so, Atahualpa brought down a curse upon his family. He had broken the true and sacred line of the Inca kings, and as a punishment, the gods sent the Spanish Conquistadors to destroy the empire and bring five hundred years of darkness to the land."

Josh glanced at Olly, noticing the fascination on her face. She knew all about families and curses — in fact, her own family was supposed to be cursed! It all had to do with a sacred scroll that had been taken from an ancient Egyptian tomb over one hundred years ago. According to the writings on the scroll, unless it was replaced, the first born son in each generation of the Christie family would die a premature death. And the creepy thing was that people *had* died. In fact, a great-uncle of Olly's had been killed in a shipwreck while trying to take the scroll back to Egypt and return it to the tomb.

"The conquistadors arrived here in the sixteenth century," Olly said, interrupting Josh's thoughts, "so I suppose the five hundred years of darkness are almost up."

"That is true," Beatriz agreed, nodding. "It is said that when the Amulet of Quilla is found, the darkness will be lifted."

Josh looked up in surprise, his weaving temporarily forgotten. "We're here to try and find the Amulet of Quilla!" he explained.

"Then may good fortune go with you on your quest," Beatriz declared solemnly.

"I don't suppose you know any legends that say *where* the amulet was hidden, do you?" Olly asked.

Beatriz began to speak in a soft, low voice, her eyes great pools of blackness very deep and dark as she looked from Josh to Olly. Josh's hands fell still and he watched her intently, hardly remembering to breathe as he listened to the strange tale.

"It is said that Quilla's handmaiden, the beautiful and virtuous Coyata, was guided on her journey by a sacred puma," Beatriz intoned. "It was the puma who told her to leave the Temple of the Moon and then Tiahuanaco, and seek refuge in the forest. After several days of traveling, they came to a deep valley with high walls of rock that could not be climbed by man or beast. Their way forward was blocked by a curtain of fire that filled the valley from side to side. Coyata despaired of getting through, and she was about to turn back when the puma walked into the flames and vanished from her sight. Coyata's faith in her guide was so strong that she followed him into the flames and walked — unharmed — to the other side. Beyond the wall of fire, she found the puma waiting for her beside a temple, hidden among the trees. Within its walls, she placed the Amulet of Quilla. And there it has remained, undiscovered, for all these long, dark years."

"Does the legend say exactly where all this took place?" Olly asked, her voice a breathless whisper.

There was a moment of silence. And then the old lady nodded and smiled.

Josh's eyes widened. "You know where Coyata hid the amulet?" he breathed.

"Yes," Beatriz said. "It is in a very secret place."

Josh could hardly believe his ears. Did the old lady really know where the Amulet of Quilla was hidden? Had the answer been part of an old legend all along?

"But *where*?" Olly asked, her voice cracking with excitement.

Beatriz smiled a secretive smile and leaned forward to whisper. "The legend says it is in the Lair of the Anaconda King!"

Chapter Four: Worrying News

"The Lair of the Anaconda King," Olly murmured. To her, it seemed like the whole world held its breath in the few moments following Beatriz's astounding announcement.

Josh stared at the old woman. Wrinkles mapped her face, but her skin shined like polished wood, and her deep black eyes sparkled like distant stars. A profound silence pressed against Josh's ears, making his head ring. Olly, too, was gazing at Beatriz with her mouth open, frozen in amazement.

And then Beatriz laughed and the spell was broken. Reality came rushing back. Josh heard again the clack and rattle of the weaving, and the everyday sounds of the nearby marketplace.

"And where is the Lair of the Anaconda King?" Olly asked.

Beatriz laughed again and shook her head, lifting her hand to shake a finger at Olly. "No, no," she said. "I do not give away the secret." She put a finger to her lips, still shaking her head.

"Beatriz, *please*," Olly begged.

Fabiola's face broke into a wide smile. "She is teasing you, Olly," she said. "No one knows where the Lair of the Anaconda King is." She spread her hands. "It is just a legend. Maybe it does not even exist. You want my opinion? If there ever was such a thing as the Amulet of Quilla, then the conquistadors took it long ago. It's gone forever."

"No," Josh put in. "I don't think that's true. Olly's father has seen letters from Hernando Pizarro to the Spanish king. Pizarro spent years searching for the amulet — but he never found it."

"Or maybe Olly's father has not yet found the letter in which Don Pizarro tells the king that he *did* find it," Fabiola pointed out.

Josh looked at her uneasily — that was a disturbing thought. And it was quite possible, too. If that one vital document was simply missing from the five-hundred-year-old archives, it would change everything. The Amulet of Quilla could have been found and sent back to Spain, then melted down to fill the gold vaults of the insatiable conquistadors. After all, thousands of other Incan artifacts had met a similar fate.

Beatriz frowned at Fabiola and said something to her in the Aymara language.

Fabiola smiled and shrugged. "Beatriz says I have no faith. She says the amulet is still hidden in the forest and that one day it will be found. Maybe she is right."

"I hope she is," Olly said fervently. "Otherwise we might as well pack our bags and go home."

~~~~

It was early evening, and Olly and Josh were setting the table on the veranda of Jazmine's house. They were going to eat dinner outdoors. The sun was just sinking behind the mountains, and cool shadows were spilling across the valley. It was still pleasant under the clear, pale sky, and heaters lined the veranda to ward off the oncoming chill of night. Lanterns, hanging from the roof, gave out a warm yellow glow, and mouthwatering cooking smells drifted from the kitchen where Jazmine's cook was preparing the evening meal.

Olly had discovered — by poking around in the kitchen — that they were going to be eating chicken and rice, accompanied by *oca* and other local vegetables. The cuts of chicken were bubbling gently in a homemade, spicy sauce called *llajhua*, while the cook shredded lettuce for an accompanying salad.

The growl of an approaching car caught the attention of the two friends.

"It's Jonathan and your dad," Josh said, leaning over the veranda and waving as the Land Rover came rumbling up the dirt road. "I hope they've had a good day."

Olly peered down at the vehicle as it came to a halt. She thought that the expressions on the faces of the two men did not look hopeful as they climbed out. They were talking animatedly as they came up the steps to the veranda.

"I'm sorry, Jonathan," the professor was saying. "But those pictures you took of the formations on the lake bottom don't convince me that there was a civilization in these parts twenty thousand years earlier than is currently believed. Analysis of core samples of the soil has proved that the size of the lake is constantly changing. If those lumps and bumps are the remains of a city, then it must have been built when the lake was much smaller than it is today."

"I agree," Jonathan argued. "But it's thought that Lake Titicaca has been shrinking for the last four thousand years. So if they are buildings, when could the city have been built? Surely, it must have been well before the first people were thought to have arrived here."

Professor Christie shook his head. "Not

necessarily," he said. "The earliest finds show human occupation in this area as far back as six thousand years ago. A catastrophic landslip or earthquake could have inundated a shoreline city at any time over that period. I need far more evidence before I'm going to believe that everything we understand about the evolution of human civilization is wrong!"

"But if it's true," Jonathan urged, "then the talismans themselves could be thousands of years older than we currently think they are."

Professor Christie smiled and rested his hand on his excited young assistant's shoulder. "It is possible. And perhaps the truth will come to light when all the talismans are brought together," he said. "In the meantime, let's not get sidetracked by unproven theories."

Olly greeted them at the top of the steps. "Hello, you two," she said. "How did it go?"

"Doctor Vargas wasn't able to help us very much, I'm afraid," her father replied. "He agreed that the Puma Punku Stone tells the legend of Coyata's flight from the Temple of the Moon, but beyond that, he knew no more than we do."

"And I don't suppose you happened to trip over the missing piece of the stone tablet?" Olly asked.

"No such luck," Jonathan said gloomily. He sniffed, his face brightening a little. "That smells good," he added.

"It'll be ready in a few minutes," Olly's grandma told him as she stepped out onto the veranda. "By the time you two have washed the grime off and changed out of those grubby clothes, it'll be on the table."

Olly linked her arm through her father's, looking up into his weary, disheartened face. "Don't worry, Dad," she said optimistically. "The five hundred years of darkness are almost up. You'll find the Lair of the Anaconda King. I know you will."

Her father stared at her. "What are you talking about, Olivia?" he asked.

Olly grinned. "I'll tell you all about it over dinner," she said. "You may have had a boring day, but Josh and I have learned some really interesting stuff." Her eyes shined. "Stuff that just might help us make the legends come true. . . ."

〜〜〜

Later that evening, Josh was in his room, typing out an e-mail on the laptop he had borrowed from his brother. He yawned. It was nearly bedtime, but first he wanted to write to his mother.

From downstairs drifted the sound of Jazmine

playing a guitar and singing a local song, the melody as haunting and beautiful as the Altiplano landscape itself. Through the window, the lights of the town were a friendly glow in the wide darkness. And above the dark mountain peaks a million stars seemed to shine in the sky, shining more brightly than Josh had ever seen before. It was at night that he really got the feeling they were living on the roof of the world — as the Altiplano was sometimes known — and that the stars were almost within reach.

There was a knock on his door, and Olly burst in without waiting for a response. She was in her pajamas.

Josh gave her an inquiring look.

"I just want to borrow that Aymara phrasebook of yours," she said. "I'd like to be able to say a bit more than 'yes,' 'no,' and 'hello' before we leave."

"It's by the bed," Josh told her.

She climbed across his bed and retrieved the book from a small table. "What are you doing?" she asked, sitting down and flicking idly through the pages.

"I'm writing to my mom," Josh told her. "I'm telling her what we've been up to so far." He glanced over his shoulder at Olly. "She likes to be kept up to date."

"And what's *she* doing?" Olly asked. "Is she still hacking her way through the Australian bush with our old friend, Ethan Cain?"

"Yes, as far as I know," Josh replied.

Ethan Cain was his mother's rich, American computer-genius boyfriend. On the surface, he seemed charming and friendly — an open, trustworthy man with a harmless amateur interest in archaeology. But Josh and Olly knew better. Under the pleasant facade, Cain was ruthless and treacherous — and he wanted the Talismans of the Moon for himself. Twice now, the two friends had thwarted Ethan's underhanded attempts to reach the talismans before Professor Christie's team found them. In both cases — in Egypt and in China — it was only Olly and Josh's quick thinking that had stopped Ethan.

But the real problem for the two friends was that no one believed Ethan Cain was a criminal. He had smiled and lied his way out of trouble very smoothly, and they had actually been reprimanded for making accusations against him. It was particularly upsetting for Josh to know that his mother was dating a lying, cheating creep like Cain, but to be unable to prove it.

Olly and Josh had been very relieved when they had learned that Natasha Welles and Ethan Cain were on an adventure holiday on the far side of the world. The last Josh had heard from his mother, she and Cain were camped near Ayers Rock. She had even sent a few digital photographs, showing the two of them standing with their backs to the rock, looking cool and glamorous, like a celebrity couple from a glossy magazine.

"The farther away Ethan Cain is, the better I like it," Olly announced. "Oh — say hi to your mom from me."

Josh added a few final words to his e-mail and then pressed send. He grinned at Olly as the e-mail vanished. "I've told her we're hot on the trail of the amulet," he said. "That should drive Ethan wild!"

∼∼∼∼

As soon as Josh woke up the following morning, he opened up the laptop to check for a reply from his mother.

He sat up in bed with the computer on his knees, yawning as he checked his e-mail. There was one new message. He smiled — it was from his mother. But his smile faded as he read her brief note.

Dearest Jonathan and Josh,
I'm feeling a little disappointed right now — Ethan's just had some bad news from California and he's had to

rush off to catch a plane home! Apparently, there's some big problem at the office that he has got to deal with in person. Typical, isn't it? Still, we only had four days of our vacation left, so it's not a total disaster. I'm going to take the opportunity to spend the rest of my time here sunbathing — you know how much Ethan hates that!

Anyway, that's all for now. I'm off to Alice Springs in the morning. I'll bring you home a didjeridoo if I can fit one in my luggage.

Love to everyone,
Mom

Josh frowned. Only a few hours after he had sent an e-mail telling his mother that they were on the trail of the amulet, Ethan had suddenly had to leave Australia. Josh had a nasty feeling that the two things might be connected.

Grabbing the laptop, he leaped out of bed and raced into Olly's room. "Olly! Wake up!" he said, shaking her violently.

Olly let out a wordless shout and struggled into a sitting position, rubbing her eyes. "What are you doing?" she growled when she noticed who had woken her.

Josh knew that Olly wasn't at her best in the early morning — but the bad news from Australia couldn't wait. He set the computer on her lap. "Read that!" he said.

Olly glared at him for a moment, then turned her head to read Natasha's e-mail.

There was a short pause. Olly's eyes narrowed as she read the e-mail through a second time. She looked at Josh. "I don't like the sound of that," she declared, echoing his own thoughts. "Do *you* think it's true?" she added. "About him having to deal with a work problem?"

"It might be," Josh began dubiously. "But I think it was a mistake to mention the amulet in that e-mail I sent last night."

Olly nodded.

"I think Ethan probably made up that story about work as an excuse to leave Australia," Josh went on darkly. "I reckon he's been waiting to find out how we were getting along — and now he's going to sneak over here and try to find the Amulet of Quilla before we do."

Chapter Five:
The Puma Punku Stone

Following their morning lessons, Olly and Josh were out on the veranda finishing their lunch, when Jonathan came roaring up the dirt road in the Land Rover. He and the professor had driven down to Tiahuanaco after breakfast; they weren't expected back for several hours yet. Jonathan brought the vehicle to a halt and came running up the steps.

Olly stared at him. "What are you doing back so early?" she called.

"I forgot the GPS," he said, disappearing into the house.

Olly knew what he meant. The GPS was a handheld, computerized device that used satellite technology to give pinpoint accuracy when recording the position of anything — from a single rock to a whole city.

She nudged Josh. "This is our chance to see the ruins," she hissed. "We can go back to Tiahuanaco with him."

It was only a couple of minutes before Jonathan reappeared and Olly was able to make her suggestion.

"Why not?" he said, climbing back into the Land Rover. "All aboard."

Olly didn't need telling twice. She quickly gulped the rest of her lunch and ran inside to tell her grandma where they were going. Then she and Josh piled into the Land Rover.

It was a seventy-mile drive to the ancient ruins, traveling a dusty, bumpy road that cut sharply through rolling hills. To their right, when they got a good view, they could see the sparkling blue waters of Lake Titicaca.

"Rats!" Josh said suddenly. "I should have brought my camera." His mother had given him a new digital camera, but he had left it sitting on his bedside table back at Jazmine's house.

"Don't worry about it," Jonathan told him. "We've taken plenty of pictures."

Olly was feeling slightly queasy. Rushing the end of her lunch seemed to have given her indigestion. But it wasn't too bad, and she decided not to mention it to Jonathan. She didn't want him to tease her, the way she had teased him in the motorboat — or worse, insist on taking her home before she'd seen the ruins!

As they approached the outskirts of the Tiahuanaco ruins, Olly fought her indigestion and stared out the window. Huge, shaped slabs of glossy, dark-gray stone lay half-buried in the ground.

"Those stones are basalt," Jonathan said. "Some of them weigh over four hundred thousand pounds. We don't really know why they're here. They could be collapsed buildings, or they might be stones that were abandoned on the way to the city, for some reason. They had to be brought in from the other side of the lake — and that's a pretty amazing feat considering the size and weight of the stones." He looked at his two passengers. "When the Spaniards asked the local Aymaras how the city had been constructed, they said the stones were moved with the help of the gods."

A little farther on, Jonathan parked the Land Rover and they scrambled out eagerly, to enter the enclosed site of the ancient ruins. There were a few tourists wandering about in ones or twos, but most were being herded around in big groups by their guides.

Jonathan pointed to a vast mound of earth.

"That's the Akapana Pyramid," he told them. "There's not much of the original structure left now — most of the stones were taken away and used in the village."

More impressive to Olly's mind were the wide, red stone walls that stretched away to the right of the pyramid. Jonathan explained that they surrounded the Kalasasaya — a ritual platform where important ceremonies took place.

They climbed the broad steps, passing between massive stone towers and under a huge square doorway. The sheer size and weight of the immense structure made Olly feel small and frail. It was easy for her to imagine that this was a city built with the help of the gods.

They came into a wide inner courtyard scattered with fallen stone blocks, from which a second stairway led them to another plateau. A big stone doorway stood imposing and solitary at the end of this platform — but it was an entryway without a purpose, for it seemed to lead from nowhere to nowhere.

Olly walked toward it, curious. It was shaped from a single block of stone that towered above her. The crosspiece at the top of the gateway was covered in intricate carvings, and above that was a stylized human figure, its strange, square face staring out over the land as it must have done for thousands of years.

The carved forehead was wrinkled, as though deep in thought. Olly gazed up at it, imagining the amazing sights it must have seen when the city was alive, and wondering what it had been thinking about since the city had fallen and the people had vanished.

"The Gateway of the Sun," Jonathan announced.

Olly jumped. She had been so mesmerized by the ancient stone face, that Jonathan's voice surprised her. She turned away from the face the spell of its outlandish features broken.

"The people who built this temple worshipped the sun," Jonathan told her. "They believed that it rose every morning from the Island of the Sun in Lake Titicaca."

"And at night the moon rose from the Island of the Moon," Josh added.

Olly nodded. "Where's Dad?" she asked.

"At Puma Punku," Jonathan said, pointing away over the ruins. "It's not part of the main site. We'll go there now."

Olly and Josh followed Jonathan out of the enclosed site and across a railway line.

"Puma Punku means Gateway of the Puma,"

Jonathan explained. "We think it may have been a wharf. Lake Titicaca was much bigger two and a half thousand years ago, when Tiahuanaco was built. Then it came right up to the city."

As breathtaking as the main site had been, Olly found the sights that met her at Puma Punku more awesome still. It was an area of immense stone slabs — huge beyond belief. They looked as if they had once been a building, until a giant hand had come smashing down on them, breaking them into a jagged heap of rubble.

"The largest stone here weighs an estimated four hundred and forty tons," Jonathan said. "We have absolutely no idea how the stones were moved."

"With the help of the gods," Josh murmured.

Jonathan smiled. "Possibly," he agreed. "And if they weren't moved by magic, then it was certainly a technology we know nothing about. The quarry they come from is nearly twenty miles away." He led them to a small area that had been cordoned off with yellow tape.

"Hi, Dad!" Olly called, catching sight of her father, who was squatting on the ground a little way off, hunched over a notebook. He was surrounded by chips and fragments of stone.

There was no response. It was not until they reached the professor's side that he became aware of their presence.

"Found the missing piece yet?" Olly asked.

Her father straightened up, shaking his head. "None of these pieces are made from the same type of stone as the slab," he said, gesturing at the rubble that surrounded them. "This is all sandstone and basalt, but the Puma Punku stone is granite."

"Can we see it?" Josh asked.

Professor Christie pointed to the far corner of the taped-off area. A dark-gray slab of stone lay on the ground, broken at the bottom right-hand corner. The two friends went over to look at it, leaving Jonathan and the professor deep in conversation.

Olly knelt to examine the carvings that covered the entire face of the Puma Punku Stone. The slab was about three feet high, and half that wide. A border ran around the edges, divided into squares. The rest of the stone was carved with a grid of different symbols that, for those who could read it, told the story of Coyata's flight with the Amulet of Quilla.

Olly had read books explaining how the ancient people of this area related stories and legends with these stylized pictures — but she couldn't remember

441

enough to be able to translate the carvings herself. She ran a finger along the broken lower edge of the stone. It was maddening to think that the answer to their search was missing. "Do you think it would do any good to dig around a little here?" she asked Josh. "Just in case?"

He didn't reply. She looked around and up at him. He was staring at the stone with a curious expression on his face — almost as if he couldn't quite believe his eyes.

"Are you OK?" she asked.

"Stand up," he told her. "You're too close."

Puzzled, she got to her feet.

Josh pulled her a step back from the stone. "Look!"

"At what?" Olly asked.

"Just *look!*" Josh told her, urgently.

She looked. For a few moments, she stared down at the stone without understanding what it was that had caught Josh's eye. But then the pattern of carvings along the border began to remind her of something.

The main intricate design was edged with a deep double groove and surrounded by a border of squares. Some of the squares contained squat, stylized human figures, with their arms raised in different positions.

Olly's eyes widened and her hand flew to her mouth as realization dawned. "Josh — it can't be!" she gasped.

"I think it is," Josh replied.

"The pattern on the stone is the same . . ." Olly went on.

"Yes."

". . . as the pattern on the mantra in Fabiola's house!" she finished.

"*Yes!*"

Olly's head was swimming. She took a long, deep breath to calm herself. "OK," she said slowly. "Let's see if I've got this right. The patterns inside the border tell the story of Coyata's escape from the Island of the Moon — and explain where she took the Amulet of Quilla, right?"

Josh nodded.

"And the reason Dad can't work out where she took the amulet is because the bottom corner of the stone is missing." She stared at her friend, her voice bursting with excitement. "But Josh — Fabiola's mantra has the complete pattern. The design must have been copied from the stone way back when it was still in one piece. We have to tell Dad!"

Josh caught her sleeve. "Wait," he said. "The pattern on the mantra is very similar to this, but I'm not sure that it's *exactly* the same."

"Of course it is!" Olly said. "It's got those little men with the crooked arms and everything."

"The little men aren't important," Josh pointed out. "It's the writing on the rest of the stone that matters."

"I think it's the same," Olly said, sounding less certain now. "Don't you?"

"I think so," Josh replied, his voice maddeningly calm. "It certainly looks very similar. But we have to be absolutely sure that the two patterns match before we say anything. We don't want to go rushing up to your dad like a couple of excited kids, and then have him say: 'Oh, yes, I noticed that. Actually it's not the same at all'."

Olly nodded, her enthusiasm waning a little. "You're right," she agreed. "So, what do we do?"

"We take some pictures of Fabiola's mantra," Josh said, his eyes gleaming. "Then, we check them against the pictures that Jonathan took of the Puma Punku Stone — they're all on the computer. If the pictures match, we show them to Jonathan and your dad, and look like geniuses!"

Olly thought for a moment and grinned. It was

a good plan. "OK," she said. She looked at her watch. It was three o'clock. She glanced over to where Jonathan and her father were deep in discussion. "But we're not going to get away from here for hours," she sighed. "And by the time we get back, Fabiola's place will probably be closed for the day. Then we have lessons in the morning," she looked at Josh, "which means that we won't be able to check whether we're right till tomorrow afternoon!" Her voice trembled slightly. "Josh — my brain will explode into a million tiny pieces if we have to wait that long. It really will."

"We can't make our own way back though," Josh said. "We have to wait till Jonathan and your dad have finished — unless you have any bright ideas."

Olly frowned. "Well, I have had a stomachache ever since we left the house," she said. "It's not too bad, that's why I didn't mention it. But I could pretend it's worse than it really is and ask Jonathan if he'd mind taking me home."

"It sounds like a plan to me," Josh said.

Olly grinned, then clutched her stomach and tried to look as mournful as possible. "Here goes . . ."

~~~~

Olly's grandma was sitting on the veranda when they arrived back at Jazmine's house.

"That was quick," she said, as the three of them came up the steps. She looked sharply at Olly, who was still doing her best to look more ill than she really felt. "Is something wrong?"

"Olly's not feeling very well," Jonathan told her. "A stomach flu, or something."

Mrs. Beckmann became very brisk and efficient. She sat Olly in a chair on the veranda with a cool drink at her side. "I'm sure you'll feel better soon if you just sit quietly," she said firmly.

"Thanks, Gran," Olly replied, feeling a little guilty about the undeserved attention she was getting. But it would be worth it, she thought. They were back in town, and that evening, when they showed Jonathan and her dad a photograph of Fabiola's mantra, she'd be forgiven for overplaying her illness — she hoped.

Once Jonathan was sure that Olly was OK, he headed back to Tiahuanaco. Josh sat down beside Olly, and they both tried to be patient.

After half an hour, Olly decided it was safe to say she felt better and to suggest to her grandma that she and Josh go into town. Mrs. Beckmann wasn't convinced that this was such a good idea, but Olly was persuasive. "I feel fine now," she said. "I think a walk would do me good."

"Very well," Mrs. Beckmann agreed. "But if you feel the slightest twinge, I want you to come straight back. And in any event, I want you back here by six o'clock."

Olly nodded. "Don't worry," she assured her. "We will be."

Her grandma went back into the house.

Olly looked at Josh. "That wasn't too tricky," she murmured. "Now, let's go."

"I just have to get my camera," Josh said, bounding up the steps.

Olly sat on the bottom stair while she waited for him to come back. She crossed her fingers. "Please, please, please," she whispered, her eyes tight shut. "Please let the patterns be exactly the same."

~~~~

"Josh! Olly! How lovely to see you again!" Fabiola beamed at them, her dark eyes sparkling. She looked searchingly past the friends as they stood in the doorway. "Is Audrey with you?"

"No," Olly said. "We've come on our own this time." She looked at Fabiola. "We're on a mission."

Fabiola gazed at her in surprise.

"We'd like to take a few pictures of one of the mantras you showed us yesterday," Josh put in,

447

taking the small digital camera out of its pouch. "If that's OK."

"Of course," Fabiola agreed. "Which one?"

"The one you told us your great-grandmother made," Olly said. "You know — the one with the little men all round the edge."

Fabiola gave them a curious look, her hand rising to her mouth.

Sensing a problem, Olly looked across the room. The patch of wall above the door to the courtyard was bare. Olly stared in disbelief at the place where the mantra had once been.

"I'm sorry," Fabiola said. "A man came into the shop only this morning. He was interested in the mantra. I told him that it was not for sale, but he offered me a great deal of money — far, far more than it was worth. I didn't want to sell the mantra — it has great sentimental value for me — but I couldn't refuse so much money. And I do have other things woven by my great-grandmother." She looked from Olly to Josh. "I'm sorry, but he took the mantra away with him. It's gone."

Chapter Six:
Fire!

It took a few moments for the truth to sink into Josh's brain. The vital mantra was sold! Gone!

"Do you have another mantra with the same pattern?" Olly asked anxiously.

"No," Fabiola replied. "It was a very old design. I doubt if there is another like it in the entire town." She looked at the two friends. "I thought that was why the man was so insistent on buying it — and why he paid so much money."

"Do you have a copy of the pattern?" Josh inquired.

Fabiola shook her head. "I'm afraid not. The design is not used these days — people prefer more straightforward patterns."

Olly was standing with her eyes closed, swaying slightly. "This isn't happening," she murmured under her breath. "This is *not* happening!"

"What is wrong?" Fabiola asked, looking puzzled. "There are many other beautiful mantras." She gestured around the walls. "Could you not take photographs of them?"

Josh took a deep breath. "That one was kind of special," he explained. "I don't suppose you know the name of the man who bought it? We'd really like to find him, if possible."

"Certainly, I do," Fabiola replied. "I wrote it down in our sales book."

Hopeful, Josh and Olly followed Fabiola to a desk in one corner of the room. She pulled a battered old ledger out of a drawer and laid it open on the table.

"There," she said, pointing at an entry near the bottom of the page. "His name is Benedito da Silva, and he is staying at the Hotel El Ray." She smiled at them. "It is a very good hotel — the best in town. Señor da Silva, he was a foreigner. He spoke no Spanish. We talked together in English, but he had a strong Portuguese accent. I would say he is a Brazilian gentleman."

"The Hotel El Ray," Josh repeated. He looked at Fabiola. "Can you tell us how to get there?"

"Of course," Fabiola responded. "It is easy. Turn right from here and follow the road. The hotel is at the far end. You can't miss it. But you may be too late — Señor da Silva told me he was leaving town today. He said he was catching an airplane from La Paz. He may have left already."

Olly let out a gasp of dismay.

"Thanks for everything," Josh called back to Fabiola as he and Olly darted to the door. They took a sharp right turn and raced along the street as if their lives depended on it.

~~~~

The Hotel El Ray was an imposing Spanish colonial building several stories tall, set in the more modern part of the town. A uniformed man stood at the entrance. He gave the two friends a disapproving look as they came hurtling up the wide stone steps and flew in through the open doors.

Josh glanced around the impressive foyer. The décor was Spanish-influenced, the ornate architecture gilded with gold leaf. Wide, sweeping stairways led to the upper floor.

"There!" Olly gasped, pointing to a long curved reception desk. A young woman eyed them curiously from behind the desk as they ran over to her. "*Buenas tardes*," she said politely as they almost cannoned into the desk.

"*¿Dónde está Señor Benedito da Silva?*" Olly pronounced carefully. *Where is Mr. Benedito da Silva?*

The receptionist replied with a stream of Spanish that Josh didn't understand.

Olly shook her head. "*¿Habla inglés?*" she asked hopefully. *Do you speak English?*

"Certainly," the young woman responded. "I asked whether you can tell me in which room Señor da Silva is staying."

"We don't know," Olly told her frantically. "But he's definitely staying here."

"Could you check your books?" Josh asked. "It's really very important."

The receptionist nodded. With agonizing slowness she flicked through a stack of file cards. "Yes," she said at last. "Señor da Silva is in room two-one-four."

"Thanks," said Olly as she headed for the stairs. "That's all we need to know!"

"Please wait!" the young woman called. "If you wish to speak with Señor da Silva, I will call him." She gestured for them to stay where they were, while she picked up the phone and punched in some numbers.

"Hello, Señor da Silva," she said into the phone. "I have two young people here who wish to speak with you." She listened for a few moments. "Very well, sorry to have troubled you," she finished and put the phone down.

"Señor da Silva cannot see anyone now," she told Olly and Josh. "He is preparing to leave. He has to take a taxi to La Paz Airport. He has no time. I am sorry."

"We only need to see him for a few minutes," Josh pleaded.

The young woman shook her head. "It is not possible."

"Can't you call him again?" Olly begged.

The young woman frowned. "No," she said firmly. "I am very sorry, but Señor da Silva cannot be disturbed."

Temporarily defeated, the two friends headed back to the street.

Olly stared thoughtfully at the hotel doors. "We've got to see him, somehow, Josh," she murmured. "We have to get a photo of that mantra."

"Perhaps if we wait here till he comes out," Josh suggested. "We can explain everything to him in person. I'm sure he'll let us take just one photo."

Olly shook her head. "You've got to be kidding," she said. "We can't tell him that the mantra he just bought holds the secret to finding the priceless Amulet of Quilla."

Now that Olly had spelled it out, Josh realized it

probably wasn't such a good plan. But what else could they do?

"Wait here," Olly said suddenly. "I have an idea."

Before Josh could reply, Olly jogged to the corner of the hotel and darted out of sight down a side alley. Josh stared after her, wondering what she was planning. He walked to the end of the alley and waited for her to come back.

"Josh! Quick!" He turned his head to see Olly leaning out of a side entrance to the hotel, beckoning him urgently. He hurried over to her.

"I think this must be the worker's entrance or something," she said. "But from here, we can make our way up to the main rooms."

"How does that help, if Mr. da Silva won't let us in?" Josh asked.

"Come with me," Olly replied with a crafty grin.

Josh followed her into a small hallway, where she pointed to something on the wall. It was a small red box with a round glass panel in it.

"See?" Olly said triumphantly.

"It's the fire alarm," Josh remarked. "So what?"

"So, what happens when a fire alarm goes off?" Olly prompted.

"There's a mad rush to get out of the building," Josh said. Then he stared at her, suddenly realizing what she had in mind. "No!" he said adamantly. "Olly, we can't set off the alarm. People will think the place is on fire."

"Yup!" Olly agreed cheerfully. "And the hotel will be completely deserted until they realize that it isn't. That'll give us time to get up to Mr. da Silva's room and photograph the mantra."

"But what if he takes it with him?" Josh asked.

Olly frowned. "Josh, if a fire alarm goes off, you don't stop to collect your luggage, you run for it. Trust me — this will be easy. We'll be in and out of his room in thirty seconds."

Josh looked at her doubtfully. But he saw that familiar, dogged glint in her eye that meant she wouldn't take no for an answer. He sighed and nodded.

Olly stepped up to the fire alarm. She lifted the small metal rod from its cradle and smashed the glass panel.

For a split second, there was silence. Then the entire hotel erupted with the shrill scream of the alarm. Josh heard the staff shouting at each other. Then Olly grabbed him and pulled him into a space under the stairs, where they ducked down behind a pile of empty sacks.

Josh heard voices approaching, then the clatter of feet rushing down the stairs. He huddled farther down behind the sacks, listening to the confused chatter of Spanish voices as people flooded past his hiding place and out through the side door.

At last, Olly lifted her head to peer over the barrier of sacks.

"I think everyone's gone," she hissed. "Come on. We don't have much time."

She led the way up the stairs to the second floor. A door brought them out into a richly decorated corridor. Several doors to hotel rooms stood open. The fire alarm was still ringing loudly. Olly grinned. The whole floor seemed deserted.

Olly and Josh ran along the corridor, checking the room numbers as they passed. Josh had the horrible feeling that at any moment someone would appear in the corridor and stop them.

"This is it!" Olly said eventually. The door to room two-one-four was wide open. The room inside was luxurious, with a huge double bed and red flock wallpaper. A suitcase lay open on the bed, half filled. Items of clothing lay scattered where Mr. da Silva had left them when the alarm interrupted his packing. Several smaller leather bags stood waiting on the carpet. Draped between the handles of one of them was a roll of woven, colored material.

Olly recognized the mantra and snatched it up. "Got it!" Her eyes shined as she smiled at Josh. "What did I tell you? Am I a genius or what?"

Josh closed the door. The lock clicked. He took his camera out. "Unroll it and hold it up," he said nervously. He wanted to be out of that room as soon as possible. The thought of Mr. da Silva — or some member of the hotel staff — finding them in there was not pleasant.

Olly held the roll up to her chin and let the mantra unfurl.

Josh stared for a moment at the familiar grid of storytelling symbols within the border of squares. They were very similar to the carved patterns on the Puma Punku Stone — but were they *exactly* the same? He simply couldn't tell — the design was far too intricate for him to be sure.

"Josh, take the picture!" Olly said urgently.

Josh held the camera to his eye. He clicked and the flash bleached the room. "I'll take a couple more just to be on the safe side," he said. The camera flashed twice more. "OK. That's it. Let's go."

Olly rolled the mantra up again and put it back

between the handles of the bag. She grinned happily at Josh. "I said it would be easy, didn't I?"

Josh nodded and turned toward the door. He was just reaching for the handle when he saw it move. Above the constant wail of the fire alarm, he heard a man's voice give a sharp, angry exclamation in a foreign language.

Josh turned to Olly in alarm. Her face was frozen in dismay.

The handle rattled again.

Josh backed away from the door. Someone was trying to get into the room — and there was no way for the two of them to get out. The plan had gone spectacularly wrong.

Chapter Seven: ~
The Aerie of the White Eagle

Josh stared desperately around the hotel room. He could hear the man outside fumbling with his room key. In a few seconds he would come bursting in on them.

Meanwhile, Olly was calmly sliding under the bed. She looked up and beckoned to him.

Josh dropped to the carpet and squirmed under the bed to join Olly. She pulled the valance down straight, making sure that they were completely hidden.

In the small gap between the valance and the carpet, Josh could see a thin slice of the room, including the leather bags, and the stretch of carpet in front of the door. As he watched, the door opened and a man stood poised for a moment in the doorway. Josh wriggled quietly into a better position so he could see the man's face. The newcomer, presumably Mr. da Silva, was tall and slim with a gaunt, tanned face and a mane of pure white hair. Josh guessed that he was in his fifties or early sixties. He was wearing a white suit, and Josh had the oddest feeling he had seen the man before.

Mr. da Silva ran toward the bed, muttering something in a language Josh didn't understand. A second later, he headed back toward the door. Josh saw him dash through the doorway and vanish into the corridor. He had the rolled-up mantra tucked under his arm.

Josh waited a few seconds to make sure the man was out of earshot before he spoke. "He's gone," he gasped. "Let's get out of here!"

The two friends squirmed out from under the bed and hurried out of the room. They ran along the corridor and tumbled down the back stairs. They paused for a moment at the side entrance, and Josh peered out cautiously, but the coast was clear. The people evacuated from the hotel had gathered at the front. He could see them milling around at the end of the alley.

Josh and Olly slipped out the side door and ran in the opposite direction.

〰〰

"What kind of an idiot runs into a burning building, grabs one thing, and then runs out again?" Olly gasped.

"The building wasn't actually burning," Josh pointed out.

"He didn't know that," Olly responded.

They were seated on a low stone wall in a plaza several streets away from the hotel, catching their breath.

Olly looked at Josh. "Was it Mr. da Silva?" she asked.

"I think so." Josh nodded. "He must have run for his life when he heard the alarm go off. But then for some reason he decided to come back and grab the mantra." He frowned. "Why would he do that?"

"Fabiola said he paid her a small fortune for it," Olly said. "Maybe he didn't want to see his brand new investment go up in smoke."

Josh nodded thoughtfully. "I suppose not."

Olly shoved him. "Well?" she said eagerly. "Have you checked whether the pictures came out?"

Josh took the camera out of its pouch and switched it on. The small back panel lit up. He clicked to review the pictures and saw tiny, bright images of Olly holding the mantra. "Yes," he said, smiling. "We've got it!"

"Great!" Olly declared, grinning back.

"Just one thing, though," Josh added. "I don't think we should tell anyone about what we had to do to get these pictures."

He could imagine how Olly's grandma would react if she knew they'd set off a fire alarm when there was no fire, and then gone sneaking into somebody else's hotel room. Somehow, he didn't think she'd be impressed.

"Good thinking," Olly agreed. "We'll tell Dad and gran that we saw the mantra at Fabiola's place — and let them think we photographed it there." She stood up. "Now let's get back. I want to see the pictures Jonathan took of the Puma Punku Stone — and the look on his face if the symbols on the stone turn out to be the same ones as on the mantra!"

~~~~

Josh and Olly were in Josh's room. Josh sat at the table while Olly perched on the corner watching his every move. The camera was in its cradle, and the cradle wire was plugged into the laptop. They were waiting for the program to open.

"Oh, come on," Olly urged. "Why is it so slow?"

Josh looked at her. "It's only been about five seconds," he said. "Chill out, Olly."

The page opened up on the screen and a series of

small images appeared. Josh clicked the first image, which promptly expanded to fill the screen.

The picture clearly showed Olly standing with her hands up level with her shoulders, the colorful mantra hanging down in front of her body.

"It worked!" Josh cried, rocking back in his chair.

Olly scrutinized the picture. A grin spread over her face — every little detail of the pattern on the mantra was visible. "Well done, Josh," she said. "Now open one of Jonathan's pictures of the Puma Punku Stone, so we can compare the two."

She watched anxiously as Josh found the folder where his brother had put his pictures. There were a lot of them — dozens of pictures of Inak Uyu on the Island of the Moon, and many more of Tiahuanaco. But finally, as Josh scrolled down the page, he came to a set of pictures of the granite Puma Punku Stone.

He enlarged the best one, and they both leaned forward to examine it closely.

"It's the same," Olly breathed at last.

"Is it?" Josh asked. "Are you sure?"

"Of course I'm sure!" Olly declared. "Print them out, Josh. Now!" She bounced off the table and did a triumphant dance around the room. "We did it!

We did it!" she crowed. Then she ran to the window and shouted. "Hey, Ethan Cain, King of the World! You might as well head home! Olly and Josh are way ahead of you!"

The door to Josh's room opened. "For heaven's sake, what's all this noise about?" asked Olly's grandma. "It sounded like a herd of elephants was jumping around up here!"

Olly ran over to her grandma and danced her around the bed. "We need to call Dad!" she said excitedly. "He has to get back here right now! Josh and I have found something amazing!"

～～～

More than an hour had passed. Olly, Josh, Audrey Beckmann, Jonathan, and Professor Christie were seated around the table on the veranda. Jonathan and the professor were staring at the two pictures that Josh had printed out — one picture of Olly holding up Fabiola's mantra, one picture of the broken Puma Punku Stone. The two men seemed flabbergasted.

"They're the same, aren't they?" Olly demanded, unable to wait any longer for Jonathan or her father to speak.

Jonathan didn't take his eyes from the pictures. "Yes, I think they are," he confirmed. "I can't believe

464

it!" He began to laugh. "Why didn't you say something when we were at Puma Punku?"

"We weren't sure that we were right," Olly explained. "We wanted to be absolutely certain before we said anything."

"Can you translate it?" Josh asked eagerly. "Do you know what the missing part says?"

Professor Christie looked up. "Jonathan, would you fetch me Hugo Rojo's book, please? And we'd better have the Poznansky translations, too."

Olly recognized the names — the men were leading authorities on the meanings of Inca and pre-Inca storytelling symbols. Jonathan and her father had been consulting their works extensively both before and during the trip.

Mrs. Beckmann looked sternly at Olly. "I take it that this was why you wanted to go for a walk into the town?" she said. "And why you asked Jonathan to bring you home early?"

Olly nodded sheepishly. "But I really did have a stomachache," she added quickly. "It just wasn't quite as bad as I led you to believe." She gave her grandma a hopeful look. "It was worth it, though, wasn't it?"

Mrs. Beckmann raised an eyebrow. "Hmmm," she murmured dubiously.

Anything further that Olly's grandma might have wished to say on the subject was interrupted by the arrival of a car. Jazmine emerged with some shopping. "It's madness down there," she said, gesturing back toward the town as she came up to the veranda. "Complete chaos!" She slumped into a chair. "It's taken me three quarters of an hour to get through."

Olly gave her an uneasy look. "Why? What's wrong?" she asked.

"Apparently some fool set off the fire alarm in the Hotel El Rey," Jazmine explained. "The whole place was evacuated, and the police and the fire service turned out in force, only to discover it was a false alarm. But the hotel is on the main through-road. It was blocked solid. It'll be hours before things get back to normal."

"Do they know who set the alarm off?" Mrs. Beckmann asked.

Olly winced.

"A couple of kids, apparently," Jazmine replied. "They were seen hanging around the hotel just before the alarm went off."

Olly forced her face into its most innocent expression and tried to look angelic. Out of the corner of her eye, she saw Josh hurriedly lean over the table to examine the photos again. The business

466

with the fire alarm at the Hotel El Rey was one part of the story that neither of the friends was excited to explore.

Mrs. Beckmann frowned. "Some children do the most stupid, thoughtless things," she sighed. She looked at Olly and Josh. "I'm glad you two have more sense."

~~~~~

The night pressed in at the windows of Jazmine's sitting room. It was actually well past the time when Mrs. Beckmann would usually have suggested Olly and Josh go to bed, but everyone was still up.

Jazmine was seated at one end of the room, quietly playing the guitar. Olly's grandma was seated in an armchair, reading. And Olly and Josh were playing Scrabble. But Olly couldn't concentrate — and judging by Josh's pathetic word tally, he was as distracted as she was.

Every few minutes, Olly would glance at the door to the study. Her father and Jonathan had been locked up in there for hours, poring over the text books, examining the photographs of the mantra and the Puma Punku Stone, trying to solve the final piece of the puzzle.

"Squink isn't a word," Josh declared, staring down at the board where Olly had just placed her tiles.

Olly looked at him. "It isn't? Are you sure?"

"Mrs. Beckmann?" Josh called out. "Squink?"

Olly's grandma looked up briefly from her book and shook her head.

"Rats!" Olly said, picking up the tiles again. She let out a deep breath and stared impatiently at the door. This time, her father was standing in the doorway, with Jonathan right behind him.

Olly and Josh both sprang up, the Scrabble game forgotten.

"Well?" Olly demanded.

The guitar fell silent. Mrs. Beckmann looked up from her book.

A grin spread across Jonathan's face. "We've cracked it," he announced. "According to the writing on the lower right corner of the mantra — that's the part missing from the stone — Coyata hid the Amulet of Quilla in the temple known as the Lair of the Anaconda King."

Olly hardly dared ask the next question. "And do you know where that is?"

Her father smiled. "It's beneath an outcrop of rock referred to as the Aerie of the White Eagle."

"We're not exactly sure where the Aerie of the White Eagle is yet," Jonathan put in. "But the writing on the mantra places it in a forested region of the Beni River. Our maps show several outcrops of rock near to the town of Rurrenabaque — the locals call it Rurre — on the Beni River."

The professor nodded, his smile widening. "Rurre is nearly three hundred miles from here, in the northern Bolivian lowlands. We are hoping that the local guides will be able to tell us which of the outcrops is associated with eagles. Once we have that piece of information, we should be well on our way to locating the temple." He looked across the room toward their hostess, his eyes shining. "I'm sorry to have to leave you so abruptly, Jazmine," he said. "But tomorrow morning we hope to take a flight from La Paz to Rurre."

Olly wasn't sure whether it was she, Josh, or Jonathan who let out the loudest yell of triumph. The hunt for the Amulet of Quilla was on!

Chapter Eight: ~
A Dangerous Road

Olly woke early the next day, filled with excitement and anticipation. She dressed quickly and went out onto the balcony. The air was still cool under the shadow of the roof, but the sky was bright and clear and promised another fine, hot day. She leaned on the parapet and looked out over the town. Beyond the buildings and the brown parched hills, Lake Titicaca shined like sapphire as the upper rim of the sun cleared the mountains, filling the great valley with shimmering light.

She walked along to Josh's room. He was up already, too, sitting on his bed with the laptop on his knees.

"Mom has sent another e-mail," he told Olly. "She's in a place called Alice Springs." He turned the laptop to show Olly a map of Australia's Northern Territory. "It's in the middle of a desert, apparently," he added.

"Did she mention Ethan?" Olly asked.

"She says they've spoken on the phone a couple of times," Josh replied.

"And is he in California?"

Josh shrugged. "She doesn't say." He looked at Olly. "But I'm not going to tell Mom where we're going," he said. "Not just yet." He frowned. "Maybe we've got it wrong, and Ethan isn't coming here at all, but . . ."

"But if he is," Olly finished for him. "It would be better if your mom wasn't able to tell him the latest news." She nodded. "Good thinking."

A moment later, the door opened and Audrey Beckmann looked into the room.

"Ah, here you both are," she said.

Olly frowned at her. "Not schoolwork — not this morning?" she said.

"No. No lessons," her grandma replied.

"You see, we have to pack and stuff," Olly continued persuasively. "And I was . . . Oh! What did you say?"

"No lessons today," Mrs. Beckmann told her, smiling. "Breakfast is ready."

Olly and Josh looked at each other.

Olly grinned. "Excellent!" she said. "This is going to be a perfect day. Off to La Paz Airport. An airplane to Rurre. And by evening we'll be in the middle of the rain forest! Very exciting!"

～～～

On their way out to the veranda, where the table was set for the usual breakfast of orange juice and sweet pastries, they passed Jonathan. He was sitting on the stairs and speaking into the phone. His Spanish was fluent, and Olly could only make out a few words here and there, but from the look on his face and the tone of his voice, she guessed that he was speaking to someone at La Paz Airport — and that the conversation was not going well.

Jazmine, Audrey Beckmann, and Olly's father were already outside. The professor's part of the table was scattered with open books and documents. Olly and Josh sat down and began to eat.

It was about ten minutes later that Jonathan emerged from the house. "It's not good news," he said, sounding exasperated. "As far as I can make out, the baggage handlers are on strike at the airport. No planes can land or take off till the dispute's been settled."

Professor Christie looked at him anxiously. "And have you any idea how long that will take?" he asked.

"The woman on the phone said, '*mañana*,'" Jonathan replied.

"That means 'tomorrow,'" Olly said. "That's not too bad."

Jazmine shook her head. "We don't always mean tomorrow when we say *mañana*," she told them. "It can mean tomorrow, or the day after, or next week, or next month."

Professor Christie frowned. "I have to be back in England in eight days," he said. "We can't afford a delay."

"Can't we go by road?" Josh asked.

"There is one road north through the mountains," Jazmine said, "but I would not recommend it."

"Have you any idea how long this dispute might last?" Audrey Beckmann asked Jazmine.

"I will make some calls," Jazmine said. She got up and went into the house.

She was only gone a few minutes, but the look on her face when she returned was not encouraging. "I'm afraid the strike will not be over quickly," she declared. "Negotiators are expected in the next few days — but the talks could take days or even weeks."

"Then we will have to travel by road," sighed the professor.

"I'll hire a van," Jonathan said.

Olly looked curiously at Jazmine. "Why did you say you didn't recommend the road?" she asked.

Jazmine hesitated for a moment before answering. "The only way to travel north from here is to take the mountain road that leads from La Paz to Coroico," she explained. "The people of these parts have a name for that road — they call it *El Peligroso*."

Jonathan frowned at her. "That just means 'dangerous,'" he said.

Jazmine nodded. "It has a bad reputation," she warned. "It is a gravel road that goes down the mountains. It is little more than ten feet wide, and there is a drop of many hundreds of feet on one side."

"Wow!" Olly exclaimed. "That sounds cool!"

Jazmine looked at her. "About twenty-six vehicles a year are lost on that road," she said somberly. "That is one every two weeks. I do not think you will be so happy once you see *El Peligroso*."

Olly and Josh exchanged a glance. It *was* a little unnerving to have to take such a notorious road, but it struck Olly that the journey to Rurre was going to be exciting to say the very least.

"Woah!" Olly breathed.

"Is *that* the road?" Josh asked, sounding awe-struck.

Audrey Beckmann's eyes widened and her back became a little stiffer.

Professor Christie was too busy with a lapful of documents to even look up.

Jonathan pressed his lips together, but said nothing.

They were in a battered, dusty old minivan, hired in La Paz. They had left the busy city behind them some time ago, and traveled out into the mountains. The road was rough and uneven, but at first there had been no sign of the dangerous cliff edges Jazmine had mentioned. Then they had rounded a towering outcrop of rust-colored rock. A stunning sight had opened out ahead of them.

They were on the crest of a steep-walled valley, plunging down through the parched mountains. Olly gazed along the road ahead as it started to descend from the crest, winding down the valley wall, like a thin white scar cut into the sheer mountainside.

From this point, the high ridges of the Altiplano

tumbled down in crags and peaks to the distant lowlands of the Amazon Basin — hazy and blue on the very edge of the horizon.

Olly could see tiny vehicles moving up and down the road, seeming to cling, like ants, to the rock-face.

Jonathan only hesitated for a moment. "Here goes nothing," Olly heard him mutter under his breath, and then he drove over the crest and down onto the steep, narrow mountain road.

The scenery was breathtaking — towering cliffs of sunburned, red rock reared up around them, arid and scorched by the brutal sun.

The road zigzagged slowly downward. Olly leaned out of the window and stared into the dizzying chasm. Usually, she had no fear of heights, but the immensity of this fall dried her mouth and made the hairs on the back of her neck stand on end.

Jonathan was hunched over the steering wheel, peering ahead, his face tight with concentration. Olly's father was speechless in the seat beside him. The most unnerving moments came when they had to move out onto one of the broader turning points in the road, to allow ascending vehicles to pass them. At these times, Jonathan had to take the van to the very brink of the cliff, the wheels only a foot and a half from the crumbling edge. Then they had to wait, holding their breath, as a truck rumbled past — shaking the ground and filling the air with choking red dust — before they could move back into the middle of the road and continue their journey.

Jonathan wiped sweat out of his eyes. Even with all the windows open, the van was becoming uncomfortably hot. Mrs. Beckmann handed out bottled water as they continued to crawl down through the mountains.

Olly leaned farther out, gazing in fascination into the gulf. Far, far below, she saw the tangled, rusted wreckage of a truck. She thought of the poor people who had been in the vehicle, and swallowed hard. Then she felt her grandma's hand grip her shoulder and pull her back into the seat.

"Not so far out, Olly, please," Mrs. Beckmann said quietly.

They crept around a wide shoulder of rock. Olly could see the road plunging ahead, empty of oncoming traffic. "How much farther is Coroico?" she asked.

Josh had a map spread open on his lap. "It's difficult to tell," he replied. "Coroico is about eighty miles from La Paz. I think we've gone about halfway." He looked up. "What's that noise?" he asked, frowning.

Olly listened. She could hear the growl of the engine and the crunch and grind of the wheels on the gravel track, but Josh was right, there was a new sound — a distant rumble, like prolonged thunder.

She stared up through the dusty windscreen into the clear, blue sky. And then the whole world turned red and the roof of the van began to clang and echo with the terrifying impact of a hundred small stones. Through the enveloping cloud of dust, Olly could see rocks and stones spilling down over them, bouncing off the hood and cracking on the windshield. They ricocheted and scattered as they came hurtling down from some unguessable height. Some were just small pebbles, but others were much bigger. They crashed down onto the van like hammer blows as it rocked and shuddered under the impact.

Jonathan flicked the windshield wipers on and fought with the wheel, his foot hard on the break, his face strained and ashen as he labored to keep the van under some kind of control. The wipers struggled to sweep the debris away, but more and more poured down to replace it. The roar and thunder of the rockfall was deafening.

Olly could hear her father shouting something —

and her grandma and Josh, too, but their voices were all drowned out by the terrible noise of the rocks on the roof. She let out an involuntary scream as she saw a boulder smash into the road only a foot and a half ahead of them. Never in her life had she been so utterly terrified.

Jonathan spun the wheel, desperately trying to avoid crashing into the boulder, but anxious not to drive over the edge of the mountain at the same time. Unfortunately, the rubble on the road was moving under the van's wheels, and he could not get any traction.

Olly hung on grimly as one wheel hit the boulder with a bone-jarring crack and the back of the van began to slide away. Dust cascaded in through the open window, filling her nose and mouth and stinging her eyes. The rockfall was pushing the van to the outside edge of the road, and through a sudden gap in the avalanche of dust and stones, she saw the abyss yawning only inches away from them.

The wheels spun. The engine roared shrilly. The van teetered on the very brink of the mountain, and under the constant hammering of falling rocks, it slowly began to tip up. Olly clung to her seat and closed her eyes in terror. The van was slithering over the precipice.

Chapter Nine: Journey's End

"Everyone, over to this side!" Jonathan shouted above the clamor, his voice cracking with fear.

Olly threw herself across the van, squeezing herself against Josh so she could grab on to the door handle next to her grandma, whose arm was tight around them both. In the front, the professor grasped the back of Jonathan's seat as his assistant leaned toward the window and wrenched at the steering wheel.

Olly saw the shock and panic in their faces. But their combined weight worked a miracle. The van righted itself, and the wheels found some traction on the gravel road. There was a violent shudder, and suddenly the van leaped forward, back onto the road.

A few seconds later they had pressed beyond the rockfall and Jonathan brought the van to a halt. He leaned against the steering wheel, cradling his head in his arms. Olly could see the sweat dripping from his face.

"Well done, Jonathan. Well done!" gasped the professor, patting his assistant on the back.

"Is everyone all right?" asked Olly's grandma, her voice trembling.

Josh had squirmed around in his seat to stare out through the filthy rear windshield. "That was close!" he exclaimed.

Behind them, the road was strewn with rocks and boulders and drifts of rust-colored silt. A cloud of red dust still hung in the air.

Jonathan lifted his head and peered over his shoulder. "No one else is going to be traveling this road today," he remarked. "It's completely blocked."

Suddenly Olly needed to get out of the van. She wrestled with the handle and threw the door open. Then she jumped down onto the gravel road and fell to her knees, panting wildly. Her legs felt like jelly, and her stomach was turning over and over.

"Olly? Are you all right?" Olly opened her eyes at the sound of her grandma's voice. "Look at you — you're filthy. Here, drink this." A bottle of water appeared under her nose.

Olly realized her mouth was desert-dry. She took a swig of water.

"Better?" her grandma asked, smiling.

Olly nodded, her spirits beginning to revive a little. "Yes, thanks." She clambered to her feet.

Jonathan and Professor Christie had gotten out of the van. They were circling the vehicle, checking for damage.

Josh jumped down to join Olly. "I thought we were going over the edge," he said, his voice slightly shrill. "Look at the size of some of those rocks!" He walked toward the debris.

"Josh, keep away from there," Mrs. Beckmann called sharply.

Josh crouched and picked up a small rock that fit into his hand. He stood up and held it out. "A souvenir," he declared.

Olly gazed at him. "Were you scared?" she asked.

He nodded. "You?"

She laughed. "Just a bit!"

"I think it would be a good idea for us to get off this road as quickly as possible," Olly's grandmother called to the two men. "Is the van all right?"

"I think so," Jonathan replied. "It's got a few more dents than it had before, but the tires are OK."

They all climbed back into the van. Olly instantly felt apprehensive. She swallowed hard, determined to master her fear.

Jonathan turned the key in the ignition. The motor coughed into life. The noise made Olly jump. She bit her lip and clenched her fists in her lap.

"So far, so good," Jonathan said. He put the van into gear and they began to move.

The gravel road took them around an outcrop of rock, and the site of the rockfall disappeared. Olly heaved a sigh of relief.

A few minutes later, they skirted another jutting rock, and Olly saw the rooftops of a small town, no more than two miles ahead of them, perched on the side of the mountains. And beyond the town lay great forested canyons and green valleys stretching away into the distance. They had reached Coroico. They had descended six thousand feet out of the Altiplano, and they had survived *El Peligroso* — the most dangerous road in the world.

Olly grinned around at everyone. "Well, that was a piece of cake," she said. "Anyone want to do it again?"

~~~~

They arrived in Coroico in the early afternoon and found a quiet, friendly restaurant where they could have a good meal and take some time to recover from their ordeal on the road.

As they ate, Mrs. Beckmann studied a travel guide, and Jonathan and the professor discussed plans for the next stage in the search for the amulet. Josh and Olly talked rapidly together, reliving the perilous journey and the rockfall.

"If one of those big chunks of rock had hit us, it would have gone right through the roof," Josh said cheerfully as he forked up his pasta. "We'd have been pulped!"

"Not while I'm eating, please," Mrs. Beckmann said. "We're going to have to start using bug spray from now on," she added. "There are some extremely unpleasant bugs in these parts."

Olly laughed. "After what we've just been through, insects don't bother me."

"They will if you get stung, Olivia," her grandma said severely. She read from the guidebook. "'The bites of infected mosquitoes can cause malaria, the symptoms of which include loss of appetite, fever, chills, and sweating. If it is not treated quickly, it can prove fatal.'"

Olly blinked at her. "Bring on the bug spray!" she exclaimed.

〜〜〜

The rest of the afternoon was spent driving out of the mountains and through the lush Bolivian lowlands. Occasionally, white mists rose from the deep, forested valleys. The warm, dry air of the Altiplano was being replaced by a humid, stifling heat that sent the sweat running in rivulets down their faces.

But the landscape that unfolded around them made the discomfort of the hot van bearable. They passed through wide orchards of oranges and lemons, and dense coffee plantations dotted with small, picturesque villages. Rivers tumbled through forested gorges, breaking into sparkling waterfalls wrapped secretively in ribbons of mist.

As the afternoon waned, they came out of the hills and began the final stretch of their long journey. Now, they were driving through endless green pampas grass, past cattle ranches and logging operations that had made great, unsightly holes in the rain forest.

It was already evening when they caught their first glimpse of the Rio Beni. It spread out below the road like a glittering black ribbon, winding between thickly forested banks. And then the road crested a final broad hill, and suddenly they were looking down on the town of Rurrenabaque. The sun was setting like a ball of red fire in a sky streaked with gold and orange and purple. The river was cloaked in a blanket of white fog, and the lights of the town twinkled invitingly.

Their long journey was at an end — they had reached the tropical rain forests of the Amazon Basin. The next stage of the hunt for the Amulet of Quilla was about to begin.

~~~~~

Josh woke with a start. He had been dreaming he was back in the van. Rocks and rubble were raining down on it, and then he was falling. . . .

He sat up, trembling slightly. It was pitch dark. Frogs croaked in chorus outside his bedroom window. But he was safe. There were no rocks.

He remembered the drive through Rurre, the climb to the hill behind the town, and being greeted at the door of the hacienda by a friendly European woman. They had cleaned up and eaten a quick meal before being shown to their rooms. Then, exhausted by the long journey, he had thrown his clothes off and fallen into bed.

He lay back again on the soft pillows, and listening to the singing frogs, he soon fell into a dreamless sleep.

~~~~~

Early the next morning, Josh stood on his balcony, gazing down in delight at the broad, silver-blue

Rio Beni as it flowed north through the forested hills. The hacienda where they were staying was to the north of the town, perched on an outcrop of rock that overhung the river. The beautiful rain forest seemed to stretch on forever — fading away into misty blue distances under the burning white sun. The air was filled with the scents of the forest.

The frog chorus was gone, but Josh could hear other noises — now the shrill shriek of birds, the rustle of the warm wind in the trees, the splash of animals in the water, the call of creatures deep in the forest. The whole place teemed with life.

Beautiful orange and black butterflies fluttered on the breeze like tiny kites. A toucan sailed by on outstretched wings, its head and chest vivid splashes of yellow against the blue sky, its huge beak patterned with all the colors of the rainbow.

Josh tore himself away from the view and ran downstairs to join the others in a wide, airy dining room.

"Here he is, at last," said Jonathan.

"We were wondering if you were ever going to wake up," Olly muttered, her mouth full of food. She pointed to a plate of sweet pastries. "Try one of these — they're amazing!"

Josh sat down beside Mrs. Beckmann, who was

there sipping coffee and reading her travel guide. Just then, their hostess came gliding into the room, a slim young woman with long black hair and dark eyes. Her name was Katerina. She smiled at Josh and poured him some fresh juice.

"Where's your dad?" Josh asked Olly as he started eating.

"He's gone off to talk to some local guides," Olly replied. "He shouldn't be long." Her eyes gleamed. "And then we can all head off into the jungle to find the amulet!"

"We'll have to see about that," said Mrs. Beckmann, and Josh noticed that her voice sounded strangely weary.

He looked at her curiously. She did seem a bit pale, and there were dark circles under her eyes.

"Are you OK, gran?" Olly asked.

"I'm fine, Olly," Mrs. Beckmann replied. "Just a little tired."

Katerina gently rested her hand against Mrs. Beckmann's forehead. "I think you have a little touch of fever," she said.

Olly stared at her. "Fever?" she repeated anxiously. "Gran — you haven't been bitten by a mosquito, have you?"

"I don't think so," said her grandma, laughing. She smiled at Katerina. "The journey was a little wearing," she said. "I think maybe I'll lie down for a bit."

"That's a good idea," Katerina agreed.

Mrs. Beckmann lifted herself out of her chair. She looked sternly at Olly and Josh. "You two behave yourselves, all right?" she said.

"Of course," Olly replied indignantly.

"I hope you feel better soon," Josh added.

"Thank you, Josh. I'm sure I will," said Mrs. Beckmann as she left the room.

"Don't worry," Katerina told the friends. "I'll make sure she's OK."

A few minutes later, Professor Christie came in. Jonathan and the two friends looked up hopefully. The professor looked pleased.

"Did you find a guide?" Jonathan asked.

Professor Christie sat down and took out a map. Olly and Josh cleared the table so he could open it. "I have hired a man called Sandro," he said. "I met him on my way into town. He was coming up to the hacienda to offer his services to any tourists. He is a local guide, and he seems to know the area very well. I asked him about the Aerie of the White Eagle. He said there are *two* places that fit the description, but only *one* is associated with eagles. It is on this side of the river and has always been known as Eagle Mount by the locals." Professor Christie pointed to the place on the map.

The others leaned over to look.

"That's farther away than we thought," Jonathan commented. "Didn't the writing on the mantra suggest that it would be much closer to the river?"

"Yes," the professor agreed. "But it is still within the bounds of possibility, and it matches the description in all other respects. Sandro says it will take us two and a half days to get there. We will set off tomorrow, but he has warned me that it will be a difficult journey." He looked at the two friends. "I'm sorry, but I'm afraid that means you can't come with us."

Josh's heart sank. It had never crossed his mind that they would be left out of the final stage in the search. The thought of sitting around for five days or more, while Jonathan and the professor were exploring the Lair of the Anaconda King without them, was crushing.

"You can't leave us behind!" Olly exclaimed. "That's not fair."

"I'm very sorry, Olivia," her father said firmly. "But it's going to be a hard trek through dense jungle. It's no place for you and Josh."

"The professor is right," Jonathan said sympathetically. "I know the two of you would love to join us, but this time, you're going to have to be patient."

Josh could see by the look on Olly's face that she felt as disappointed as he did.

They had come all this way, solved the riddle of the Puma Punku Stone — and now, they were going to be left behind at the very end of the quest.

It was almost too much to bear.

Chapter Ten: ～
The Brazilian Again

It was a depressing day for Olly and Josh. Jonathan and Professor Christie were busy making arrangements for their trip into the jungle. It wouldn't even be possible for those left at the hacienda to keep in contact with them by cell phone; deep in the pathless heart of the rain forest, they would get no reception.

Audrey Beckmann got up in the afternoon, but everyone could see that she wasn't well. She sat quietly in an armchair on the wide veranda that overlooked the river, looking pale and drawn.

Olly was worried. Her grandma was never ill. She fussed over her, bringing her cool drinks and snacks, constantly checking to see if she needed anything.

"Olivia, please, I'm not an invalid," her grandma said. "I feel a bit run-down, that's all."

"Are you sure that's all it is, Mrs. Beckmann?" Jonathan asked. "It's not wise to ignore these things. I've been talking with the professor, and he thinks you should see a doctor."

"You should, gran," Olly urged. "Just to be on the safe side."

The old lady lifted her hands in surrender. "Very well," she said wearily. "I'll see a doctor."

The doctor came that afternoon and saw Mrs. Beckmann in her room.

Olly waited outside anxiously. "What if she's got malaria or some other horrible disease?" she asked Jonathan. It was very disturbing to think of her grandma being ill — she was the person who held things together. Olly couldn't imagine how anything would work properly without her grandma at the helm.

The doctor was a small, well-dressed man with a goatee and bright black eyes. He spoke to the professor while Olly listened. "It is nothing to worry about," he said in thickly accented English. "Mrs. Beckmann has a mild fever. She must rest. I will write a prescription for her. Katerina will get the medicine and ensure she takes it." He smiled at the worried faces. "I believe you will see a great improvement in forty-eight hours."

Olly let out a sigh of relief. "I'll go and sit with her," she said. "I could read to her or something."

She went up to her grandma's room and found her lying in bed, propped up against the pillows.

"The doctor says you're not to lift a finger for two days," Olly said sternly. "And you've got to do as you're told."

Her grandma smiled. "You're the boss," she said quietly.

Olly nodded. "You bet I am," she agreed. "Now, do you want anything to eat or drink?"

"I don't think so," Mrs. Beckmann replied. "Not right now."

"OK." Olly sat down on the side of the bed. "I'll read to you for a while, then." She picked up the book that her grandma had been reading. It was the chronicle of a journey into the jungle made by explorers in the nineteenth century.

Her grandma settled back into the pillows and closed her eyes as Olly began to read.

〰〰

The next day dawned with an eerie beauty. Ghostly sheets of fog had come curling up the river, giving the water a silvery sheen. The fog coiled slowly through the town, too, so that from the hilltop hacienda, the rooftops of Rurre seemed to be afloat on a rolling silver sea. A warm wind raked the forest, making the treetops ripple and rustle in waves.

The cries and calls of animals and birds were

carried on the breeze. Olly watched as a scarlet macaw flew past her balcony, its feathers as bright as newly spilled blood. It let out a cry that made her shiver. Insects danced on the warm air. A huge, shining, blue-and-green dragonfly startled her as it darted past. An iridescent beetle hovered for a moment, then went zigzagging back into the trees.

In less than an hour, Jonathan and her father would set off with their Indian guide. She had taken note of every detail of the trip as they had discussed it. They would strike inland just north of the town, following a clear path at first. But they would soon have to leave the path and head northeast into uncharted jungle. For two and a half days they would hack their way through to the outcrop of rock known as Eagle Mount.

And then they would know if the story on the mantra, copied from the Puma Punku Stone, was true.

Olly sighed. She was sure they would find the Amulet of Quilla. In five or six days, they would step triumphantly out of the jungle, and the quest for another Talisman of the Moon would be over. And she and Josh would have missed it all!

She sighed again, her spirits sinking as she brooded on the injustice of it.

Then she heard Josh's voice calling from somewhere in the hacienda. "Olly! Come on — they're leaving."

She straightened her back and fixed a smile on her face. It was time to wave the adventurers off with as brave a face as she could muster.

~~~~

Later that morning, Olly made sure her grandma was comfortable in bed with fresh water and a book in case she wanted to read. "We'd like to take a look around the town," Olly said. "That's OK, isn't it?"

"Of course," her grandma replied. "Give me my purse; you'll want some money for lunch."

Olly handed the purse over. "Can we have an advance on our allowance — in case we want to buy some souvenirs?" she begged.

Smiling, Mrs. Beckmann handed the money over. "Now then," she said, "no madcap ideas about exploring the jungle." She eyed Olly's lightweight linen trousers and cotton top. "You'll ruin your clothes. Keep to the town and the riverbank. And I want the two of you back here before nightfall, or there'll be trouble."

"No problem," Olly said. "We won't go anywhere near the jungle."

~~~~

Josh was ready to go when Olly came back downstairs. His digital camera hung in a canvas bag on one shoulder, and he was wearing a loose cotton top and cargo pants with large pockets. The friends set off into Rurre.

The town was an attractive, bustling place, with long, straight, earthen roads running between white adobe buildings. It was a charming mix of the old and the new — with reed-thatched wooden buildings and colorful adobe shops lining the main streets. There were plenty of hotels, restaurants, and cafés to cater to intrepid tourists who came to sample the delights of the surrounding rain forest and to canoe along the Rio Beni.

Olly quickly cheered up as she and Josh wandered through the town. It was impossible for her to stay gloomy in such a lovely place, and she resolved to make the most of a disappointing situation. They made their way down to the river's edge and watched the wide waters flow by. Local children played in the shallows, splashing each other as they swam and dived.

Groups of tourists were also gathered on the riverbank, waiting their turn to climb into the long, slender canoes that would take them on tours up the river. Olly and Josh decided that later on they would also take a canoe ride.

"Did you know that the word *beni* means 'wind' in the local language?" Josh asked. "So the Rio Beni is the River of the Wind."

Olly smiled at him. "You're a mine of information, aren't you?" She frowned. "I'm thirsty," she said. "Let's go and find something to drink."

They made their way back into the town.

"How do you ask for a drink in Spanish?" Josh asked.

"Well, drink is —" Olly began.

"Olly, look!" Josh's fierce whisper stopped her in mid-sentence.

She followed the line of his pointing finger. "What?" she asked, staring blankly at the people on the far side of the broad street.

"It's *him!*" Josh hissed.

Olly searched the crowd for a familiar face. "Him who?" she asked. "What are you talking about?"

"It's Mr. da Silva," Josh told her. "From the hotel. The man in the white suit."

Now Olly saw who Josh meant. The tall, silver-haired man was standing outside a shop. "Are you sure it's him?" Olly asked.

"Of course I am."

"I wonder what he's doing here," she said thoughtfully. "Wasn't he supposed to be catching a flight to Brazil?"

"Exactly!" Josh replied.

Olly blinked at him. "I suppose he must have got caught by the strike," she said, "and decided to travel around a bit until he could get a flight out." She stared hard at the tanned Brazilian. "It's quite a coincidence that he should turn up here, though, isn't it?" she added. "I wonder what he'd say if he knew that the design on that mantra he bought could lead him to a hidden treasure."

Josh looked sharply at her. "What makes you so sure he doesn't know?" he asked.

Olly started. "What?"

"Think about it," Josh continued. "Didn't Fabiola say he was desperate to buy that particular mantra from her? He paid her a lot more than it was worth. Why would he do that?"

"Because he liked it?" Olly offered.

"Maybe," Josh said. "But then he ran back into

the hotel to save it — even though he thought the building was on fire. And now he's *here*, Olly. I bet that's more than just coincidence." Josh's eyes suddenly widened. "I'm such an idiot!" he gasped.

Olly frowned at him. "Why?"

"I just remembered something," Josh told her. "In the hotel room, I had the feeling that I'd seen Mr. da Silva before. And I remember now — he was in the market the day we first went to Fabiola's place. I saw him watching us. I didn't think anything of it at the time — but what if he was deliberately following us?"

"You mean *spying* on us?" Olly breathed. Her eyes narrowed. "You know who would want us spied on, don't you? Ethan Cain!" She looked back at the tall, slim Brazilian.

"But even if he does know about the amulet, he's too late," Josh pointed out. "Jonathan and your dad have already left."

Before Olly could respond, they noticed a short, dark-haired man approach Mr. da Silva and speak to him. Da Silva nodded, then frowned and shook his head. The shorter man spoke again and then the two walked away together.

"I know that man," Josh whispered. "I saw him with Sandro this morning when he came to pick up your dad. I think his name's Lucho. He's a guide, too." He looked at Olly and frowned. "If Mr. da Silva is going to hire Lucho to guide him to the Eagle Mount, he'll only be a few hours behind Jonathan and the professor!"

"Let's find out if that *is* what he's doing," Olly suggested. "Let's spy on the spy!" She darted across the road, with Josh right behind her. Together, the friends trailed the two men as they made their way through the crowds.

When Mr. da Silva and Lucho turned down a side street, Olly and Josh dropped back a little to keep from being spotted. From the corner of the street, they saw the men sit down at a round, white table in front of a café. Tall ferns in terra-cotta pots marked out the forecourt of the café, and Olly figured she and Josh could use these as cover to draw closer to their quarry.

They sneaked toward the café until they were close enough to eavesdrop on Mr. da Silva's conversation. Olly listened intently, ready to try and work out his plans from the small amount of Spanish she understood. But she soon discovered that the conversation was being conducted in English. Mr. da Silva was Brazilian, she remembered. Fabiola had said that he didn't speak Spanish — only

Portuguese. English was obviously the only language that the two men had in common. She grinned happily at Josh.

"When did they leave?" Mr. da Silva was asking.

"Early this morning," Lucho replied. "Sandro will take them far into the forest, do not worry. They will not return for many days — five, maybe six."

Olly stiffened and threw a quick glance toward Josh. He nodded sharply, as if reading her thoughts. The two men were talking about Jonathan and her father.

"You're sure they didn't suspect anything?" Mr. da Silva demanded.

"Yes, quite sure." Lucho said firmly. "Sandro told them that the Aerie of the White Eagle was probably Eagle Mount, which is to the northeast. He did not tell them that the nearer outcrop, overlooking the Rio Beni, is known as Eagle's Nest. Eagle's Nest is sure to be the *real* Aerie of the White Eagle."

Olly's head swam. Sandro had deliberately lied to her father. The Aerie of the White Eagle was really much nearer to the river — just as Jonathan and her dad had first thought.

"It will be many days before they realize that they are looking in the wrong place," Lucho continued. "And by then, your friend will have done what he came here to do. He left yesterday with a team of men. He will be at the Aerie of the White Eagle now."

"I want you to take me there, too," da Silva.

"I will need more money," Lucho told him.

"That's not a problem," replied da Silva. "When can we set off — and how long will it take us to get there?"

"We can set off immediately, if you wish," said Lucho. "And once we have crossed the river, it will only take us three hours to find the place. We will follow the tourist trail for a short distance, then strike out north into the jungle."

"Good," said da Silva. "Finish your coffee. I want to leave immediately."

Olly and Josh backed away as the two men got up from their table and headed off along the street.

Olly was stunned by what she had just overheard. "Dad and Jonathan have been sent in the wrong direction!" she gasped.

"I know," Josh agreed, looking shocked.

"And now Lucho is going to take Mr. da Silva to the *right* place," Olly went on thoughtfully. She turned to her friend. "Let's follow them, Josh! If they lead us to the Aerie of the White Eagle, we may still be able to find the Amulet of Quilla."

Chapter Eleven: ∿
Into the Jungle

Olly stood at the water's edge, one hand up to shield her eyes from the river's silvery glare. There were many crafts on the Rio Beni — a ferry taking tourists to a popular beach upriver, canoes, and small fishing boats. But her attention was focused on one canoe in particular. It was halfway across the river, heading for the far bank.

A sturdy man paddled expertly. In the back of his canoe sat the guide, Lucho, and the tall, silver-haired Brazilian, Benedito da Silva.

"We mustn't lose track of them," Olly said, anxiously.

Josh frowned. "We can't just take off into the jungle, Olly," he said. "We're not really wearing the right kind of clothes. Plus we don't have any water or food."

Olly nodded and pointed to one of the many riverside restaurants. "Go and buy some bottles of water," she said. "I'll hire a canoe."

"And the clothes?" Josh inquired.

"No time."

Josh stared after da Silva's canoe for a moment, then turned and ran up the shoreline.

Olly scanned the riverbank for a canoe to hire. She spotted a skinny young man sitting on the bow of his canoe and hurried over to him.

Josh was right about their clothes, Olly thought, but there wasn't time to go back to the hacienda and change. If they lost sight of Mr. da Silva and his guide, then they might as well forget the whole plan. She knew that once the two men had melted into the jungle, it would be impossible to track them.

She and Josh had to act quickly.

~~~~

The wiry young man paddled the canoe with ease, and the slender craft cut swiftly across the waters of the Rio Beni. Further along the shoreline, Olly saw a group of capybara wallowing in the shallows, looking a little like furry pigs. Insects circled the canoe, buzzing and whining. Their guide ignored them, but Olly and Josh wasted a lot of energy trying to swat them away. Olly couldn't forget the warning her grandma had read from the guidebook.

As they approached the far bank, Olly spotted

Lucho and da Silva talking with their boatman on the shore. She got the impression they were arguing about money, and she smiled grimly — that delay was exactly what she and Josh needed.

The canoe bumped ashore, and Olly and Josh clambered out. Lucha and da Silva were just disappearing into the trees ahead.

The friends had disembarked in a shallow bay of white stones and brown earth, which sloped gently up to a steep ledge of wiry grass and overhanging trees. They ran up the beach and cautiously entered the forest.

The two men were following a well-worn trail that snaked through the trees. Olly remembered what Lucho had said: They would follow the tourist trail for a while, then head north into the deep jungle. She knew that she and Josh would have to keep their wits about them. They had to keep within tracking distance of the two men, but far enough back so that they wouldn't be spotted.

For half an hour, the two friends followed the men, keeping close to the tree line, ready to duck out of sight if either man should glance back. They met no one else, but the jungle around them was full of life. Olly heard the chirp and whir of insects, the screeching of birds, and the busy rustle of small mammals. Sometimes, a startlingly loud chattering would ring out, and she'd turn in time to see a small golden monkey skittering away through the branches.

Sandflies droned, gathering in whirling clusters under the trees. Olly was glad that they had taken her grandma's advice and covered all their exposed skin with bug spray.

The trail grew narrower — becoming a dark, six-foot-wide tunnel through overhanging trees. There was a series of zigzag bends, following a natural depression in the folded hills.

Olly and Josh jogged from one point of cover to the next — always checking ahead before coming out into the open, until, suddenly, they peered ahead and found that the path was empty.

"They're gone!" Olly whispered. She ran forward, with Josh close behind. There was no sign of the men — it was as if the jungle had just swallowed them up.

"You're in front. Didn't you see where they went?" Josh hissed.

Olly shook her head. She lifted her hand for him to be quiet, and listened intently. The innumerable sounds of the jungle filled her ears — but from close by she heard the distinctive sound of a twig snapping.

She ran off the trail and up a steep ridge, using the tree roots to help her clamber up the slope.

The ridge came to a sharp crest. Olly stared down the slope ahead and grinned. She could just make out da Silva's white jacket through the tangle of green leaves.

She caught hold of Josh's arm as he arrived beside her. She pointed ahead and he nodded. As quickly as they could, they scrambled down from the ridge, trying to move quietly through the undergrowth. Olly could hear the men's voices. She smiled grimly — da Silva seemed to be doing most of the talking, Lucho's voice only drifted back to her now and then.

Olly looked at the forest around her. Progress was a lot slower now that they had left the path, but the jungle was indescribably beautiful. The tree canopy spread out above their heads. The light that filtered through was golden and dappled with shadows. Thick, woody lianas hung from the trees like twisted ropes, and all around, exotic flowers bloomed like pink and crimson stars, their scent sweet and strong. Huge bees hummed as they moved from blossom to blossom, dodging the great sprawling ferns that grew to shoulder height beneath the towering trees. At times, Olly thought, it was like wading through a deep, green sea.

She glanced back at Josh. His face was running with sweat, and striped and smeared with dirt. His hair was sticking to his forehead. She guessed she must look the same.

Olly could no longer see the two men — she was following their disembodied voices. Although she could make out little of what was being said, she got the impression that da Silva was complaining.

Suddenly, she realized that she could hear the conversation more clearly. She caught a glimpse of white through the foliage and stopped quickly. Josh was at her shoulder. Da Silva's voice was belligerent. Lucho sounded apologetic.

"There is no other way," Olly heard him say.

Da Silva let out a curse, and the voices began to move on again.

"What was that about?" Josh whispered.

"I don't know," Olly replied. She pushed through a dense curtain of leaves and almost stepped out into midair. With a stifled gasp, she drew back, clutching onto branches as the ground dropped away at her feet.

She found herself looking down into a steep

ravine, about sixty feet deep — it was as though a giant machete had cut down through the jungle. A tumbling gush of white water ran along the bottom of the cleft. For a moment, Olly was at a loss. There seemed no way across the chasm. But where had Lucho and da Silva gone?

Then she heard a curious creaking noise. She drew back a veil of leaves and saw, just a few feet away, that a rickety rope bridge had been strung out across the gulf. Two figures were crossing the bridge, one moving quickly and easily, the other, da Silva, clinging on grimly and shuffling forward as if he expected at any moment to be sent plunging into the rushing torrent below.

Now Olly knew what da Silva had been complaining about.

Josh's grimy face appeared next to hers, and the two of them watched from the safety of the trees as da Silva reached the far side of the bridge. Moments later, the jungle had swallowed both men up again.

As soon as they were out of sight, Olly made her way to the rope bridge and examined it dubiously. Ropes as thick as her arm were wound around two wooden pillars set in the ground a few feet from the edge of the ravine. The narrow walkway of planks dipped and rose to the far side — at least thirty feet away. Olly could understand why da Silva had been reluctant to use the bridge. In places, the planks were missing or broken. The whole thing looked old and rotten and ready to fall apart.

She stood on the brink, clinging to the hairy ropes, her heart pounding in her chest as she gingerly took the first step onto the bridge. The plank creaked under her, the ropes rasped and groaned. She looked over her shoulder at Josh. His mouth was set in a thin, determined line.

Holding on with both hands, Olly took a second, cautious step. The rope bridge swayed. Stinging sweat ran into her eyes, but she didn't dare let go to wipe her face. The bridge dipped lower in the middle. Several planks were missing there, and Olly had to take a long step to cross the gap. Below her the rushing water hissed and spat.

Olly felt movement behind her and realized Josh was following her. She began the climb up to the far side. It was steeper than she had anticipated, and a kind of panic began to creep over her. There was a whir by her left ear, and a small, bright blue bird flashed past. Its rapid flight seemed to urge Olly to move more quickly. She was suddenly desperate to get off the bridge — convinced that it was about to fall away beneath her.

But her haste betrayed her. One foot slipped, and Olly came thumping down on her knees, her arms wrenched backward as she clung to the ropes. There was a dry crack, and the plank under her broke. For a moment, she hung in space, supported only by her hands. She saw a shard of rotten wood spiraling down into the water below. Watching it made her feel dizzy. Her fingers started to come loose, and she closed her eyes. She was going to fall.

Then she felt an arm around her waist, and she was dragged backward. She sprawled on the bridge, struggling to breathe.

"Are you OK?" Josh asked.

"Yes," Olly panted. "You can let go now."

She hauled herself to her feet, looking at Josh. "That was close," she breathed.

Josh nodded.

Olly could see by his expression that her accident had scared him. *But not half as much as it scared me*, she thought. "OK," she said firmly. "Let's try that again."

She took a long, careful step over the broken plank. This time there were no mistakes. In a few moments she was on solid ground, holding out her hand to help Josh.

Ahead of them, the jungle stretched out forever. Olly listened for voices. There was nothing.

She stared through the undergrowth. There was no sign of the two men.

She pushed forward through the leaves, her eyes straining for a telltale glimpse of white, her ears alert for any sound of human voices.

A sudden movement on the ground startled her. A long, sinuous yellow shape slithered past and was lost in the undergrowth.

"That was a snake," Josh said under his breath.

"Yes. I know," Olly replied softly.

She pushed on through the forest. "Where are they?" she muttered.

"They couldn't have gone far," Josh replied. "Just keep going straight ahead."

Olly swallowed and nodded. "What if we don't find them?" she asked.

Josh looked at her for a moment, then glanced down at his watch. "Lucho said it was a three-hour march, right?" he said. "Well, we've been walking for nearly three hours now."

"So we should be reaching the Aerie of the White Eagle soon," Olly remarked. "And it's a big outcrop of rock. We ought to be able to find it."

"Let's hope so," Josh responded.

They made their way down into a valley. In front of them, the land folded up in a high ridge.

"Along or up?" Olly asked.

"I think we should go up," Josh said, staring up at the ridge. "We might be able to see something from the top."

They each took a long drink of water, and then began to climb up the hillside. They were a few feet from the top when Olly heard the sound that she had been longing for — a human voice. She couldn't make out the words, but it was a man's voice, speaking sharply, as though issuing orders. She looked at Josh. "It's them!"

Josh frowned. "Is it?" he asked uncertainly. "It doesn't sound like their voices."

"Who else could it be?" Olly asked.

She forced her way to the top of the ridge and peered through the trees. The scene below her took her breath away.

Olly found herself staring across sixty feet of empty air at a man-made structure. It was a huge pyramid, overgrown with dense green foliage. The walls rose in steps to a crowning block that was almost at a level with Olly's line of sight. Lianas, creepers, and other plants covered the entire structure — except for the lower section of the wall facing her, where a dozen or more men were busy clearing the plants away from a monolithic stone entrance. From the square opening spilled a mass of rubble that completely blocked the doorway.

Olly knew exactly what she was looking at: It was an Inca temple, possibly the Lair of the Anaconda King, and the resting place of the Amulet of Quilla. As she stared at it in wonder, the same voice that she had heard before sounded again. She inched herself a little farther forward and stared down the cliff-face.

A man stood on a boulder about thirty-six feet below her. "Steady there," he called. "I want that entrance cleared before dark."

Olly's mind reeled. She knew that voice — and she recognized the man below her.

It was Ethan Cain.

Chapter Twelve:
The Inca Temple

"Olly?" Josh called softly to his friend. She was lying full-length on the ground, her head and shoulders above the crest of the hill that overlooked the temple. "Olly? What can you see?"

She didn't reply.

Frowning, Josh crawled up next to her. He soon realized why she hadn't answered.

He stared in stunned silence at the impressive pyramid in front of him. He saw the men working to clear the entrance, hacking and chopping the undergrowth with machetes, then hauling the cut foliage away from the huge stone doorway.

He was still trying to come to terms with this discovery when he saw Benedito da Silva and Lucho, clambering up a mound of white rubble to join a man standing on a large rock. He was watching the workers like a king surveying his armies.

Ethan Cain.

Josh caught his breath in amazement.

Cain's voice drifted up to him. "Da Silva? What

are you doing here?" the voice was sharp and cold — the voice of a man used to giving orders, and used to having them obeyed.

Josh's eyes narrowed — he knew only too well how that voice could change to honey when Ethan wanted to turn on the charm.

Benedito da Silva paused to mop his brow. He was panting, clearly exhausted by the trek through the jungle. "I wanted to see the temple for myself," da Silva replied.

"You don't trust me, is that it?" Ethan asked. "You think I'd take the amulet and not pay you your share?"

Da Silva raised his hands in protest. "I must protect my interests, that is all, Mr. Cain," he said. "Without me, you would not have gotten this far. Did I not find the mantra for you?"

"You were only an errand boy, da Silva," Ethan responded contemptuously. "It was Vargas who found out what Christie was doing. And it was Vargas who made the connection between the carvings on the stone and the old Aymara weavings."

Vargas! Josh remembered the name — Dr. Vargas was the expert that Professor Christie had called in to look at the Puma Punku Stone. So, he had been working for Ethan Cain. That explained a lot.

"But it was I who followed the boy and the girl to the weaver's house and saw the mantra on the wall," da Silva wheedled. "It was I who bought it and brought it to you."

"And you will get your money, once I have the amulet," Cain said dismissively. He turned to Lucho. "Have Christie and Welles been taken for their little walk?"

"Sí, señor," Lucho replied. "They will be gone many days, I think. Sandro knows what you expect of him."

Olly edged backward down the slope, and Josh went with her. They looked at each other. Josh could see fury and dismay in his friend's eyes.

"How did he get here so soon?" Olly hissed.

Josh shrugged. "He probably hired a private plane. He's a millionaire — he can do whatever he likes." He sat on the ground with his head in his hands. "He's really beaten us this time," he went on. "We're on our own, in the middle of the jungle, and he's got a dozen men down there. We can't do a thing to stop him!"

"Oh, no?" Olly demanded. "Well, we're not going to let that rat walk away from here with the Amulet of Quilla. It's not going to happen."

Josh stared at her. "So, what do we do?" he asked.

"We have to get into that temple and find the amulet before Ethan does," Olly said. "Then we have to sneak away again without being seen."

Josh's face lit up. "That's great!" he declared. "So, how do we get into the temple without Ethan knowing about it?"

"I haven't completely figured out that part yet," Olly replied.

Josh looked at her thoughtfully. "You mean you don't have a clue!" he decided.

"You could put it that way, I suppose," Olly admitted.

"We can't do much from here, anyway," Josh pointed out. "Maybe we should make our way around to the other side. That way we can get a lot closer to the pyramid without being seen. If Ethan's men are all concentrating on the front entrance, maybe we can slip in the back door."

Olly stared at him. "Do you think there is one?"

Josh shrugged. "There's only one way to find out," he said.

Olly nodded. "Let's do it."

〰〰

It took them a while to force their way across the hillside and to circle around behind the temple. But eventually, they broke through a curtain of ferns and found themselves right next to it. From there, the ancient building was a lot more imposing. It towered over them, the massive brown stone blocks showing through a green web of creepers and vines and lianas that straggled all the way to the high peak. Beautiful, brilliant blue butterflies pirouetted in the air, their wings the size of Josh's outspread hand.

In the distance they could hear the sounds of the men working. Every so often Ethan Cain's voice would ring out, shouting instructions.

"So?" Olly asked, wiping the sweat out of her eyes. "See a back door?"

Josh stared at the long base wall of the pyramid. It was entirely enveloped in foliage. They would need machetes to hack their way through to the stonework.

"No."

Olly peered up at the side of the Inca temple. "I think I can see holes," she said.

Josh looked up at the stonework.

"See?" Olly said, pointing. "Those dark areas? I think there are some stones missing. Let's climb up and see if we can find a way inside."

They used the thicker branches and creepers for help as they climbed up the first stone step. It was easily twelve feet high. Where patches of stone were visible through the undergrowth, they could see carved patterns and designs. Occasionally a face would stare out from between the leaves and grimace at Josh.

There was a fierce hiss, and Josh drew back in alarm. He had disturbed a large lizard, and it glared fiercely at him with bright eyes before turning its scaly green body and scuttling away.

Eventually, they found themselves standing on the broad platform of the first shelf. They went on to climb the second and third steps of the pyramid — but Josh was tiring rapidly, and he could see that Olly was also exhausted. Of the two bottles of water Josh had brought, one was empty and the other had only a few mouthfuls left.

The sun beat down on them as they stood panting wearily on the fourth step. The climb so far had proved futile. None of the missing stones had revealed a way down into the temple, and Josh was afraid that they were wearing themselves out for nothing.

Olly gazed upward. "Come on," she panted. "We have to keep going."

Josh peeled a large black caterpillar off his arm.

Scores of bright red legs waved as he placed it carefully on a branch. "I think this is a waste of time," he said.

Olly frowned at him, so he shrugged and began to climb again.

Flies whined in Josh's ears and buzzed irritatingly around his face. A large brown spider dropped onto his hand, and he jerked his arm away quickly to dislodge it. The spider fell onto a creeper, but the sleeve of Josh's shirt snagged on a twig. He tugged at it and the cotton ripped, leaving the lower half of his sleeve hanging by a thin strip of material.

"Oh, great!" he groaned, tucking the dangling sleeve up out of the way. He called back to Olly, who was behind him. "Maybe we should give up. We're never going to find a way in like this. Not in a million years."

"No way!" she replied. "If you think —" she broke off with a sudden, startled yelp.

Josh looked over his shoulder. Olly had completely vanished.

"Olly?" Concerned, Josh clambered carefully back down the way he had just come. There was a gap in the foliage. He spread the leaves and saw Olly's grimy face peering up at him from a hole in the stonework. She was clinging to some roots. Josh leaned down and closed his fingers around her wrists.

"I'm OK," she gasped. "There's something under my foot. Just keep hold of me for a second." She twisted and wriggled. "There. I've got it. I'm fine, Josh — you can let go now."

Josh released his grip, and Olly ducked down out of sight.

Curious, Josh kneeled and began clearing the undergrowth away. He saw that Olly had slipped down a wide crack between two of the stone blocks. The crack ran from the edge of the step right in under the next platform. She was bent over, staring down into the hole. Her head bobbed up again — she was grinning.

"Not in a millions years, eh?" Olly laughed. "I can see a way down. Follow me."

She disappeared into the crack again. Josh peered in after her. There was a ledge of stone a few feet down, and then another a little way beyond that. Below him, Olly was clambering lower and lower.

He followed cautiously. The footholds were firm, and once through the heavy roof, Josh was easily able to climb down the half-ruined wall to where Olly was waiting.

"Did you bring your flashlight?" she asked eagerly.

"Of course." Josh put his hand in his pocket and drew out the small pencil-flashlight he always carried. He switched it on, and a thin, bright beam lit the room.

They were in some kind of corridor. The stone floor was traced all over with a carved zigzag design, and the walls, cracked by pale roots and wound about with creepers, were covered in carvings of men and animals. Josh could make out the shapes of scorpions and birds, snakes and pumas, lizards, and other creatures he didn't recognize.

Josh set off along the corridor. The flashlight beam revealed a stone doorway set in the inner wall. He stared into a small, dark chamber while Olly peered over his shoulder. There were no other doorways, and nothing to be seen in the chamber except for the ever-present carvings on the walls and the white roots of creepers that had pushed their way in through the roof and now hung in hairy knots that trailed almost to the floor.

Josh withdrew, and the friends continued along the corridor. They had obviously reached a corner of the pyramid, because the corridor turned sharply to the left before running on straight ahead of them once more. The inner wall was marked by more dark doorways. The second chamber Josh looked into was an exact replica of the first — dark and covered with roots. But the next chamber held a surprise.

It was as dark and creeper-clogged as the others, but beyond the trailing roots, there was a ragged patch of bright light.

Josh and Olly crossed the room to take a closer look.

The far wall of the chamber had a long vertical fracture running down it from roof to floor. Stones had broken and fallen away, and a golden light was spilling in through the gap.

Josh stuck his head through the fissure and gazed into the light. He let out a gasp of sheer amazement.

He was staring down into a huge, lofty chamber, its patterned stone floor about twelve feet below him. It was filled with sunlight that streamed in through cracks in the high roof.

They had reached the heart of the Inca temple.

Chapter Thirteen: The Lair of the Anaconda King

Olly pushed in next to Josh so that she could see through the gap. She had expected to see a room on the same level as the one they were in and of a similar scale. When she saw the fabulous chamber at the heart of the pyramid, she was spellbound. Shafts of sunlight pierced the broken roof and made pools of golden light on the geometric designs carved into the floor. The light illuminated what at first appeared to be a lush, exotic garden of rich, green ferns and jewel-bright flowers. But, on closer inspection, Olly realized that the garden was not a deliberate creation but merely the natural result of the jungle's invasion. Green lianas and tumbling vines cascaded from holes in the roof, scattering clusters of fragrant blooms down the walls, in vibrant rainbow colors of red, violet, orange, yellow, and pink. Their scent filled the room, drifting in the bright air and attracting the turquoise butterflies that fluttered from flower to flower.

The chamber itself was oblong, with high walls of dark gray stone that glimmered as though polished. Olly saw a single stone doorway set in the wall at the far end of the chamber. Its mouth was entirely blocked by rubble.

Squat statues lined the walls. They were made out of a greenish stone that glowed in the glorious sunlight. They surrounded a carved rectangle that filled the floor of the room, and their arms stuck out at odd angles, while around their feet — and circling the entire chamber — was a barbed-wire tangle of dry, dead creepers and vines.

"You see what that is, don't you?" Josh said suddenly, pointing down at the patterns that were carved into the floor.

Olly nodded as she looked and recognized the designs. "It's the writing from the Puma Punku Stone!" she exclaimed.

The carvings in the middle of the floor were an exact replica of the Incan symbols on the Puma Punku Stone that told the story of Coyata's flight with the Amulet of Quilla. And the squat, green statues with the curious arms were great sculpted versions of the figures that had filled the border of the stone.

"Have you still got those pictures of the mantra on the camera?" Olly asked.

Josh took the camera out of its pouch and flipped the button to activate it. The small screen on the back lit up. Josh flicked through the stored pictures, until he found the best one of Olly holding the mantra.

The friends peered at the tiny image, their heads together as they tried to make out the details on the photograph.

Olly frowned and looked down into the chamber. "There are the swirly shapes," she said, pointing to one part of the floor. "And there are the squarish parts that look like a maze, and the zigzags, too." She looked at Josh. "It's definitely the same."

Josh shook his head. "The statues are different," he said. He held the camera up close to his eyes. "It's not easy to tell, but I'm sure the positions of the arms aren't the same as they are on the mantra. That's weird."

"The design on the mantra was copied from the Puma Punku Stone." Olly pointed out. "Maybe the people who carved the stone got it wrong." She leaned out of the cleft and peered down. The head of one of the statues was only a few feet below her. "Let's climb down," she said.

"OK," Josh agreed. "Me first."

Olly frowned at him. "Why?"

"Because if I fall, you'll know what *not* to do," Josh told her.

"That's ridiculous!" Olly said, but Josh had already put his flashlight away and was now scrambling through the fissure.

He straddled the wall, reaching down with one leg until his toes just touched the statue's head. He transferred his weight. Olly held onto his collar as he lowered himself carefully onto the statue's broad, flat head.

"OK, let go now," he said.

Olly released him, and Josh crouched down, then turned and eased himself slowly past the statue's face. Olly could see that there were clefts and projections in the statue that made it a fairly easy climb, and it wasn't long before Josh was walking through the crackling dead branches and out into the middle of the chamber and its flourishing garden.

He turned in a long, slow circle, his arms spread out. "Olly! It's amazing!" he called. His voice echoed.

Olly sat astride the broken wall and prepared to follow Josh. "OK," she murmured under her breath. "Here goes." She twisted around, gripping the cracked stonework with both hands and feeling for something solid with her feet.

Josh shouted up to her. "Left a little. That's it. You're almost there." A few moments later, she brought her feet down firmly on the statue's head. She dropped carefully to her knees and stretched one leg down over the huge face. The toe of her shoe lodged safely on a point of carved stone, and Olly lowered herself, reaching for the statue's great upraised arm.

She transferred her weight to the huge stone arm. But then, just as she was about to continue her downward climb, the stone arm began to move.

Olly let out a yell as she felt herself swinging downward. As the statue's arm shifted downward, she completely lost her grip and fell.

She landed on her back in an uncomfortable tangle of dry, spiky branches.

Josh peered down at her. "Are you OK?" he asked.

She hauled herself to her feet and clambered out of the dead undergrowth. "I'm fine," she replied, frowning up at the statue. "That thing deliberately threw me off," she added. "Whose stupid idea was it to make statues with moving arms?"

"I'm not so sure it was a stupid idea," Josh said slowly. "Take a look." He held out the camera for her. "See? Now that the arm has moved, it's in exactly the same position as shown on the mantra and the Puma Punku Stone!"

Olly frowned. "That's odd," she muttered.

A slow grin spread across Josh's face. "It's not odd," he said. "It's brilliant!"

Olly recognized Josh's look of triumph. "OK," she said. "What have you figured out?"

"The pattern on the Puma Punku Stone is the code to finding the Amulet of Quilla," Josh explained excitedly. "The people who built this temple wanted to make sure that no one could get to the amulet without knowing the code — so they built in some safeguards: They put the arms of the statues in the wrong positions."

Olly frowned. "You mean all the statues have moving arms?"

"Exactly," Josh agreed.

"And if we put them in the right positions — somehow that will lead us to the amulet?"

"Yes."

Olly looked around. Fourteen of the great squat

statues lined the walls of the chamber: one in each corner, three on the long walls, and two along the shorter walls. Rearranging all those arms was going to take some time.

Olly jogged over to the wall and listened. She could hear distant, muffled sounds — the unmistakeable thud, crash, and rumble of rocks being moved.

She ran back to where Josh was standing, peering at the camera. "We don't have much time," she said. "I'll climb the statues, you call out the positions the arms should be in." She looked anxiously over her shoulder at the entranceway. "And let's hope we get it done before Ethan Cain's men break through."

~~~~~

It was not an easy task to adjust the arms on all the statues, and nearly half an hour had passed by the time Olly reached the final green figure. Josh could see that she was worn out, but there was no time to rest — the sharp sounds echoing from the entranceway were getting louder all the time. Ethan Cain's men might appear at any minute.

"OK," Olly called down breathlessly. "What do I move?"

"The left arm should be twisted downward," Josh instructed. He watched as Olly climbed the statue until she could reach its raised left arm. She tried to tug it down. Nothing happened.

Josh heard a loud noise from the entrance. Cain's men were getting close. They were running out of time.

"It won't move," Olly panted. "It's stuck."

"It's the last one, Olly," Josh urged. "Give it another try."

Olly sighed. "I'll . . . try . . . something . . . else . . ." she gasped. She climbed higher and stood precariously on the statue's narrow shoulder. Hanging on to its head as best she could, she kicked at the arm.

There was a grating sound. Olly kicked again. The arm rotated suddenly and came sweeping down.

Josh stared at the mantra on the camera screen. Yes! Now all the statues were positioned exactly as they were on the weaving copied from the Puma Punku Stone.

Olly was looking around hopefully. "Well?" she called. "Now what?"

"I don't know," Josh replied. And then he heard a low rumble.

He looked over his shoulder, assuming that the sound had come from the entrance. But then he realized that it was coming from the floor beneath his feet. He felt the stones vibrate under his shoes. "Uh, Olly . . ." he breathed, staring down at the quivering floor. "Something's happening!"

A moment later, the rumbling became a loud grinding noise as the floor began to disappear from underneath Josh. He threw himself backward, falling full length on the ground. The massive stones in the very center of the room were pivoting and falling away to leave a large square gap. Josh pushed himself frantically away from the hole with his heels.

As he watched in amazement, a gigantic snake came thrusting up out of the gap. It was yellow, its back and sides spotted with black, its eyes bright, its scales gleaming. It reared over Josh, its mouth open and fangs bared, as if about to strike.

For a terrifying moment, Josh thought it was real, but then he realized that the scales were carved from shining yellow stone, and the powerful head was fixed in position.

The dust of centuries rained down from the massive stone snake as it quivered for a moment. Then all was still again.

Josh got to his feet, his heart hammering. He stared up dizzily at the huge snake. There was something very majestic about the arch of its neck and its glittering black eyes. But, most impressive of all, on top of its head was a huge, faceted crystal that caught the sunshine streaming in through the roof and sent brilliant beams of light scattering in every direction.

This, Josh realized, was the Anaconda King.

~~~~~

Olly was nearly sent tumbling from her perch on the statue's shoulder, as the middle of the floor opened up and the monstrous snake rose into the chamber. She clung on for dear life as the great stones of the temple shuddered and shook.

And then the room was still again. Olly stared, speechless, as dust filtered down through the air and daggers of light stabbed out from the jewel on the snake's head, raking the chamber.

"Josh?" she called down, after a moment. "Are you OK?"

"Yes," he replied. "Olly, look! *Look!*"

He was staring at the walls. Between the statues in the two longest walls, square entrances had opened up — two in each wall.

Heedless of falling, Olly scrambled down the statue and ran out onto what remained of the floor.

Each of the entrances was made up of four doorways, one inside the other — leading about six feet deep into the walls. Then there was nothing but a blank wall of smooth-set stonework. They were exactly the same as the niches they had seen on the Island of the Moon — the niches in the walls of Inak Uyu.

But here there was a symbol set into the facade of each door — a sun with eight rays radiating from it, a crescent moon, a five-pointed star, the face of a puma.

As Olly gazed in awe at the massive doorways, she was only half-aware of faint smoke beginning to rise from the dried creepers that surrounded the room. The dead vegetation was smoldering in the fierce beams of focused sunlight that darted from the crystal crown of the Anaconda King.

"What do we do now?" Josh asked.

"We have to choose which doorway will lead us to the amulet," Olly breathed. "And fast."

A sudden rumbling sounded from behind them. They both turned in time to see a cloud of dust billow out from the entrance tunnel. And then they heard a voice shouting, "I see light! Stand back there — let me through."

Olly and Josh looked at each other in horror.

"It may be dangerous," called the voice. "Keep back till I call."

Stones spilled out of the entrance, rattling on the temple floor. And then a figure emerged from the dust. Ethan Cain came scrambling down the rubble and into the chamber with a look of triumphant delight on his face.

They had not been fast enough, Olly thought in despair, their enemy had broken through.

Chapter Fourteen:
A Leap of Faith

Olly and Josh watched miserably as the man clambered through the tangle of dried branches and strode out into the chamber. He was smiling, and his eyes shined with greed. For several seconds he didn't notice the friends.

"Hello, Mr. Cain," Olly said wearily.

The smile vanished from Ethan's face in an instant, to be replaced by a look of disbelief — of utter astonishment. But he swallowed the shock quickly, and his face hardened.

"Olly and Josh," he remarked. "You never cease to astound me."

A sharp crackling interrupted their conversation. In several places, the smoldering branches had burst into flame under the intense heat of the light beams coming from the Anaconda King's crystal crown. Smoke was rising up the walls, and the fire was spreading rapidly, the flames running swiftly along the tangle of dead branches.

Ethan Cain stared around the walls. "Where is the amulet?" he shouted, his voice shrill with panic.

"We don't know," Josh yelled.

"And we wouldn't tell you if we did!" Olly added.

Ethan Cain ran into the middle of the chamber, his eyes scanning the walls. "Four sacred niches," he hissed. "Sun — moon — star — animal. But which one holds the amulet?" He glared up at the carved symbols, and then a fierce grin spread across his face. "Of course, Quilla was the goddess of the moon!" he exclaimed in delight.

He bounded across the chamber, kicking and dragging the smoldering branches away from the niche with the moon symbol.

The flames were leaping all around the chamber now. A wall of hissing and spitting fire completely blocked the entranceway so recently cleared of rubble.

But Ethan had managed to clear a narrow path through the dead branches. He stamped out the few flames that licked around the gap. Then, with a final victorious glance at Olly and Josh, he stepped through the opening he had made and approached the niche.

Walking in under the four stepped doorways, he stood facing the solid wall of stones and spread his hands out over the blocks, running his fingers over them carefully.

Josh started to run toward him, as if he hoped to somehow stop Ethan. But Olly caught hold of his arm and held him back.

"Let him try," she said quietly. "I think he's got it wrong."

Josh stared at her in confusion.

"Just watch!" Olly told him. Her eyes were focused intently on the man as he examined the stones. She remembered the legend that Beatriz had told them — of the puma that had led Coyata to the temple. She felt certain that the crescent moon symbol would not lead to the Amulet of Quilla — the puma was the guide.

She saw Ethan's hands come to rest on a single point in the wall. He seemed to press something, and Olly saw one of the stones slide away to reveal a gaping hole. She caught her breath, suddenly filled with doubt. Ethan had found something! Was it that simple? Did the doorway of the crescent moon really lead to the lost Amulet of Quilla?

The answer came swiftly and suddenly.

As Ethan reached into the hole, a slab of stone

came sliding down behind him, shutting the niche off — and imprisoning him inside.

Josh let out a gasp of shock as the stone block came crashing down — and Olly heaved a sigh of relief.

Josh broke free from Olly's grip and ran toward the gap in the wall of flaming branches. Apart from that one gap, the fire completely encircled the chamber now, the flames licking and dancing around the shoulders of the impassive statues.

Olly ran after Josh. He was already at the niche, pressing his ear to the stone. "Mr. Cain? Are you all right?" he called. Josh hadn't noticed the small oblong cavity in the face of the stone. It was at waist height.

Olly kneeled and put her mouth to the hole. "Can you hear me?" she asked.

Quick as a striking snake, Ethan's arm shot out of the hole and his fingers clenched Olly's throat.

"Get me out of here!" Ethan bellowed. "Call my men!"

Olly couldn't speak — the fingers were choking her. She clawed at Ethan's wrist, trying desperately to pry his fingers off.

Then Josh's fist suddenly came hammering down on the disembodied forearm. "Let her go!" he yelled, battering at Ethan's arm.

The fingers lost their grip and Olly scrambled away.

"Did he hurt you?" Josh asked as he helped her up.

Olly touched her neck. It was a little bit sore, but otherwise intact. "No, I'm fine," she replied.

She turned and ran back through the breach in the wall of flames. "Ethan's men will get him out of there as soon as the fire dies down," she said. She looked at Josh. "He's safe enough for now. We have to find the amulet."

Josh stared at her in disbelief. "Look at this place, Olly!" he shouted. "We're surrounded by fire. We can't get at any of the other doorways, even if we knew which was the right one."

Olly smiled. She felt curiously calm and clear-headed. "Remember that old legend Beatriz told us?" she said.

Josh frowned. "Yes — why?"

"Coyata went into a valley," Olly reminded him. "And there was a wall of flames blocking her way. She was going to turn back, but her puma guide led her on through the fire."

"Yes, I remember," Josh agreed in confusion. "But . . ."

Olly turned and pointed to the niched door with

the symbol of the puma set in it. The golden face was just visible, shining brightly in the leaping flames. "That's where the Amulet of Quilla is hidden," she said quietly.

"But we can't reach it," Josh argued. He stared into the roaring wall of flame and frowned. "How is that stuff burning so fiercely anyway?" he asked. "It's just a lot of dried twigs — it should have burned away to nothing by now."

"Maybe it's not an ordinary fire," Olly suggested.

"I think you're right," Josh agreed, his eyes opening wide. "I think these branches were put here on purpose. It's some kind of booby trap. They were probably treated with some kind of chemical to make them burn longer."

"The puma led Coyata through the flames," Olly murmured, taking a step closer to the wall of fire. Her eyes were fixed on the shimmering golden puma face behind the leaping flames.

"That was just a legend," Josh said. "We have to wait till the fire goes out."

Olly didn't turn away from the puma. "Cain's men will be able to get in here then," she replied. "We can't wait that long." She took another step toward the flames.

"What choice do we have?" Josh asked desperately.

Olly bit her lip, summoning her courage. It wasn't logical — it made no real sense — but somehow she knew that she had to go through the flames.

She remembered the shard of pottery with the puma face on it that she had found at the bottom of Lake Titicaca. She remembered Beatriz's voice as she had told the legend of Coyata and her puma guide. She fixed her gaze on the carved puma face above the massive stone niche. And then she ran forward and leaped into the flames.

~~~~~

Josh let out a horrified yell as Olly jumped. For a moment, she seemed to hang in the air, engulfed by the hungry flames. And then she was through. He saw her land lightly and turn toward him, her slim shape seeming to twist and writhe as the fire danced between them.

"Olly?" he called.

"It's fine, Josh," she shouted back to him. "Come through. You won't get burned."

Josh stared at her. It was impossible. He could feel the terrible heat of the flames already.

"What are you waiting for?" There was something wonderfully normal in the impatient tone of

Olly's voice. "Are you going to help me find the amulet, or are you just going to stand there?"

Josh let out a gasp of amazed laughter. "OK, OK," he said. "I'm coming."

He backed off a few paces, trying not to think about the impossibility of what he had just seen — and of what he was about to do. He rocked on his heels. "Three . . . two . . . one . . . go!" he yelled, and ran at the flames.

He leaped high. The fire was all around him. The heat was terrible. His head swam. And then he was through the flames.

Olly looked at him. She was smiling. "Easy, wasn't it?"

Josh gazed at the barrier of fire and then at his smiling friend. The flames were dancing in Olly's eyes. "How did you know it would be safe?" he asked.

"I didn't *know*," Olly told him. "But I remembered what Beatriz said — that the five hundred years of darkness would soon come to an end — that it was time for the amulet to be found." She looked sharply at him. "Don't you dare laugh at me, Josh, but I think we're meant to find the amulet."

Josh simply shook his head and shrugged. He didn't know what to say.

Olly turned and walked through the doorway until she reached the flat stone wall at the back. She ran her hands over the stone as Ethan had done. Josh joined her, and together they felt for something that might open a way through.

Olly pressed against each stone block, and found one that moved slightly. She pushed more firmly, and it slid back with a small grating sound. She reached into the gap. And then, with a much louder grating sound, the whole wall opened up in front of them — splitting down the center, from floor to lintel, and sliding apart to let the friends through.

"Can I have your flashlight?" Olly asked.

Wordlessly, Josh took it from his pocket and handed it to her.

The thin, white beam illuminated a small, dark chamber, no more than nine feet square. The walls were green with lichen and moss. Lying in the middle of the chamber was a casket of polished black stone about three feet long, and half that wide. It was carved all over with Incan designs.

Olly walked into the chamber and knelt before the casket. She grasped the lid and tried to lift it. It wouldn't budge.

She looked over her shoulder at Josh. "Help me," she groaned. "It's heavy."

Josh went around to the other side of the box and grasped the cold stone lid. They heaved and it came open a crack. Josh heaved again, putting all his strength into the effort. The lid rose and fell back.

But, as it did so, with a great rumble, the door crashed shut again, sealing them inside the chamber.

Josh stared at it in horror. "We're trapped," he gasped.

Olly stared at the wall that had once been a door. "We came here to find the Amulet of Quilla, Josh," she said, her voice strangely calm. "We'll worry about getting out once we've found it." She shined the flashlight into the stone casket. "Is this silver, do you think?"

There was another box inside the first that did indeed appear to be made of silver. Its lid was finely etched with stylized animals — llamas, lizards, hummingbirds, eagles, dogs, monkeys — there were scores of them, all grouped around representations of the moon in its various stages from crescent to full.

"It's amazing," Josh said, gazing at the beautiful engraving. "How did they do all this?"

"I don't know," Olly replied. "But I bet it took ages! Can you help me lift it out?"

The box had handles on both sides. It was heavy, but together the friends managed to pull it up and out of the stone casket. They set it down on the floor. There was no lock, so Olly lifted the lid and shined the flashlight inside.

The light played over another box. This one was made from some kind of white crystalline stone that sent sparks of light dancing across the roof and walls of the chamber.

Olly gasped in wonder, and Josh saw that the crystal was covered in carvings of pumas. The beautiful animals were shown in various positions — some running and leaping, others sitting or lying with their paws outstretched. He leaned forward to look more closely. The detail was incredible — the pumas even had tiny, needlelike claws and whiskers.

Olly reached in carefully and pulled out the crystal box.

Josh crouched by her side, and together they opened the lid. The casket inside was a rich yellow gold that burned with a deep luster as the beam of the flashlight ran over it. The box was a few feet long, and covered with more of the fine etchings — this time of simple spirals, triangles, stars, and squares, and series of parallel lines that Josh recognized as ladders.

"Ladders have something to do with death," Josh murmured. "I remember reading about it. Maybe we shouldn't open this one, Olly — we might not like what we find inside."

Olly looked at him. "I'm not giving up now!" she said. Silently, she lifted the lid of the golden casket — and let out a yell of shock and dismay!

Josh looked inside with curiosity, and shuddered. There was a dried, withered arm resting on a cushion of reeds. It was quite small and slender — Josh guessed it was a woman's arm. The skin was as brown as old leather and shrunken to reveal the shapes of the bones beneath. But the fingers were curled like dry, brown twigs around a crescent-shaped amulet of bright gold. It was covered with engravings and inlaid with diamonds and emeralds and rubies and sapphires that sparkled magnificently in the flashlight beam.

Olly smiled at Josh, her face patterned with a rainbow of colored lights reflected from the jewels. "We've found the Amulet of Quilla!" she breathed in awe.

Josh nodded, realizing that it was true. He was looking at the Amulet of Quilla, held in the shriveled hand of Quilla's loyal handmaiden, Coyata.

He reached into the casket, and jumped in

surprise as the bony fingers snapped open. His heart pounding, he lifted the amulet out of Coyata's hand. It felt heavy — heavier than he had expected from such a delicate object.

A small, sharp click sounded from the far end of the chamber. Olly shined the flashlight at the wall, and they saw that a stone near the floor had slid aside to reveal a dark passageway.

"That must be our way out," Olly remarked softly.

Josh nodded. "We should wrap up the amulet," he said. "To keep it safe." He tore off the ripped sleeve of his shirt and carefully wrapped the amulet in it, watching as the fabric smothered the spinning rainbows of light. Then he slipped the precious package into his shoulder bag. "Let's get out of here," he said.

They kneeled at the entrance of the tunnel and peered inside. The passage was narrow — only just wide and high enough for them to crawl through.

Josh took his flashlight back from Olly and, on all fours, crawled in under the wall. He aimed the flashlight ahead and saw that the square, stone tunnel ran straight ahead for as far as he could see. There was no light at the end, and no suggestion of how far it went.

Josh crawled silently on along the tunnel with Olly following. It was cool, but airless and stifling. Olly didn't say anything, but Josh knew that she must feel the same as he did — there would be no celebrations until they were safely out of the Inca pyramid.

The tunnel dipped at a shallow angle, and Josh guessed it was taking them beneath the massive temple walls. But a little while later, the tunnel showed no sign of finishing, and Josh became puzzled. "We can't still be under the temple," he panted. "We've come too far."

"We still have to keep going," Olly said. "What other choice do we have?"

She was right, of course — they had to follow the tunnel to its end, but Josh was beginning to wonder where exactly that end might be. And a more disturbing thought had occurred to him — did the architects of the ancient temple have any more tricks in store for them? So far, they had passed every test, but what if the tunnel was the final trap — what if it led nowhere?

The tunnel began to narrow alarmingly, and then they came to a place where it widened and split in two. Josh stopped and sat back on his heels, playing the flashlight beam along both channels. The tunnel to the right was by far the wider of the two. The left-hand one was tiny by comparison, and its sides and roof were jagged so that it looked like the open mouth of a hungry animal. The only way through that cramped entrance would be for them to lie flat and wriggle along on their bellies, squeezing in under the stone teeth.

And there was something else that Josh noticed: the stone teeth were angled inward down the throat of the tunnel, like the teeth of a predator, allowing prey in, but preventing escape.

Josh started forward toward the larger, right-hand tunnel. Olly didn't follow. He turned and looked at her. "This must be the way," he said.

"No, I don't think so," she disagreed. "Look." She took the flashlight and pointed it at a spot just above the entrance to the smaller tunnel. The pool of light picked out a carving on the stone that Josh hadn't noticed before. It was the face of a puma.

Josh frowned. "But we can't go through there," he said.

"The puma has led us this far," Olly pointed out. "It won't send us the wrong way now."

Josh stared at her. She looked tired — but there was a determined light in her eyes. "Are you absolutely sure?" he asked.

"Yes. This is the right way," Olly declared firmly. "Trust the puma, Josh."

He watched as Olly flattened herself on the ground and squeezed into the tunnel. Slowly, her body slid into the hungry mouth. The flashlight beam faded, and Josh found himself in absolute darkness. He could hear Olly's breathing, and the scrabbling noise of her body edging deeper into the tunnel.

Josh sighed and felt his way to the mouth of the left-hand tunnel. He stretched out and crawled in after Olly. Stone teeth scraped his shoulders and head. He stopped for a moment and tried backing out of the passage, but the stone teeth snagged in his clothes, stopping him.

"You had better be right about this, Olly," Josh muttered under his breath as he began to edge forward again. "Because if you're wrong, there's no way back."

Chapter Fifteen: ⟍
The End of Darkness

Olly dragged herself along the tunnel, grazed by the sharp stones that pressed in all around her. She had entered the narrow stone passage, driven by the absolute conviction that the puma would always lead her the right way, and that she and Josh were somehow *meant* to find the amulet. But as the tunnel burrowed on and on, growing no wider and showing no sign of reaching an end, her faith began to wane. Could she have been wrong? The significance of the angled stone teeth had dawned on her, too. If she *was* wrong, she had led them into a deadly trap from which there could be no escape.

And then a new problem appeared. The flashlight shined on dangling roots that began to clog the tunnel, making progress even more arduous. Olly pushed on, but the pale, hairy roots crowded in around her, smelling ripe and feeling unpleasantly soft.

She paused, fighting for breath, taking a moment

or two to gather her strength for another push forward. She felt Josh at her feet.

His voice came up to her in a muffled croak. "What's wrong?"

Olly took a deep breath. "Nothing," she replied, trying to ignore her doubts and fears and struggle on. But the flashlight was shining on a tangle of pale vegetation ahead that almost completely blocked the tunnel. Roots bent and snapped as Olly dragged herself past them — but there were so many ahead that she feared they would form an impenetrable barrier.

For a moment she despaired completely. They would never get through. They would die in this terrible tunnel, their bodies would never be found, and it would be *all her fault*.

But as her spirits reached their lowest ebb, she suddenly realized that she could see a faint green light ahead — and it had nothing to do with her flashlight.

The foliage that was blocking the way wasn't just more of the sickly white roots — it was green and lush, with leaves and curling green tendrils. Olly gave a sound that was half-gasp, half-shout and heaved herself into the dense barrier of greenery.

Her head emerged into bright sunlight. It dazzled her, and for a few moments she was totally disoriented. The ground seemed to be missing, and all she could see was a blur of brown that seemed to dance in the air many feet in front of her. She blinked and rubbed her eyes, and suddenly everything snapped into focus.

Olly gasped. The ground *was* missing — it fell away in a cliff-face. And thirty feet below, the foaming white waters of a narrow stream leaped and crashed over knife-sharp rocks. The brown in front of her was the far wall of the gorge, topped with trees and sprawling ferns and alive with blue and red butterflies.

Directly beneath her, Olly saw that a ledge had been cut into the rock-face. She wriggled carefully out of the tunnel and stood on the narrow shelf, leaning back against the cliff. She could see the ledge snaking its way slowly down to the rushing water below. A treachorous path, but a path just the same.

Josh's grimy face appeared through the greenery covering the mouth of the tunnel beside her. Olly helped him to crawl out, and they both stood in silence for a few moments, just relishing the sunlight, the clear, fresh air, and the sound of the racing water.

"Do you know what's really strange about the last part of that tunnel — the section after the split?" Josh said at last.

Olly looked at him. "What?"

"It's too narrow for an adult to get through," Josh told her. "And that's strange, because it means no adult could ever have escaped with the amulet."

Olly turned her head to look along the cliff-face. About nine feet to the right of where they were standing, there was a black cleft in the rock. She pointed at it. "I think that's the mouth of the other tunnel," she said.

Josh nodded. "You see, there's no ledge there, no path," he pointed out. "And it's too far away for anyone to climb from there to here. Anyone who chose that tunnel would be stuck. There's no way up. And no way down unless they jumped."

"You couldn't jump from this height," Olly said. "You'd be killed."

"Yes," Josh agreed.

"Is the amulet safe?" Olly asked eagerly.

Josh took the folded bundle out of his bag and carefully unwrapped it. The golden crescent moon glittered and gleamed. It was far more beautiful in the bright sunlight, where the jewels blazed like colored fire.

Olly touched it gently. "Put it away," she said, her voice soft and reverent. She turned her head and stared across the ravine. "Now we have to get back to Rurre," she murmured. "If we can."

Josh grinned. "I have an idea about that," he said. He pointed down to the rushing water. "I think that if we follow the stream, it will lead us to the Rio Beni. And then we can follow that out of the jungle!"

They followed the ledge down to the noisy white water. Near the bank, the stream was only ankle deep, and it wasn't difficult for the two of them to pick their way over the slippery rocks. Gradually the stream widened and calmed, so that the friends were sometimes picking their way over dry stones, and sometimes walking on mud-banks.

They saw an iguana sprawling on the brown rocks, basking in the afternoon sun. Sandflies danced wildly in swarms over the water, and the frogs watched them hungrily from wet hollows. The air was full of butterflies and the sound of monkeys chattering in the treetops.

Olly almost stepped on a salamander. "Sorry!" she said, watching as it slipped into the water and made off across the stream, leaving wide ripples in its wake. She saw movement farther downstream. "Look," she said. "Fish." There was a whole shoal of them. They were about twelve inches long, and their gray backs shined like polished steel under the clear water. Their heads were large and blunt.

Josh peered at the fish suspiciously. "Piranhas!" he declared after a moment. "I wouldn't try making friends — they'd eat you alive."

"Oh!"

After an hour or so, the steep banks of the stream began to broaden and fall away. Soon, the friends were walking along a rocky shoreline under tall trees.

Olly was thoughtful. She looked at Josh. "I guess Ethan's men will have rescued him by now," she said. "It won't take him long to realize we've got the amulet — not once he takes a look in that room with all the boxes." She frowned. "I wonder what he'll do."

"He'll go crazy," Josh said with a grin. "And I wish I was there to see it."

"Me, too," Olly agreed. "But what are we going to tell everyone? We know that Dr. Vargas and Mr. da Silva and Sandro were all working for Ethan — but you know what he's like. He'll find a way of making it all sound completely innocent."

Josh nodded. "It'll be our word against his," he said. "Jonathan and the others will think we've got it all wrong."

"We've found the Amulet of Quilla," Olly sighed. "That's the most important thing." She gave a growl of frustration. "But we still can't prove Ethan is a rat. If we try, it'll only get us in more trouble." She sighed again and thought for a few moments. "We'll tell them we overheard someone saying that there was a rocky outcrop near town known as Eagle's Nest. And we thought it might be the Aerie of the White Eagle — so we went to check it out. We'll say we found the temple, and Ethan and his gang were already there — but we got to the amulet first." She looked at Josh. "And we'll leave everything else out, right?"

Josh nodded.

"But one day," Olly added, "we'll find some way of proving what Ethan's *really* like."

Josh smiled grimly. "Yes, we will," he agreed fervently. "But not today."

The friends followed the stream for another half an hour, and then they found themselves standing on the banks of the great Rio Beni. The river curved away from them in a wide loop. Fingers of white mist curled out of the jungle and hovered over the glimmering water. The sun was low and red in the sky behind them. It was nearly six o'clock.

"How far do you think it is to Rurre?" Olly asked. "Gran will worry if we're not back soon."

"I don't know," Josh said. He pointed to the right. "But I think it must be that way."

They began to walk along the riverbank, feeling tired but happy. They had found the long lost Amulet of Quilla — Olly just wished they didn't have such a long walk home.

And she was in luck; they had only been stumbling along beside the Rio Beni for a few minutes when a canoe glided into sight through the silvery evening mist. They waved and shouted. The man in the canoe spotted them and grinned. He turned the boat and paddled toward them.

~~~~~

Olly leaned back in the prow of the canoe, delighted to be able to rest at last and watch the jungle slip past. Josh sat facing her, looking along the river in the direction they were traveling.

Their rescuer was gazing out over their heads, his arms working smoothly as he paddled. Olly closed her eyes, listening to the steady splash of the paddle. She trailed her fingers in the cool water.

"Piranha!" Josh cried suddenly.

Olly sat up with a jerk, snatching her hand out of the water and peering over the side of the boat in alarm. There was no sign of any fish — let alone piranhas.

Olly looked at Josh — he was grinning. She laughed and flicked water at him.

But Josh was momentarily distracted by something else.

Olly looked over her shoulder. Around a long curve, she could see buildings spilling down to the shoreline.

They had reached Rurre.

It was only a few minutes later that Olly and Josh were climbing wearily up the steps of the hacienda, relieved that their long adventure was almost at an end.

"Good heavens — look at the state of you!" said a familiar voice.

Olly looked around to see her grandma sitting on the veranda with a magazine, a drink, and a horrified expression on her face.

"Gran — you're up," Olly remarked happily. "Are you feeling better?"

"I was until I saw the two of you," her grandma replied. "What on earth have you been up to?

You're absolutely filthy." Her eyes narrowed. "You've been in the jungle, haven't you? And I specifically told you —"

Olly held up her hands. "Before you yell at us, Gran," she said. "Can I just say it was for a really good cause? And you'll be pleased when we explain it all — but could we have a drink first? Our water ran out hours ago and we're really thirsty."

Audrey Beckmann held out her glass. Olly half-drained the cool mango juice in one long gulp, then passed the glass on to Josh. He finished it.

"Now then," Mrs. Beckmann said. "Would one of you like to explain exactly why you decided to go into the jungle when I expressly asked you not to? You look as if you've been wallowing in mud like a pair of hippos."

"Well," Josh began. "It's a long story. You see . . ." His voice trailed off as a new figure emerged from the house.

Olly's eyes widened in surprise. "Jonathan?" she said, staring at Josh's brother. "What are you doing back?"

"We had some back luck," Jonathan told her. "I don't want you to worry — everything's under control — but your father was bitten by a snake."

"Where is he?" Olly gasped.

"He's lying down in his room," Jonathan replied. "But . . ."

Olly didn't wait to hear any more. Her father was hurt! She sprang through the door, ran up the stairs three at a time, and burst into his room.

Professor Christie was in bed, propped up on pillows and busy making notes on a sheaf of documents that spilled over the sheets. "Olivia!" he gasped as she came flying across the room. "Look at your clothes! What in the world have you been up to?"

She flung her arms around his neck. "Are you OK?" she panted. "Jonathan said you got bitten by a snake. Was it poisonous? Have you seen a doctor?" She frowned at him, her voice full of fear and concern. "How could you let yourself get bitten by a snake?"

Her father hugged her. "Calm down, Olivia," he said. "I'm perfectly all right. Katerina called a doctor, and he's examined the bite. The snake wasn't poisonous, and I'll be fit as a fiddle in no time. We only came back because Jonathan insisted."

"Yes, I did," Jonathan said, coming into the room. "We didn't know how serious it might have been."

Josh and Mrs. Beckmann followed him in.

"I think your father could do with some peace and quiet," said Olly's grandma. "And he certainly doesn't need you covering him in mud, Olivia."

Olly sat back and looked at Josh. "Show them," she said.

Josh took the precious bundle out of his bag and slowly unwrapped it. The sparkling jewels sent rainbows of light flying around the white walls.

"It's the Amulet of Quilla," Josh said, reverently holding it up for everyone to see.

Papers cascaded to the floor as Professor Christie leaped out of bed. He limped over to Josh and carefully took the amulet out of his hand. Jonathan and Audrey Beckmann stared over Josh's shoulder, their eyes filled with amazement.

"Where did you find it?" the professor breathed.

"In the Lair of the Anaconda King," Olly said proudly. "Ethan Cain was already there, but we beat him to it!"

Jonathan, Mrs. Beckman, and Professor Christie looked even more confused.

"Ethan Cain?" the professor queried. "Olivia — what are you talking about?"

"You should sit down, Dad," Olly told him firmly. "It's quite a story!"

It was nearly seven o'clock that same evening. Everyone was out on the veranda. The professor had his leg propped up on a spare chair. Olly and Josh had showered and changed clothes. And they were all digging in to a delicious meal that Katerina had provided for them.

Jonathan was examining the amulet with an eye-piece and making copies of the intricate engravings in a notebook.

Olly looked up as a figure suddenly rushed out of the trees toward the veranda. It was Ethan Cain.

Everyone stared at him in surprise. Olly could hardly believe her eyes — the handsome business-man showed no signs of his ordeal in the jungle. His clothes were clean and smart, and he bounded up the stairs as though full of energy.

At first, his face was filled with anxiety. But then he caught sight of Olly and Josh, and a look of abso-lute astonishment replaced the concern. "Josh! Olly! You're here!" he gasped. "That's such a relief! I was afraid you'd got lost in the jungle. Why did you run off like that? What happened to you?"

It was such a perfect act, Olly could almost have fallen for it herself — if she hadn't known Ethan Cain as well as she did.

Professor Christie stood up to greet him. "Olivia and Josh told us they met you in the jungle, Ethan," he said, limping forward and shaking the American's hand. "But I don't understand — what are you doing here? Jonathan told me you'd been forced to break off your vacation with Natasha to deal with a work crisis in California."

Ethan Cain nodded. "That's exactly what happened," he confirmed. "But things were nowhere near as bad as I'd been led to believe. In fact, by the time I got to California, the whole thing had blown over." He smiled. "It was too late to travel all the way back to Australia, so I decided to come and see how you were getting along with your search for the Amulet of Quilla." He smiled at Josh. "Your e-mail to Natasha made it sound as if you were really on to something." He looked at Professor Christie. "Then I had some real luck. I met up with a local guide who knew of an Incan temple hidden in the jungle not far from here. It's an amazing place." He gestured to Olly and Josh. "These two can tell you all about it. They got there ahead of me." He grinned. "I take it you did find the Amulet of Quilla?" he asked.

The professor picked up the golden amulet and held it out. Ethan Cain took it carefully in both hands. Olly saw greed and desire shining briefly in his eyes.

"Marvelous!" he said softly. "It's even more beautiful that I'd imagined." He put the amulet down, his fingers lingering on the surface for a few moments, as if he could not bring himself to let it go. Then he turned and Olly saw that he wore his usual charming, guileless smile. "I think we should celebrate," he declared. "I would like you all to join me at the Hotel Safari tonight. Olly and Josh will be the guests of honor!"

〰〰〰

It was, of course, the best hotel in Rurrenabaque. Ethan Cain had taken a luxurious apartment with a balcony overlooking the Rio Beni. The western horizon glowed with the last few threads of purple light, and a full moon was riding high in the velvet sky, making the river mists gleam like silver. The jungle spread out around them, dark and mysterious.

Ethan stood on the wide balcony with his guests, pouring champagne into their glasses. Mrs. Beckmann had given Olly and Josh orange juice for the toast.

"To the Amulet of Quilla," Ethan Cain said, raising his glass. He looked at Olly, and for a moment she caught, deep in his eyes, a flash of anger and resentment that sent a chill up her spine. "And to Olly and Josh for finding it!" Ethan finished.

Everyone drank.

"I'd like to make a toast, too," Olly said, her eyes resting defiantly on the American. "Here's to my dad, and here's to him finding the next Talisman of the Moon."

She watched as Ethan Cain drank the toast. He put the glass to his lips and drank heartily without a glimmer of annoyance.

"This is the third time we've beaten him," Olly whispered to Josh. "He must be furious, but you wouldn't know it by looking at him."

Josh stared at the suave businessman. "He is smooth," he growled under his breath. "How else would he be able to fool my mom the way he does?"

"We'll find a way to prove what he's really like," Olly said. "Look at him now, sweet-talking my dad! I bet he's already planning how to get his hands on the next talisman. But we're on to him. Ethan Cain had better watch out."

The two friends moved to one end of the balcony. Olly leaned on the rail, gazing down into the jungle. A subtle movement caught her eye. A long dark shape was padding out of the trees and slipping silently down toward the river.

Olly caught her breath. "Josh, look!" she breathed.

The sinuous, dark animal was at the river's edge now. As they watched, it lowered its head to drink.

"What is it?" Josh whispered as he peered into the gloom.

Can't you see?" Olly replied, her eyes shining. "It's a puma!"

At that moment, the beautiful creature lifted its head — and Olly could have sworn that it looked straight up at her — before it turned and stalked majestically back into the unfathomable jungle.

CHRONICLES OF THE MOON

LEGEND OF THE GOLDEN ELEPHANT

Chapter One:
A Dramatic Encounter

Josh Welles huddled in the doorway, clinging tightly to its frame as the deck of the riverboat rocked and swayed under him. The vessel was gathering speed as it sailed on down the river. Josh knew there was no one on the bridge. The captain was fighting alongside his few remaining crew members for control of the vessel. Josh heard gunfire from on deck as the attackers advanced on the captain's position. He noticed that a fire had broken out in the stern — red flames and billowing black smoke rose high into the clear blue sky.

He looked around frantically for his friend, Olly Christie. Everywhere, passengers cowered behind chairs, under tables, and in stairwells as bullets tore overhead. He spotted Olly crouched beneath the stairs leading to the upper deck, not far from him.

Suddenly, there was an explosion below deck and the whole boat shuddered. The iron stairs above Olly were wrenched from their fixings in two places. They creaked and groaned, listing ominously.

"Olly!" Josh called. "Get out of there! Fast!"

Olly nodded and ran to the shelter of the open doorway.

Josh could see a few men wearing crew uniforms still fighting back — but it was a very one-sided battle. Most had already been defeated — some looked as if they were dead, others wounded. A fight erupted on an upper deck as three crewmen sprang on one of the gunmen. They wrestled his gun from him, but in the struggle he lurched backward over the rail and fell — a long scream trailing behind him. Machine-gunfire rattled from above. There were more screams. Another explosion.

This mayhem had erupted in just a few minutes. Before the first shots had rung out, Josh and Olly had been lounging on the deck of the passenger cruiser, basking in the sunshine and watching the beautiful scenery of the forested north Indian valley slip slowly past. Then the gang of armed men had moved into action.

"Agent Jack Kelly! Show yourself or we will kill her!" shouted a voice above the noise of the battle.

Josh peered out along the foredeck from his hiding place. He saw his mother. She was being held hostage. Josh could also see the agent the gunman was calling to. He was crouched behind the rail on the upper deck. Josh watched breathlessly as he drew a pistol from his shoulder holster and leaped over the rail.

Then a terrified voice screamed from the prow, "We're heading for Elephant Falls!"

Olly and Josh ran to the rail and leaned over the side of the boat to peer ahead. Sure enough, the boat had traveled well past the jetty where it should have docked. Now it was speeding toward Elephant Falls, where the rushing torrent of the river plunged into a haze of sunlit mist. A rainbow arched through the rising clouds of vapor, and the water shined like silver as it tumbled over the lip of a mighty waterfall and plummeted ninety feet down a rugged cliff face.

It was so close, Josh thought. Surely nothing could stop the boat from plunging over the waterfall. They would all be smashed to pieces on the rocks below.

∿∿∿

"Cut!" The amplified voice rose above the noise.

Olly and Josh were almost jolted off their feet as the boat was brought to an abrupt halt by powerful steel cables anchored to the riverbank. The gunfire stopped. The dead men got up. And the terrified-looking passengers relaxed as cameras ceased rolling.

Several stunt coordinators ran forward with extinguishers to put out the flames.

The actor playing the part of Jack Kelly had landed on a large, inflated plastic mattress. He clambered off, grinning and waving to general applause.

"That was great, Ben," cried the film director. "Thanks everyone — good work. That's a wrap for today."

Olly and Josh ran over to join the glamorous Natasha Welles, who was standing chatting to her kidnappers and to her handsome costar, Ben Wilder.

"So — how do you two like being in the movies?" Natasha asked, smiling at her twelve-year-old son and his best friend.

"It's cool!" Olly replied. She looked at Ben. "Do you think they'd let me do one of those neat dives onto the mattress?" she asked. "It looked fun!"

"You'll have to check that with Giovanni," he said. Giovanni Bosconi was the director of *Collision Course*, a multimillion-dollar, continent-hopping action thriller.

"Hey," Ben continued, pulling a small writing pad out of his jacket pocket. "I've been meaning to ask — could I have your autographs?"

Olly and Josh stared at him.

"Excuse me?" Josh said. "*You* want *our* autographs?"

Natasha laughed. "Didn't I tell you?" she said. "Ben is a big fan of yours."

"I'm really into archaeology," Ben explained. "Natasha's told me how you and Olly's father have been traveling the world, hunting for the lost Talismans of the Moon. And you two were right there when three of the talismans were found!" He pushed the pad and pen into Olly's hands. "That's why I want your autographs. It has nothing to do with your future film careers."

Olly grinned as she signed and handed the book to Josh. The two friends had been a big part of Professor Christie's search for the ancient talismans. "Do you think someone might make a movie about the search for the talismans?" she asked.

"It would certainly make a great story," Natasha said. "Just think of the exotic locations — a tomb in the Valley of the Kings in Egypt, a lost city in a volcano in China, a temple in the Bolivian rain forest . . ."

"And now the Mandakin Valley in Uttaranchal in India," Olly finished, her eyes shining with excitement as she gazed around the rolling, green country at the base of the foothills of the mighty Himalayan Mountains.

"So, tell me, which talisman is the professor looking for now?" Ben asked.

"The Elephant of Parvati," Josh told him. "The legend says that it's a small statuette of an elephant, made of solid gold and covered with diamonds and rubies and emeralds and sapphires! But it wasn't Professor Christie's idea to search for it in the Mandakin Valley," he continued. "We're here because of an ancient parchment that was found close by a few weeks ago."

"Only a few people have seen it so far, and none of them can translate it," Olly added. "There's going to be a big conference at the Peshwar Palace, starting tomorrow — all the top archaeologists in the world will be there." She sighed. "Of course, the discussions won't really get going till Dad arrives since he is an expert on the Talismans of the Moon. He's been held up in Oxford with some boring college business, but he'll be here in a day or two. That's when things will really take off."

Natasha smiled at Ben. "Olly's very proud of her father, as you can tell," she said. "And with good reason, but Ethan has played an important part as well. It was one of Ethan's researchers who discovered the parchment in the first place, and it's Ethan who's organized the conference at the Peshwar Palace."

Olly and Josh exchanged a private look. What Josh's mother said was quite true — her American boyfriend, Ethan Cain, had organized the conference and was footing the bill for the expedition to find the fourth Talisman of the Moon. But they would both have preferred it if he was not involved at all.

Olly and Josh had good reason to dislike the American millionaire. They had seen a side of him that he had managed to hide from most people. Ever since Professor Christie had started his search for the four fabled Talismans of the Moon, Ethan Cain had been somewhere in the background — desperate to get to the talismans first. He was ruthless and cunning and perfectly prepared to use criminal means to get his way — but the worst of it was that Josh and Olly had absolutely no proof of his underhand dealings. Without hard evidence, no one would believe that the good-looking and charming businessman wasn't just as he appeared: an enthusiastic fan of archaeology. But Olly and Josh were sure Ethan was as selfish as he seemed. And this time, he was in complete control of the expedition to find the final talisman known as the Elephant of Parvati.

It wasn't simply because the Talismans of the Moon were of immense archaeological value that they had attracted so much attention; there was also a legend attached to them. It was said that if all the talismans could be gathered together, then they would reveal a great secret. It was Olly and Josh's belief that Ethan Cain wanted to learn that secret and use it for his own purposes.

"But what I don't get is why Ethan won't let anyone see the parchment before the conference starts," Olly said.

"He's invested a lot of time and money in this project," Natasha replied. "He has to keep control of the information, otherwise people could take advantage of him." She shook her head and laughed. "Sometimes, Olly, you almost sound like you're still suspicious of him."

Olly and Josh had tried once before to convince Natasha and the other adults not to trust Ethan — but the millionaire had talked his way out of it, making Olly and Josh look like foolish, overly imaginative children in the process. Olly knew there was no point in starting up that old argument again.

She was still trying to think of a tactful way to respond to Natasha's comment when there was a shuddering bump. The riverboat had returned to the dock. Olly was happy for the distraction.

"OK, people," called Giovanni Bosconi. "Please make your way safely off the boat. We'll be doing some pick-up shots tomorrow, so I want everyone involved to be ready by seven o'clock in the morning. And please remember that we're relocating to the Temple of Ganesha the following day. We only have access to the temple for the one day, so I need everyone to be on their toes."

Olly, Josh, Natasha, and Ben joined the stream of people disembarking. Crowded all around the dock were trailers, trucks, and jeeps, carrying all the cumbersome equipment and supplies needed for shooting such a big-budget film on location.

The assistant director met Ben as they walked off the jetty, talking at high speed about interviews and TV promo appearances as she led him away. Ben smiled at them over his shoulder and gave a helpless shrug.

Josh's twenty-one-year-old brother, Jonathan, was waiting for them at Natasha's trailer, sitting on the steps that led up to the door. Jonathan was Professor Christie's assistant — and a brilliant archaeological student in his own right. But since

Professor Christie was still in England, Jonathan had some time off.

He smiled as they approached. "How did it go?" he asked. "Did everything explode in the right places?"

"It was awesome!" Olly replied. "I'm expecting an Oscar nomination for 'Best Frightened Extra.'"

"It went very well," Natasha said, her arms resting around Olly's and Josh's shoulders. "And these two were great."

Jonathan laughed. "So — are you two planning a career in the movies now? Do you think you could handle being international celebrities?"

"It would be great to be rich and famous," Olly confessed, "but I still think I'd rather be an archaeologist, like Dad. Helping him find the rest of the talismans is much more important to me than being on the cover of *People*."

"I don't see why you two can't be glamorous celebrities *and* legendary archaeologists," Natasha said with a laugh.

"That would be great," Olly said thoughtfully. "But if I had to choose, I'd be an archaeologist."

Josh grinned. "That's so she can finally get rid of the creepy Christie family curse," he said.

Natasha looked interested. "You don't believe in the curse, do you, Olly?"

Olly frowned. "Well, to be honest, I don't really know," she explained. "But the parchment that William Christie, my great-great-grandfather, took from that tomb in Egypt said that the firstborn son in each generation would die young — and so far that's exactly what's happened! William's oldest son died. And then Great-uncle Adam — who was the firstborn son of William's *second* son — died in a shipwreck while he was trying to take the parchment back to the tomb. And then, most recently, Dad's older brother died young, too — in a car crash in 1964."

"But your father is a scientist," Natasha pointed out. "Surely he can't believe in curses?"

"He says not," Olly agreed. "But he first got interested in archaeology while he was researching stuff about the curse." She shrugged. "And you never know. It is odd that they all died."

"Those family deaths are just coincidences," Jonathan said reassuringly. "Don't worry, there are no such things as curses."

Olly looked at him. The sensible part of her knew he had to be right — but there was another part of her that wasn't so sure. And the thing that sometimes worried her was the uncomfortable knowledge that, for the first time since William Christie had removed the cursed writings from the ancient tomb, there was no firstborn son to suffer the Christie curse. Olly was an only child — her mother had died in a tragic plane crash two years previously. And there were no other kids in her generation.

If there really was a curse, and if there was no firstborn son, Olly wondered what would happen. Would the curse die out, or would it come down on her instead?

It wasn't a very pleasant thought.

Chapter Two: ☾
The Peshwar Palace

Jonathan was at the wheel of a rented jeep as it bounced its way down the unpaved road that led to the Peshwar Palace, some six or seven miles below Elephant Falls. Josh was beside him and Olly was in the back, kneeling on the seat and looking back the way they had come — staring into the far, far distance where the jagged, snowcapped peaks of the Himalayas reached up to the sky in a misty blue haze.

Closer, but still many miles away, the rumpled brown mountains of northern Uttaranchal gathered in crags and ravines. The nearer mountains became greener and greener as they tumbled down into forested foothills and lush river valleys.

Olly could see how this astounding place had caught Natasha's eye when she and Ethan had first flown over it in his helicopter. Natasha had suggested it to the producers of *Collision Course* as an excellent location for a dramatic action sequence — and within weeks the whole crew had been sent here.

The filming of the hijacked riverboat had taken place on a wide stretch of the Nintal River, as it flowed through the Mandakin Valley. To the north, the Nintal wound its way between steep valley walls, where pilgrim trails led to remote temples deep in cedar forests.

The jeep bounced and jolted as Jonathan carefully steered it along the path that snaked back and forth down the steep cliffs bordering Elephant Falls. They had reached the point where the trail came closest to the falls. Here, the road took a hairpin turn on a shelf of black rock that was permanently wet with spray. Jonathan brought the jeep to a halt and the three of them gazed in wonder at the curtain of white water that cascaded over the thirty-yard fall of the cliff face.

Olly rolled down the window, leaning out to feel the spray on her face and to hear the roar of the rushing water. "It's amazing!" she shouted over the thunder of the waterfall.

She had seen many wonderful and astonishing sights in her travels with her father, but the power and beauty of Elephant Falls took her breath away.

Down below, the falls flowed into one end of a long, oval-shaped lake. At the far end of the lake, the river flowed on, channeled by rocky banks into a long stretch of stony white water that tumbled away out of sight around a shoulder of the hills.

"I love this place!" Olly shouted, her heart pounding. "Oh, look!" she yelled, leaning out even farther and pointing to something even more wonderous on the far shore of the lake. "Elephants!"

Olly counted five full-grown elephants, as well as three calves, walking with slow majesty toward the crystal water of the lake. There were half a dozen men with them, two seated high on the backs of the lead elephants, the others walking alongside.

"There's an elephant orphanage over there," Jonathan said, pointing to the east. "There's a real problem with poachers in this region. They'll kill anything that will make them a quick profit — elephants, rhinos, tigers — you name it. So they have a shelter for the orphaned animals."

"How could anyone kill an elephant?" Josh wondered aloud, staring down at the huge creatures. "Do you think we could go down there and see them close-up?"

"Not right now, but I don't see why you couldn't come back," Jonathan replied. "It's not too far from the Peshwar Palace, but you'd have to watch out for the monkeys. I'm told they're great pickpockets. They'll snatch your things before you know what's happening — especially if you're carrying food."

They watched the elephants for a few minutes, then Jonathan started up the engine and they set off again. The jeep rounded a rocky cliff and then the waterfall, the lake, and the elephants were out of view.

Far ahead in the distance, where things were pale and hazy, the friends could just make out the town of Tauri, where the cast and crew of *Collision Course* were staying. But their destination was much closer at hand. Nestled in a small valley less than a mile ahead was the beautiful and impressive Peshwar Palace, shining like a jewel among the tall cedar trees.

It was a tall, square building of white stone, its walls punctuated by arched windows and ornate balconies. The high roof was adorned with slender white towers, extravagant domes, and golden minarets that flashed in the sunlight. The palace was surrounded by wide ornamental gardens of green, velvety lawns and flowerbeds blooming with color.

Fifty years ago, the palace had been transformed into a luxury hotel. And it was here that Ethan Cain had arranged for the archaeological elite from around the world to gather and discuss the parchment that he believed would guide them to the priceless Elephant of Parvati.

"The palace was built by the Mughal emperor in 1647," Josh told Olly. "It was supposed to be for his oldest son, but he died young and the emperor's second son, Balaram, inherited it instead. But then he was killed when the Chand Rajahs invaded and took over the country. Lots of different people have dominated this area over the past few hundred years, but the British managed to stop the final invasion in the 1800s."

Olly stared at him. "Josh, you can be kind of weird," she said. "How do you know all that?"

Josh grinned at her. "I looked it up on the Internet last night. Anyone could have done it."

Olly laughed. "Yes, but no one who is normal would have memorized it!"

The mountain path joined a more substantial road as it winded its way down to the hotel. Jonathan brought the jeep to a stop in a gravel parking lot, and then the three of them made their way to the front of the palace and up the broad marble steps to the wide veranda.

Ethan Cain was seated at one of the white, wrought-iron tables near the magnificent archway into the palace. He was working at a laptop, but he stopped and stood up with a smile and a wave, as Jonathan and the two friends came toward him.

"I've just been speaking to Natasha on the phone," he said, smiling from Olly to Josh. "She says the two of you should be looking for high-class Hollywood agents to run your future movie careers."

Olly managed a thin smile. "Far from it," she said. "All we had to do was run around looking scared and then cower in a doorway."

"Stay and have a drink with me," Ethan Cain suggested. "You can tell me all about it." He snapped his fingers and a white-clad waiter appeared from nowhere and hovered silently at his shoulder.

"That'd be nice," Olly said. "But I want to go and check with my grandmother and find out if Dad's been in touch yet. I expect you're anxious for him to arrive — I mean, you can't really start the conference without him."

Ethan Cain smiled at her. "Of course. We desperately need your father's expertise, Olly," he said smoothly. "But I really can't keep all these important people waiting around, you know. It wouldn't be fair to them."

Olly frowned. "You mean you *are* going to start without him?"

"I think we can manage a few preliminary discussions before your father arrives," Ethan replied. He looked at Jonathan. "I believe you will be acting as Professor Christie's stand-in until he gets here?"

Jonathan nodded. "That's right," he said. "And I'd like to have a quick word with you about that, if I may."

"Of course." Ethan looked at Olly and Josh. "I think we'll have our first full meeting tomorrow morning," he declared. He lifted a tall glass from the table. "Here's to a successful outcome. Here's to us finding the Elephant of Parvati!"

Olly and Josh exchanged an anxious look. Olly certainly wanted the talisman to be found — but not by Ethan Cain!

～～～

The reception area of the Peshwar Palace was very elegant. The high, domed ceiling was decorated with thousands of small mirrors that sparkled like trapped stars. Golden pillars framed the arched doorways, and rich blue draperies were swathed over the white walls. Olly and Josh walked across the dark blue-and-white mosaic floor toward the white marble staircase that swept in a long curve to the upper floors.

"Ethan is such a creep," Olly hissed to Josh as

they headed up to the suite of rooms allocated to the Christie party. "I know what he's up to. He's hoping to get that parchment translated before Dad arrives, so he can find the talisman all by himself."

"But even if he does," Josh pointed out, "he'll only have one of them. The professor is still in control of the other three."

"But if Ethan gets even one of the talismans," Olly responded, "it'll mean he can insist on being involved when the rest are found and they're all brought together so that the big secret can be revealed."

Josh frowned. "I wonder if there really is a big secret," he said thoughtfully. At first they had thought there might be just four talismans, but recent research suggested there could be many more — and they all would have to be found before anyone could discover their true purpose.

Olly shrugged. "Dad thinks so," she answered. "According to what he's read, the secret is the location of the lost Archive of Old — and you know what's supposed to be in there, don't you?"

"Copies of every ancient document that has ever been written," Josh confirmed. "Scrolls and parchments and books that have been lost for thousands of years."

"And remember what Jonathan says," Olly added. "He thinks there might be documents in there that prove human civilization has been around for at least twenty-five thousand years longer than anyone realized."

Josh nodded. "Yes, but your dad doesn't think that's very likely, does he?"

"No," Olly admitted. "But once the Archive of Old is found, we'll all know for certain, won't we?" She looked at Josh. "And I really, really don't want Ethan Cain to be in on it!"

"Neither do I," Josh agreed vehemently. "He's not an archaeologist. He's a fake. And he wouldn't be here if he weren't rich. He bought his way in."

"So, our job is to keep a close watch on him and make sure he doesn't get away with anything," Olly declared.

"Agreed."

~~~~~

There was a small brass plaque on the wall outside the double doors of the suite where Olly and Josh's party was staying.

In these rooms, the eminent archaeologist, Sir Oliver Gordon-Howes, lived and worked during his exploratory expedition to the region in 1903.

"Considering how famous Sir Oliver was, I'm

surprised Ethan didn't want these rooms for himself," Olly said.

"He's taken over the biggest suite of rooms in the whole place," Josh told her. "The Maharajah's Suite. It covers almost the whole top floor."

"He would!" Olly replied. "But I bet it's not as interesting as the rooms he gave us."

She opened the door and they stepped into a large sitting room with many doors leading out of it. The room was almost a museum to Sir Oliver Gordon-Howes.

A bookcase held copies of his published works, and a glass-topped cabinet displayed his diaries, open at pages filled with a pale scrawl and rough drawings. Another tall cabinet held Sir Oliver's compass, an old box camera in a cracked leather case, and the hat from the photos. Alongside these were a few of the artifacts he had discovered: small dancing figures sculpted from black stone; carved images of the elephant-headed god, Ganesha; and a brown pottery elephant with a small, mouselike animal sitting on its curled-up trunk. Olly wondered if these were recreations — or the real thing.

A large, framed map of the region hung on the wall, showing Sir Oliver's travels marked out in red ink. Many more maps, some much older, were kept in a special room on the ground floor of the hotel. Olly and Josh planned to investigate that room as soon as they got the opportunity. In fact, they intended to thoroughly explore the whole palace — it would give them something interesting to do while Jonathan and the others were working on translating the ancient parchment.

"Ahh, here you are." Olly's grandmother stepped in from a side room. Audrey Beckmann was a tall, elegant woman with gray hair cut in a neat bob. Ever since the death of Olly's mother, she had been looking after Olly and her father on their travels. When Natasha Welles's lifestyle had proved too erratic to provide her younger son with a stable home life, Josh had joined his brother and the Christies. Now Mrs. Beckmann was tutor to both Olly and Josh. As an ex-teacher, she was, in Olly's opinion, just a little too intense when it came to schoolwork. She insisted on lessons every weekday morning, even when there were far more exciting things to do.

"Josh and I have decided we're going to run away and be movie stars," Olly joked. "If that's OK with you, Gran."

Mrs. Beckmann raised an eyebrow. "I take it you enjoyed yourselves today, then," she said.

Olly grinned widely. "It was great!" she replied. "There were people firing guns, and bombs going off all over the place, and Ben did this amazing leap off the top deck."

"Good, then I'll look forward to a five-hundred-word essay on it as your homework assignment," Mrs. Beckmann said firmly. "That will make up for you both missing lessons this morning."

Olly sighed but she knew better than to argue the point. "I don't suppose you've heard from Dad, have you?" she asked.

"As a matter of fact, I have," Mrs. Beckmann told her. "I spoke to him on the telephone about an hour ago."

"When's he coming?" Olly asked eagerly. "He'd better get here soon. Ethan's planning on having the first meeting tomorrow."

"According to your father, his work in Oxford should be finished the day after tomorrow," her grandmother said. "And he's going to take the first flight he can. So we can expect him here in three days' time."

Olly smiled. "That's great," she sighed, relieved. "They're never going to be able to figure out what the parchment says that quickly."

"I wouldn't be too sure about that," Jonathan

said as he came through the door. "There are going to be some real experts around the conference table tomorrow morning."

"Not as expert as Dad," Olly said confidently.

Jonathan laughed. "We'll see."

"You're so lucky," Josh said gloomily. "I'd really like to be in there with you."

Jonathan smiled. "Oh, didn't I mention it?" he teased. "I asked Ethan if it would be OK for the two of you to attend some of the talks — and he said yes. So he's going to set out two chairs for you at the table tomorrow morning. As long as your grandmother approves, of course."

Olly and Josh both looked eagerly at Mrs. Beckmann.

"I think that would be a very good idea," she responded.

Olly grinned. This was great! Now, Ethan Cain wouldn't be able to get up to anything underhanded in her father's absence, at least not without her and Josh knowing all about it.

Chapter Three: ☾
The Whispering Shrew

It was quarter to ten the following morning. The first meeting of the International Conference on the Uttaranchal Parchment was due to begin in a quarter of an hour. Josh sat at the table in the main room of their hotel suite. Mrs. Beckmann had insisted that he and Olly wear their nicest clothes. They were waiting for Jonathan to take them down to the conference room.

Olly stood on the balcony, which provided a wonderful view of the beautiful palace gardens with their fragrant lilies, roses, and other exotic flowers. Slender, juniper-lined walkways led to sheltered arbors and to fountains and pools of still, clear water where golden carp swam. Beyond the gardens, the valley rose up into green hills and distant mountains.

Jonathan rushed from room to room, assembling his papers and pausing in front of the mirror every now and then to adjust his tie or smooth his hair.

Josh watched his brother in amusement — it

wasn't often that Jonathan showed signs of nerves, but he was clearly anxious about the conference meeting.

Mrs. Beckmann handed notepads and pens to Josh and Olly. "I want you to make notes of the meeting," she told them. "And I'd like you to write them up as minutes — you know what minutes are, don't you?"

"Of course," Olly sighed. "Minutes are a record of everything that happens."

Mrs. Beckmann nodded. "Now listen, both of you," she said. "You are very privileged to be allowed into this meeting — I want you to promise to behave yourselves."

Olly gave her an affronted look. "What's that supposed to mean?" she asked.

"I think it means that your grandmother doesn't want you telling them that they won't be able to translate the parchment without the professor," Josh said with a grin.

"That's exactly what I mean," said Mrs. Beckmann. "I want you both on your very best behavior. This will be a marvelous learning experience for you, so — mouths shut, Olly, and ears open wide."

"Why are you picking on me?" Olly demanded.

"I wonder," Mrs. Beckmann said with a half smile.

Jonathan joined them, a stack of documents under one arm, and his laptop under the other. "OK," he said, slightly breathlessly. "Is everyone ready?"

"We've been ready for half an hour," Olly pointed out.

"Then let's go."

Soon they were walking quickly down the magnificent corridors of the palace toward the tall double doors of the conference room.

Inside, they found a handful of people were already there, some going through papers, others standing and talking quietly together beside the polished, dark-wood table. On the wall at one end of the room hung a large screen, and Josh spotted a projector at the far end of the table.

A small, gray-haired Asian man walked up to them. "You are Mr. Welles, Professor Christie's assistant?" he asked Jonathan.

"Yes, Professor Wu," Jonathan replied. "And this is my brother, Josh, and Professor Christie's daughter, Olivia."

The professor bowed his head politely toward

the two friends. Josh had seen pictures of Professor Wu in his brother's archaeological magazines — he was China's foremost expert in ancient languages.

"If I may, I would like a word about Professor Christie's thoughts so far," Professor Wu said. He pulled Jonathan aside, leaving Olly and Josh standing on their own.

"I know him," Olly said softly, pointing discreetly at a large bearded man. "He's Professor Rostapov. He works in Moscow. And the woman talking to him is Doctor Johansdottir from Iceland. And that thin woman with the long hair is Judith Marx — she's from Berkeley University in California."

They stepped aside as more people entered.

Josh recognized the Nigerian Professor, Mpele, and Doctor McKenzie from Australia. He really did not know *that* many archaeologists by name and face, but it seemed all the ones that he would recognize were there.

"I don't know how Ethan managed to get all these people together in one place!" Olly whispered. "Some of them are really serious rivals. I remember my dad saying that Judith Marx and Doctor McKenzie can't stand the sight of each other. And there are plenty of others here who are always disagreeing with one another in print."

"I suppose Ethan thought it made sense to invite people with different opinions," Josh said.

"He's certainly done that," Olly replied. She gazed around the room as more renowned people came in. "This is going to be amazing. I can't wait to hear what they all have to say about the parchment."

"Good morning, Josh and Olly," came Ethan Cain's voice from close behind them.

They turned to see Ethan with a young man who he introduced as his assistant, Paul White. Paul smiled. He was slightly shorter than Ethan and looked immaculate in a tailored suit. He was clutching a briefcase.

Ethan rested a hand briefly on Olly's shoulder. "This should be interesting — plenty of lively debate, I should think. It's such a pity your father can't be here when we kick things off."

"We're expecting him in a couple of days," Olly told him.

"Really? That's great. I'm looking forward to it." He smiled. "Now, I think I should get this show on the road." He swept past the friends, closely followed by Paul.

Olly stared after Ethan as he greeted the gathered archaeologists. "I've got my eye on you," she murmured under her breath.

A couple of minutes later, Ethan brought the meeting to order. Everyone found their seats and the murmur of voices faded to an expectant silence.

Paul White laid the briefcase on the table and opened it. He took out a sheaf of brown folders and began to move quietly around the table, placing one in front of each person present — including Josh and Olly. Once he had finished, he closed the briefcase and quietly left the room.

Ethan Cain stood up. He gazed slowly around the table, and Josh saw a look of quiet triumph cross his face. The businessman was clearly reveling in the moment. *He must be in his element*, Olly thought, *being at the head of this big boardroom table.*

"I'd like to start by welcoming you all to the Peshwar Palace and thanking you for making time in your busy schedules to attend this meeting. As you are probably all aware, Kenneth Christie will not be able to join us for a couple of days, but in his place I would like you to welcome his very able assistant, Jonathan Welles, the son of my good friend Natasha Welles, the actress." He smiled. "I hope our endeavors will prove less arduous than the film that is currently being shot near here." There was a low ripple of polite laughter. "Seated with Mr. Welles are his brother, Josh, and Professor Christie's daughter, Olivia." All eyes turned to them. "Olivia, Josh, and I are old friends, and I am especially pleased to have them with us today."

Josh looked carefully into Ethan's eyes, but there was no sign that he didn't mean every word. Whatever dark thoughts he might harbor toward Josh and Olly, he kept them well hidden.

Ethan pressed some buttons on the projector, and a picture appeared on the screen at his back. It was a beautifully colored painting of a richly dressed couple. The man had a pale blue face and a golden crown. The woman's face was rose-pink and she wore an elaborate headdress. Between them, they held a baby, normal in every way but for one thing — it had the head of an elephant.

"This is the Hindu god, Shiva, with his bride, Parvati, and their child, Ganesha," Ethan Cain said. "Legend has it that Shiva did not realize the child was his own, and in a rage, cut its head off. When he learned his mistake, he replaced the lost head with that of an elephant." A second picture appeared. The human with the elephant head again — this time as an adult, with a round belly and four arms. "The child became Ganesha — the god of wisdom and learning — the remover of obstacles," Ethan continued. "You see him here depicted in his usual form, with one broken tusk, and with a discus, a club, a conch shell, and a water lily in his hands."

Another picture appeared behind him — this time it was an enlargement of a cracked and stained parchment, covered with flowing writing.

"This is the parchment that we are here to discuss," Ethan said. "It was discovered by a researcher of mine in an old shrine dedicated to Ganesha in the town of Tauri, about thirty miles south of here. Each of you will find a copy of the parchment in your folders. It is by translating this ancient document that I hope we may discover the resting place of that Talisman of the Moon known as the Elephant of Parvati."

The screen changed to show a drawing of a golden elephant covered in jewels. "The Elephant of Parvati has been lost for millennia," Ethan declared, "but it is said to resemble this artist's rendition."

Josh opened his folder and took out his copy of the parchment. He peered at it. The script was small and fine, consisting of row after row of delicate penlines, with loops and curls forming an intricate pattern that hardly looked like writing at all. At the foot of the page was a strange, simple, little illustration: an elephant, with some kind of mouselike animal that was nearly the same size, talking into its ear.

"I would like to pass the floor to Professor Indira Singh, India's foremost authority on ancient scripts," Ethan said.

A tall, slender woman in a bright red sari stood up. "Many of the symbols used in this writing seem similar to an early form of the Devanagari script used in modern Hindi," she said. "But we believe the language is a lost branch of Sanskrit, many thousands of years old. As you will see, it has many similarities to Sanskrit. However, the splitting on the sandhis is quite unlike anything I have encountered before."

Josh had jotted down Sanskrit on his notepad, but now his pen lay still as Professor Singh continued to speak. He had no idea what she was talking about, and when another of the professors interrupted to contradict what she had just said, it suddenly dawned on him that the meeting might not be quite as exciting as he and Olly had hoped.

Olly leaned close to Josh. "Have you got the faintest idea what they're talking about?" she asked.

He shook his head.

Another of the archaeologists joined in the discussion, and soon several people were all trying to speak at the same time. Professor Rostapov pounded his fist on the table to emphasize a point he was trying to make.

Josh could see that Ethan Cain was completely absorbed by the debate. "Ladies and gentlemen," Ethan called, as tempers, and voices, began to rise. "Please! We'll never get anywhere if we all speak at once. Professor Rostapov — I believe you wanted to say something."

"I think we can agree that certain words on this parchment bear a remarkable similarity to the Devanagari words for *full moon* and for *temple*," Professor Rostapov said. "We can therefore deduce that the first section of the writing concerns the Talismans of the Moon." There were murmurs of agreement from various parts of the table. "And the reference to a temple suggests that the talisman may be found in a temple in this region. Now, there is a temple only a few miles from here dedicated to Ganesha — we should surely investigate that before we get bogged down in linguistic detail."

"The Temple of Ganesha has already been thoroughly researched and explored," argued Professor Singh. "Besides which, Professor Rostapov is forgetting that the word preceding *temple* can be translated as *secret* or *hidden* or *missing* — suggesting that the talisman was placed in a temple that was already lost when this parchment was written in the early Harappan Era almost five thousand years ago."

"Surely, if the parchment mentions the moon," Judith Marx broke in, "we should search for a temple linked with the moon."

"I disagree," said Doctor McKenzie. "We need to have a much more thorough understanding of the entire script before we can proceed to search for anything."

A whole new debate erupted at this point. Josh noticed that Olly was slumped in her chair, obviously bored by all the arguing.

Jonathan raised a hand. "Excuse me," he said. "Has anyone given any thought to the illustration at the foot of the page?"

"The elephant and the shrew?" Ethan asked. "Ganesha is very often shown with a shrew companion — I doubt if the picture has any particular relevance to the Elephant of Parvati."

Oh, it's a shrew? Josh thought. *Not a gigantic mouse, then.*

"Yes, but the shrew isn't with Ganesha in this picture," Jonathan persisted. "It's with an ordinary elephant. I'm sure I've seen something similar before with Professor Christie, on a document from the

Vedic Period. It illustrated a part of a story which involved a shrew whispering secrets to an elephant."

"The Vedic Period is too recent to have anything to do with the topic we're discussing, thank you, Jonathan," Ethan said, in a dismissive tone that Josh could tell his brother found quite annoying. Jonathan simply nodded and fell silent.

The debate raged on. Josh was amazed that all these eminent people seemed unable to agree on anything. At this rate, they'd never make any progress. He noticed that the only thing on Olly's pad was a little drawing of a shrew, with a speech bubble over its head in which she had written: *How do you do? I am a shrew.*

He watched as Olly picked up her pencil and scribbled something else on her pad.

This is so unbelievably boring!

Josh looked at the drawing of the shrew. The illustration of the giant shrew and the elephant rang bells in his mind. He'd seen something like it recently — since he'd been at the palace. . . . He sat upright as his memory suddenly clicked into place. He opened his mouth to speak, but closed it again when he saw Ethan Cain's eyes on him from the far end of the table.

He picked up his pen and wrote on Olly's pad,

*I remembered something that might be important.
Let's go.*

Olly looked at him and her eyes widened with
interest as she saw his expression. She nodded.

Josh leaned over to his brother. "Is it OK if we
leave?" he asked.

"You might as well," Jonathan whispered back.
"I think we're going to be bogged down in this argument for some time."

Josh quietly folded up his copy of the parchment
and slipped it into his pocket. "We'll see you later,"
he murmured to his brother. "Have fun."

Jonathan gave him an expressive look.

As quietly as they could, Olly and Josh slipped
from their seats and padded to the door. Josh opened
it and — just as he was about to close it behind
them — he saw that Ethan Cain was staring at them
intently.

〰〰

"I can't believe the way they were arguing back
there," Olly said, shaking her head as they made
their way up to their hotel suite. "Maybe that
explains why a lot of professors and doctors and
smart people like that prefer to work on their own."
She looked at Josh. "So, what did you remember?"

"You'll see," Josh said.

There was no one in the main room when they got there — Mrs. Beckmann had left a note to say that she had taken a trip into Tauri.

Josh stood in the middle of the room. "OK," he said. "It's in here."

Olly looked at him. "What is?"

"The thing I remembered."

Olly frowned at him. "It's something to do with the parchment, right?"

Josh nodded, grinning.

"OK," Olly said. "If you can figure it out, then so can I." She looked around. "Don't say a word." She walked over to one of the display cabinets and scrutinized the contents.

"Cold," Josh said.

"Shush!" Olly hissed. She moved to another of the cabinets, looked carefully at its contents, and then moved to the next. She stared through the glass top for a few minutes and then smiled. "Got it!"

Josh walked over to join her. Lying on its side in the cabinet — just as he remembered it — was a dark brown pottery elephant, beautifully carved and covered in intricate ornamentation. Its trunk was curved up beside its head, and seated on the trunk, as if whispering into the elephant's ear, was an exquisitely carved little shrew.

"It's like that picture at the bottom of the parchment!" Olly exclaimed. "Except that the elephant and the shrew are the right size here."

"Exactly," Josh said. "A shrew whispering secrets to an elephant — just like Jonathan mentioned."

Olly turned the small gilt handle on the cabinet lid and it swung open. She gave Josh a look of surprise. Why had it not been locked?

"Careful," Josh said as she picked up the pottery elephant. "It looks really old."

"It's heavy," Olly replied.

They walked over to the table and Olly put the elephant down on its four stumpy legs.

"What's that?" Josh asked, pointing to a narrow slit behind the elephant's right ear.

Olly ran her finger along the slit — it was about an inch long and less than half an inch wide. "It's like the slot in a piggy bank," she remarked. "I wonder if there's anything inside." She lifted the elephant and shook it.

"Don't!" Josh said. "If you break it, we'll be in big trouble!"

A faint clattering sounded from inside the elephant.

"There *is* something in there," Olly declared excitedly. She turned the elephant over in her hands, and Josh again heard the sharp clink of something moving about inside. "Do you think it could be money?"

"I don't know," Josh responded. "Is there a hole in the bottom so we can get it out?"

Olly turned the heavy object around, but apart from the slot behind its ear, there was no other break in the pottery.

Josh lifted the elephant out of Olly's hands, turned it upside down, and gently shook it in the hope that the thing inside would fall out.

"That's never going to work," Olly said.

Josh held the elephant up high and tried to peer in through the slot to see what was inside — but the slot was too small and the inside of the elephant was too dark.

"There must be some way of getting it out," Josh said. He looked around. Olly had gone. "Great. Just leave me here talking to myself," he added loudly.

Olly reappeared from her bedroom with a pen-knife.

Josh frowned. "What's that for?" he asked.

"You've never had a piggy bank, have you?" Olly countered with a wide grin.

"No. Why?"

"Give it here and I'll show you," she said.

Josh handed the elephant over. Olly sat cross-legged on the floor with the elephant in her lap. She tilted it sideways and carefully slid the blade of the knife into the slot. Then she leaned sideways, angling the elephant until it was almost upside down.

Josh crouched at her side. "No way," he said doubtfully.

"You'll see."

A few seconds later, something small and slender and silvery slid out of the slot and fell onto the carpet.

Josh picked it up and stared at it. The artifact was clearly very old and he could see that it was engraved with beautiful patterns. But that wasn't what fascinated Josh most: The thing he was holding between his fingers was a tiny, silver key.

Chapter Four: ☾
The Silver Key

Olly and Josh sat at the table. The pottery elephant stood between them, and lying on the tabletop was the delicate, little silver key.

"A treasure chest filled with diamonds and rubies and pearls," Josh said, continuing their game of guessing what the key was for.

"I don't think so," Olly said. "I think it's the key to open the box where the Elephant of Parvati is hidden."

Josh's eyes widened. "Wouldn't that be great?" he said. "Imagine if we could find the box and get to the talisman while all those professors are still arguing about it."

Olly looked at Josh. "But could it really be that simple?" she asked.

Josh shrugged.

The door opened and Jonathan walked in.

"You've finished early," Olly said. "I thought you'd still be arguing for hours."

Jonathan dumped his papers on the table and

slumped into a chair. "So did I," he said, shaking his head. "There are fourteen eminent archaeologists in there — some of the finest minds on the planet — and almost every single one of them has a different idea about what the parchment says and what we should do about it." He ran his fingers through his hair. "We broke early for lunch. Paul came in and said something to Ethan. I don't know what it was, but he adjourned early for lunch. I suppose he must have had a call from California — something to do with his business, no doubt." He looked at the pottery elephant and then from Olly to Josh. "What's this doing out of its case?" he asked. "Do you have any idea how valuable it is?"

Olly placed a finger on the silver key and pushed it across the table toward Jonathan. "Josh remembered seeing the elephant in here when you mentioned that story about a shrew whispering secrets to an elephant."

"We heard a rattling sound when Olly picked it up," Josh added. "There's a little slot. The key was inside."

Jonathan picked up the key and examined it closely. "It's pure silver, I think," he said. "Look at all the fine tracery on it. It must have been made by a master craftsman."

"How old is it?" Olly asked.

"I have no idea," Jonathan replied. He held the key up to the light that streamed in through the French windows. "And here's another fascinating question: Where exactly is the lock that it was made to open?"

There was a knock at the door.

"Come in," Jonathan called.

Ethan Cain appeared in the doorway.

"I just came to check that Olly and Josh weren't too bored by the meeting," he said, smiling as he entered.

Olly stared at him in dismay. Ethan had picked the very worst moment to come to their suite. She reached across the table, desperate to get the key back from Jonathan before Ethan spotted it. But Jonathan turned toward Ethan and the key was shining brightly in his palm.

"I know all that talking can give you a headache," Ethan said. "But I'm afraid that's the price you have to pay for dealing with experts." He came over to the table. "That's attractive," he said, looking down at the key.

Olly prayed that Jonathan wouldn't tell Ethan anything about the key — but it was hopeless.

"Olly and Josh found it inside this pottery

elephant," Jonathan said, gesturing toward the little artifact sitting on the table. "It looks as if it may be quite old."

"Yes, I think it probably is," Ethan said, leaning forward to peer closely at the key.

Olly glanced at Josh. She could see from his face that he was thinking exactly the same thing she was. The very last person they wanted to see the key was Ethan Cain.

"An expert on Indian silverwork should be able to date it from the designs," Ethan said. "We should show it to Professor Singh."

"We were wondering what kind of lock it was made for," Jonathan remarked.

"That's a very good question," Ethan responded. He looked at Olly and there was an amused gleam in his eye. "It might even be the key to where the Elephant of Parvati is hidden," he said. "What do you think, Olly?"

Olly managed to keep her expression neutral. "Could be," she murmured.

"Everyone's in the dining room," Ethan said. "Shall we go and show it to Professor Singh right now? I'm sure we'd all be fascinated by her insights." He held out his hand and Jonathan dropped the key into his palm.

Olly stared in dismay. She couldn't believe that Jonathan had handed the key over so easily. She and Josh watched miserably as the glinting silver key disappeared into Ethan's fist.

~~~~

The dining room was on the ground floor. It opened out onto a wide veranda of white stone that overlooked the palace gardens.

Professor Singh was at a table on the veranda with Professor Marx and the Swedish doctor, Ingmar Froeman.

Ethan placed the key in Professor Singh's hand. "What can you tell us about this, Indira?" he asked.

She looked curiously at the key. "It is of beautiful workmanship," she said. "And very old — I'd say at least two thousand years by the designs engraved on it. It was probably crafted for the lock of a jewelry box or something similar. I have never seen an artifact quite like it. Where did you find it?"

"We found it inside a pottery elephant in our suite," Olly told her. "An elephant with a shrew whispering into its ear — just like on the parchment."

"I think the elephant might date back to the first millennium B.C.," Ethan suggested. "The Mauryan Empire Period, I would estimate. It's too recent for it to have any connection with the talisman, of course, but it is an interesting find."

"It is indeed," Professor Singh agreed. "I would advise you to put this somewhere safe. It is very fragile. Perhaps you could have a copy made. I believe there is a metalworker in the hotel who could do it for you. That way you could search for the lock that fits the key, without any fear that the original key might be damaged."

"That's an excellent idea," Ethan declared. He took the key from her and went in search of the hotel manager.

Olly watched despondently as he took the key away.

"Are you two hungry?" Jonathan asked.

"Not right now," Olly said, trying hard to mask her disappointment that their great find had just disappeared in Ethan's clutches. She looked at Josh. "Do you feel like going for a walk?"

He nodded, looking as fed up as she felt.

They left Jonathan talking with the professors and walked down the wide steps that led to the gardens.

"Leave it to Ethan to show up at exactly the wrong moment," Olly said. "Now we'll never get the chance to find out what that key was for." She sat on the raised marble edge of an ornamental pond. Silver and golden fish glided beneath broad lily pads. "I don't care what they say. I'm sure that key has something to do with the talisman," she said, dabbling her fingers in the cool water.

Josh sat beside her. He pulled out the folded copy of the parchment and smoothed it out on his knees.

Olly stared out across the gardens. A little way off, she saw a friendly face. Salila Gupta was the ten-year-old daughter of the hotel's chef. She had shown Olly and Josh around the palace when they had first arrived, and they had struck up a friendship. Olly loved the clothes that Salila wore: loose tunics and pants of brightly colored cotton, known as salwar kameez.

Olly waved and Salila came over to them. "I am feeding the fish," she explained slowly in clear and carefully pronounced English, showing them a pot of fish food. "It's fun today because they are hungry." She looked at Josh and Olly. "Are you enjoying yourselves at the palace?"

"Not much right now," Olly admitted. "But we'll get over it."

Salila looked at the paper in Josh's lap. "What is that?" she asked.

"It's a copy of an old parchment," he said. "The archaeologists are trying to figure out what it means. Apparently it's in a very old version of Sanskrit — maybe thousands of years old."

"May I see?" Salila asked, sitting down beside him.

Josh gave her the sheet of paper.

"Please tell me you can read it," Olly said with a grin. "That would make our day!"

Salila shook her head. "No," she said. "I cannot read it." Then she looked up at Olly and there was a sparkle in her eyes. "But I know someone who might be able to help."

Josh and Olly gaped at her.

"Are you kidding?" Josh said.

"Excuse me?" Salila asked, her forehead wrinkled.

"He means — are you playing a joke on us?" Olly explained.

"Oh, no, I am not making a joke," Salila replied. "Do you know of the elephant orphanage near here?"

"Yes," Josh told her. "We saw some of the elephants at the lake on our way back from the movie shoot yesterday."

"There is an old mahout there," Salila continued, using the Hindi word for elephant driver. "He is a very wise old man. His family was once rich — they sent him to England to be educated. But when he returned, he gave up all worldly things and chose instead a life of modesty and meditation. His name is Adhita Ram. He is said to be the only man alive now who can speak the ancient dialect of this region." She nodded toward the copy of the parchment. "You should show this to him — he may be able to translate it for you."

Olly and Josh stared at each other in excitement.

"What are we waiting for?" Olly cried, jumping up. "Let's go and talk to Mr. Ram!"

Chapter Five: ☾
Adhita Ram

Olly ran back to the suite to grab Josh's digital camera and to leave a note letting her grandmother know where they had gone. A couple of minutes later, she met up with Josh and Salila outside the front of the palace. Salila had told them that the mahouts led the elephants down to the lake every afternoon — and that Adhita Ram usually went with them. She suggested they go there first, and hopefully save themselves the much longer journey to the orphanage itself.

The road that led to the lake at the base of Elephant Falls wound its way through the hills for several miles, but Salila said she would show them a shortcut, a route that would take them through the hills and forests. That sounded a lot more interesting to Olly and Josh than a long, hot march along a dusty road.

Salila guided them up out of the valley of the Peshwar Palace and down through forests of rosewood and cinnamon trees, where the cool, shaded air was heavy with fragrance and the noise of insects. There were tall chestnut trees, too, and plum trees with branches heavy with fruit. In open country, thick bushes of juniper grew everywhere.

Josh pointed into the sky, to several long, elegant shapes that were moving above the hills with slow wing-beats. "Flamingos!" he cried.

"They are heading toward the sea," Salila explained. "They travel many miles to reach their breeding places."

Josh raced up to a rocky high point to take some pictures as the large, exotic birds with their vivid, pink plumage flew past.

Olly looked at Salila. "Are there any tigers around here?" she asked.

Salila shook her head. "They live farther up in the mountains — away from people," she said. "Higher up there are bears and deer and snow leopards. But where there are people, only wild dogs and monkeys are at home."

Olly sighed. "I'd love to see a snow leopard," she said wistfully.

"I have never seen one," Salila told her. "They are very rare."

The two girls carried on walking. It was a few moments before Olly noticed that Josh had not followed them.

She looked back to the ridge on which he was standing.

"Josh!" she called. "Come on — the flamingos are gone."

Josh didn't reply. He didn't even turn to look at her. Puzzled, Olly marched back toward him. "What are you doing?" she asked.

"Don't come any closer," Josh hissed at her through gritted teeth. "Go and get help."

Then she realized how strangely stiff he was, and noticed that his eyes were fixed on something on the ground just in front of him. She followed his gaze and her heart skipped a beat. A long, sand-yellow snake was rearing up from a nest of stones, its wide hood extended, its forked tongue flickering.

"It's a cobra," Olly breathed. "Josh, don't move!"

"Do I look like I'm moving?" Josh murmured.

"I'll get Salila. She'll know what to do."

Olly ran back to where the Indian girl was waiting. "Josh is face-to-face with a cobra," she gasped.

Without speaking, Salila moved quickly up the hill to where Josh stood frozen with fear. She stepped carefully up to his side and peered closely at the snake. "It is not a cobra," she said after a moment, with a grin. "It is a rat snake. It is harmless."

Josh let out a sigh of relief and backed away from the snake, wiping his sleeve across his forehead.

Olly shook her head. "Way to think it was a cobra," she said, laughing as the snake dropped to the ground and slinked away.

Josh gave her a look. "*You* thought it was a cobra, too," he reminded her.

"Rat snakes look very similar to cobras," Salila told them. "People are easily fooled. But rat snakes have no venom."

Olly looked at her. "*Are* there cobras around here?" she asked.

Salila smiled. "Oh, yes," she said. "It is wise to be careful where you place your feet."

They continued their journey, but after that, Olly found she couldn't take her eyes off the ground. She had a horrible feeling that at any moment something slithery and poisonous would rise up in front of her.

"The best way to deal with a snake is with a mongoose," Josh commented. "Mongooses eat snakes."

"Is that so?" Olly asked. "And do you happen to have a mongoose on you?"

"Not right now," Josh admitted.

"I didn't think so," Olly responded, and returned to her study of the paths ahead.

A loud chattering noise finally broke Olly's obsession with snakes.

She looked up to see a group of monkeys gathered on a rock just ahead of them. She guessed there were about twenty, a whole family troop of adults and babies.

"Those are the monkeys that Jonathan warned us to be careful about," Josh said. "The ones that steal stuff."

Olly looked at the monkeys. "Hey, listen," she called to them. "We've got no food for you guys to steal, all right?"

The monkeys were quite small — the largest of them was probably no taller than knee height — with long, slender tails. They had rough gray-brown fur and small, intelligent faces with big, dark, watchful eyes.

Olly looked at Josh. "Lend me the camera and go and stand over there," she said, pointing at the monkeys.

Josh handed her the camera and walked toward the rock. The monkeys stared at him inquisitively, and a few of the braver ones bounded over to check him out.

Olly held the camera to her eye. "Smile! That's a great pose," she said, giggling. "Josh and the monkeys — I wonder if anyone will be able to tell which is which!"

"Very funny," Josh replied with a hint of a smile.

‹‹‹‹‹‹

It was warm work, trekking through the hills on a hot afternoon, but Olly loved every minute of it. This was far more interesting than sitting in the stuffy conference room listening to the archaeologists disagreeing with one another.

It was mid-afternoon when they crested the last grass-tufted hill and found themselves gazing out at the dramatic spectacle of Elephant Falls.

"There they are!" Olly said, pointing along the lake to where a group of six elephants were drinking and bathing in the shallow water.

Salila shielded her eyes against the sun. "Adhita Ram is with them," she declared.

Eagerly, they climbed down the hill and made their way toward the elephants. The huge beasts seemed to be having a marvelous time in the shallows of the lake. The adults stood knee-deep in the water, filling their trunks and then lifting them high over their heads to send great spouts of water shooting over their backs. The young calves splashed about with water up to their shoulders, their trunks lifted like snorkels.

"They're taking showers." Olly laughed. "And look at that one taking a bath!" One of the elephants was lying on its side in the water while a young mahout scrubbed its mountainous hide with a broom.

"How close can I get to them?" Olly asked Salila.

"They are all tame," Salila told her. "They will not harm you." She called out in her own language to a young boy seated astride the neck of a massive old tusker. The boy kicked his heels and spoke to the elephant, and the creature slowly turned and moved ponderously through the water toward Olly. Its long mobile trunk reached out, its eyes small and strangely gentle in the great, gray head.

Olly stood quite still, captivated and just a little alarmed as the massive bulk of the elephant loomed over her. She held her breath as it examined her with its trunk. Then she reached out cautiously and patted the elephant's thick, tough skin. "I think he likes me!" She laughed, grinning at Josh.

"Most of them are fully grown," Josh said to Salila. "I thought an orphanage would just be for babies."

"The orphanage also looks after old elephants

who can no longer work," Salila explained. "They are brought here from the logging companies and from the mines in the east."

"Good boy!" Olly said, patting the elephant's thick trunk. "I'd love to take you home, but I don't think Gran would approve." She looked at Salila. "So, where's Mr. Ram?" she asked. As much as she was fascinated by the elephants, she had not forgotten their real reason for coming here, and she was eager to find out if Adhita Ram would be able to help them decipher the old parchment.

Salila led them to a hillock where an old man sat watching the elephants with bright eyes. He was very thin and his skin was dark brown, like old leather. His hair and beard were long and gray, and he wore a lungi — a long tunic of faded yellow cotton. Around his wrinkled neck was a necklace of dark brown bodhi beads and on his forehead were two white lines.

Salila introduced Olly and Josh. "My friends have a copy of some very old writings," she explained. "Would you look at it for them, please?"

The old man's bright eyes rested thoughtfully on Olly and Josh. Then a slow smile spread across his wrinkled face. "It will be my pleasure to help your friends," he said, his voice high and breathy.

"Thank you very much," Josh replied, unfolding the sheet of paper and handing it to him.

The old man held it close to his face in both hands. There was silence for a long time. Olly and Josh looked at each other.

"My great-grandfather was a great scholar," the old man said at last. "He would have been able to find the meaning in these words."

Olly looked hopefully at him. "But can you make sense of anything at all?" she asked.

The old man rested the sheet of paper on his bony knees and ran a long, crooked finger down the script. "This section says something like: *When all is lost, turn the key in the lock in the ear*," he murmured. "I believe those are the words, but its meaning is not clear to me. It may be symbolic. The lock may be ignorance. The key may be words of wisdom spoken into the ear to eliminate ignorance."

"I think I know what you mean," Olly said. "But we found an old pottery elephant with a slot behind its ear and there was a key inside it — an actual key. Could that be what it refers to?"

"It is possible," Adhita Ram agreed.

"Can you read anything else?" Josh asked eagerly.

The old man scrutinized the paper again. "Some of these words are familiar to me," he said. "But I have not seen writing like this since I was a small boy, and even then it was on a very ancient document." He shook his head. "I cannot translate anything else for you now. The meanings, the old words, they may come back to me — but it could take many days, and even then I would not be able to translate all of this writing." He held out the paper to Josh. "I am sorry."

"Please keep it," Olly told him, smiling. "Maybe you'll remember some more words later on. We can come back again another day — if you don't mind."

Adhita Ram bowed his head. "You are most welcome to return," he said.

Olly felt hopeful that he might be able to translate more words given time. She stood up, looking over at the elephants. "Do you think it would be OK for us to help give the elephants a bath?"

"Of course, my friend." Adhita Ram laughed. "But be warned — the elephants can be playful."

"So can I," Olly replied with a grin. "Come on, Josh — last one to wash an elephant has to sit by Ethan at dinner!"

Josh gave her a questioning look. Were they having dinner with Ethan? Not wanting to risk it, Josh picked up one of the brooms and ran down to the lake.

Chapter Six: ☾
Trouble at the Temple

It was early the following morning, and Olly was yanked out of a deep sleep by someone roughly shaking her shoulder.

Josh's voice sounded loudly in her ear. "Wake up!"

Olly opened her bleary eyes. "Go away!" she mumbled, trying to pull the covers up over her head. "What time is it?"

"Seven o'clock."

"Leave me alone!" Olly grumbled. "I'm not getting up yet. It's still the middle of the night!"

"OK, suit yourself," Josh replied. "I'll just tell the professor you'll see him later then?"

"What professor?" Olly demanded. "What are you talking about?"

Josh's voice was coming from the other side of the room now. "Your dad!" he called. "He just got here."

All the sleepiness fell away from Olly in an instant. She sat bolt upright in bed. "Why didn't you say so in the first place?" she exclaimed, clambering out from under the sheets.

"We're next door, having breakfast," Josh told her. And with that he was gone.

Olly ran into her bathroom. She splashed some cold water on her face and scrambled into her clothes. A couple of minutes later she came out into the sitting room, eager to see her father.

Professor Christie, Jonathan, Mrs. Beckmann, and Josh were seated at the table, eating breakfast.

Olly's heart lifted at the sight of her father. As always, his gray hair was an untidy thatch and his clothes were rumpled and unkempt. His glasses hung from a cord around his neck, and his corner of the breakfast table was scattered with documents.

He lived in a world of dusty books and ancient artifacts and deep thought, and when he was absorbed by his work — which was most of the time — he paid almost no attention to anything else. If she and her grandmother didn't keep an eye on him, Olly knew he was quite capable of missing meals and of wearing the same clothes for a week.

"Hi, Dad!" Olly said, giving him a quick hug and sitting down next to him. "How was your trip? Did you have time to look at the notes Jonathan made of the meeting yesterday? It just turned into one big argument. I told Ethan that he shouldn't bother starting without you, but no one ever listens to a word I say. You wouldn't think that all those doctors and professors would argue like that. Josh and I gave up in the end. We went to see an old mahout who we thought might be able to translate the parchment. He knew some of the words, but not enough to translate the entire passage. Did they tell you about the elephant with the key inside it?"

"Olly, for heaven's sake," her grandmother said. "Give your father a moment or two to catch his breath, will you? He's only been here ten minutes."

Olly looked from her grandma to her father. "Oh, sorry," she said. "I thought you'd want to know everything that's been going on."

"That's very thoughtful of you, Olivia," Professor Christie said with a smile. "Jonathan sent me his notes of yesterday's meeting and I've been studying the copy of the parchment. It's very interesting."

"Can you read it?" Olly asked. "The only part Mr. Ram could translate for us was about turning a key in someone's ear."

"'When all is lost,'" Josh quoted, "'turn the key in the lock in the ear.'"

Olly looked at her father. "Do you know what that means?"

He shook his head. "I'm afraid I don't," he replied. "But I do recognize some of the words from a document I once read in the museum in Mumbai." He took out a crumpled copy of the parchment, covered with scribbled notes. "This word is *water-fall*, I am almost sure of it," he said, tapping the paper with his forefinger.

Olly frowned. "Does it mean Elephant Falls?" she asked.

"I don't think so," said her father. "I believe it is a reference to something inside the Temple of Ganesha."

"Inside the temple, there's a shrine to Parvati," Jonathan said. "The shrine includes an artificial waterfall."

"But didn't Professor Singh say that the temple had already been searched from top to bottom?" Josh asked.

"I'm sure it has," responded Professor Christie. "But previous archaeologists didn't have the clues that are in the parchment. There are references to the moon, and to a hidden or secret temple." He frowned. "Of course, without being able to put these words in context, it is very difficult to know exactly what they refer to."

"What if it doesn't mean an actual secret temple?" Josh asked. "What if it means a secret *in* a temple?"

"And what if that key we found fits a hidden box in the temple?" Olly added. "The box with the talisman in it!"

"It's an interesting idea," Professor Christie said. "I would like to take a look at the key at some point." His forehead wrinkled. "It's possible that there is an undiscovered temple hidden somewhere in these hills," he said. "There are forested regions and mountain valleys in this area that could be protecting all manner of undiscovered treasures. All the same, I don't know of any documents that specifically mention a lost temple around here."

"So do you think we should concentrate on searching the Temple of Ganesha again?" Jonathan asked.

"I certainly think it makes sense to start our work in there," said the professor. "And this time, I think we should pay particular attention to the shrine to Parvati and its waterfall."

"I'm afraid you won't be able to visit the temple today," said Mrs. Beckmann. She looked at Jonathan. "Don't you remember? The director of your mother's movie has special permission to film there today. They're not going to welcome unexpected visitors; it took them several weeks to obtain permission in the first place, and they have only been allowed eight hours for shooting."

"Then we must be patient," said Professor Christie. "The talisman has been lost for millennia; another twenty-four hours won't make much difference." He looked at Jonathan. "And it will give me some time to talk to Professor Singh and the others. There's a great deal of information we need to discuss." He pushed his chair back. "And I'd like to see Ethan as soon as possible."

"I'll call him," Jonathan said, getting up. "I'm sure he'll want to speak with you, too."

"Can we come?" Olly asked.

"I think not," Mrs. Beckmann broke in before the professor could speak. "I let you skip your lessons yesterday to go to the meeting — and you left halfway through."

"Only because it was so boring," Olly pointed out. "It's not like we were learning anything in there."

Her grandma smiled. "Well, I can assure you that you'll learn something in here," she said, eyeing them both. "Be ready with your books in fifteen minutes, please." She got up and went to her room.

Jonathan called Ethan Cain's suite and Olly and Josh heard him making arrangements for an early morning meeting with Ethan.

A few minutes later, the friends found themselves alone at the table, picking at the last of the breakfast. Olly was thoughtful as she gazed out of the tall windows.

"It will be great if Mr. Ram can decipher some more of that writing," Josh said. "I think we could really be onto something there."

Olly frowned. "What makes you think we aren't already?" she asked.

Josh looked at her. "Because the only part he understood was about a key going into an ear. It's pretty obvious it meant that someone had hidden the key in that pottery elephant's ear. And we already knew that."

Olly shook her head. "I'm not sure that's it," she said. "I've been thinking about it ever since we met Mr. Ram." She looked at Josh. "The key we found came out from *behind* the elephant's ear."

"So?" Josh said. "It had to be put there in the first place, didn't it?"

"Yes, but the point is it was put in *behind* the ear, not *in* it," Olly insisted. "And it was a slot, not a lock." She took a deep breath. "Do you remember what Mr. Ram said? He thought that the passage in the parchment might not mean an actual key, he thought it might just have to do with someone whispering secrets into someone else's ear. We didn't agree with that explanation, because we'd just found a real key. But what if we're both right?"

Josh shook his head. "You've lost me, Olly."

"Maybe that picture of a shrew whispering secrets into an elephant's ear isn't a clue to where the key was *hidden*," she said. "Maybe it's a clue for what you should do with the key once you've found it!"

"You mean it's telling us to use the key in a lock in an elephant's ear — and that will reveal a big secret," Josh breathed. "Like where we could find the talisman!"

"That's right," Olly said. "The pottery elephant that we found the key in doesn't have a lock in its ear — I've double checked. That means we need to find another elephant — one that *does* have a lock in its ear."

"And it might not be an *ordinary* elephant at all," Josh added. "Maybe the lock is in the ear of Ganesha, the elephant-headed god."

"And if we add to that the other clues in the parchment," Olly said. "The waterfall, the secret in the temple — what happens when we put everything together?"

"All the clues seem to point toward the Temple of Ganesha," Josh replied. "That's where the talisman must be hidden. And we can find it by using the key in a lock in an elephant's ear!" He let out a groan of frustration. "Why did we ever let Ethan get his hands on that key?"

"Forget about that for now," Olly said. "What we need is some way of proving whether our theory is correct. If it is, then we can tell Dad about it, and he'll be able to get to the talisman first." She looked anxiously at Josh. "We have to go to the temple and check out any elephant ears in there, either attached to actual elephants, or to Ganesha himself."

"I've seen photos of the temple," Josh said. "It's *full* of carvings and statues of Ganesha."

"But it's still just a process of elimination," Olly pointed out. "We only need to find the one with the keyhole in its ear." She looked at him. "It's a shame we can't go there today, but the place will be full of the cast and crew of the movie."

"So what?" Josh said. "My mom is the costar — if that doesn't get us an on-location pass, then nothing will. And once we're in there, we can search around quietly while everyone else is busy making the movie."

Olly nodded. "There's just one problem," she said.

Josh frowned. "What?"

A door opened and Mrs. Beckmann's voice

drifted through from the adjoining room. "If you've finished breakfast, we can start lessons."

"That!" Olly said under her breath.

〰〰〰

Josh and Olly knew it would be a waste of time to try and convince Mrs. Beckmann to let them out of lessons. They would just have to submit to class-work for a few hours, and then quietly slip up the hillside to the temple at the first opportunity.

The Temple of Ganesha had been carved long, long ago, in the face of a rocky cliff about a mile north of the Peshwar Palace. Olly and Josh arrived there in the early afternoon to find the area outside the temple blocked by a jumble of trucks, trailers, and jeeps.

"I can't believe how many people it takes to make a movie!" Olly exclaimed, staring at the chaos of vehicles and people.

Josh laughed. He had been on location with his mother before. He knew all about the need for drivers, caterers, carpenters, electricians, camera operators, makeup artists, and props managers — and that was only the start. And there they all were — scurrying around outside the ancient temple like a bunch of frantic ants.

And there was equipment everywhere —

scaffolding and lighting rigs, sound-booms, power generators, and metal tracking for the cameras to run on. Plus, there were the true necessities: massive urns of tea and coffee.

Josh took the lead as the two friends made their way to the temple's square entrance. Above and around the doorway were astonishingly detailed carvings. Figures of men and women, animals, and gods gazed out of the cliff face. They were so skillfully chipped from the gray rock that they seemed almost real — as if caught and frozen in motion centuries ago.

There were people in the open doorway, and a loud voice could be heard from inside. Josh recognized the voice at once: The director, Giovanni Bosconi, was having a fit — or a breakdown — by the sound of it. Josh's mother had shared several stories about how Mr. Bosconi would fly into a tirade if something went wrong in the middle of a scene.

"This isn't working at all," he was shouting now. "The lighting's all wrong. Where's David? I can't work with these lights; they're too bright. I need more shadows. Am I surrounded by amateurs here?"

Olly and Josh slipped inside. The temple was crammed with even more people.

"Give me ten minutes," a gray-haired man was saying to Mr. Bosconi. "I'll fix it."

Josh recognized a young woman standing nearby. She was a production assistant. She turned and smiled at the friends, leaning forward to say in a whisper, "David Starr has two Oscars. He's brilliant, but Giovanni still isn't satisfied. He's driving everyone crazy."

"Where's my mom?" Josh whispered back.

The woman pointed deep into the temple. Natasha Welles and Ben Wilder were being given a quick touch-up by the makeup artists.

"Can we go in, if we keep really quiet?" Josh asked.

"I shouldn't let you," said the woman. "But, since you are the star's son . . ." She smiled. "Just stay out of trouble and don't let Giovanni see you."

Josh and Olly crept along the wall. Even though it was filled with people and gear, the temple was an astonishing sight. Sunlight poured in through high, arched windows, bathing everything in a rich, warm light. The main chamber was a great square room with orange-painted walls. A stone balcony carved with dancing figures stretched across the width of the roof. In the center was the sculpted elephant head of Ganesha, circled with garlands of flowers and beads.

The far end of the chamber was dominated by a six-foot-high full statue of the elephant-headed god. There was a tall golden crown on his head, and his trunk was adorned with a golden shield. He was seated on a stone platform that stood atop a long flight of wide stone steps. Ganesha sat with his four arms raised in blessing, his skin was painted a vivid red, and the expression in his large, black eyes was wise and peaceful. Carved white flowers hung in wreaths around his shoulders.

The friends worked their way to the back of the chamber. Here, a narrow passageway led to the black, wrought-iron gates that marked the entrance of the shrine to Parvati. Josh paused. One of the gates was slightly ajar. He peered inside.

The shrine was quite small and austere compared to the main sanctum. It was just a simple, unadorned chamber, carved from the dark rock. In the far wall, reached by four broad, black, stone steps, was a statue of Parvati, Ganesha's mother. She stood on the edge of a small, rocky precipice, over which a stream of clear water plunged into a wide, oval bowl. Black stone elephants had been carved all around the rim of the bowl; each had a lighted candle flickering in a holder on its back. More elephants stood underneath the bowl, as though bearing its weight on their shoulders.

A narrow sunbeam splashed in a pool of light on the stone floor. Josh couldn't see where the sunbeam was coming from, but he realized there must be some kind of window or vent high up near the roof. The pool of sunlight threw the rest of the shrine into deep shade, but the ring of stumpy yellow candles gave off a soft glow that scattered the shadows and flickered over the dark rock.

The shrine was very peaceful and calming. But then, to Josh's surprise, he saw a third source of light in the shrine. It was a flashlight! A man was running the beam of the flashlight over the elephants around the rim of the bowl. It was as if he was searching for something.

Josh caught his breath and shrank back in the shadows. It was Ethan Cain.

Josh heard Olly's voice softly in his ear. "What's he doing here?" she asked.

Josh shook his head and gestured for Olly to back up so they could speak without fear of Ethan overhearing them. So far, he was unaware of their presence — absorbed as he was in carefully examining each of the black, stone elephants in turn.

"I thought he was supposed to be chairing another one of those meetings this afternoon," Olly said quietly. "What's he doing up here?" She peeped through the gateway. "He's looking at the elephants," she added. "Why would he be doing that?"

"Someone must have told him what Mr. Ram said," Josh replied in a low voice. "He must have come to the same conclusion as we did about the key. He's looking for the elephant's ear with the keyhole in it. But why is he in here on his own?"

"Because he'd rather find the talisman all on his own, if he can," Olly muttered darkly. "I bet the others don't even know he's here." She frowned. "We can't search the shrine now — not while he's poking about in there." Her eyes glinted. "So, what do we do instead?"

Josh beckoned for her to follow him back the way they had come. "The ear with the keyhole in it might not be in the shrine to Parvati at all," he pointed out to Olly. "It could be anywhere in the temple." He looked up. "It could even be up there," he said, pointing at the sculpted head of Ganesha carved in the center of the long balcony.

Olly looked up at the balcony. "So let's go and check it out."

Narrow stone stairs wound up to the high balcony. Olly led the way this time. From up there, deep in shadows under the roof, Josh could see the movie crew getting ready for a reshoot. He peered down. His mother and Ben Wilder were being given instructions by Giovanni Bosconi. Camera operators were standing by.

Olly crept toward the middle of the balcony with Josh close behind. She leaned over the stone banister. Unfortunately, the elephant head was located at the base of the balcony, so they had to lean over the banister to even see the top of its ears.

"Can you see anything?" Josh hissed.

"It's too dark," Olly replied. She drew back. "I think I can squeeze between these," she said, edging a shoulder between the stone columns that supported the banister rail. "Then I'll be able to get closer. But you'll have to keep hold of me in case I slip."

"Are you sure about this?" Josh whispered uneasily. "That would be a nasty fall."

Olly looked at him. "Then don't drop me," she instructed.

She eased her head and shoulders between the stone pillars and squirmed around so she was on her stomach. Josh hooked his fingers into her belt, taking her weight as she edged forward to inspect the carved head.

"OK, everyone," Giovanni Bosconi called. "Scene fifty-seven, take fifteen. All quiet on set, please. I want plenty of energy, Natasha and Ben! OK — *action!*"

The assistant director snapped the clapper board.

Josh leaned forward to see what was going on down below. Ben and his mother were crouching behind the stone platform of Ganesha's statue. A strong flashlight beam was being shone around the temple from behind the cameras. The two actors ducked down as the light passed near them. Obviously, someone was searching for them in the scene.

Olly edged out a little farther. Josh tightened his grip on her belt. The beam of the flashlight slid over the walls of the temple and Josh watched the cameras follow it.

Suddenly, the flashlight beam climbed the wall and raked the balcony. Josh's heart jumped into his mouth — the beam of light was coming right toward them.

"Cut!" the director bellowed furiously.

Olly was caught on camera, right in the glare of the flashlight beam.

"What is going on up there?" Giovanni Bosconi yelled. "Who are those kids?"

"Oh, hi!" Olly called down. "Sorry — did I mess up your shot?"

~~~~~

Olly and Josh stood just outside the ring of trucks and jeeps. Olly was staring at the temple, her face clouded and her hands on her hips. "Anyone would think I'd ruined his precious shot on purpose," she moaned. "I told him it was a total accident — but would he listen?"

"I think we're lucky he didn't strangle us both with his bare hands," Josh remarked.

"He shouted at me!" Olly exclaimed. "I don't like being shouted at. I should go back in there and give him a piece of my mind."

Josh grabbed her arm. "Don't do that," he said. "We're going to be in enough trouble with my mom as it is, without you making it worse."

"Ethan Cain is still in there hunting for the keyhole," Olly snapped. "And he has the silver key, so he can open the lock the moment he finds it and grab the talisman for himself!" She stalked off angrily. "How could things possibly be any worse?"

Chapter Seven: ☾
Making Movies,
Keeping Secrets

The sun was setting, huge and orange on a golden horizon. A warm breeze wafted in from the palace gardens, scented with roses, hyacinths, and honeysuckle. Stars were just beginning to appear in the darkening sky and traditional Indian music was playing softly. A woman's voice rang out above the fluid, plaintive accompaniment of plucked sitar strings and the hypnotic rhythm of tabla drums.

Torches had been lit out on the dining-room balcony. Their flickering flames made the shadows dance. Around the table sat the entire Christie party, along with their special guest for the evening, Natasha Welles. Ethan had also joined them for the meal, but his dutiful assistant, Mr. White, had arrived at the table after only a few minutes, to say that Ethan was needed urgently on the phone. Some big problem had arisen at the headquarters of Ethan's California-based computer company.

"This could take a while," Ethan had said, apologizing. "I may not be able to get back any time soon. Enjoy your meal."

Olly wasn't sorry to see him go, but she was delighted to know that he had obviously found nothing in the temple that afternoon — his dour mood was proof of that.

There was more good news for the friends, too. Natasha wasn't angry with them for the trouble they had caused on the set. Quite the opposite, in fact. To Olly's surprise, Natasha seemed to find the whole incident highly entertaining.

"And then Olly said, 'Sorry, did I mess up your shot?'" quoted Natasha, shaking with laughter as she related the story. "Giovanni went absolutely crazy."

"It was a complete accident!" Olly exclaimed indignantly. "But he just yelled and threw us out before I could explain."

"Leave it to Olly," Jonathan sighed, grinning. "If there's an ounce of opportunity for trouble, she will find it."

"I hope you apologized properly to Mr. Bosconi," Mrs. Beckmann said, frowning.

Olly looked sheepishly at her grandmother, who obviously didn't find this nearly as amusing as Natasha or Jonathan did.

"We tried to," Josh said. "But he wasn't really listening."

"He didn't give us a chance," Olly agreed. "He was jumping around and waving his arms in the air and yelling so much that we couldn't get a word in edgewise." She looked at Natasha. "Did he *ever* calm down? We really didn't mean to wreck his shot."

Natasha smiled. "Don't worry about it," she replied. "That man is never calm. He's been driving me crazy. We were shooting a really simple scene a few weeks ago, in which my character realizes that her friend is actually working for the bad guys and was wearing a wire — you know, a bug that recorded everything I said and transmitted it to the bad guys who were listening in a van nearby. We only had a few lines of dialogue between us, and then I had to walk out of the room. But Giovanni kept changing his mind about how he wanted to shoot the scene. We ended up spending two whole days on it!" She shook her head. "And the version he used in the end was the very first one we did." She looked at Olly and Josh. "*That's* why I didn't mind you driving *him* crazy for once. He deserved it!"

"All the same, Natasha," Mrs. Beckmann put in. "I really don't think we want a repeat performance." She gave Olly and Josh a fierce look. "Do we?"

"I don't think they'll get the chance." Natasha laughed. "Despite Olly's surprise guest appearance, Giovanni got all the footage he needed. In fact, we're almost done. There are just a few scenes to be shot down in Tauri, then principal photography will be finished." She smiled around the table. "I've convinced the producers to hold the wrap party — to celebrate the end of filming — right here in the Peshwar Palace. And you're all invited. It's in three days. There will be reporters, TV cameras, everything! It should be a glamorous affair."

Professor Christie frowned at her. "I hope it won't turn into a media circus, Natasha," he said. "I don't want our work disrupted by reporters."

"I promise they won't get in your way, Kenneth," Natasha said, flashing him a dazzling smile. "But you know what they say — there's no such thing as bad publicity."

The professor gave her a horrified look.

"Don't worry about it, Dad," Olly reassured him. "The party's not for another three days — we might have found the talisman by then."

"I think you're jumping the gun a little, there," Jonathan said. "I suspect the film crew will be long gone before we get anywhere close to unraveling the text on that old parchment."

"I'm afraid Jonathan is probably right," Professor Christie agreed.

"But you already know some of the words," Josh said eagerly. "It won't take you long to put it all together, will it?"

"That's easier said than done," said the professor, shaking his head. "Without knowing the grammar of the language, the individual words can only offer glimpses into the meaning. Thanks to Olly and Josh, Adhita Ram has shed some light on one section — if he has translated it correctly — but that isn't enough to help us with the rest. We're still a long way from any real understanding of the text." He sighed. "And my colleagues have differing opinions about how we should proceed. I'm hoping that I will be able to convince them to explore the Temple of Ganesha tomorrow."

"I'm sure Ethan will be on your side," Natasha said. "He has a tremendous amount of respect for you, Kenneth."

Olly rolled her eyes at Josh, who gave her a sympathetic look. They both knew exactly how much respect Ethan Cain had for the professor! Just enough to use him to hunt down the talisman and then snatch it out from under his nose at the last moment.

"I wanted to ask you something. My costar, Ben Wilder, is a talented amateur archaeologist," Natasha was saying. She looked at Professor Christie. "He wondered if it would be possible for him to film you while he's here — to make a record of the hunt for the talisman."

"I don't see why not," Professor Christie said. "If he is careful not to get in the way of our work."

"You won't even know he's there," Natasha promised. "And just think — it means you'll have a day-by-day record of your search."

"Natasha's right, Dad," Olly said eagerly. "Wouldn't it be great to have someone right there with a camera when we find the Elephant of Parvati?"

The professor smiled at Olly, then turned to Natasha. "Tell Ben that he's welcome to join us, as far as I'm concerned," he said. "But Ethan will have to give his blessing, of course. He's in charge of this conference."

Natasha smiled. "I've already asked Ethan," she replied. "He said it was fine with him — but only if you approved. Ben will be really pleased. He's not needed on set tomorrow, so if you really are going to explore the temple, I'm sure he'd love to be there."

"Don't forget to take the silver key with you," Olly reminded her father. "Then, when you find the ear with the keyhole in it, you'll be able to open it right away."

"Professor Singh has explored the temple on several occasions," her father said. "She is adamant that there isn't any kind of hidden keyhole in there."

"Not even in the shrine?" Olly asked. "Josh and I have this theory that the keyhole is probably in Parvati's shrine."

"And why's that?" Jonathan asked.

"Well, it's obvious, isn't it?" Olly responded. "Dad said that the parchment mentioned a waterfall, and the only waterfall around here — apart from Elephant Falls — is in the shrine to Parvati. So the talisman is probably there."

"I see," Mrs. Beckmann said, looking grave. "I assume *that* was the real reason you went up there this afternoon. And you told me you just wanted to watch the movie being shot."

Olly smiled weakly at her. "Well, we did want to see the movie being made," she insisted. "We just thought we could look for the keyhole at the same time. You know, multitasking."

Jonathan laughed. "But if you thought the keyhole was in the shrine," he said, "why were you hanging from the balcony in the main chamber?"

"Because Ethan was in the shrine," Olly explained.

"And we didn't want to disturb him," Josh added quickly. "Do you know why Ethan was there?"

Jonathan shook his head. "He handed the meeting over to the professor after lunch," he said. "But I thought he had been called away because of some problem in California. I didn't know he had gone up to the temple."

"But it was you who told him what Adhita Ram had said, wasn't it?" Olly asked.

"Not me," he said. "I never had a chance to mention it."

Olly looked at her father. "Did you discuss it with him, Dad?" she asked.

Professor Christie shook his head.

"Why do you ask?" Jonathan inquired.

"Oh, no reason," Olly replied, glancing at Josh. "It's not important."

But it was very strange. She and Josh had only decided to investigate the shrine after making the link between the shrew whispering to the elephant and Adhita Ram's translation about putting a key into a lock in an ear. If no one had told Ethan Cain of the old mahout's words, then why had he been in the shrine that afternoon? And why had he been so interested in the elephants there?

It was a real puzzle.

Chapter Eight: ☾
The Hidden Temple

The meal was over. Josh and Olly sat alone on the steps down to the gardens, while the others chatted over drinks at the table.

A starry night had fallen over the valley, and the long gardens were a sea of shadows, surrounding ponds that reflected sparkling stars. The hills looked like the black backs of sleeping animals and the walls of the palace glowed with light.

Olly sipped her badan, a sweet drink made from almonds and saffron-flavored milk. Josh had chosen a masala soda, flavored with lime and spices.

"So," Olly said, her voice low so she would not be overheard at the nearby table. "How come Ethan Cain was up there checking out the elephants, if no one told him what Adhita Ram said to us?"

"Maybe Ethan heard about Mr. Ram," Josh suggested. "Maybe Ethan went and talked to him."

"I suppose that could be it," Olly agreed. "Listen, we told Mr. Ram we'd go and visit him again soon. Perhaps we should do that tomorrow — that way we can ask him whether Ethan sneaked over to worm information out of him."

"Shouldn't we go back to the temple first to try and find the keyhole?" Josh asked. "I know no one else believes it's there, but I don't think they've looked hard enough."

Olly nodded. "I agree," she said. "It's got to be there. OK, first of all, we go up to the temple with Dad and the others. If we can't find the keyhole, then we go and see Mr. Ram. He might have deciphered some more of the writing. But even if he hasn't, at least we can warn him not to talk to Ethan again."

Josh looked thoughtfully at her.

"What?" she asked.

"Oh, nothing," he said. "I was just wondering whether your grandmother would let us out of lessons in the morning, that's all."

Olly stared at him. "Of course she will," she said. "Exploring the temple is educational, isn't it? How could she refuse?"

~~~~~

It was the following morning. Breakfast had been cleared away and Professor Christie and Jonathan had gone to make preparations for their trip to the temple. Olly went into her bedroom and emerged wearing her hill-trekking clothes and a pair of stout walking boots.

Mrs. Beckmann was having a final cup of tea and reading the newspaper. Josh was leaning on the balcony, enjoying the view.

Olly stood in the open balcony doorway. "Come on, Josh, get your gear. We're not going to wait for you."

Mrs. Beckmann peered at Olly over the top of the newspaper. "And where exactly do you think you're going, Olivia?" she asked.

Olly turned cheerfully to look at her grandmother. "Josh and I are going to help explore the temple," she said. She gave her grandmother a hopeful smile. "It'll be really educational. A once-in-a-lifetime experience. We'll tell you all about it when we get back. We could even write up a report."

Mrs. Beckmann finished her tea and quietly folded the paper. "I expect you to be ready for your lessons in fifteen minutes," she said.

Olly laughed. "Very funny, Gran."

Mrs. Beckmann raised an eyebrow.

Olly looked to Josh for support, but he had an I-told-you-so expression on his face.

Olly took a deep breath. "OK," she said. "Can we make a deal, Gran? Double lessons tomorrow if you let us off today? We really have to go to the temple with Dad."

Mrs. Beckmann stood up. "I'm sure he will still be there when your lessons are finished," she replied. "And so will the temple. Now, take those boots off, Olly, and get your books. Lessons start in ten minutes."

And that was her final word on the subject.

~~~~~

Mrs. Beckmann had been right about one thing, as Olly could clearly see when she and Josh arrived at the Temple of Ganesha. There were three jeeps parked outside the entrance — the archaeologists were all still there.

Now that the trucks and other movie gear were gone, Olly could really appreciate the workmanship that had gone into carving the temple facade. She gazed up at the figures of humans, animals, and gods. The detail in the carvings was dazzling.

The two friends walked in under the square entrance. Jonathan was standing just inside, studying wall carvings and making notes. From deeper inside the temple, Olly could hear the sound of voices.

"I hope you haven't found the talisman without us," Olly said.

Jonathan gave a half smile. "Not yet, I'm afraid," he replied.

"Can we go in?" Josh asked.

"Of course," Jonathan told him. "This is a fascinating place — we've already found out a lot about it." He pointed to a carved inscription. "The temple was put together in three distinct stages over almost two thousand years, but there's something even more interesting. The earliest inscriptions say that the first stage of the building involved carving the temple out of caves that had already been used for worship for many centuries."

Jonathan led them into the main body of the temple. Over by the tunnel that led to the shrine to Parvati stood a group of archaeologists. An intense, but outwardly polite, debate was going on.

Olly noticed that someone was missing. "Where's Ethan?" she asked.

"He had to stay behind at the hotel," Jonathan told her, shaking his head. "More business problems in California, I think. I don't know how he manages to find time to organize this conference with all the other responsibilities he has."

"He's just a total superman, I guess," Olly said drily.

Jonathan gave her a sharp look, but she just

smiled innocently and walked up the steps that led to the huge statue of Ganesha.

She gazed around the temple. It seemed larger and more imposing now that the film crew was gone. The place glowed in the light that poured in through the high windows. The elephant-headed deity sat in the middle of the chamber on his stone platform, a strange-looking creature, Olly thought, but also rather magnificent and strangely calming.

"Did you find anything yet?" Josh asked his brother as Olly rose on tiptoe to peer into Ganesha's golden ear.

"Not so far," Jonathan confirmed. He nodded toward the professors. "They're still debating whether there's any point in being here at all. Half of them think it's a waste of time."

Olly moved around to the other side of the statue and looked into Ganesha's other ear. There was no sign of anything resembling a keyhole. "Rats," she breathed. "This is so annoying!"

"Still looking for the keyhole, Olly?" Jonathan asked. "It's not here, I promise you."

Olly frowned. "All the same, is it OK for us to look for it?" she said. "Just in case it was missed."

Jonathan smiled. "Be my guest, Olly. I hope you're successful."

The archaeologists were blocking the way to the shrine, so Olly and Josh separated and spent the next half hour exploring the main sanctum. They carefully examined the ears of every elephant, and of every statue and painting of Ganesha. They met together at the far side of the chamber. Neither of them had found anything remotely resembling a keyhole.

The professors had moved outside to continue their discussions, so the friends were now able to make their way along the dark passage that led to the shrine. Josh pushed open the black iron gates and they went inside.

A circle of bright sunlight marked one wall. Olly looked up at the vaulted roof. A high, narrow hole had been carved in the rock, and it was through this opening that the sunlight streamed into the shrine.

Olly felt that the shrine had quite a different atmosphere than the rest of the temple. In spite of the constant splashing of the water into the stone bowl, there was a deep sense of silence. The candles in their sconces on the backs of the elephants gave off a soft, steady yellow glow. A thin trail of smoke rose from an incense holder by the door, scenting the air with sandalwood. The subdued mood of the small chamber made Olly feel like she should whisper.

She went closer to the statue of Parvati herself. The goddess was carved from smooth, shiny black stone. She wore a headdress, and one hand was raised in welcome. There was a peaceful smile on her face, and her bright eyes, reflecting the candle-light, seemed to shine with joyful life.

The fall of clear water poured from a crack in the wall behind the statue of Parvati, and splashed softly into the broad stone basin. Olly couldn't see where the water went after that, but she assumed it flowed away through some hidden pipe. The constant rippling of the water threw reflected light over the dark stone walls, giving the impression that the whole room was deep underwater.

Olly walked slowly around the bowl, examining each elephant in turn. Then she knelt and looked into the ears of the elephants that supported the bowl.

She turned to Josh, who was gazing up into Parvati's lovely face. "There's nothing here," she murmured.

Josh sighed. "Maybe our key really doesn't have anything to do with the talismans," he said.

Olly shook her head. "No," she argued. "I'm not going to accept that — not yet, anyway."

"But we've searched the entire temple," Josh pointed out. "What do we do now?"

"We do what we agreed," Olly told him. "We go and see Mr. Ram again." She gave him a hopeful smile. "You never know — he might have remembered something else."

~~~~~

It wasn't a long trek across the hills to the lake at the foot of Elephant Falls. The elephants from the orphanage were there, wading in the shallows with their mahouts, and cooling themselves off with great spouts of water. Sitting watching them on the same grassy hill as last time was the unmistakeable figure of Adhita Ram.

"Ah, my young friends," he said as Josh and Olly approached. "I am glad you have come — I have some news for you."

Olly's heart jumped. She scrambled up the hill and sat in front of the elderly man. "What is it?" she asked eagerly.

Josh sat beside her, looking hopeful.

The old man drew the crumpled copy of the parchment from his clothing. He pointed to a section of the strange writing at the top of the page. "I think this is an old saying," he told them. "I remember it from a long time ago. It is not used much these days. It says . . ."— his finger moved along the writing as he spoke — "*To see beyond the moonlit veil, the seeker must look without looking*." He pointed to another section. "And this says: *The seeker must crack the nutshell in order to discover the kernel within*."

Olly frowned. "I'm sorry," she said. "What do those sayings mean?"

Adhita Ram smiled gently at her. "Only the seeker can answer that question," he replied.

"The seeker of the Elephant of Parvati, you mean?" Josh asked.

"Possibly. I do not know," the old man said. "Only the seeker knows."

Olly looked closely at him. "We're looking for the Elephant of Parvati," she said slowly. "So that makes us the seekers, right?"

Adhita Ram shook his head. "I do not know," he repeated. "Only the seeker knows."

Olly closed her eyes. This was making her head spin.

"Have you managed to figure out what anything else means?" Josh asked.

The old mahout shook his head. "The words are lost to me," he said, making a curious fluttering gesture with his hand, like a bird flying away. "It has been too many years."

"Has anyone else spoken to you about the parchment?" Josh asked.

"No, only you, my friends," Adhita Ram replied.

Olly frowned. "Well, is there anyone else around here who might be able to translate any of it?" she asked.

The old man's face cracked in a wide smile and his long, thin hand came up to touch his chest. "Only Adhita Ram knows," he said proudly. "Only Adhita Ram remembers. No one else remembers. I am the oldest. Only I remember the old words and the old writings." The smile became slightly crooked. "Although Adhita Ram does not remember it all, and for that he is truly sorry."

Olly and Josh exchanged a puzzled look. If Ethan Cain had not spoken to the mahout, then how come they had found him snooping around the elephants in the shrine?

"Don't apologize. You've been really helpful," Olly told the old man. "Honestly, you have."

"I come here to Parvati Falls with the elephants every afternoon," the mahout responded. "Maybe you can come and speak with me again? Maybe I will remember more."

"We'll come again when we can," Olly said. "But please don't worry if you can't remember anything else. We appreciate all your help." She stood up to leave, but she noticed that Josh was still staring at the old man.

"This is *Elephant* Falls, isn't it?" Josh asked. "You just called it *Parvati* Falls."

"It has been called Elephant Falls for many years, because the elephants are brought here to drink and to bathe," Adhita Ram told him. "But in the old days this waterfall was sacred to Parvati. The pilgrims would come here to honor Parvati and to fill the lake with lotus blossoms. It is long forgotten by my people now, but my great-grandfather was a scholar; he read the ancient texts. He told me that there was an old tale of a temple by the waterfall — a temple to Parvati."

Olly's eyes widened. "A temple?" she breathed, gazing around. "Where?"

"The temple was hidden," Adhita Ram replied. "And besides, this was many centuries ago."

"Hidden where?" Josh asked eagerly.

The old man smiled mysteriously and shook his head. "I do not know the answer to that question, my friend," he said. "Maybe only the seeker knows the answer."

Chapter Nine:🌙
An Important Discovery

"So there really is a secret temple," Olly breathed, staring at Josh over the table in the main room of their suite back at the Peshwar Palace. They were alone in the suite, and all was quiet, save for the singing of birds in the gardens and the occasional cry of a peacock.

"You mean there *was*, centuries ago," Josh replied. "There's nothing there now."

Olly frowned. "Even if the temple was torn down — surely there must be some clue to show where it was," she said. "A few stones or some of the foundation. Come on, Josh, you've been on plenty of archaeological expeditions by now. There's always *something* left."

Josh looked at her. "You're assuming that it was made of stone," he said. "Not all temples were. It might have been wooden. There could have been a fire."

Olly shook her head. "If there had been a temple there that was either knocked down or destroyed in a fire, why would Adhita Ram's great-grandfather have referred to it as a *hidden* temple?"

"Hmm, good point," Josh agreed. "It would be more likely to have been called the *lost* temple or something like that. But there are forests and ravines all over this area. We could search for years and never find it — especially if it was hidden in the first place."

"Jonathan told us that the Temple of Ganesha started off as a small cave in the cliffs," Olly said. "But then more people came along and made it bigger and bigger. What if this hidden temple was always just a cave in the cliffs somewhere near the waterfall?"

"And what if there was a landslip or an avalanche?" Josh added excitedly. "And the entrance was blocked. Then, as time went by, people remembered that there used to be a temple there — but they forgot exactly where it was. Olly, you're right. That could be it!"

"And the waterfall mentioned in the parchment might not be the waterfall in the shrine in the Temple of Ganesha. It could be the real waterfall — Elephant Falls," Olly said. "That would explain why we couldn't find the keyhole in the other temple. It's not in the Temple of Ganesha at all — it's in the hidden temple by Elephant Falls.

And *that's* where we'll find the Elephant of Parvati!" A grin spread across her face. "Josh, we are amazing! This hotel is stuffed full of expert archaeologists, but it's the two of us who worked this out!" She laughed. "Ethan will go crazy!"

Josh laughed. "We don't know if we're right yet," he pointed out. "All we've got so far is a good theory. I don't think we should go yelling it from the rooftops just yet. If we tell Jonathan and the professor about this, they'll just go and tell Ethan right away. And then he'll hire a load of digging gear and start searching."

"And when he finds the temple, he'll get all the glory," Olly agreed gloomily. "You're right — we'd just be handing the talisman to him on a plate." She looked at Josh. "But what else can we do? It would take us forever to search the hills near the waterfall. And if the cave is blocked off, we'd never find it anyway without a bulldozer or something."

Josh rested his chin in his hands and stared thoughtfully out the window.

Olly leaned back in her chair, her arms folded over her chest. "It's a pity the people who made that parchment didn't include a map!" she grumbled.

Josh stared at her. "There's a map room downstairs,"

he said. "Some of Oliver Gordon-Howes's maps are down there. And there are some much older maps, too — maps of this area that go back hundreds of years."

Olly looked at him dubiously. "You think there might be a map with an arrow and a little sign saying 'Hidden Temple This Way'?" she said. "I think someone would have noticed it before now, if there was."

"They would if it was like that," Josh agreed. "But remember what Adhita Ram said? It's been centuries since pilgrims came to the temple. But there would have been some kind of road or path that they used. Even if the old maps don't mention the temple, they might still show the old road."

"So, we'd be looking for a roadway that just seems to stop dead at the cliff face somewhere near the waterfall," Olly said thoughtfully. "And if we find it, then we'll know exactly where the temple is. Josh, sometimes you're almost clever!"

"And once we can pinpoint the place," Josh said, "we can tell Jonathan and the professor all about it. Even if Ethan does supply the men and machines to dig the temple out again — everybody will know it was the two of us who found out where it was. And Ethan won't be able to claim it for his own."

"I love it!" Olly crowed. "Let's go and look at the maps right now. Ethan has been ahead of us all the way so far, but this time, we're in the lead."

~~~~

The Map Room was on the ground floor of the palace, at the end of a long hallway with walls painted ivory and decorated with peacock feathers and cascades of purple and white flowers.

Josh frowned and caught hold of Olly's wrist as they approached the tall doors of the Map Room.

"What?" she asked, looking at him curiously.

Josh pointed ahead — one of the room's heavy doors was slightly ajar.

Olly walked forward more quietly now. She had a bad feeling about this, although she could not have said exactly why. The room wasn't kept locked — anyone in the hotel could get access to the maps — and the palace was full of archaeologists, any one of whom might decide that a visit to the Map Room would be worthwhile. Still, Olly couldn't escape the feeling that there was something wrong.

A moment later she heard a voice from beyond the doors. She stopped in her tracks and looked at Josh. "That's Ethan's voice," she whispered.

"It can't be," Josh replied.

Olly's eyes narrowed warily as she crept up to the doors. She peered in through the narrow gap.

The Map Room was long, with a high ceiling, and as ornately decorated as were all the rooms in the palace. Tall, arched windows let in a flood of light. Framed maps hung on the walls behind glass. Others were stored safely in heavy cabinets which lined the walls.

Two figures were bending over the open drawer of a cabinet near the center of the far wall, apparently absorbed in studying its contents. Olly recognized the figures immediately: It was Ethan Cain and his assistant, Paul White.

Olly drew back and beckoned for Josh to look, too. Together, the friends watched the two men pore over the maps.

"Do you see anything?" Ethan asked his assistant.

"Nothing," Paul replied.

"Neither do I." Ethan closed the map drawer and opened the one below.

Olly and Josh moved away from the doors.

"What are they doing here?" Josh whispered.

"That's what I'd like to know," Olly hissed. She beckoned for Josh to follow her back along the hallway and out through the dining room. They sat on the steps overlooking the garden.

"There's something weird going on here," Olly said. "This is the third time Ethan has managed to spoil our plans — and I'm getting sick of it!"

Josh nodded. "It's almost as if he knows what we're about to do and gets there first," he said. "We'd only just found the silver key when he turned up out of nowhere. Then he was in the shrine to Parvati ahead of us. And now he's in the Map Room just a few minutes after we decided to go there."

"I can't really see Ethan snooping through keyholes," Olly said. "But how else could he know?"

"It must be a coincidence," Josh said. "A really annoying coincidence."

"*Three* annoying coincidences," Olly reminded him. And then a thought struck her. She looked at Josh. "Remember that story your mom told us the other night? It was about a scene that Giovanni Bosconi made her do over and over again."

Josh frowned. "The scene where she realized that her so-called friend was wearing a microphone," he said. "Yeah, so?"

"What if Ethan has hidden a microphone somewhere in our hotel room?" Olly suggested.

Josh snorted with laughter. "Oh, please!" he said. "What is this, a James Bond movie? You seriously think Ethan bugged our suite?"

"Why not?" Olly demanded. "He's perfectly capable of pulling a dirty trick like that. And it would explain why he's always one step ahead of us. And if you think about it, in each case, we've talked things through in the sitting room up there. We were in that room when we found the silver key. We were in there with Dad and Jonathan when we were talking about Adhita Ram, and we were just there when we said there might be something useful in the Map Room."

Josh gazed at her. "We should go and check," he said firmly.

〰〰

Olly paused outside the door to their suite. "We have to do this really quietly," she said. "If you find anything, just wave your hand, OK?"

Josh nodded. He didn't really believe that they would find a bug. It seemed too far-fetched an idea, even for Ethan Cain.

Olly opened the door and they walked silently inside. She began to search behind the large wooden cabinet that stood by the door. Josh carefully lifted some pictures down off the walls and checked the backs. He found nothing suspicious.

Josh watched as Olly squeezed herself between two display cabinets and stretched her arm down the back. Then he walked over to the heavy velvet curtains that hung beside the balcony doors. He moved them aside and examined the door frame. Again, he found nothing.

Olly was now stretched full-length over one of the cabinets, reaching down the back, her legs waving in the air. Josh had to stifle a burst of laughter. This was silly — they weren't going to find anything.

He went to the table and ran his hand around under the top. Nothing. *Of course not*, he thought to himself. *There isn't anything here.* And then his fingers touched on something smooth, protruding slightly from the underside of the table.

Josh crouched under the table and peered upward. A small gray object was attached underneath the tabletop, near the center. It wasn't much bigger than a bottle top, it seemed to be made of metal, and it was stuck to the table by some kind of adhesive patch.

Josh realized that he was staring up at an electronic listening device. Olly was right: Ethan Cain really had bugged their room!

Chapter Ten: ☾ Wild Goose Chase

Olly and Josh crouched together under the table, staring up at the small gray metal disk.

What do we do with it? Olly mouthed silently to Josh. She acted out smashing it, but Josh shook his head. Olly gave him an inquiring look, and he crawled out from under the table, beckoning to her.

She followed him out into the hallway and Josh closed the door firmly behind them. He stared up and down the corridor before speaking in a low, urgent voice.

"If we smash it, he'll know we've found it," he said.

"I don't care," Olly snarled. "I want him to know we've found him out — the big, slimy rat! He's been listening to everything we've said in there right from the start. No wonder he was always one jump ahead of us. He was planning on using us to do all the hard work for him — and then he was just going to stroll off with the Elephant of Parvati after we'd figured out where it was."

Josh nodded. "I'm sure that's exactly what he planned on doing," he said. "But you know what he's like, he'd never admit the bug had anything to do with him." A sly grin spread over his face. "But if we leave it where it is, he won't know we've found it."

Olly looked blankly at him. "So?"

"So, we can have some fun with him," Josh explained. "We can invent some stuff and send him off on a wild goose chase."

Olly's eyes widened in delight. "We can say we know where the talisman is," she breathed, grinning. "Josh, that's a great idea. Let's do it now."

"No, let's wait," Josh argued. "We have to be convincing. Let's do it tomorrow after our schoolwork. We can pretend we've been to see Adhita Ram again, and that he's translated some more of the parchment. In the meantime, we can take a look at a local map, and see if we can find a really good place to send him."

‸‸‸‸

Later in the afternoon, Olly and Josh went down to the Map Room again. This time the doors were closed and the room was empty. They spent half an hour or more pulling out the long shallow drawers and examining the maps. The more recent maps were highly detailed and very accurate — and they showed nothing to indicate either a hidden temple or a pilgrim track anywhere near Elephant Falls. The most ancient maps were several hundred years old, but although they were beautifully drawn — with small colorful pictures and explanations in the old Devanagari script — none seemed to indicate the existence of a temple or an old road near the waterfall.

"There's one good thing about this," Josh pointed out as they left the room. "If we didn't find anything useful, then neither did Ethan."

Olly nodded. "I wonder if Dad and the others are back from the temple yet?" she said. "I'd like to know if they found anything up there." She smiled. "And I'd *really* like to get all those professors together and tell them what we've figured out!"

Josh looked anxious. "We can't do that," he said. "They'll just tell Ethan."

"I know," Olly replied. "Don't worry, I won't breathe a word. I want to see Ethan's face when he finds out that we've outsmarted him again."

〰〰〰

The Christie team met up for dinner out on the moonlit balcony of their suite that evening. As Olly and Josh had suspected, the investigations up at the temple had not been particularly successful.

While they ate, Olly and Josh looked at some printouts of digital photographs that Jonathan had taken of the temple and the shrine.

Professor Christie spent most of the meal going through his notebook, reading and rereading the notes he had been making ever since he arrived in India.

"Kenneth, you must eat something," Olly's grandmother told him eventually.

He gazed distractedly at her. "Hmmm?"

"Eat some food," she said. "You'll waste away."

Olly smiled fondly at her father — when he was on the track of an elusive piece of information, it was as if he were on another planet.

Nibbling at a popadum, Olly flicked through the printed digital photographs. She spread out a few pictures of the shrine.

"It's weird that they bothered to cut that little window through all that rock," she murmured, looking at the white pool of sunlight that glowed on the wall. "I mean, it's not like it lets much useful light in," she continued. "You still need candles in there to actually see anything."

She looked up. Her father was staring at her. "What?" she said. "What did I say?"

He didn't reply. Now everyone at the table was looking at him.

"Professor?" Jonathan asked. "What is it?"

Without answering, Professor Christie turned to a clean sheet in his notebook and began to draw. As he worked, Olly saw a look of understanding and delight come over his face.

"Dad!" she demanded. "What's going on?"

He looked up at her, smiling widely. "Well done, Olly!" he declared. "It's been staring me in the face all along, but I didn't make the connection till you mentioned it." He turned the notebook around to show them the sketch he had made. It was rough, but Olly could see that it was Parvati's shrine. It showed the little window in the roof, from which her father had drawn an arrow extending downward.

"Olly was quite right," the professor said. "That aperture was never intended to be a source of sunlight. I think it has an entirely different function. And if I'm right, it's one that doesn't reveal itself until after the moon has set."

"It's for moonlight!" Josh gasped.

The professor laughed. "Exactly!" he confirmed. "The parchment contains a section that refers to the full moon. We all just assumed it was a reference to the talisman, but I think it means much more than that. If I'm right, then the hole in the roof of the shrine was cut to allow the light of the full moon in."

Jonathan stared at the drawing. "So when the full moon is in exactly the right place in the sky," he said slowly, "it will shine down onto a particular point in the shrine."

"What do you think it will shine on?" Olly's grandmother asked.

"The place where the talisman is hidden, of course!" Olly exclaimed.

"We can't be sure of that until we test my theory out," said her father. "But it must illuminate something important for them to have cut through so much rock."

Josh looked up at the night sky. "It will be a full moon tomorrow night," he said.

"Indeed it will," agreed Professor Christie. "I think we should arrange with our colleagues that we all take a trip up to the Temple of Ganesha tomorrow night, and then we'll see where the moonlight falls."

"A night in the temple," Olly breathed. "That will be so cool."

"I don't think you and Josh will be able to go," put in Mrs. Beckmann.

Josh and Olly both stared at her in horror.

"But we have to!" Olly exclaimed. "They can't do it without us."

"Listen, you two," Mrs. Beckmann said quite kindly. "If it was just Jonathan and the professor, then I'm sure some room could be found for you. But the others will be going up there, too, and I doubt they will be as tolerant as the professor is about having young people underfoot. I'm afraid you'll have to sit this one out. I'm sorry."

"But, Gran!" Olly wailed.

Her grandmother raised a silencing finger. "If anything is found, you'll learn all about it first thing in the morning," she said firmly.

Olly didn't bother arguing with her grandmother right then, but she planned on having plenty to say about it before the following night. Only over her dead body would she let the archaeologists head up to the temple and find the Elephant of Parvati without her!

⁓⁓⁓

Olly managed to have a chat with Josh after the meal, before they went to bed. They sat on Olly's bed in her room and whispered softly together.

"If the professor is right," Josh said, "it wrecks our theory about a hidden temple near Elephant Falls."

"I'm not so sure," Olly replied. She had been doing some thinking, and she had come up with a theory of her own. "What if he's right about the hole letting in moonlight, but what if the moonlight doesn't fall exactly on the place where the talisman is hidden?"

Josh looked puzzled. "I don't understand."

"Do you remember what the inside of the shrine looks like?" Olly asked. "Parvati is standing on a kind of cliff, isn't she? And the water runs over the edge of the cliff and pours down into the bowl. Now, does that remind you of anything? Maybe something like a *real* waterfall?"

Josh looked at her. "You mean Elephant Falls," he said.

Olly nodded. "*Parvati* Falls," she corrected him. "What if the waterfall in the shrine is meant to represent Parvati Falls?"

"Like a kind of model, you mean?" Josh asked. "A three-D map?" His eyes widened with excitement. "So the moonlight wouldn't be shining down on the actual hiding place of the talisman — it would just show you where to look on the *real* waterfall. Olly, we have to tell Jonathan and the professor!"

Olly shook her head. "I don't think we should do

that," she whispered. "They'll just go off and tell Ethan. They'll feel like they have to since Ethan organized this whole thing. Then all Ethan has to do is wait for the moonlight to show him where to dig. And before we know it, he'll have found the hidden temple and the talisman."

Josh frowned. "You're right," he agreed. "But even if we don't say anything, the professor's bound to work out what the moonlight is really showing." He sighed heavily. "So, Ethan's going to win either way."

"Not necessarily," Olly said. "If the waterfall in the shrine is a copy of Parvati Falls, then maybe whatever happens in the shrine will also happen at the real falls. Isn't that possible?"

Josh looked dubious. "I guess so," he said. "But that hole was carved in the temple to let just a thin beam of moonlight shine through and pinpoint one spot. The moon won't have the same effect out in the open, will it?"

"Maybe not," Olly replied. "But there's one good way to find out."

Josh raised his eyebrows. "You mean, you want to go up there?"

Olly nodded. "Tomorrow night," she told him. "After dinner, we wave good-bye to Dad and the others, putter around for a while — play a game of

Monopoly or something with Gran — and then pretend to go to bed as normal."

"And then we slip out while no one is looking," Josh continued, "and head toward Elephant Falls."

"Where we see something utterly marvelous and unbelievable," Olly finished. "Which leads us to the Elephant of Parvati! What do you think?"

Josh grinned at her. "I think it's crazy," he said. "But it's our only chance. Let's do it!"

〰〰〰

It was the following day and their schoolwork was finally over. Mrs. Beckmann had gone to sit on the veranda, with a tall cool drink and a newspaper. Olly and Josh sat huddled together in Josh's room, planning out what they intended to say for Ethan Cain's benefit.

Looking at maps the day before had served them well. They had found the perfect place to send Ethan: an abandoned village called Gamsali in a nasty, swampy area, thirty miles to the east.

"Remember, you have to sound really convincing," Olly told Josh. "If he thinks you're faking, he won't fall for it."

Josh looked at her. "One of us has a mother who is a famous actress, right?" he demanded.

"Yeah," Olly replied.

"Don't worry about my acting talent," Josh said. "I've got this under control."

Olly stood up. "OK, then — let's go and win some Oscars!"

Josh walked to the door of the sitting room and grasped the handle. "Scene one, take one," he whispered. "Our intrepid heroes enter the room."

Olly rolled her eyes.

⌁⌁⌁

"Dad still thinks the talisman is probably hidden somewhere in the Temple of Ganesha," Olly said as they walked into the room. "But if what Adhita Ram has just told us is true, then the Elephant of Parvati isn't anywhere *near* that temple." Olly and Josh sat down at the table.

"Yes, but yesterday he told us that there might have been a hidden temple by Elephant Falls," Josh pointed out. "So why should we believe him now, when he says he thinks the hidden temple is over at Gamsali? It's at least twenty-five miles away from here."

"He told us about the possibility of a temple near the falls before he realized what the rest of the parchment meant," Olly replied. "Most of the writing on the parchment is a list of directions for how to get *from* the waterfall to the place where the talisman was hidden. He's absolutely convinced that the Elephant of Parvati is in a lost temple over at Gamsali."

"Then I suppose we should tell Jonathan and the professor all about it," Josh suggested.

Olly smiled — now for the really brilliant part of their scheme. "I don't think we should tell them right away," she argued. "They'll only tell Ethan — and we don't want him to know about it before we've had time to do some double-checking." She managed to sound totally convincing; Josh gave her the thumbs-up as she continued. "I don't know how, but Ethan has been ahead of us all along. Now we know something he can't possibly have found out. I think we should ask Gran to take us for a ride tomorrow. We can get her to drive over to Gamsali, and once we're there, we can take a look around."

"Great idea," Josh agreed. "Adhita Ram said the temple was in the hills about three miles southeast of the town. It should be easy enough to find it with those directions."

"And when we do, we'll have beaten Ethan again!" Olly declared triumphantly.

"Are you hungry?" Josh asked, signaling that their little act was over.

"Yes, I am," Olly said. "Let's go and eat."

They left the room. Outside in the hall, Olly turned to Josh. "Do you think we were convincing?" she whispered.

Josh nodded. "I think we were brilliant," he replied. "We might make it as movie stars after all."

"I'll be an archaeologist–movie star," Olly said thoughtfully. "I don't think there are many of those around." She laughed. "Now we have to keep our fingers crossed that Ethan takes the bait."

"Oh, he will," Josh said. "Just you wait and see."

~~~~~

The two friends didn't have to wait very long to see that their little act had done the trick. About half an hour later, they were sitting on the front steps of the palace, chatting with Salila, when they saw Ethan Cain leave the hotel in a rented jeep.

Olly nudged Josh. Ethan was taking the road to the east — the road that led to Gamsali.

The friends grinned as they watched the jeep disappear.

"Why do you smile?" Salila asked.

"Our friend Ethan is going on a day trip to Gamsali," Olly began.

Salila frowned. "But there is nothing there," she said. "The village has been abandoned for years. Why would he go there?"

Olly and Josh looked at each other. "I think we may have given him the impression that there's something interesting there," Josh said with a grin.

Salila shook her head. "All he will find is an unpleasant swamp and a lot of hungry mosquitoes."

Olly laughed. "Great!" she said. "This just keeps getting better and better."

"We're playing a kind of practical joke on Ethan," Josh explained to Salila. "Trust me — he deserves it!"

Chapter Eleven: ☾
Breaking and Entering

"Do you know what would be even better than Ethan getting stuck in a swamp and bitten half to death by bloodthirsty mosquitoes?" Olly asked.

"No," Josh replied. "What?"

They were stretched on lounge chairs on the hotel veranda, sipping cold drinks and soaking up some afternoon sunshine.

Olly sat up and peered at Josh over her sunglasses. "If we could prove to everyone what he's *really* like," she said.

Josh looked at Olly curiously. "And how would we do that?" he asked.

"Well," Olly began. "Why won't anyone believe that Ethan is a creep?"

"Because he always charms everyone into thinking he's innocent," Josh replied. "And because there's never any proof."

"Exactly!" Olly agreed. "But this time we *do* have some proof. We have the bug!"

Josh sat up. Olly had a good point. Ethan Cain

had always managed to sweet-talk his way out of trouble in the past, but what if they produced the hidden microphone in front of everyone?

"But how could we prove he planted the thing?" Josh asked, suddenly seeing the big flaw in Olly's idea. "You know what he's like. He'll act as shocked as everyone else when he sees the bug, and they'll all believe he didn't know anything about it."

"Rats!" Olly hissed, throwing herself back on the lounge chair. "You're right. Of course he will."

"Wait a minute, though," Josh said. "If he's been listening in on everything we've said, then he must have some kind of a receiver hidden in his suite."

A slow grin spread over Olly's face. "So, we tell everyone about the bug, march them all up to Ethan's suite, show them the receiver, and — *wham!* — he's busted! I like it, Josh. I really like it."

Josh shook his head. "They'd never agree to search his suite," he said. "The only way it'll work is if we can tell them exactly where the receiver is."

"Then, we have to find the receiver first," Olly said. She chewed her bottom lip thoughtfully. "How long do you think it'll take Ethan to get to the swamp and back?"

"A couple of hours, at least," Josh responded.

Olly clambered up off the lounge chair. "So that

means we've got about forty-five minutes left. Josh, what are you loafing around for? We've got some breaking and entering to do!"

〰〰〰

The opulent Maharajah's Suite took up most of the top floor of the hotel. The corridor outside seemed deserted as Olly and Josh made their way stealthily across the thick carpet toward the grand doorway.

There was a brass plaque attached to the wall. It said: *The Maharajah's Suite. Designed by Buland Darza for his son, Akbar, in the year 1647.*

"It must be nice to have a dad who can afford to build you a place like this," Olly said quietly.

"It didn't do him much good," Josh reminded her. "Akbar died before he even moved in."

The friends stood before the door and stared at the heavy brass lock.

Josh glanced around at Olly. "How are we going to get in?" he asked.

"We could call room service," Olly suggested. "We could pretend we're calling from inside the suite and order something to eat. The waiters will have pass keys. When they come up to deliver the food, we'll slip in while they're not looking."

Josh stared at her. "That's ridiculous," he said.

"If a waiter comes up here and knocks on the door but doesn't get an answer, he'll just go down and tell management there's something funny going on. Then they'll send security people up to check it out."

Olly glared at him. "You come up with a better plan, then."

"There must be an unlocked door somewhere on this floor," Josh said. "We could go into that room and out onto the balcony. Then we could climb across to one of the Maharajah's Suite's balconies and go in the window."

"Or we could fall off the balcony and go splat on the ground!" Olly pointed out. "Which is a whole lot more likely, if you ask me." She stared at the door. "And we assume it's actually locked, right?"

Josh gave a scoffing laugh. "Of course it is!" he said. "Do you think Ethan is the kind of person to wander off without locking up behind him?"

"All the same," Olly insisted. "We should check."

"Really, Olly, how did you get so stubborn?" Josh said, stepping up to the door. He grasped the handle, turned it, and leaned against the door. It swung smoothly inward and Josh promptly fell through the doorway and landed flat on his face.

Olly crouched down beside him. "Are you OK?"

"Yes," Josh groaned. "I'm fine."

"Good. Then stop messing around and get up."

Josh clambered to his feet and looked around.

They were in a large room with deep blue curtains framing ornate latticework windows. The ceiling was decorated with more gold, and a rich, thick carpet covered the floor. The furniture was lavish and obviously antique.

"I told you it was fancy up here," Josh murmured.

"OK, let's start searching," Olly said. "What exactly does a receiver look like?"

"In the movies, they're like big reel-to-reel tape recorders," Josh replied. "But it's more likely to be a small digital device. It might even be a computer. It's possible Ethan's got a laptop with the right software on it to act as a receiver."

Olly stared at him in confusion.

"Basically, anything electronic," Josh said. He pointed
to the left. "You go that way. I'll look over here."

Olly headed for the huge, mahogany desk by the balcony doors. None of the drawers were locked, but none contained anything suspicious. She did find one interesting thing, though. In the top, right-hand drawer there was a small black box. She opened it to see the silver key that they had found in the pottery elephant.

She considered taking the key, but quickly realized that it wouldn't be a good idea. Ethan would be sure to notice that it was missing, and the last thing she wanted to do was put him on the alert.

She closed the drawer again and looked around. There was a large old cabinet by a set of double doors. Quickly, she moved over to search it. It was full of exquisite, old china and sparkling wineglasses, but no laptop and no electronics of any kind.

Olly opened the double doors and went through into another large, luxurious room. The furniture was very grand, with long couches, deep armchairs, and small round tables holding statues of the Hindu gods.

The golden afternoon sunlight streamed in through the tall windows, giving the room an otherworldly look, and making Olly feel as if she was walking through an ancient Indian fable. She imagined herself as the daughter of a wealthy Maharajah from hundreds of years past. She'd be dressed in silks and satins, with scores of servants at her beck and call. She walked regally toward the next door, smiling to herself.

She was just reaching for the door handle when the door swung open and she found herself staring into the startled eyes of Ethan Cain's personal assistant.

Olly let out a squawk. It had never occurred to her that there might be someone in the suite. But clearly there was, and now she was caught!

Paul glared at her with narrowed eyes. "What are you doing in here?" he snapped, stepping into the room and closing the door behind him.

The thought sped through Olly's mind: *It's in there! The receiver is in there!* But she couldn't think what to say. "Well, the thing is . . ." she began, racking her brains for a plausible excuse.

"We were just exploring," came Josh's voice from behind her. "The door was open; we didn't think Ethan would mind."

Olly glanced over her shoulder. He must have heard her stifled yell and come running, she realized. *Good for Josh!* "That's right," Olly said, picking up on Josh's lead. "I'm sure Ethan wouldn't mind us looking around. It's amazing up here. Prince Akbar would have loved it if he hadn't been killed before he could move in." She smiled her most innocent smile. "Isn't that a shame?" she went on. "His father must have been really upset." She walked over to an old chest and ran her hand over the carved wood. "Do you know how old this is? Would it have been here at the time — or maybe it was added later. What do you think?"

Paul stared at her, confusion mixed with anger on his face. "I'm afraid I really don't know," he answered. "But you shouldn't be in here without Mr. Cain's express permission."

Olly gave him an innocent look. "Why's that?" she said cheerfully. "Has he got something to hide?"

Her attitude seemed to take him aback. "That's not the point," Paul said sharply. "Mr. Cain doesn't allow anyone to come in here without his permission."

Olly could tell he was annoyed, but he was doing his best to keep it under control. After all, Josh was the son of his boss's girlfriend.

"Oh, well, if that's the case," Josh said calmly, "I guess we'd better be leaving."

Olly nodded. "Yes — sorry to have bothered you," she added.

Mr. White looked hard into her face, but she just smiled back at him.

"I'm sure Mr. Cain will be only too happy to give you a tour of the suite," Paul said, clearly doing his best to remain polite. "But please ask next time."

"Will do," Olly said as she and Josh headed for the door.

Paul followed them all the way.

"Bye, now," Olly said. "Have a nice day."

Paul closed the door behind them and they heard the sharp scrape of the key turning in the lock.

Josh put his finger to his lips and gestured that they should get out of earshot.

"Oh! He almost scared me to death!" Olly said once they were a safe distance away. "Do you think he suspected anything?"

"I don't know," Josh replied. "But he's bound to tell Ethan — and there's no way Ethan is going to believe we were just up there to have a look around. He knows us too well for that."

They made their way down the stairs and out into the gardens.

"I don't suppose you had time to find anything interesting, did you?" Olly asked hopefully as they sat on the edge of one of the fish ponds.

"Not a thing," Josh sighed.

"I bet the receiver was in that room Paul came out of," Olly said. "What do you think Ethan will do when he hears we were up there?"

"Whatever he does, we've blown our only chance of finding out where the receiver is," Josh said. "And that was our only proof that he's been listening in on us."

"We still have the bug," Olly pointed out. "If we show that to Dad and Gran — and tell them that we're absolutely certain Ethan planted it — we *might* be able to convince them."

Josh's eyes brightened. "At the very least, they'll want to set up an investigation. They might even call in the police," he said thoughtfully. "And then, with any luck, there might be some clues that will lead back to Ethan."

"It's worth a try," Olly declared, jumping up. "Dad and Jonathan are in another of those meetings, but Gran should be around somewhere. Let's go and get the bug and show it to her."

They ran up to their suite. As they turned into the hallway, they saw someone slip quietly around the corner at the far end.

"Who was that?" Olly asked.

"I don't know," Josh answered.

"It looked like Paul White," Olly said. She stared at Josh. "What's he doing here?" A horrible thought flashed across her mind. She rushed to the doors of the suite and threw them open. Then she ran across the carpet and ducked under the table, peering up at the underside of the tabletop.

Olly let out a yell of frustration. Her suspicions had proved right: The bug was gone.

Chapter Twelve: ☾
Peril by Moonlight

The late afternoon sun was throwing long shadows as Olly and Josh sat at a table in a quiet corner of the long veranda that ran along the front of the hotel. The disappearance of the bug was a real blow, made all the worse by the fact that they felt they should have seen it coming.

"I can guess exactly what happened after Mr. White got rid of us," Josh said. "He got right on his cell phone to tell Ethan all about it. And Ethan guessed why we were up there."

"And told him to go down to our suite and take the bug away," Olly sighed.

Josh's face brightened. "At least one good thing's come out of it," he said. "Ethan can't listen in on us anymore."

Olly nodded. "And we did manage to send him off into a nasty swamp, looking for a nonexistent temple," she added with a smile. "So, the day hasn't been a complete disaster." She chuckled. "He's not going to be a very happy bunny when he gets back."

As if in response to her words, a jeep came roaring up to the front of the hotel in a cloud of dust. One of the hotel porters ran down the steps to open the car door.

Ethan Cain emerged, looking disheveled and furious. He said something to the porter, who climbed into the jeep and drove it around to the parking area at the side of the hotel.

His face thunderous, Ethan stalked up the steps to the veranda. Olly watched him with a cheerful smile on her face.

As soon as Ethan caught sight of Olly and Josh, his face miraculously cleared. He took a moment to straighten his clothes and smooth his hair and then strode toward them with a wide smile on his face.

"Have you been anywhere interesting?" Josh asked innocently.

"Oh, here and there, you know," Ethan replied, leaning on the back of a chair. "We have to follow up on all kinds of leads. Some of them are useful, and others are kind of a waste of time."

Olly watched his face. She had to admit that he was a great actor. There wasn't a glimmer of anger in his expression now.

"It must be annoying when you think you're onto

something big, but it turns out to be a miserable swamp," she said.

A gleam came into Ethan's eye. "What makes you mention a swamp, Olly?" he asked.

She pointed to his mud-caked boots and trousers. "You look like you've been in a swamp, that's all," she said. "Was it nasty?"

"It was a little uncomfortable," Ethan admitted. "But I learned something really interesting while I was there." He smiled from Olly to Josh. "And I figured something out, too — so it wasn't a complete waste of time."

"What did you figure out?" Josh asked.

Ethan smiled. "Oh, I just put one and one together and made two," he told them. "By the way, Paul called. He said you were having a look around my rooms." Olly opened her mouth to speak, but Ethan raised a hand to silence her. "I don't mind at all," he went on. "It would be more polite of you to ask first, that's all. Oh, and any time you'd like another look around, just let me know and I'll be happy to give you a guided tour — in case there's anything up there that you missed." He straightened up. "And now, I think I'd better freshen up; I've got work to do this evening."

"I suppose you'll be going up to the Temple of Ganesha with the others?" Olly inquired.

Ethan smiled. "Actually, no, I'm going to have to miss that," he said. "I'm sure your father will be able to deal with anything they might find up there. I've got some other business to deal with." He turned and walked toward the entrance of the hotel. "In fact, if my business tonight works out, I'm expecting to have some really big news for everyone in the morning," he called back. "Catch you guys later."

Olly and Josh looked at each other as the amateur archaeologist disappeared into the hotel.

"What do you think he meant by that?" Olly asked.

"Beats me," Josh replied, frowning.

"I don't like the sound of it," Olly said. "He has contacts all over this area. What if he's been told something we don't know about? Something about the hidden temple?"

"Well, if he has, there's nothing we can do about it," Josh sighed. "We should stick to our plan and go up to Elephant Falls. Let's just keep our fingers crossed that something exciting happens up there tonight." He lowered his voice. "Because otherwise I've got a bad feeling that Ethan is going to get to the Elephant of Parvati first!"

Olly and Josh stood on their balcony, watching as the small convoy of jeeps wound its way up the road toward the Temple of Ganesha. Every one of the professors and doctors had wanted to be there to see if Professor Christie's theory was correct. Ben Wilder had also come up from Tauri to record the whole adventure.

It seemed that, apart from the hotel staff and Olly's grandmother, the whole of the Peshwar Palace was deserted.

Josh watched the jeeps move up into the night-dark hills, the beams of their headlights gradually fading away in the darkness. There was a knot of excitement in his stomach at the thought of his own plans for the evening. He knew Mrs. Beckmann would be livid if she found out that he and Olly had left the hotel without her permission. But, as Olly had pointed out, if they found the talisman all would be forgiven. And if they found nothing, they would just creep back to the hotel and no one would be any the wiser.

The friends turned away from the night and walked back into the sitting room. Olly's grandmother was seated in an armchair, reading her book.

"They've gone," Olly said, flopping down onto the couch. "Some people get all the fun."

Her grandmother looked up. "I hope you're not going to mope around the place all evening," she said.

Olly gave her a smile. "No, Josh and I are going to play some games on Jonathan's laptop," she replied. Then she yawned and stretched. "Although I think I might need an early night, tonight. I'm exhausted." She looked at her grandmother. "How about you? Are you feeling sleepy at all?"

Mrs. Beckmann glanced at her wristwatch. "It's only five past eight," she remarked, looking rather surprised.

"Come on," Josh declared, grabbing Olly and hustling her out of the room before she could say anything else. "We'll set the computer up in my room."

He closed the door between them and Mrs. Beckmann. "Really subtle, Olly," he hissed. "Why don't you make it even more obvious that you want her out of the way? You just need to be patient for a while!"

Olly threw herself down on the bed. "Yes, yes," she said. "I'm great at being patient!"

Josh grinned at her as he opened the laptop and

booted it up. He had a feeling it was going to be a long, long evening.

~~~~~

Josh lay in bed listening to Mrs. Beckmann's footsteps in the living room. He looked at his watch. The luminous dial glowed in the darkness; it was almost eleven o'clock. He sat up, listening intently and staring at the thin line of light under his door. Suddenly, the light went out. A moment later, there was the click of a door closing — and then silence.

Josh slipped out of bed. He was fully clothed except for his shoes. He tiptoed to the door and put his ear to the wooden panels. There wasn't a sound from the sitting room: Mrs. Beckmann had finally gone to bed.

He found his shoes in the dark and put them on. He was just tying the laces when his bedroom door opened and a shadow slipped inside.

"I thought she was going to stay up all night," Olly whispered. "I've brought a flashlight with me. Are you ready?"

"Yes," Josh whispered back. "But I've been thinking. We've forgotten all about the key. If we find the hidden temple and manage to get inside, we might need it."

"Ethan probably has the copy that he had made," Olly said. "But the original is up in his desk. I saw it. It's in a little black box in the top right-hand drawer."

"Perfect!" Josh said. "Then we should go and get it."

"What if we get caught in Ethan's suite again?" Olly asked.

"It's worth the risk," Josh replied. "We need to have that silver key."

~~~~~

The door to the Maharajah's Suite was locked this time.

"I know how we can get in," Josh whispered as they stood in the corridor. "I know you thought it was a stupid idea last time I mentioned it, but when we were down on the veranda earlier I noticed that all the balconies on the top floor are linked together. We can do what I suggested: Go into another room and climb across."

They found an unlocked door farther along the corridor. It was a small room that was being used for storage and it didn't have a balcony. But the window had a wide ledge, and it was only a single long step from there to the main balcony of the Maharajah's Suite.

"I'll climb out and go in through the balcony doors," Josh said, eyeing the gap uneasily. "You wait by the main door — I'll come and open it for you."

"Be careful," Olly warned.

Josh nodded. He climbed onto the windowsill, and keeping a tight hold on the masonry, got gradually to his feet. A cool breeze drifted over his face. Even in the darkness, he was well aware of the long drop to the paving stones below.

He turned so that he was facing the wall. It was only a few feet to the edge of the balcony. He clung to the stonework and carefully extended a foot. Once he had a firm footing, he reached out an arm, gripped the top of the balcony, and started to swing himself across.

But his shoe slipped on the stone and for a moment Josh found himself hanging by his arms, his feet dangling in midair. Olly squawked in alarm, but then Josh regained his footing and quickly threw himself over the banister. He lay panting on the floor of the balcony, praying that the doors onto it were unlocked — he didn't want to have to go back the way he had come.

Eventually, Josh got to his feet and tried the doors. To his relief, they swung open easily. He crept into the room, carefully closing the doors behind him. The place was in darkness, but a sliver of light under an adjacent door showed that someone was still awake. Josh swallowed hard — he knew he would need to be quick and silent.

The big desk was in front of him. He tiptoed to the top right-hand drawer and slid it quietly open, wincing at the soft scrape of wood on wood. He paused, for a moment, listening for any sign that he had been overheard. But all he could hear was the roar of his own blood surging through his temples. He inched the drawer farther open — there was the black box, just as Olly had described it. Josh lifted the lid. The little silver key was still there, gleaming in the moonlight. Quickly, Josh picked it up and slipped it into his pocket.

Smiling, he closed the drawer again and padded over to the main door of the suite. The key was in the lock. He turned it and started to push the door open. But, suddenly, the door swung inward toward Josh, and Olly came tumbling into the room.

She closed the door behind her. "I heard the elevator — there's someone coming," she hissed, her voice a sharp whisper in the gloom.

"Who?" Josh breathed.

"I don't know." Olly pressed her ear to the door. "I can hear the elevator doors opening now."

A few moments later, there was a sharp rap on the door and a voice called out, "Room service!"

"I'm coming!" answered a voice from the adjoining room where the light was on.

Josh and Olly exchanged a look. They had both recognized the voice as Paul White's. They heard Paul get up and head toward the main room to answer the door.

Josh looked at Olly in despair — they were trapped.

Chapter Thirteen: ☾
The Moonlit Veil

It was Olly who saved them from discovery. She dived for cover down by the side of a large, old cabinet, pulling Josh along with her. A split second later the lights came on and they heard footsteps crossing the room.

They stared at each other, hardly daring to breathe, as Paul approached. They heard him turn the key in the lock and try to open the door.

Olly groaned inwardly. Josh had unlocked it — which meant that Paul had locked it again when he thought he was *un*locking it. He would only need to put two and two together to realize that something strange was going on.

"It's room service, sir," came the voice from outside. "I have the food you ordered."

"Wait a moment," Paul replied, wrestling with the door.

They heard him turn the key again, and grunt with surprise as the door opened.

Paul spoke briefly with the man outside and then

they heard the door close again. Olly waited breathlessly for the footsteps to move back across the floor — but there was a tense silence in the room. Ever so carefully, she peeped past the corner of the cabinet to try and see what was going on.

Paul was standing with his back to the door and a silver tray in his hands, frowning in thought. After a moment, he shrugged, turned back to the door, and twisted the key in the lock. For one dreadful second, Olly thought he might take the key with him, but he didn't. He headed back to the room he had come from, switched the light off in the main room, and closed the door behind him.

Olly let out a long sigh of relief. "That was close!" she said.

"I've got the silver key," Josh whispered. "Let's get out of here."

Olly led the way across the room, turned the key, and eased the door open. She and Josh slipped out and Olly silently closed the door again.

Josh took the silver key out of his pocket and held it up for Olly to see.

"Great," she said. "Now, let's go to Elephant Falls!"

~~~~~

It took them an hour or more to make their way to Elephant Falls. They used the shortcut that Salila had shown them, up and down the rolling hills and in and out through the forests in the bright moonlight. Even under the canopy of the trees they could still see quite clearly. The full moon was huge in a sky teeming with stars. Its light cast shadows that seemed to dance mysteriously around them.

The waterfall was fabulously beautiful in the silvery light — the endless cascade of water glinting and sparkling, the rising mist like a silver cloak around the shoulders of the hills. The lake itself shimmered and gleamed like liquid silver in the starlight.

"Oh, wow!" Olly breathed as she gazed at the moonlit falls. "It was worth coming here just to see this."

"It is pretty amazing," Josh agreed. He walked on down to the edge of the lake, while Olly stood staring at the spectacle of Elephant Falls.

"You coming or what?" Josh called, after a moment.

"I'm coming," Olly replied, and took one last look at the waterfall in all its moonlit splendor. She was just about to run down and join Josh by the lake, when something caught her eye. As she stared at the waterfall, she thought she could glimpse something in the curtain of water. It was a shape —

visible one moment, gone the next. She stared for a few moments more but the shape seemed to have vanished.

"Olly, come on," shouted Josh.

Olly looked down at her friend, and as she glanced away from the waterfall, the curious shape caught the corner of her eye again. It looked like a silver arch in the water. But when she looked straight at it again, there was nothing there.

"Josh," she called. "Come back up here. I want you to look at something."

Josh clambered back up to where Olly was standing. "What is it?" he asked.

She pointed to the place where she had seen the phantom archway in the water. "Don't look straight at it," she told him. "Just focus your eyes to one side, and then tell me what you see."

Josh did as she instructed. "What am I looking for?" he inquired.

"I'm not going to tell you," Olly replied. "I want you to see it for yourself."

"This is dumb," Josh argued. "I can't see any-thing . . . Oh!" He stared hard at the waterfall. "That was weird."

Olly smiled. "What did you see?"

"It was like a kind of arch in the water," Josh

explained. "But I can't see it when I look directly at it. I suppose it must be some kind of optical illusion. There can't actually be anything in the waterfall, though, can there? It's just the way the moonlight is shining on the water."

"Do you remember what Adhita Ram said?" Olly breathed. "'To see beyond the moonlit veil, the seeker must look without looking.'"

Josh stared at her. "That's right," he said. His eyes widened. "It must mean the veil of the waterfall."

"And you can only see it if you don't look directly at it," Olly said. "Josh — I think the hidden temple is behind the waterfall!"

Josh stared at the rugged cliffs. "Is there a way up there?" he asked.

Olly pointed. "Yes," she said. "Look!" It wasn't obvious unless you were searching for it, but a rugged path did seem to wind its broken way along the cliff face toward the waterfall.

The two friends hurried around the lake, and up to the place where the path seemed to start. It led them up through the rocks beside the waterfall. They scrambled along as quickly as they could climb, sometimes side by side — helping each other over the tricky parts — sometimes in single file between boulders or clefts in the cliff.

Always, as they climbed, the silver moonlight shined down upon them and the roar of the waterfall echoed in their ears.

Olly clambered up a final steep slope and found herself standing on a precarious ledge. She helped Josh up beside her and the two of them stood there for a few moments, recovering from the climb.

Olly glanced back the way they had come. Bone-breaking rocks tumbled down some sixty feet into the valley below. Ahead, the path toward the waterfall rose and fell. Sometimes it was no more than the width of a cautiously placed foot, sometimes it was wide enough to walk along with comparative ease. It looked old and worn, and as if it might crumble away at any time, but Olly wasn't going to let that stop her.

She couldn't see the silver arch in the water anymore — but she was absolutely certain that it was there and that it would lead them to the hidden temple. She edged onward along the path, with Josh right behind her.

As they drew nearer to the falls, they felt fine spray on their hands and faces. The powerful torrent of water was only a few feet ahead of them now, waiting to sweep them off the narrow path and impale them on the jagged rocks below.

But the path ran *behind* the waterfall, and Olly found herself edging under an overhang of rock and along a ledge that echoed to the noise of the cascading water. It was impossible to converse, and almost impossible to think.

She glanced back at Josh. He was right behind her, his hair dark with spray, his face spangled with water droplets, and his eyes glowing in the strange silvery light.

Olly moved farther along the ledge behind the waterfall. The rock beneath her feet was slick with water, but it formed a smooth and level pathway — on one side, the sheer cliff face, on the other, the curtain of constantly falling water. And through the shining water, Olly could just make out the bright disc of the full moon.

Suddenly the pathway shot off to the right, tunneling its way deep into the cliff face. Here there was a beautiful archway of fine silverwork. Olly took out her flashlight and switched it on. The beam shined along the tunnel, and Olly let out a gasp of wonder and delight. At the end of the tunnel — about thirty feet away — the flashlight beam gleamed on a pair of tall silver gates.

Olly and Josh walked forward together and gazed at the exquisite gates. They were etched with an intricate design of blossoms and vines, with sculpted silver flowers and dancing figures. The gates were three or four times Olly's height as she stood underneath them, gazing upward in speechless amazement.

Olly thought about the little silver key — could such a very small thing have been used to lock such immense gates? She looked at the silver panels where the doors met — but she couldn't see a keyhole and there were no handles. So, how did the doors open? Before she had time to share this puzzle with Josh, he pushed against the doors.

Smoothly they swung open, allowing Olly and Josh to step, in rapt silence, into the hidden Temple of Parvati.

The light from Olly's flashlight revealed an awesome sight. The center of the chamber was dominated by a towering statue of Parvati. The beautiful goddess was seated cross-legged on a deep plinth of beaten silver. She was wearing a painted pink sari, edged with golden braid. There were gold, bejeweled bracelets on her arms and wrists. A golden belt gleamed at her waist and a necklace of pearls hung around her neck. On her head was a high golden crown, studded with jewels in all the colors of the rainbow. Her face was beautiful, smiling, and serene, and in her outstretched hands she held a carved wooden elephant.

As Olly approached the statue, other wonders were revealed in the beam of the flashlight. The walls and ceiling were entirely paneled in silver and gold, engraved with a multitude of figures that danced and fought, walked and talked, or sat in contemplative silence. The decorations were so lavish and so detailed that Olly could only take in a fraction of the designs revealed in the scattered flashlight beam.

Stone pillars supported the golden roof. They were painted in bright colors and decorated with inscriptions and carvings of lotus flowers and fruit.

Olly knew the temple must be very, very old, but she saw that somehow the colored paint had remained bright and vibrant. She guessed that it had been protected from the bleaching power of the sun by the darkness of the hidden cavern.

Behind her the tunnel echoed with the sound of the waterfall, but in the fabulous chamber it was possible for Olly and Josh to speak without shouting.

"I wonder how long this has been here," Josh said.

"A very long time," Olly replied, her eyes fixed on the polished wooden elephant that rested on the two enormous hands of Parvati. The carved elephant was about a foot and a half long from trunk to tail. It was unadorned and quite smooth, the natural grain of the wood showing up clearly in the flashlight beam.

"This must be the Elephant of Parvati!" Olly breathed, as she walked toward it. She handed Josh the flashlight and stepped up to the broad silver dais on which the statue sat. Parvati towered over Olly, her beautiful face high above Olly's head, but her outstretched hands just within reach.

"Be careful," Josh said, as Olly stretched up toward the wooden elephant. "It's probably really heavy."

"Yes," came another voice from the shadows. "Be very careful, Olly — I wouldn't want you to drop it."

Startled, Olly turned toward the familiar voice.

Ethan Cain stepped from a dark corner of the chamber and switched on his flashlight. He held up something between the fingers of his other hand, shining the flashlight on it so that Josh and Olly could see it clearly.

It was the copy of the silver key.

"I thought this might come in handy tonight," he said, smiling. "I see you have the original, Olly. I will have to have a stern word with Paul when I get back. He was supposed to be on guard."

Olly glared at Ethan, speechless with anger and dismay.

He stepped forward, his arms spread wide. "What? No questions?" he asked. "I thought you'd want to know how I got here first."

"I can work that out for myself, thanks," Olly told him, her voice cold with contempt. "You listened in on us, and then guessed the rest."

Ethan smiled. "Once I knew you'd found my little device, I realized that what Adhita Ram had told you about a hidden temple by Elephant Falls must be true," he said. "And so I came here while the others went to the Temple of Ganesha. And I saw the silver archway through the water — as I imagine you did, too." He smiled. "The moonlit veil! Very poetic." He looked at the wooden elephant. "I assume we're all thinking the same thing? That the talisman is inside the elephant? I had a few moments to look at it before I heard you coming — I think you'll find it opens up." He took another step forward. "Olly — be a friend and hand it down to me, will you?"

Olly glared at him and didn't move.

"Oh, come now," Ethan said. "Be fair. We both wanted the prize and we both used rather underhanded methods to get it. After all — you did send me off to that swamp this afternoon. Now that wasn't very fair, was it?"

"The only reason you're here is because you were listening in on everything *we* said," Josh put in. "We worked the whole thing out — you didn't do a thing."

Ethan's eyebrows rose. "Really?" he said. "But, Josh — it was one of my employees who found the parchment in the first place. And it was I who funded the conference and brought all those people together. And it was I who arranged for your room to be bugged." He spread his hands again. "And you tell me I didn't do anything? On the contrary" — his voice suddenly took on a sharp edge — "I did *everything!*"

"No," Olly said. "We worked it all out for you."

The American laughed. "That's right, Olly," he said. "Like puppets on strings — and *I* was pulling the strings."

Olly stared down at him in horror. The terrible thing was that he was right — he had set the whole thing up, and they had fallen into his trap, solved the mystery, and found the Elephant of Parvati for him.

"We'll tell Jonathan and the professor everything," Josh said. "We'll tell them all about the bug."

"You're welcome to do that if you wish." Ethan

laughed. "But do you really think anyone will even believe that there *was* a bug? Let alone that *I* planted it? I will be suitably horrified when you tell everyone about it. In fact, I'll organize a thorough investigation . . ."

Olly's heart sank because she knew Ethan was right. No one would believe that he had planted a bug in their suite. And as for finding the talisman — he could just say that he followed the trail of clues in exactly the same way that she and Josh had.

This time, it seemed he really had beaten them.

"Now then," Ethan snapped. "Give me the elephant, Olly. I can make life very uncomfortable for you if you don't." His eyes narrowed. "Who knows, with the right words whispered in the right ears, I might arrange it so you never get to travel with your father again," he continued. "How does life in a boarding school appeal to you, Olly? Exciting enough?"

Olly glared at Ethan Cain, too angry to reply. She turned and grasped hold of the elephant. Josh had been right — the wooden statue was very heavy. She could only just manage to lift it out of Parvati's hands.

But as she did so, something startling happened. The statue's hands rose sharply with a loud creak.

Olly staggered backward with the heavy wooden sculpture clasped to her chest.

Another strange sound began to reverberate around the chamber. A scraping sound, like stone rubbing heavily on stone. Ethan, Olly, and Josh stood transfixed as the strange noises echoed back and forth between the temple walls.

And then there was another sound: the harsh clang of metal striking metal. The silver gates had slammed shut.

Josh turned and ran to the gates. He tried to drag them open, but there were no handles. He tried to get his fingers between them, but the panels met seamlessly. He grasped at the projecting parts of the silver carvings and hauled on them with all his strength, but the gates would not move.

And now a new and far more frightening sound began to echo through the cavern. The sound of rushing water.

Ethan flicked his flashlight around the chamber. Long dark slots had opened up in the walls, and as Olly stared at them in alarm, great spouts of water came pouring out.

Ethan gave a howl of fear and ran to join Josh at the gates, but water swept his feet from under him and he vanished in the flood. Olly saw his flashlight glowing for a few moments through the water, then it was gone.

Josh pressed up against the gates as the water rose to his knees. He began to climb, but Olly could see that the water was rising with him, and threatening to pull him down again.

For a few moments, Olly found herself on an island amidst the flood. But then the rising water came lapping over the dais, cold and dark and deadly. She gazed around frantically, clutching the wooden elephant to her chest as the water began to rise up her legs.

The water level was rising swiftly and there was no way out of the chamber. Soon the flood had reached Olly's waist. She pressed herself against the statue of Parvati, as if hoping the goddess would somehow save her.

But then an undercurrent tugged at her feet and Olly fell, losing her grip on the elephant as her head plunged beneath the rushing water and everything went black.

Chapter Fourteen: ☾
Floodwater

Josh scrambled up the gates, his fingers and the toes of his shoes only just finding a hold on the ornate silverwork. But the deadly floodwater pursued him relentlessly, swirling around the gates, rising ever higher. Terrified, Josh grasped his flashlight and pointed it around the echoing chamber. He saw that water was still pouring in through the vents high in the walls.

When Olly had lifted the carved elephant out of Parvati's hands, it had triggered some ancient, protective mechanism that opened sluice gates to the river. Its intention was hideously clear: to drown anyone who attempted to take the wooden elephant from Parvati's keeping.

Josh was at the top of the gates and he could clearly see that there was nowhere else to climb to. The water level was still rising, and even if it stopped, there was no way to escape from the temple chamber now that the gates had shut.

Josh aimed the flashlight at the place where

he had last seen Olly, clinging to the goddess as the water swept around her. The statue was now shoulder-deep in water — but Olly was gone.

Josh gasped. "Olly!" he shouted over the thunder of the water. "Olly!"

Water dragged at his legs, trying to pluck him off his precarious perch on the gates. He shined the flashlight over the heaving surface of the water, desperate for some sign that Olly was still alive.

And then he saw something moving in the water. Somebody was splashing around, sending up white spray. It was Olly — still near to the statue of Parvati and trying to make her way back to the comparative safety of the statue's shoulders. But she was caught in the clashing currents of the flood.

Olly was a competent swimmer, but Josh knew he was better. Alone, she might not survive. With his help, he thought they might both make it to the statue. Josh didn't hesitate. He secured the cord of the flashlight around his wrist and then launched himself off his perch into the water. In the darkness, he could see nothing, but he knew which way to go. He struck out strongly for the statue and his friend.

When he reached Olly, he treaded water, holding the flashlight beam on her face.

She just had breath left to spit out a few words. "I'm OK, but I've lost the elephant."

"Don't worry about that now," Josh gasped. "Try to get back to the statue." She nodded and they began to swim together.

The water was breaking over Parvati's shoulders now — the temple was half-drowned and still the water was rising.

Josh made sure that Olly was secure on Parvati's left shoulder before swimming around to the other side and hauling himself up onto the right. He sat astride the ridge of stone, his legs dangling in the water, his arms clinging to the great head.

He heard Olly's voice over the roar of the water.

"Now what?" she shouted.

"Have you seen Ethan?" Josh yelled back.

Olly shook her head.

Slowly Josh scoured the surface of the rising tide with the flashlight beam. He had no wish to see Ethan drown, not if there was some chance of helping him. But there was no sign of him. Josh had the horrible, sickening feeling that Ethan might have drowned.

"Josh?" Olly called again. "Do you think we'll be able to stay afloat till the water stops rising?"

Josh aimed the flashlight at the high vents

through which the water was still pouring. Soon, the statue of Parvati would be covered by the rising water and there would be nothing for them to cling to. They would be able to keep their heads above the surface for a certain amount of time — treading water, helping each other. But for how long? Eventually their strength would run out, and if the water rose to completely fill the chamber, they'd drown in the temple for sure.

He summoned his courage, determined to keep Olly's spirits up, and called back to her. "We'll be fine," he told her. "The water can't rise much farther. Then we just need to hang on till it drains away." He hoped he sounded more convincing than he felt.

As he began to realize the hopelessness of their situation, Josh felt himself give way to despair. His head fell forward against the head of the goddess. And then he saw something that chased despair from his mind. He sat up and shined the flashlight on the side of Parvati's head. Within the intricately sculpted curves of Parvati's ear, he saw a small dark slot. A keyhole.

Adhita Ram's words came back to Josh: "When all is lost, turn the key in the lock in the ear." He and Olly had assumed that the parchment was referring

734

to an elephant's ear, or perhaps to Ganesha's ear —
but it looked like they had got it wrong. At least,
Josh *hoped* they had got it wrong.

He pushed his hand into his pocket and felt for
the silver key. Carefully, he pulled it out and slid it
into the hole. He gave a shout of triumph — the
key fitted perfectly.

"What's going on?" he heard Olly shout. But
Josh was too excited to respond.

He tried to turn the key. It resisted for a moment,
but then it turned smoothly in the lock. At first,
nothing seemed to happen, but then Josh felt a faint
shuddering from deep within the statue — as if age-
old mechanisms were shifting into gear. Then there
were deeper, louder sounds and the whole statue
started to vibrate.

"Josh!" Olly howled. "What's happening?"

"It's the silver key!" Josh yelled. "There's a keyhole in Parvati's ear, and the key fits! I think —"

But the rest of Josh's words were drowned out by
a cacophonous rumbling from all around the chamber. He stared at the walls — the vents were closing!
The flood of black water dwindled to a stream and
then a trickle, and then it stopped altogether.

A strange silence fell over the chamber.

"So the keyhole wasn't in an elephant's ear, after

all — it was in the statue of Parvati!" Olly cried. "Josh, you're brilliant." Her voice bubbled with relieved laughter. "We're saved!"

Josh leaned around the huge head to look at her. "We still have to get out of here," he pointed out.

Olly stared back at him, her hair clinging to her face in wet strands, her eyes shining. "Have you turned the key all the way?" she asked.

"I think so." Josh took hold of the key again and gave it another twist. As he pushed, the key suddenly clicked and twisted farther in the lock. This time, Josh could clearly hear mechanisms moving within the head of the statue, as the farther turn of the key set some new device in motion. There was a low grumbling from beneath the water, and then silence.

"What happened then?" Olly asked.

"I don't know," Josh replied slowly.

But then they heard a booming clang and saw the tall silver gates swing open. The trapped floodwater went streaming out of this new exit and Olly was swept away in the rush.

Josh saw the water drag her off the statue's shoulder, and he lunged forward to catch her. But Olly's weight only served to pull him away from the statue, too.

Josh felt himself dragged along in the flood of water. He tried to keep hold of Olly, but she slipped from his grip. And then his head went under the water and Josh had to concentrate all his energy on trying to find the surface again. The water swept him along, turning him over and over until he was utterly disoriented. His head broke the surface for a moment and he was vaguely aware of being carried back along the tunnel that had led him and Olly to the temple. But the next second, the force of the water dragged him under again.

He held his breath, his head pounding as he was tumbled in the flood. He expected to be dashed against rocks at any moment. But then he saw a kind of brightness through the water and felt himself falling in a powerful cascade. The flood had taken him over the waterfall!

The sensation of falling seemed to last forever. But then Josh felt himself plunge into more water. He struggled upward, toward light and air, and eventually broke the surface to find that he was in the lake at the foot of Elephant Falls. The thunder of the falling water threw spray into his face and threatened to force him back underwater. So Josh swam away from the waterfall itself as quickly as he could. As soon as he was out of immediate danger, he turned in the water to search for any sign of Olly. His flashlight was lost — but now there was the bright moonlight to help him search.

After a moment, he spotted her over on the other side of the falls, and she was clinging to something — a large round shape that seemed to be buoying her up in the water. Josh swam toward her.

As he got closer, he realized what it was that she was hanging on to — it was the carved wooden elephant, but it had split open on a hinge along the spine.

"It banged against me in the rush," Olly gasped. "I just grabbed hold of it. I think it saved me. But it broke open when we hit the lake."

"Let's get to dry ground," Josh said.

"Josh!" Olly shouted. "Look! I think that came out of the wooden elephant when it split open." She was pointing to a small, round white shape bobbing on the surface of the lake a few feet away. Curved and buoyant, it slowly moved out of the eddies, turning in circles as the current caught it and carried it down to where the river flowed out from the far end of the lake.

"Get to dry land," Josh said. "I'll find out what it is."

He headed toward the white object. Glancing

over his shoulder, he saw Olly heading for dry land. She was safe — now he could concentrate on the white thing. But as he drew closer, something else took his attention. Something terrible. It was a human figure, floating facedown in the water.

Forgetting the bobbing white object, Josh swam strongly toward the floating man. He had passed his life-saving exam two years before, but until now he hadn't had much need to use the techniques he'd been taught.

He treaded water, using all his strength to turn the limp form over. He couldn't tell whether Ethan was breathing or if he was alive, but there was no time to think about that now. Josh swam around behind him, lodged his hand under Ethan's chin, and then struck out landward.

It was a difficult journey, and Josh was already tired, but he refused to give up. If there was any chance that Ethan had survived, then Josh was going to save him. He became aware of a frantic splashing behind his head and looked back to see that Olly had waded out into the lake to help him.

Together, they managed to drag Ethan out of the water.

"Is he dead?" Olly asked, her voice trembling.

Gasping for breath, Josh knelt by Ethan's chest.

The man's face was pale in the moonlight and water trickled from his mouth and nose. Josh tried to remember what he had learned. He turned Ethan onto his front and knelt astride his waist, pushing down hard on his back. Water gushed from his mouth.

Josh pushed down again. There was more water and then a weak cough.

Josh looked at Olly. "He's alive!" he said. He climbed off and together they turned Ethan into the recovery position. He was breathing normally now and his pulse felt strong.

Josh pushed the wet hair out of his eyes. "I think he's going to be OK," he said.

Olly gave a gasp of relief. "I thought he was dead," she said in an undertone.

"Another minute or two and he would have been," Josh told her. He stood up, trembling all over.

Olly went over to the wooden elephant which lay at the lakeside. She bent over and closed it with a sharp snap. "Whatever that white thing was from inside here, it's gone now," she sighed.

Josh turned and stared out over the lake. "Not yet!" he cried, excitement rising in his voice. "Look!"

If it wasn't for the bright moonlight, they would never have seen the small white blob at the far end of the lake. It was moving swiftly with the water now, heading down to where the river followed its winding course through the hills.

"We might still be able to get it," he said. "Come on!"

"What about Ethan?" Olly asked.

"He'll be fine for a minute or two," Josh said. "We'll come back for him."

Side by side, they ran along the bank of the long lake. Every now and then the white thing would be lost among the waves — but each time Josh thought it had vanished for good, it would come bobbing back into sight.

The lake narrowed between steep hills, and the river flowed down over rocks, the water foaming white as it raced along. Josh was slightly in the lead as the two friends bounded from rock to rock, desperate to keep up with the white thing in the water.

Josh redoubled his efforts and managed to edge slightly ahead of it. He jumped out onto a large boulder that jutted into the river and dropped to his knees. For a moment the thing bobbed tantalizingly within reach. Josh made a grab for it, but he couldn't get a grip and it bobbed away to be swept on down the river.

Olly came racing up to him. "Did you get it?" she panted.

"No. Almost," he gasped.

She gave a cry of frustration and ran on past him. Only a few feet ahead, more boulders pushed out into the river.

"There!" Josh yelled, pointing. "See it?" The thing had been caught in a swirling eddy. It was spinning around in the lee of a large rock.

"I see it!" Olly shouted. She leaped onto the rock and lay down on her front. She reached out and her fingers touched the smooth white object, but it bobbed and drifted away from her.

"Careful!" Josh shouted, as Olly leaned perilously far out over the churning water.

Her fingertips touched it again, and this time she managed to ease it toward herself. A moment later, she had a firm grasp on it. She sat up, cradling the thing in her lap. "Got it!" she gasped, grinning up at Josh as he ran to join her.

Olly got to her feet and held the thing out in triumph.

It was a white pottery elephant, quite stylized with its head tucked in and its trunk curled up to one side. It was fat and round, smooth and shiny, and no more than seven inches long. The legs and other features were shaped in quite a rudimentary way. Seated high on the curve of the animal's trunk was a tiny shrew.

Olly turned it over, frowning. The shiny porcelain had no holes or slots in it. She looked at Josh. "There's no way of getting into it," she said. She gently shook the elephant. There was no sound from inside. She frowned. "I don't think there's anything in it."

Josh gently took it out of her hands and slowly examined every inch. She was right — there were no slots, hinges, or holes in the smooth surface of the elephant.

"What should we do?" Olly asked. "This can't be the Elephant of Parvati, can it? That was supposed to be made of gold and jewels."

"I don't know," Josh said. "It might be. We did find Parvati holding it. We should take it to the Temple of Ganesha. The professor, Jonathan, and the others should still be there."

Olly nodded and the two of them began to trek back up the river toward the lake.

"We should check on Ethan first," Josh said. "If he's conscious he might be able to come with us.

If not, we'll have to leave him here and send help when we get to the temple." He shivered. "I'm looking forward to getting into some dry clothes."

Olly trudged along beside him. "Who cares about clothes! Just think about what we've found, Josh! Maybe we haven't got the talisman yet — but we found the hidden temple!"

They arrived back at the lake. Josh frowned. He was sure they ought to be able to see Ethan by now. They weren't far from where they had left him.

As they got closer to the place where they had dragged the half-drowned man from the lake, they realized that he was gone.

"He must have recovered," Josh said, staring all around. "But why did he wander off?"

"There's something else," Olly pointed out. "Wherever he's gone, he's taken the wooden elephant with him."

She was right. Both Ethan Cain and the elephant were gone.

Chapter Fifteen: ☾
Cracking the Nutshell

It was a long trek through the hills to the Temple of Ganesha in the dark, but the excitement of their discovery kept Olly and Josh in high spirits, despite their wet clothes and exhaustion.

Finally, they came to a familiar stretch of roadway, winding upward between rocky cliffs. They ran up to the crest of the hill and found themselves looking down at the facade of the temple. The moonlight threw strange and eerie shadows, making it seem to Olly as if all the human and animal figures on the carved rock-face were watching and waiting for her and Josh.

The jeeps that had come up from the palace were parked outside, but there was no other sign of life. Everything was silent under the huge full moon.

"I guess they're still in there," Olly said. She was clutching the white elephant protectively to her chest. "Let's go and show them what we've found."

Her own voice broke the mystical spell of the

place and, together, she and Josh walked down the hill to the temple.

"Where do you think Ethan went?" Josh asked.

Olly shrugged. "I don't know and I don't care," she said. "He's alive, but he didn't get his thieving hands on this." She lifted the elephant in her two hands. "And that's all I care about."

"But what is it?" Josh wondered. "It doesn't have any markings on it — and it doesn't fit the description of the talisman."

"It must be important, or it wouldn't have been inside the wooden elephant," Olly replied thoughtfully. "Maybe there's something about it that we can't see in this light." She looked up at the full moon, riding high in the star-bright sky. "It has to be something to do with the talisman, Josh — perhaps it's another clue."

As they approached the entrance to the Temple of Ganesha, they began to hear voices from within. They walked in through the heavy wooden doors just as a single voice rose above the others.

They looked at each other — the voice belonged to Ethan Cain.

Josh put his finger to his lips and Olly nodded. Before they made their presence known, they needed to know what Ethan was up to now.

They waited in the shadow of the doorway. The archaeologists were gathered at the foot of the stairway in the main sanctum. Lanterns stood on the ground, throwing out a soft yellow light that filled the chamber with leaping shadows. Ethan Cain was standing on the top stair, holding the wooden elephant in his hands. At his back, Ganesha gazed out over the temple with calm, untroubled eyes. Ben Wilder stood halfway up the stairs, filming Ethan on a camcorder.

"Again, I wish to apologize for not keeping you all up to date with my private researches into the parchment," Ethan was saying. "But I wanted to make sure that I was heading in the right direction before I drew too much attention to my findings. That is why I decided to investigate Elephant Falls alone tonight. An elderly mahout from the local area was able to make translations of a few sections of the parchment. This led me to believe that there was a lost temple to Parvati near the waterfall now called Elephant Falls, but once known as Parvati Falls. And, ladies and gentlemen, I was right — as this extraordinary artifact proves." He held the wooden elephant up for the camcorder. "I have only had a brief chance to study it," he continued. "But it is obvious that it is constructed in two halves and that it can be opened. I have no doubt that there is something of great significance within."

Olly's eyes narrowed with anger — Ethan was playing to the crowd of archaeologists, and to the camcorder, and making out that the discovery of the hidden temple and the elephant had all been down to him. *Typical!* she thought. She turned to look at Josh.

"Boy, is he in for a surprise!" Josh whispered.

Olly nodded and turned back to watch Ethan's next move. He had rested the elephant on the top step of the platform, beside the statue of Ganesha, and was crouching at its side with the iron copy of the silver key. Jonathan stood beside him, holding the elephant steady, while Ethan searched for a keyhole that wasn't there. The others watched in fascinated silence. Olly saw her own father among them, as thrilled as any by the find.

"Here!" Ethan said eventually. "I was expecting a keyhole, but this wooden clasp seems to be holding it together." He pressed his fingers against the wooden carving. There was a sharp click and the two halves fell open in Jonathan's hands.

Professor Christie climbed the steps to look at the relic. He stooped for a moment and then straightened up. "I'm afraid it's empty," he said.

"I don't understand," Ethan said in the profound silence that followed this revelation. Olly could almost have hugged herself with delight at the dumbfounded expression on his face. She grinned — it was time for a dramatic entrance.

"I think you're looking for this!" Olly announced loudly. She stepped out of the shadows, holding the porcelain elephant high in her hands. Josh was at her side as the archaeologists murmured in astonishment and parted to let them through.

"Olivia?" her father said. "What on earth are you doing here?"

A poisonous look came and went very quickly in Ethan's eyes as he glared at Olly and Josh. For a split second he looked as if he wanted to pounce on Olly and tear the prize out of her hands. But he recovered himself very quickly. "As I was about to tell you," he said, standing up, "Olly and Josh were on the same track as I." He looked at Professor Christie. "I'm sure you'll forgive them for leaving the hotel without permission, when you hear how helpful they were to me in locating the hidden Temple of Parvati." A smile spread across his face. "In fact, they saved me from drowning. They're a couple of heroes!"

"What have you got there, Olly?" Jonathan asked.

"Well, the temple filled with water when I took the wooden elephant out of Parvati's hands," Olly explained. "But Josh found the keyhole for the silver key, and all the water flooded out. We ended up in the lake at the bottom of the waterfall. The wooden elephant broke open." She nodded to the porcelain elephant in her hands. "And this was inside. We had to chase it down the river to catch up with it." Olly saw that Ben Wilder had turned the camcorder toward her and Josh. This wonderful moment was being captured on film! No matter what lies Ethan Cain told, no matter how he twisted the truth — she and Josh were the ones presenting this artifact to the world.

Almost giddy with pride and excitement, Olly ran up the stairs toward her father. But she missed her footing and stumbled on the stone steps. Her first instinct was to protect the porcelain elephant. She twisted, trying to fall onto her side. But her elbow slammed against the stone, and the elephant was jolted from her grasp.

She let out a cry of dismay as the elephant hit the step with a loud crack. But it didn't break. It rolled over the edge and struck the second step, still rolling. Olly watched, frozen in horror as the thing rolled and bounced down the stairs.

Josh lunged forward, trying to catch the tumbling elephant as it fell, but he moved a moment too late. The elephant rolled off the final step and struck the stone floor. This last impact was too much for the porcelain and it shattered into a hundred pieces.

Olly was too stunned even to cry out. She couldn't believe that this had happened. She had dropped the elephant that was the final clue to the whereabouts of the Elephant of Parvati, and now it lay in pieces. And, even worse, Ben Wilder had caught the whole humiliating, horrifying incident on film!

Olly put her head in her hands and groaned in absolute despair. When she looked up again, Josh was kneeling beside the broken relic, looking as wretched as her. But then something seemed to catch his eye and his expression changed. He leaned forward, spreading the porcelain fragments with his fingers, and picked up something, which he held out to Olly.

She stared at it in disbelief as it sparkled and flashed in the warm lantern light. It gleamed with gold and glittered with a thousand points of colored light.

Her despair and embarrassment forgotten, Olly got to her feet and walked slowly down the steps toward this wonderful shiny object. Josh laid it reverently in her hands and now Olly could see it properly.

It was a golden elephant, the size of Olly's hand. Hundreds of jewels adorned the elephant, making it sparkle and gleam with all the colors of the rainbow. It was beautiful beyond words.

Olly turned, holding the elephant up toward her father, speechless with joy.

She and Josh had found the Elephant of Parvati.

～～～

It was the evening following the dramatic discovery of the fourth Talisman of the Moon. Olly was in her bedroom in the Peshwar Palace, standing on a footstool while Natasha and Salila busied themselves with wrapping her in a sari of scarlet silk.

Under the sari, Olly wore a tight-fitting, short-sleeved shirt, and a narrow silk petticoat. She watched herself in the mirror as the beautiful material was wound around her. The dazzling strip of silk was about fifteen feet long and almost three feet wide. She couldn't quite work out how it could be transformed into a dress, but as Natasha and Salila tucked and pleated it expertly into place — without any buttons or pins or fastenings — it all began to make sense. Finally, Natasha lifted up the one free end of the sari and draped it elegantly over Olly's shoulder.

Olly gazed at the result. "I look amazing!" she breathed in delight.

"Yes, you do," Natasha agreed with a smile.

"How many people did you say this broadcast would be going out to worldwide?" Olly asked.

Natasha grinned. "Oh, only about eighty million — something like that."

Olly couldn't really picture 80 million people all sitting in front of their TV sets to watch her and Josh appear on the news. It didn't really seem real. But it was!

As soon as news of the discovery of the talisman had leaked out, the producers of *Collision Course* had seen the potential for some huge publicity for their movie. And things had moved very quickly after that. Arrangements had been made for a big joint party to announce the end of filming and the astounding discovery of one of the lost Talismans of the Moon.

The party was due to start in about half an hour. Already there were dozens of people downstairs, gathering in the palace ballroom. All day, Olly and Josh had watched the TV vans arriving and lights, cameras, and other equipment being unloaded into the hotel.

"What if my mind goes blank and I can't think of anything to say?" Olly asked in a sudden attack of nerves.

"That won't happen," Natasha replied calmly, looping the final length of her own sari over her shoulder and tucking it into place. "Just relax and imagine you're chatting to your friends."

Olly looked doubtfully at her. "I don't have eighty million friends," she said.

Natasha laughed. "Josh will be with you — and Jonathan and your father. It'll be fine, just you see."

Olly frowned. "I'm not so sure Dad will want to be there," she said. "He hates this kind of thing. He said it was all a 'pointless distraction' taking him away from his proper work of investigating the Elephant of Parvati." She looked at Natasha. "He's really not into wearing a dinner jacket, either. Even if you do manage to drag him to the party, he'll probably turn up wearing a big sweater and a pair of old corduroy pants. You know what he's like!"

"Ethan has all that under control, don't you worry," Natasha assured her. She smiled at Olly. "I'm so proud of the way you and Josh helped him with this whole thing," she said. "He might not have even been here tonight, if it wasn't for Josh. You're both very brave."

Olly gave a quick smile. It was pointless for her to ruin the evening by trying to tell Natasha what had really been going on since their arrival in India. She would never believe that her boyfriend was a scheming rat who only wanted the talisman for himself.

As far as Olly could tell, Ethan was lapping up the media attention. It was he who had coordinated the whole party and the live news broadcast with the producers of *Collision Course*. He had been pulling strings and using all of his considerable influence to make sure everything went with a spectacular bang.

Natasha looked at her watch. "Speaking of Ethan, I'd better go and check that he's ready," she said. She gave Olly a final once-over. "You look gorgeous. And remember, just relax and be yourself." And so saying, she left the room.

Olly gazed thoughtfully after her for a few moments, and then turned to Salila. "But what if being myself includes tripping over the sari and landing flat on my face?" she demanded.

Salila grinned. "I don't think you will do that," she replied.

Olly sighed and climbed down off the foot stool. She looked at herself in the mirror one last time. "OK," she said. "Let's go and make a big entrance!"

The reception area of the hotel was crowded with a throng of people. Olly met Josh at the head of the stairs. He was dressed in a dinner jacket.

"Nice sari," he said, grinning at her.

"Thanks," she said. "You look very suave — very James Bond."

"Ethan organized it," Josh replied. "Ethan organized everything."

"I bet he did," Olly murmured under her breath.

Josh leaned in close. "Don't worry about it," he whispered. "Remember: We were the ones who found the talisman — not Ethan."

Olly looked at him. "Are you nervous at all?" she asked.

Josh looked thoughtful. "I don't think so," he said. He gestured down the long stairway toward the crowds. "All this doesn't seem real, if you know what I mean. It's like it's not really happening. And I certainly can't get my head around the idea of sixty million people watching us on TV. That's totally mind-blowing!"

"Eighty million," Olly corrected him.

"Is that right?" Josh grinned at her. "You know," he said, "somehow, the extra twenty million doesn't bother me at all."

Audrey Beckmann appeared and gave Olly a hug. She was wearing a sari of deep blue silk. Jonathan and Professor Christie were with her. Olly stared at her father in amazement — he was wearing a tuxedo. Although he looked slightly uncomfortable in it, he was smiling and had a look of quiet pride on his face.

Olly turned to see Natasha and Ethan down below, surrounded by a crowd of people. Just then, Ethan swung around and looked up at them. He smiled and waved. Gritting her teeth, Olly waved back.

Ethan made his way to the foot of the stairs and called for silence. "Please welcome our guests of honor," he declared. "Olly and Josh — two intrepid young people who I am proud to call my friends! Olly and Josh, everyone!"

Applause broke out as Olly's grandmother whispered in Olly's ear. "That's your cue," she said. "Down you go."

Olly and Josh looked at each other.

"Come on," Josh said. "Our public awaits!"

Side by side, they began to descend the broad marble staircase.

"I'll trip," Olly whispered. "I haven't had much luck with stairs recently."

"This time, you won't trip," Josh told her.

And Olly found that he was right. As she walked slowly down the stairs with the applause ringing in her ears, her nerves evaporated in the thrill of the moment.

\~\~\~\~

The live TV broadcast was due to begin in a few minutes. Olly and Josh were sitting on the steps that overlooked the garden. Once again, the moon was riding high in a clear, starlit sky.

"I could get used to all this media stuff," Olly said. "Just think, in a few minutes, we're going to be in an interview that will be seen all over the world."

"We'll be famous," Josh said softly. "Isn't that a weird thought?"

Olly frowned. "Yes," she said. "Very weird." She grinned. "But still totally amazing!"

"When we've done our part, Jonathan and your dad and Professor Singh are going to be interviewed, too," Josh said. "And so is Ethan, of course."

"I'm not worried about anything he might say," Olly said firmly. "We know the truth, and that's all that matters."

"*And* we beat him again," Josh added.

Olly nodded. "It's about time he realized he's never going to get the better of us." She laughed.

Josh gave her an anxious look. "Don't say that — you might jinx it!"

"It's a pity Mr. Ram wouldn't agree to come," Olly sighed. "We wouldn't have gotten anywhere without him."

"I don't think this is really his kind of thing," Josh replied, looking over his shoulder and in through the open French doors to where the party was in full swing. "I think he's happier up in the hills with his elephants. But we have to mention how much he helped us."

"Of course we do," Olly agreed. "I've just thought of something. Remember what he said — about the seeker having to crack the nutshell to find the kernel within? Do you think that meant I was *supposed* to drop the china elephant in order to find the talisman?"

Josh smiled at her. "As Mr. Ram would say, 'Only the seeker can answer that,'" he replied.

"Just think," Olly said, "if I hadn't dropped it, the Elephant of Parvati might never have been found."

Just then, Salila came running out of the hotel. "The news reporters are ready for you now," she said excitedly. "The broadcast will begin in five minutes."

Olly and Josh stood up and followed her back into the room. A huge plasma screen had been set up at one end, and as they walked through the crowds of people, Olly saw their own faces filling the screen as a camera tracked them.

Olly leaned over to whisper to Josh. "You know something," she said. "We'd better get used to this. If we find any more talismans, I can see us becoming international TV personalities."

Josh nodded. "Maybe Mom was right," he said. "Maybe we can be glamorous celebrities *and* legendary archaeologists, after all!"